1ª-OP-#40⁰⁰

D1121889

Out of the House of Life

Tor books by Chelsea Quinn Yarbro

Ariosto
Blood Games
A Candle for D'Artagnan
Crusader's Torch
A Flame in Byzantium
Hotel Transylvania
Out of the House of Life
The Palace
Path of the Eclipse

Chelsea Quinn Yarbro 1DC90

Chelsea Quinn Yarbro

Out of the House of Life

TOR
HORROR

A TOM DOHERTY ASSOCIATES BOOK
NEW YORK

This is a work of fiction. All the characters and events portrayed in this book are fictitious, and any resemblance to real people or events is purely coincidental.

OUT OF THE HOUSE OF LIFE

Copyright © 1990 by Chelsea Quinn Yarbro

A Tor Book
Published by Tom Doherty Associates, Inc.
49 West 24th Street
New York, N.Y. 10010

Printed in the United States of America

Library of Congress Cataloging-in-Publication Data

Yarbro, Chelsea Quinn
    Out of the house of life / Chelsea Quinn Yarbro.
        p.   cm.
    ISBN 0-312-93126-3
    I. Title.
  PS3575.A709   1990
  813′.54—dc20   90-38900
                                                         CIP

First edition: December 1990

0 9 8 7 6 5 4 3 2 1

Since this novel
has two separate story lines
it follows that it should have
two separate dedications:

for

the incomparable
Roger Zelazny

and

the memory of
George Sheviakov

treasured friends, the both of you

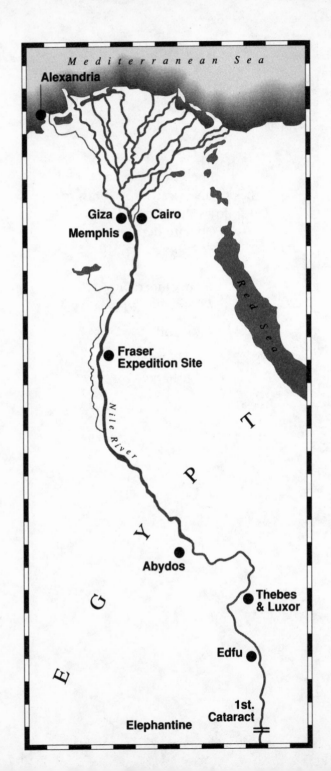

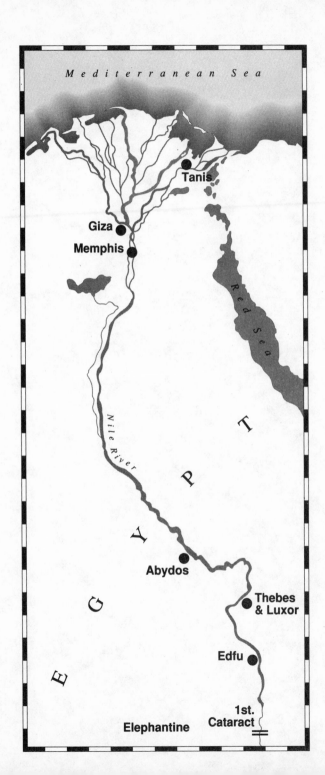

Author's Notes

Of the Seven Wonders of the Ancient World, only the pyramids at Giza remain standing to this day. The Hanging Gardens of Babylon are gone, and the Lighthouse at Alexandria has long since fallen; neither the Colossus of Rhodes nor Phidias' Statue of Jupiter exists anymore; Mausolinus' Tomb and Diana's Temple are dust; but the temples at Luxor and Thebes are rising, phoenix-like, out of their rubble. Few vanished civilizations have left such impressive monuments as the Egyptians; few have attracted such fascination or proved so puzzling to those caught by their mystery. And mystery they were—silent and enigmatic. Until Jean-François Champollion successfully translated the Rosetta stone in 1823 and cracked the language code of those ancient people, the Egyptians had been a cypher for more than fifteen hundred years.

Pharaohnic Egypt endured for more than 2,700 years, far and away the most stable culture in the ancient world, and was surpassed in durability only by China; against such a backdrop, even a semi-immortal vampire might feel a trifle dwarfed: by the time Saint-Germain's recollections of his Egyptian past begin at the height of the Glorious Eighteenth Dynasty, Kufu's pyramid and the Great Sphynx are about eight hundred years old. For more than a thousand years, Saint-Germain remains in Egypt, and the integrity of the culture continues through that time and beyond.

Before archeology became a formal study and the word entered the language in 1890, before the excavations in Greece and Turkey, there was an enduring preoccupation with Egypt. Those enormous buildings and colossal figures compelled admiration and amazement if nothing else. Romans from the time of the Caesars went to Egypt as tourists to stare in awe at the temples and pyramids and statues. Tourism continued from that time to the present, in spite of hardship, hostile religious and political leadership, wars, disease, and the exigencies of travel. From time to time over the years, the tourists remained in Egypt to study the monuments of that lost civilization, to search for the hidden tombs in the cliffs beyond the swath of the Nile, to explore ruins half-buried in sand. These antiquarians, as they were called, were the first to chronicle the treasures of the Pharaohs, and their records continue to be of use today, especially in regard to artifacts that have disappeared or have been destroyed.

Study of ancient Egypt stepped up sharply once Champollion published his work and the Egyptians emerged from silence. In the decades immediately following the decoding of the hieroglyphics, many antiquarians seized on Egypt as a way to establish reputations and intellectual fiefs, and at that time there were theories about the ancient people of Egypt that would today be laughable, but at the time were debated as passionately as paleontologists now debate the nature and temperament of the dinosaurs. Scholarly understanding of the Egyptians has changed since those early days of Egyptology; the abundance of material has increased formidably and the organization of the information has improved, as has the concern of the current government of Egypt with the restoration and preservation of the ancient artifacts. The politics of antiquarian expeditions of the early nineteenth century often required accommodation of several levels of power-brokering and corruption, and was encountered at every phase of the ventures, from Europeans inception to the actualities of on-site chicanery; in addition standards of academic integrity were of secondary interest on expeditions.

Thanks to Napoleon's expedition to Egypt, French involvement in Egyptian antiquities was very high in the 1820s, and with Champollion's accomplishment to fuel the fire, several antiquarian expeditions were sent to Egypt. Although most of these went to

Cairo—the easy access to Giza, the Pyramids and the Sphynx—
and Memphis, a few went the four hundred miles upstream to
the tremendous temples at Thebes and Luxor as much to record
inscriptions as to attempt any restoration on buildings that were
largely in ruins. Along with the French antiquarians there was
also a contingent of British during that time, though they were
more interested in tombs across the Nile on the west bank; their
work brought the Temple of Hatshepsut to light, and eventually
led to the discoveries of tombs in the Valley of the Kings and the
Valley of the Queens.

In the portion of this novel taking place in the 1820s, every
effort has been made to stay within the understanding of Pharaohnic Egypt as it existed at that time, which by current standard
was scant and inaccurate. Saint-Germain's memories are based on
his experience and his subjective interpretation instead of scholarly theory and are often at odds both with Egyptology of the
period of the book and current thought as well.

For help and insight in preparing this novel, the writer would
like to extend her thanks to J. K. Pearl and Elaine Thomas for
information on Egypt in the 1820s, to Dave Nee (as always) for
finding more obscure references than either of us thought possible, to members of the Egyptology department of the University
of California at Berkeley who patiently answered dozens of questions, and to the good people at Tor for their continuing interest.

Berkeley
October 1989

Out of the House of Life

PART I

Senh
Demon

Text of a letter from le Comte de Saint-Germain between Switzerland and the Netherlands, to Madelaine de Montalia in Egypt, dated April 17th, 1825.

Madelaine my heart;

So you have arrived at Cairo; your description of the pyramids brings back many memories, though my nostalgia has faded in the last three thousand years. Yes, they are the most wonderful and sad monuments, now: when I first saw them, they were not the rough bricks you describe, but were sheathed in white limestone, and they shone like enormous jewels. Not that I appreciated them then.

If it were anyone but you, I would not speak of those times; believe this. I put the past behind me long ago, because the burden was too great. I am chagrined, and worse than chagrined, by what I was; I can only excuse myself because I understand in retrospect how I came to be what I was.

Not that Egypt saw the worst of me—far from it. By the time I came to Egypt I was too numbed to be the horror I had been before. I did not raven as I had once; I did not crave terror anymore. I have told you that there are things in my life I do not like remembering, and your questions awaken them. I do not want to tell you what I was, for fear of what you will think of me, and for fear of what I must accept. The words are repugnant, and the acts are loathsome. Yet if you are to under-

3

stand how I came to Egypt, I suppose I must tell you, and hope
you will not despise me for those times. I swear to you by all
the forgotten gods that I would embrace the true death rather
than be such a monster again.

So. In Nineveh and Babylon they thought I was a demon; not
without reason. They kept me chained in an underground dungeon, like a deep well, throwing me a victim at every new moon
for sacrifice. Most of the time I was alone in stench with the
rats. In those endless dark hours I would vow not to kill all at
once, not to fall on the next offering. But the time was long,
and I grew famished; the victims, when they came, were terrified
to madness, and I had no hope. Hunger as much as isolation
deranged me, and I lusted for the dread I spawned, to have
something to sustain me through the empty darkness. The priests
were satisfied with me for two centuries or so before they decided
I was too dangerous to keep. They hauled me out into the full
glare of sunlight, bound me as I screamed and gibbered from
shock and pain, then confined me with chains in a huge cage,
the better to protect themselves while they sought a way to be
rid of me at last.

It was as a demon that I was sold to the High Priest of Judea,
who kept me bound, but not in an underground dungeon: he
confined me with enormous nets and sunlight. From time to
time he tried to speak with me, to show how great his power was
over demons, and to provide proof of his magical skills. Some
thought that he was taking a terrible chance to have me, and a
few whispered that the High Priest was in league with me, though
most were too frightened to do more than whisper. After a time
he died and his successor, who had no wish for commerce with
demons, made up his mind to banish me, and I was given as
tribute to Pharaoh Hatshepsut while she was in Judea. She fascinated the High King and troubled the priests because she did
not worship as they did and was foreign. It was assumed, I have
come to think, that I would make short work of her.

How odd it is, to write of those times. I do not want to recognize
myself in that blood-crazed unhuman thing, but I do. I detest
what I remember, but I cannot deny it. I wonder if telling you
all this will purge me of my loathing and despair? We shall see.

Hatshepsut's entourage carried me overland to the sea in an open wagon, the sun making me howl in agony. I recall how I had longed for the light all those years in that Babylonian abattoir, and I cursed my folly. At night they provided me with a goat and a half-dozen armed guards to surround me while I had my feast, which was the greatest kindness I had known in nearly three hundred years. Pharaoh Hatshepsut watched me as I slaked my thirst and gave me a carnelian scarab afterward. To this day I do not know what she intended by her gift. When we set sail, they bound me in the hold. I am grateful for that: had they chained me on the deck with the other slaves I refuse even now to imagine what torture it would have been, with the water and the sun.

At Memphis the priests had come aboard, and after offering thanksgiving to Hapy and Atan for the safe and prosperous journey of Pharaoh Hatshepsut, they were given the chance to inspect the many gifts presented to her by the High King of Judea, along with the tribute of other, less favored, dignitaries.

"Where did these come from?" asked the most venerable of the priests, who wore a huge pectoral representing the head of a jackal, as he looked over the slaves. "They are stalwart enough. Anubis will take three of these. We will have the biggest, to handle the bodies."

"What about this one? They say he is a demon; he drank all the blood in a goat, I have been told," his scribe remarked, indicating the unkempt figure double-chained to the wall.

"No," the priest of Anubis said with a decisive turn of his head. "Let the House of Life have him. It will not matter to them what he is. He will be no loss, and his death will be a credit to the gods." He passed on, signaling the others in his train to follow.

Another priest, less impressively arrayed, paused in front of the demon. "Dark hair, dark eyes. Skin like a Thracian." He tapped the demon on the shoulder with a short staff. "Where do you come from?"

"Don't make me go outside," pleaded the demon, but in a

tongue no one but himself spoke or understood. He repeated the words in the language of Babylon but without success.

"Uncouth babbling," murmured the priest, shaking his head. "I suppose I could expect nothing more." He signaled to the single acolyte who accompanied him. "Well, since Anubis has been good enough to permit us a little of the spoils, I suppose we ought to be grateful. We know how jealous a jackal can be of carrion." He stepped back, regarding the manacles that bound the demon's hands. "You are strong, and that is something. It's a pity you cannot speak intelligibly, but among the dying..." He shrugged. "We will carry you to the House of Life; Imhotep will find a use for you before the end."

The demon drew back as the priest tried to grab his hair; he showed his teeth and babbled, "Don't touch me." He snarled as much for the futility of speaking to these arrogant Egyptians as for a threat.

"Is it possible that he belongs to a god already?" the priest asked his acolyte. "There are times that the gods put their mark on their slaves, but..." His large, kohl-rimmed eyes narrowed. "Are you without wits, or are you a messenger gone astray?"

Now the demon was restless, moving about as much as his double load of chains would permit. He said nothing, but there was an expression in his dark eyes that was more arresting than the most eloquent words would have been.

"We'll probably have to bring more men; it won't be safe for you and me to try and carry him to the temple." The priest shook his head as he continued to stare at the demon. "Without the beard and that mess of hair, he might be passable. We can't send him among the dying like that. See that he and the two others we've been allotted are bathed and shaved properly." He started to move away, then glanced back at the demon. "Tall, deep chest for strength, yet such small hands and feet. Those scars are terrible. I wonder where he comes from?"

It is misleading to call the House of Life the Temple of Imhotep, although that was its name: this was a sanctuary for those in failing health, and the work of the priests was more in the care of the ill and injured than in chants and offerings given to their deity, and while worship continued endlessly so that the medicines they offered might prove effective, most of those in the House of Life ministered to those in need of healing. All but the highest priests confined their worship to the study of treatments and the tending of those who were beyond the reach of medicine and prayers and would die.

That is where I went: among the dying.

Amensis stood at the entrance of the courtyard, out of the House of Life. It always saddened him to see those unfortunates who gathered there, each with Anubis, Maat and Thoth waiting for them. As High Priest of Imhotep, he was required to visit this place twice a day. Of all his duties, this was the most onerous, the most futile, and the one that haunted him more than all the rest. In spite of his resolution not to, he found himself watching the foreign slave some called the Demon moving among those lying on pallets. "Senh," he said, using the name the slave had been given, the only one it was appropriate for him to use: no one would call him Demon aloud, to his face.

The slave paused in his task of sponging a man delirious with fever. His demeanor was impassive, showing neither concern nor revulsion. "High Priest," he said, his accent atrocious, his words without emotion.

"What is the matter with him?" He did not need to ask; Amensis had ordered the man out of the House of Life three days before when it became apparent that the medication applied to his broken hip had not restored him to health; now there was a discolored swelling larger than a clenched fist just where the bone snapped and the man could no longer walk.

"He is burning," said Senh, the Demon, finding the words with difficulty. It had been three days since he had last been shaved, yet there was little stubble on his scalp and arms, less than would have been expected in other men. "Fever."

Amensis nodded, smelling the infection that filled the delirious man even ten steps away from him. "How long have you been here now, at the House of Life?"

It took Senh a short time to work out the question and his answer. "Two years, more, High Priest."

"Two years and more," Amensis repeated, though he knew this already. "You have been here two years, two years and three months." He shook his head. No wonder the foreigner was called Demon. No slave out of the House of Life had survived so long. Before now, the longest anyone had lived as a slave out of the House of Life was eight months: Senh had been here more than three times as long. Amensis stared at the wide swath of scars that crossed Senh's skin just below the ribs and was hidden by the waist of the short kalasiris all slaves wore at the House of Life. In order to avoid his speculations, Amensis straightened himself and said, "He will be dead by morning. It is beyond us to help him. The priests of Anubis are to be told, so they will be ready to take him."

"I stay here," Senh said in the same flat, uninflected way that he said all things.

"So it seems," responded Amensis, glad for the excuse to walk away from the disturbing slave, and eager to be back within the walls of the House of Life, where there was hope.

Serving out of the House of Life I had no means to hide my identity or my history, nor did I try. I could not have hidden had I wished to and there was no reason for such precautions, not there, not then. Amensis and all the other High Priests entered my name and my tasks in their records, and this did not trouble me, for it was the same with everyone within the House of Life. You might find this strange, considering what the world is become, but in Egypt at that time it was believed that immortality was possible and could be within the grasp of those who traversed certain rituals. That I, a foreigner, survived against formidable odds and through unorthodox means did not rouse the hatred of the priests of Imhotep, or not most of them. It was later—much later—that I discovered my mistake, and learned that if I wanted to survive I would have to conceal my name, my origins and my nature.

For many years I tended the dying much the same way a good farmer tends his chickens, though they meant less to me than the chants of the priests. From time to time I would take what I required from one too lost to know or care what I did, preferably one who was caught up in splendid dreams, for their fancies fed me as much as their blood. But for the most part I was satisfied with the goats I was brought; it was all nothing more than fodder and the quality did not matter.

To this day, I recall how I came to change: it is as clear to me as my recollection of the music I heard last night, and no matter how long ago it happened, it pulls at me still. It was during the turbulent years following the famine in the reign of Thutmose III. Increasingly I had been left on my own, for some of the priests were afraid of me, and a few of them wanted to turn me over to the Temple of Anubis, to work with the dead. But Neptmose, who succeeded Amensis as High Priest, was a pragmatic man who knew he would never have such another slave as I, and would not give me up; and I remained out of the House of Life.

There was a child, a girl no more than seven or eight, who had been bitten by a mad dog. The priests had rubbed her with the fat of oxen, as they did in these cases, and then they had brought her to me for there was nothing else to do. They knew she could not be saved. And she knew what was happening, of course: that was what made in unbearable.

Her face was slick and dried foam crusted her lips. She stood by the low bed prepared for her. "Will I die?" She looked up at the slave who served out of the House of Life.

Senh nodded. "Yes."

The girl sat down on the bed staring at a point an arm's length beyond the wall. "Soon?"

The slave's answer startled him more than it did her. "I hope so."

She looked at him quickly, critically. "Why do you say that?" There was more anger than fear in her eyes, and if her hands had not been shaking where she clutched them at her sides, it would have been impossible to know she was afraid.

"Because it is a hard way to die," said Senh.

"For kindness?" She considered his answer and accepted it. "I have two brothers."

Senh said nothing.

In the silence she lifted her hand and began to gnaw at her fingernails, though they were ragged already. "If I live, will they let me marry?" she asked after a time.

"You will not live," said Senh.

Again she was silent.

"I . . . regret," said Senh as if the words had spikes on them, "I can do so little."

Before sundown she had another fit, and during the night two more, each lasting longer than the one before. Senh held her, and no matter how she strained and kicked and struggled he would not let go of her.

"She cannot live another day," one of the priests said when he came upon Senh tending the girl in the morning. "Imhotep guard us! She has bitten you. There!"

"It's nothing," said Senh, frowning as he looked at the small trail of blood at the top of his arm.

"You will madden as well," the priest said, becoming more alarmed and starting to back away from the foreign slave. "You will take the madness."

"No," said Senh. He tried to think back, to recall when during the night she had bitten him, but he could not bring it to mind. He rubbed absently at the blood, flaking it away. "I can take no hurt from her."

The priest was new to the House of Life but he knew the rumors about Senh, who was called Demon when he could not hear. He had been told of the times Senh had walked through the courtyard when there were so many dying that there was hardly a place to step, and had come away unscathed. He had heard others swear that when fevers came that felled Egyptians, Senh remained untouched by them. He had been told that those who shaved Senh said that his hair grew far more slowly than it ought, and that in spite of his many years, none of it was white. He regarded the foreign slave uneasily. "How can we be sure of that? How can you know that you will not be maddened?"

"Because I never have," said Senh. His eyes rested on the priest a moment, then flicked away. "I must go; she cannot be left alone." He broke away from the priest, a thing no slave would dare to do, and strode back through the courtyard, looking neither to the right or left, his back straight and his stride long and clean. No one knew how much the sunlight pained him.

"You were gone," said the child when Senh came to her side.

"I'm back now." He put his hand to her forehead and felt the madness tainting her blood.

By midafternoon, as the heat lay over the Black Land as insistent as an impassioned lover, the frequency and severity of the girl's seizures had driven her beyond exhaustion. In her last lucid moments, she stared up at Senh, her eyes enormous in their dark sockets, all deception burned away by the ferocity of her disease. "I didn't mean to bite you."

"It is nothing," he said, holding her now to support rather than restrain her.

"You will suffer as I have; I'm sorry."

He smoothed the side-lock of her hair. "It's nothing," he repeated. She weighed so little. She was so young.

She lifted her hand in supplication. "Tie me to the bed and leave me. I don't want to hurt you anymore." Her voice was hoarse and low, and each time she breathed her ribs showed taut against her skin.

"You cannot hurt me," Senh told her, and found it difficult to admit this to a child who was so vulnerable. Wondering at himself, he pulled her closer to him, as if he could protect her from her approaching death with his own, more durable body.

"No?" Her eyes accused him but she did not protest; in a little while another seizure raged through her, and when it was gone Senh sent word to the Temple of Anubis so that she could be prepared for burial. He stood in the middle of the courtyard out of the House of Life and he looked up at the vast dazzle of the night sky; for the first time since his own death, he missed some-

one. In his despondent state the indifference and beauty of the
sky angered him. He missed the girl who died of the bite of a
mad dog, and he mourned her. He rubbed his arm where she had
bitten him and wondered if his blood had passed any of his nature
to her. It was the first time that possibility had entered his mind
in more than a century. It was the first time he hoped that it had,
and knew it had not.

*I never knew her name, and I have never forgotten her. No
fate required she die; it was blind chance. No god had demanded
that death of her. And because of that, because no one could
change what happened, I felt I owed her an answer for her dying.
That was not possible, but the feeling that life had cheated her
has never entirely left me. She was no human livestock, much
as I wanted to think her so, and her dying left me desolate in
a way I had not known since I saw my family slaughtered when
I was taken captive by our enemies, before I came to this life.
She was so mortal. She was so lost.*

*Have a care, my heart, while you are in that place. The Black
Land is beautiful but it is also unforgiving; take no chances
while you are there. As much as the loss of that child has haunted
me down the ages, the pain of it is nothing compared to the
agony I would know if any harm came to you. And there is
harm in Egypt, never doubt that. Perhaps it is because I have
longed for you so many, many centuries that I want to guard
you; perhaps it is my certainty that what you and I have found
is found only once, if you are very fortunate and have the
courage to accept it.*

*Now that you have decided to go to Thebes, give me permission
to provide you some assistance. Do this to please me, if not for
your own safety. I will not interfere with your discoveries, I will
not cheat you of the knowledge you seek, and I will not do
anything to compromise your position with the antiquarian
expedition: my word on it. I know how precious learning is to
you, for that is a part, a very small part of what makes you
precious to me. But that is also the reason I am apprehensive.
You are an unmarried woman, alone, in a Moslem country,*

and working with a party of European men. Your wealth and position cannot protect you, for they have no bearing where you are going. All those considerations are sufficient to trouble me, but given our nature, I am more anxious: I do not want to alarm you, but I urge you to be cautious. I cherish you for your courage and I dread where it might lead. Let me have news of you often, Madelaine; be sure you are eternally in my thoughts, as your blood, your life, lives in my veins.

                              Saint-Germain
                              (who was once Senh)
                              (his seal, the eclipse)

May through September, 1825

Text of a letter from Jean-Marc Paille in Cairo to Honorine Magasin in Poitiers, through the good offices of her cousin Georges in Orleans.

My most adored Honorine;

Thank the Good God who has provided you such a cousin as Georges! Surely he is a saint among sinners. How would I be able to have contact with you if it were not for him? He told me himself that he thinks your father is being cruel to you and unkind to me in prohibiting our marriage for no better reason than my lack of money. He promised me before I left that he would do all in his power to continue his association with you so that he might be able to carry my messages to you and send yours to me. How infuriating it is that we should be reduced to this subterfuge. This is not the Medieval world, yet your father is worse than the puissant lords who sold their serfs for gaming debts. And now he contrives to keep us from the consolation of letters. I cannot imagine what it would be like for me if I could not find some way to correspond with you while I am away from France. It would eat my soul as the worm devours the body. When I return, we will decide what to do.

We landed at Cairo two days ago, and I found a room at the hotel recommended by Baundilet, supposedly one of the best for Europeans, but nothing like what I have come to expect in accommodations. I know that it will be far more primitive when I join the rest of the expedition, but that is nothing unexpected. Here, in this city, I had hoped for better, though the price is not too high, which I had feared it might be, for one hears tales of these foreign places. It is good to know that in this instance I worried for no reason.

The heat here is unspeakable, as if some enormous, invisible beast has wrapped itself around oneself. The breath of the desert, one Englishman at this hotel called it, and I must concur. It is a living, deadly heat. With it are sand and dust. I find them everywhere, even in clothes folded and locked in my luggage. That silky grit gets through the smallest space. Also, as I was warned, there are flies. The air is sooty with them, and you cannot step into the street but that hundreds of them are buzzing around you. The people who live here do not seem to notice them, nor their livestock. I suppose it is what they are used to.

I have at last met Alain Baundilet, the leader of this expedition. He was waiting for my arrival at the hotel, having come down-river five days ago. Ever since I had his letter accepting me into the venture, I have imagined what he would be like in my mind. Such a scholar, I determined, would be old and dried out with hunting through desert ruins, crabbed from bending over, and preoccupied as so many enthusiasts are. That was what I expected. So you may imagine my surprise when Professor Baundilet presented himself to me, a young man for so great a scholar, no more than thirty-five. He is well-set-up and articulate, very witty and erudite. He kept me quite entertained throughout the dinner we shared, giving me his impressions of what he has uncovered so far. Mind you, he has no great discoveries to his credit as yet, but he is confident that within the year he may make such claims. His demeanor lends credit to these assertions, and I feel more than ever that I have found a valued mentor in him. Even his clothes are quite fashionable, and when I remarked upon it, he told me at once that he keeps two separate wardrobes: one for scrabbling about in the ruins and one for polite company. Those are his words.

Everything he has related to me has fired me with new hope for the both of us. Now that we have the Champollion translation of the hieroglyphics, this ancient world, which previously was a maddening puzzle, is coming to light. I cannot say what pride I have in knowing I will be able to play a small part in that great process. There are writings enough on these ancient walls to keep scholars occupied for a good twenty years or more, which assures my future. By the time we have answered the riddle of the Egyptians, every major university in France will be eager for my services. It is apparent to me that Baundilet is determined to make a concerted study of all he finds, and that convinces me I have allied myself with the right man.

Once I have demonstrated how genuine my determination is, I am convinced that your father will relent and give his permission for our marriage. Since he will accept me on no terms but his own, I will demonstrate my worldly worth to him in such a way that he cannot ignore what I have accomplished. It sickens me to think that he has you on an auction block as much as any miserable slave has been. To determine a suitor's acceptability entirely on his financial prospects is as repugnant to me as it is to you. If there is any attempt to sway you, to make you entertain one of those wealthy old men you have complained of, remain steadfast, knowing that I will strive the more determinedly for you.

Should there be such a need, your Cousin Georges has said that he will offer you refuge in his house if you require it. He has convinced me of his utter sincerity, for he has told me that your happiness has been the first order of his concern since you were children. Do not feel that you have no one to turn to because you are in France and I am in Egypt. Your Cousin will open his doors to you whenever you have need, and he has sworn to me that he will guard you as if you were his beloved.

I go tomorrow morning to see the sunrise at the Pyramids. You cannot conceive what monuments they are. No description can do them justice. No matter how awe-inspiring the drawings of them are they are nothing to the reality. When I approached them for the first time, at dusk, I could well understand how the Egyptians felt they were in the presence of a god. It is not only their enormous size, it is their inestimable age. One day, my darling, you will see this amazing sight with me. You will stand at my side and together we will share the majesty of these stones.

When we reach Thebes, I will meet the other members of this antiquarian expedition. There are nine of us in all, though the names Baundilet has mentioned are not familiar to me. He tells me that some work has already begun. Everything is arranged. The day after tomorrow we will begin the journey up the Nile. Imagine! I will see the river the Pharaohs rode on, the river that brings life to the land of Egypt, and go as Egyptians have gone for hundreds and hundreds of years, to the heart of that ancient civilization. It may even be possible to have the opportunity to meet the great Jean-François Champollion, for he is gathering an expedition with Ippolito Rosellini of Pisa, or so I have been told. I do not know yet if they have set out or arrived or, indeed, anything more. News moves slowly here, and you will have to excuse my occasional tardiness on that account.

Remember me in your prayers and your dreams, dearest Honorine, as I will you in mine. When I return, you need never fear again. I will make myself a bastion between you and the rigors of the world. I will take on the burden of all your cares, making your happiness my happiness. I may not have money now, but I swear to you I will cover you in jewels and furs when I come back from Egypt. There is nothing your father can do to keep us apart once we have pledged our faith to each other. This separation is nothing more than an inconvenience which allows me to pave my way to you with gold and acclaim. Thus, with my name I send you a thousand kisses and the sweetest, most sacred vows for our continuing love.

With my heart in my hands,
Jean-Marc

3 May, 1825, Cairo

1

"Are you still up? Paille? It must be close on three." Alain Baundilet was sitting on a sack of grain toward the aft of the dhow, his features unreadable in the light of the waning moon.

Jean-Marc Paille started at the unexpected words, then did his best to appear calm. "I didn't see you there," he said.

"Small wonder," Baundilet sighed. "There's another sack, a little way along the deck, if you want it." He took his huge linen handkerchief and swabbed at the back of his neck. "I can't sleep when it's like this, so hot and still."

"It's like suffocating," said Jean-Marc, trying to sound more experienced than he was. He pulled out his watch and squinted at it in the sudden glare as he struck a lucifer and held it near the face. "I make it two forty-nine."

Baundilet chuckled. "Suffocating at two forty-nine. Or smothering. The sheets were more weight than I wanted to bear. The air is weight enough. Well, at least my wife isn't with me. Can you imagine anyone lying close to you in this heat? It's unthinkable." He smoothed his lapels. "She's one to droop in the heat, in any case. I'd never bring her here; it wouldn't be right."

"You left your wife at home?" Jean-Marc asked, horrified that anyone could do such a thing.

"Better than having her here." He sensed the younger man's disapproval and raised his hand placatingly. "Good God man, look around you. You see what the Moslems are. Look at this place. This is no country for a Frenchwoman. We have other things to occupy our thoughts. Wives get underfoot, Paille, as you'll find out as soon as you acquire one." He slapped at his neck suddenly. "Damned mosquito. Big as a beetle." He stared at his fingers, but could not tell if he had killed the insect or not. "Lots of beetles in Egypt, and they're not all scarabs, either. I found one digging, last month. Thing was as big as my hand, I swear it was. It gave off the most appalling stench."

"Oh," said Jean-Marc, the matter of wives forgotten; he was

enchanted by what he heard, though he was not very fond of beetles; he was caught up in the thrill of his adventure.

"You've got to be careful digging," Baundilet went on, enjoying the way Jean-Marc listened to him as if mesmerized. "It's not just beetles you have to look out for. Scorpions, now they're what you have to be careful of out here. They're deadly, for one thing, and you don't always see them. One of the natives took a bite from a scorpion not long ago; his suffering was dreadful. So take no chances. Be careful of scorpions. Snakes, too, though some of them aren't very dangerous. Don't take risks with them, either, whatever they're like. Better safe than sorry, that's my way." He looked up at the sails. "The designs haven't changed very much, you know. That lateen-like rig, and the long reach up the river. Going upstream, the wind's almost at your back. Coming down, you must use the current and the boats are harder to control. This river shapes everything in Egypt. It always has. The ships of the Pharaohs wouldn't look too out of place today, at least not the ordinary ships."

"Have you found any references to ships in your studies?" Jean-Marc asked it eagerly, and cursed himself for sounding naïve. He changed his tone, making it more confident, or so he hoped. "Have you some proof of that? Have you found a ship from the time of the Pharaohs?"

"Some. You see them in the wall paintings. There's been broken bits of gilded wood, and they might be ships, or catafalques or ... who can tell?" Baundilet sighed and shook his head, folding his handkerchief with care before returning it to his pocket. "Can't keep linen crisp here. It's useless to try." He squinted at the steersman, who was pointedly paying them no heed. "He speaks a little French, you know. Not a lot, but enough to get along. He listens to us. So think about what you say when you see these fellows about. Most of them are ignorant and only a little removed from savagery, but there are those who are crafty and capable, who seek to profit from us and the things we do. It would be unwise to forget that."

"Thanks. It's good to be warned," said Jean-Marc, not knowing how he was to determine which of the Egyptians he encounterd actually spoke French and which did not.

"Oh," said Baundilet as he got to his feet, stretching a bit. "One more thing. I suppose I ought to mention that we have another person joining our expedition, just recently arrived, in fact." His smile—if it was a smile—was gone almost before it began. "There's a woman: young, wealthy, one of those aristos who got through the Revolution and has been allowed to remain French. Her family probably bribed someone or made a pact with the Church. Whatever the case, she has lands and money and some sort of title. She has said she has a genuine antiquarian interest, and so far as I know, it's true. She's rented a villa near Thebes, and she's paying handsomely for the privilege of digging in the sand with us. Her fees have assured us another six months here, no matter what the university may decide. I don't suppose she'll find it interesting for long, which is why I demanded so much money at the first, but while she's along, we won't be bored. We've an opportunity for variety, that's my assumption."

"A young woman? What would she be doing here?" Jean-Marc thought of his beloved Honorine and how he had felt about her accompanying him on this expedition, even if it had been possible. "Why did she come?"

Somewhere off near the shore there was a splash and a thrashing. Jean-Marc looked toward the sound, his eyes wide; Baundilet went on as if he had not heard.

"The guess within the group is that she's run away from her husband. You know what the aristos are like. Why else would a woman set herself up in a villa outside Thebes? This is no place for someone like her. Moslem law won't give her much more satisfaction than her husband, and if she imagines herself with a sheik for a lover, she'll have a long time by herself. Foreign women don't appeal to Moslems. Most of the Egyptians have wives to spare and take their outside pleasures with boys."

Jean-Marc could think of nothing to say. He nodded several times to encourage Baundilet to go on.

Baundilet was growing more pleased with his own observations. He moved a little closer to Jean-Marc. "I've given her some thought these last several days. She might be one of those women who seeks her own sex for pleasure, of course, but Egyptian women are cloistered as nuns, most of them. If they are inverted, they express it behind walls, where other women are. Besides, they do things to them when they're children—take out part of their female apparatus, the little nib, you know, and the inner lips; sometimes sew the mons veneris partly closed to ensure virginity—that don't lend themselves to women's perversions." His laughter was derisive.

"Then what is this Frenchwoman doing?" asked Jean-Marc, trying to consider everything Baundilet had said so casually.

"She is amusing herself. What else can it be?" Baundilet announced this as if it were his most recent discovery. "Aristos are like that, even now. She wants something new in her life, something that she can boast of when she is in high company. She wants a reasonable excuse to keep away from her husband without compromising herself. A trip to Egypt is just the thing, now that we have a little clue to the meaning of all those endless inscriptions." He took out his handkerchief again and swabbed his forehead. "In a month or so, she'll know enough to make it possible to return to Paris with her pride intact, a trinket or two, her reputation as a scholar assured, and her husband will dare not question her about her time in Egypt." He laughed, this time not at all nicely.

"What if she really does care? Couldn't she have a serious interest in antiquarian scholarship?" asked Jean-Marc.

"She would not be a pretty creature with money if she were. Women who care about scholarship are crabbed and ugly, disappointed by family and without hope of a husband, and none of those words fit la Montalia. Strange name, isn't it? From Savoie, or so I have been told, where they're almost Italian, some of them. Dark hair, a neat figure, the most amazing eyes, almost like violets, and an elegant manner. A century ago they would have fought duels over her." He laughed again. "Well, that is the woman who is joining us. You will want to make your bow to her soon, for I miss my guess if she is not one to stand by form."

Jean-Marc nodded, his mind distracted. "I will call on her."

"Fine; fine." Baundilet started along the deck, then looked back at Jean-Marc. "Have you brought any shaving soap with you? Proper shaving soap? We're almost out, you know."

"Actually, no, I haven't," said Jean-Marc. "I didn't realize we would need outside supplies of soap. But I believe I have three bars packed with my things. Will that do?" This shift took him by surprise and he answered with more candor than he had intended.

"Let me have one, will you? I want to freshen up in the morning, look my best. I'm afraid my jaw is about to turn to a complete rash with the muck I've been using. They don't understand about proper soap here. Everything is oil and sandalwood." He rubbed his hand over his chin to make the point, and then he added, "I hope you do well with Mademoiselle de Montalia. Someone ought to, and she does not seem to trust me, no matter how much money she has paid me."

"Trust you?" Jean-Marc was genuinely surprised. "What is her explanation for that?"

"She doesn't offer one. Women of her sort don't." He folded his arms and cleared his throat, preparing to make a crucial statement. "Someone is going to have to keep watch on her, but not too obviously. She isn't one of these women who can be left alone. She's too curious."

Jean-Marc frowned. "But why is that a problem?"

Baundilet wagged his finger at Jean-Marc. "We do not need someone of her sort keeping track of what we do. It isn't fitting. We're reasonable men, not from her class. We don't go on these expeditions solely for amusement." He touched his watchfob. "It's one thing to have her digging with us, so long as she doesn't collapse in the sun, but it's quite another if she starts interfering with our work."

"Yes," said Jean-Marc after a moment. "I see that."

"Well, then, I suppose I can rely on you to keep me informed of everything she gets into." This time his smile was wider, hungrier. "Mind you, there are a few things she might get into that would suit me very well."

The implication was not lost on Jean-Marc, who tried to hide his astonishment with a wordly laugh. "Because you have left your wife at home, is that it?"

"Certainly in part," said Baundilet, then concealed a yawn with his hand. "I've told you she's an attractive woman. It is better than taking chances with whores, isn't it?" He cleared his throat. "I think I'll try to get some sleep. It won't be easy, but . . ."

Jean-Marc rose at once. "I was thinking the same myself," he told Baundilet. "It will take me a while to get used to this climate."

"Yes; it's hard for all of us at first," said Baundilet. "Well, Paille, good-night, then." He turned away with no more comment and made his way toward the narrow cabin door. There he paused, but whether it was to look at Jean-Marc or to cast a last glance at the steersman, it was impossible to tell.

After another half-hour of sitting on the deck watching the moon drop down the night and listening to the groan of the sails and lines, the occasional indefinable noises from the shore, and the endless slap of the river against the prow of the boat, Jean-Marc decided to renew his attempt at sleep. He returned to his cabin and made sure that the shutters were adjusted to let in what little breeze there was. As he undressed, he considered what Alain Baundilet had told him, and could not make up his mind if he thought the leader of the expedition was joking or not. Surely a man like Baundilet would not compromise his standing as an antiquarian by seducing a woman of wealth and position, married or not. He arrived at no satisfactory conclusion before sleep at last overcame him.

Well before ten, the morning was hot, the sun bright off the surface of the Nile as it burned along the sky. Unfamiliar birds coasted over the water, their cries like the sound of lambs calling to their mothers. Jean-Marc stood at the side of the dhow, his eyes shaded as he followed the progress of the birds, wishing he knew what they were. He felt a bit light-headed, as if he had drunk a tot too much brandy. The only excuse he could offer himself was fatigue, for he had not been able to sleep more than four hours; he did his best to concentrate on the progress of the dhow up-river.

"Liking what you see?" The speaker at his arm was Ursin Guibert, the expedition's man-of-all-tasks who had accompanied Baundilet down-river.

"I don't know yet," Jean-Marc confessed. He was a trifle disoriented, and so did not wonder that Guibert should speak to him; ordinarily he would not converse so easily with a servant.

"It takes time," said Guibert, who had come to Egypt as a sergeant in Napoleon's army, remaining as a civilian guide when the troops left. Now, though his clothes were fairly European though years behind the fashion, he covered his head with a kind of turban and his face was as dark and weathered as that of the steersman. He was thirty-nine and looked sixty. "The first three years I was here, I thought I'd never know it, never feel a place for myself. I thought I only wanted to go back to France. But that changed." He smoked a pipe, the long-stemmed sort made of clay. He filled it now, tamping the tobacco with care. "I've never learned to like these water pipes the natives smoke. I don't like what they put in them much, either. I'll take my intoxication from wine and brandy, thank you, and not from a handful of herbs." He lit up and drew in the smoke. "There's tobacco in the supplies. I made sure of that."

Remembering what Baundilet said the night before, Jean-Marc asked, "What about shaving soap?"

"Alain is worried about that again, is he? Shaving soap!" Guibert chuckled through his clenched teeth, and the pipe quivered. "He is forever afraid that he will not be able to give himself a decent shave. I've never failed him, but he continues to fret. He must always have something to bother him." This was more amusement than complaint, and he did not continue to comment on his employer. "Ah. Look." He pointed across the river toward the western bank. "Look there. Shadufs, they're called. They use them to irrigate the fields. The counterweights lift the waterbuckets, you see."

"Yes," said Jean-Marc, looking at the devices with fascination. "How ingenious."

"Baundilet thinks the ancients used something like them, as well. He's found a wall painting that shows something like them, in any case. He'll be preparing drawings of it for presentation, along with sketches of the shadufs we see now, to make his point. He's never been one to overlook an advantage. Very ambitious is our Alain. He's got his sights set high." Guibert rested one hand on the rail, swinging around to watch the wake of the dhow. "And what about you, Paille? What are you looking for in Egypt?"

"Why, antiquities," said Jean-Marc, too promptly.

"Of course," Guibert said, then added, "But what besides? There must be something more. If all you wanted was antiquities, you could arrange to purchase them in Paris."

"Oh, no," Jean-Marc protested. "No, buying them is nothing. Anyone with *money*—he said the word bitterly, for he had so little of it—"can purchase anything if he has patience and determination. It means nothing to buy antiquities. What is important is to discover them, to find what has not been found before, and to bring it to the attention of the world."

"Ah," said Guibert with a single nod. "Fame. It is fame you want. Well, there is fame to be had here, of a sort, that's true enough." He laughed. "But it is not for everyone, is it?"

Jean-Marc flushed, and tried to make himself believe it was the heat and not his vanity that caused it. "Fame is trivial," he said, wishing he meant it. "The discoveries are important, the learning. These ancient people have much to tell us. To be able to come here when so much is new, well, it is an opportunity few teachers have. It must be an honor to any scholar to add to the knowledge of the world."

"And his own reputation, incidentally," said Guibert with a smile and a nod. "You need not be ashamed of what you seek. If you are willing to come this far and to labor like the meanest peasant under the most grueling conditions, you will earn your fame, your reputation. I have no reason to cavil with you for what you want." He took his pipe from his mouth, seeing the hard set to Jean-Marc's mouth. His manner grew more amiable. "Best to stop this before it gets started. I have nothing against you, Paille, or your goals. We will be part of the same expedition for quite a while, you and I. In places as isolated as Thebes, we cannot afford rancor. It's not wise to take what I say now in offense, for it will only lead to problems between us, which neither of us wants. Do we?" He held out his gnarled hand. "It's the East, don't you see? It changes you if you stay here."

Jean-Marc took Guibert's hand reluctantly. "I'm sorry if I misunderstood you. I hope we will work well together."

"Very tactful," approved Guibert. He remained silent for a few minutes, then remarked, "You'll want to get your hat. If you stand in the hot sun without something on your head, your brains will broil." With that warning, he strolled away down the deck, humming to himself.

As he watched Ursin Guibert move away, Jean-Marc attempted to discover for himself what their exchange—for he could hardly call it a conversation—had been about. Was Guibert putting him on warning? Of what? Why? Try as he would, Jean-Marc could make no sense of it. He ambled toward the prow of the boat, doing his best to appear nonchalant. There was so much new to him that he could not quite keep from staring. At last he came to a halt and stood watching the curl of the water where the boat parted the river.

"Finding anything?" Alain Baundilet asked as he came up behind Jean-Marc.

Jean-Marc shook his head as he glanced over his shoulder, then shrugged. "Nothing. I think the heat is making me a bit silly."

"It can do that," said Baundilet with scant interest. Seeing that Jean-Marc was bareheaded, he added, "Just guard against it." He indicated the sun. "Ursin told you about hats, didn't he?"

"He said something, yes," was Jean-Marc cautious answer.

"Well," Baundilet said, indicating his own hat, "you'd do well to put yours on. The day isn't going to get any cooler until several hours after sundown." His smile was so facile that it had almost no reality at all. "I don't want you left prostrate by the heat."

"I'm hardy enough," said Jean-Marc, adding indignantly, "Why is it that everyone thinks all Europeans cannot endure the desert?"

"Because most can't," Baundilet said curtly. "I certainly wouldn't come out without this." He tapped the brim. "Go on. Get your hat. Then join me in my cabin and I'll show you what we've been working on. That'll give you a notion of what we're trying to do." He clapped Jean-Marc on the shoulder, adopting an attitude of good fellowship. "It's easy to feel lost when you first arrive in Egypt. It's an overwhelming place. But if you let me have a little of your time, we can avoid the worst of that, I hope. Once you're acquainted with the project, you'll settle in well."

"Of course," said Jean-Marc at once. He nodded to Baundilet. "You're right about the hat. I suppose I've been stubborn."

"Not difficult when you're first here. It's strange to us, and we don't want to give up the ways we know," Baundilet said with greater geniality. "I remember how I clung to the best French ways when I first arrived here. I thought I was being sensible; I supposed it was correct, to insist that Egypt be Paris, or at least Marseilles."

Jean-Marc's laughter was as polite as it was expected. "I'll try to accustom myself to Egypt."

"Good," Baundilet approved. "No sense fighting the place." He indicated the shore where almost a dozen cattle stood half-submerged at the edge of the river, guarded by two scrawny under-sized boys. "Even the people here now, they don't quite belong. No one can. It's older than any of us."

"It's older than any of us," Jean-Marc repeated under his breath as he followed Baundilet down the deck, wondering for the first time at his audacity at coming here.

Text of a letter from the Coptic monk Erai Gurzin at Edfu in Upper Egypt to le Comte de Saint-Germain in Rotterdam.

To the Teacher of the Great Art, Saint-Germain, greetings in the Name of God and the Eucharist;

Your letter reached me at last, taking longer than might be expected because the first messenger went to the First Cataract at Aswan, thinking to find the monastery there. It is, as it has been since its founding sixteen hundred years ago, near the ancient temples of Rameses II. The messenger was three weeks late making the delivery because of this misunderstanding.

We have done as you requested, and marked the grave of Niklos Aulirios with a stone that is not Christian. The inscription you provided, in Greek, has been carved into it. The monks here were not wholly pleased, but they accept that Aulirios was a good man, living a Christian life without benefit of baptism, and so they agreed at last to let him lie at the entrance to the monastery garden, near the wall. It may be that his death played some part in their decision, for he would not have faced that firing squad if he had not stopped those French soldiers from destroying those ancient inscriptions. Most of the monks believe that he did a right thing in protecting the inscriptions, though they were from the time of Rameses II and not Holy Writ. We pray for the repose of his soul, as well.

I have obtained permission to travel north to Thebes, and I will endeavor once I am there to make contact with this Madelaine de Montalia who is there to discover what she can about the Egyptians of the Pharaohs. Your description of her is intriguing; I have not met many European women, and those I have were not of her sort, or so I suppose from what you tell me. I find it difficult to believe that she is as serious in her scholarship as you claim, but I have never known you to err in your judgment. If this woman is of your blood and has your capacity for knowledge, I ought not hold her in suspicion because she is French and young.

There have been an increasing number of Europeans coming to see the ancient monuments here. Last winter there were over thirty of them at Philae, all rapt at what they saw, though they had no understanding of it. I was hired by one party because of my knowledge of French and English, which money I have given to my monastery. I doubt they realized I am a Christian, for the faith of Coptics is not expressed in ways familiar to them. These Europeans were amazed at everything they saw, but aside from their own outrageous speculations, had no real desire to know anything of the Egyptians who built Philae, or any of the rest. I suppose we must expect more visitors, and accept that most of them do not wish to know more than that the language is strange and the people who made these things are gone.

From the tone of your letter, I dare to hope that your Madelaine de Montalia is not the same as these. Assuming she is willing to accept me as her tutor, there is a great deal I can impart to her. As you know, for you have greater knowledge than I, she can discover much if she is able to see beyond her own country and language into the hearts of strangers. Her dedication to the study of vanished peoples, you tell me, is deeply felt. That would be a welcome change from showing pylons to Europeans who wish only to stare. How worthwhile it may be, if she is half the scholar you describe. It would please me to be able to do this, for it might in part repay all that you have been willing to teach me, and for which I pray for your benefit every morning. God will show favor to those who guide His servants, and you have opened the door for me as no other teacher but God's Word has done.

I will supply you with reports on the progress of this Madelaine de Montalia. You have my word before the altar that I will not let her being young and French blind me to her abilities. I vow that if it is my power to prevent it, no harm will come to her.

In the Name of God,
Erai Gurzin, monk

According to the European calendar, June 29th, 1825
Monastery of Saint Pontius Pilate, Edfu

2

Long, spiked shadows raced ahead of them as Madelaine de Montalia and Claude-Michel Hiver pushed their horses to a gallop in the first brilliance of sunrise. They could see Thebes and Luxor ahead of them, the pylon and obelisks acting as targets for their ride.

"Pull in!" Claude-Michel shouted as he saw a number of camels ahead, already following his own order. He disliked the occasional encounters he had with the Egyptians who lived at Thebes, and did not want so pleasant a morning to be marred by threats and anger.

Madelaine laughed, and brought her horse down to a trot, allowing Claude-Michel to catch up with her. "I told you, you ought to have taken the other Barb." She patted her dark chestnut on her glossy neck. "Good girl."

"You do this every morning?" Claude-Michel asked, panting a little from the excitement of the run. He had seen her on several occasions, but until her invitation of three days ago, it never occurred to him that this was her regular exercise.

Madelaine considered her answer. "Most mornings, not every single one of them. I stay indoors through the worst of the day's heat, so this is the most reasonable time for a ride. Once I settle in with my books, I'm useless until it's dark, which is no time to be out. It's easier on the horses, too, in the early morning." The mare was willing to walk, mincing as the first of the camels went by. "It's odd," Madelaine remarked, doing her best to give the camels a wide berth. "I've been thinking how informal the expedition has made us all. I would never considered calling you Claude-Michel if we were in France, but here, where there are so few of us, and we are working so closely, it would seem ... incorrect to call you Professor Hiver."

"It's not what I expected. When I return to France, it may seem odd to me that I cannot be as informal." He wrinkled his nose. "Christ, those animals stink," said Claude-Michel, confident that none of the men riding or leading the bad-tempered beasts would know what he said.

"They spit, as well," said Madelaine, hoping she and her mount were out of range. "Take care."

"Oh, most surely," said Claude-Michel, waiting until the camels were by before saying, "Are you going to Baundilet's house now, or are you returning to your villa first? I'd assumed you were going to the morning discussion, but that may not be the case." Although he had been in Egypt four months, he still retained his good humor and excellent manners that made him so popular as a teacher in Anjou.

"I might as well hear what Baundilet has planned for today. He seems determined to get the whole of that wall copied before the end of the week." She made a bit of a face. "I want to see it copied as well, but not as if finishing it were some kind of race. The inscriptions have been there a long time. They will wait a week or two for us to copy them." She looked at the sandy track which was now a dusty street. "Are you going to come, or do you have other studies to keep you busy?"

"Oh, I might as well hear what Baundilet has to say." He showed her his most cheerful smile. "Do you think that he's right? Do you think those ancient people did use those counterweight things to load boats and bring water into their houses?"

"Why not?" Madelaine asked. "They use them now." She adjusted her leg over the horn, wishing they could have galloped longer.

"But the ancients had such skills and more," said Claude-Michel. "None of us are capable of what they have accomplished. We're all agreed on that." His fresh, fair face was turning slightly ruddy as the first heat of the day reached him. "Who can say how they built all these things?"

Madelaine smiled slightly. "They weren't magicians, Claude-Michel. They were men, as you are a man. They knew how to use what they had. They wanted these temples more than they wanted . . . oh, I don't know . . . powered plows or enormous ships. They agreed on the worth of the gods, if nothing else." She said this with such conviction that she held Claude-Michel's attention. "We credit them with wonders because we have not devoted our knowledge to the things they studied. You do not see a steam engine in the wall paintings, or a railroad, though they might have found both useful. They put their knowledge to moving heavy objects, and their discoveries made all these monuments possible." They were nearing the houses that clustered near the ancient buildings of Thebes. Reluctantly Madelaine tied her neckcloth over the lower part of her face.

"You have very little wonder in you, Madame," chided Claude-Michel.

"On the contrary," said Madelaine, her voice now muffled. "I am forever filled with wonder, not because I assume miracles, but because I do *not* assume miracles. Where is the wonder in magic making these temples? It is nothing more than a conjuring trick on a large scale. But to realize that men, ordinary men, raised everything that you see here, or anywhere else in the world, that is cause for wonder." She gave a swift smile which he could not see. "It's my favorite thesis. Forgive me for subjecting you to it."

"Not at all," said Claude-Michel as he brought his horse ahead of hers.

"The next street is where Baundilet has his house, isn't it?" Madelaine called, raising her voice so that Claude-Michel would be certain to hear her.

"Yes. We'll put the horses in the courtyard. He has servants who'll hold them and make sure they have water." Claude-Michel hesitated, then said, "It's not a bad house he has—God knows, it's nicer than the one I've leased—but it's nothing like your villa."

Madelaine laughed. "Well, I was fortunate, and the purchase price was reasonable. Besides, I doubt my villa would be convenient for Baundilet, being so far from Thebes itself. It's almost four miles from here—three from el-Karnak." She lowered her voice as she saw a merchant frown at her angrily. "Quite a trudge each morning and evening, if you don't have horses, or the horses are lame." It was the one real disadvantage she had discovered about the villa, and so far it did not trouble her.

"Those are considerations, certainly," said Claude-Michel as he drew up in front of the walled courtyard of Alain Baundilet's house. He tapped the bell that hung by the gate, and waited for one of the servants to answer its summons.

"Fortunately I do not have to consider everyone in this expedition; if I had Baundilet's position to occupy, then I would have to be at pains to find housing near the work, for questions might arise any time of the day or night and I would need to be close at hand." She did not mention that one of the attractions of the villa she had purchased was that it was far enough away from the expedition site that she need not worry about having her privacy disturbed.

"That German fellow—he has taken that villa near yours, hasn't he?" Claude-Michel asked, rising in the stirrups as he heard footsteps approaching on the other side of the gate. "Hello there. Open up. It's Professor Hiver and Madame de Montalia."

"Falke, his name is. I haven't met him. I've been told he's a physician," said Madelaine, breaking off any other comment as the gate was pulled open and Hassan, the senior servant of Baundilet's household, stood aside to admit them.

"Morning, Hassan," said Claude-Michel as he dismounted. He nodded in response to Hassan's bow. "Madame de Montalia and

I have come for the morning discussion. Is Professor Baundilet prepared to talk with us yet?"

"He is dressing," said Hassan, his French good enough to be understood, but limited to a few phrases.

"Then we'll go into the drawing room and wait for him there. I don't suppose any of the others are here yet?" He held out the reins to Hassan and went to assist Madelaine.

"No others here," said Hassan, frowning with disapproval as Madelaine permitted Claude-Michel to catch her by her waist as she dropped out of her side-saddle. He accepted the second set of reins grudgingly.

"Well, they should be here soon," said Claude-Michel, unaware of how his actions had offended Hassan. "If there's coffee . . . "

"It will be served," said Hassan, his frown deepening as he watched Madelaine remove her scarf from her face.

"Good," said Claude-Michel, letting Madelaine enter the house ahead of him. The next servant was known not to speak anything but the local dialect, and so Claude-Michel said nothing to him, but indicated where he and Madelaine were going. "Coffee." He told this servant in the hope the fellow might know the word. "Two." He held up two fingers.

The servant bowed and moved away, but whether he would bring the coffee was uncertain.

As Claude-Michel crossed the entry hall into the drawing room, he glanced out through the tall windows into the garden, where a fountain gurgled and splashed. "I've heard these things help keep the place cool."

"If the house is correctly designed, I suppose they do," said Madelaine, looking at the two large tables that were set up. Charts were strewn across them, along with a profusion of sketches and a number of pocket-sized notebooks. "They must have worked last night again, after supper."

"They do, occasionally. I haven't sat in. Most of it is about the digging. They don't need me for that." He took his place on the longest of three sofas. "They're comfortable, I'll say that."

"What?" Madelaine asked, turning toward him. "Oh. The furniture. Yes, quite comfortable." She went back to the tables and looked down at them. "I see that Jean-Marc has made more notes about the pylon and obelisk. He's captivated by them."

"Well, they are impressive. Most of the people coming here on tour want to see them." Claude-Michel took out his handkerchief and swabbed his face and neck. "They say the heat gets worse through the summer. It's worse than southern Spain already. I find it very hard to believe it will be hotter." He tucked the handkerchief back in his breast pocket. "I don't know if I can stand it much hotter."

"Then you will have to be careful," said Madelaine, looking at the charts and following one of the routes of the temple streets there with her finger. "I wish I knew which temple this is. There must be an inscription somewhere that tells us. They can't all be to the sun god—Amun, Aton, Re, whatever they call him—can they?"

"Of course not," said Claude-Michel at once, then went on less confidently. "By the time we discover more about the language, we'll know more about the character of the temples. It's going to be very exciting, finding out about these temples. Champollion has made a tremendous contribution, I don't mean to imply that he has not, but there are matters about the ancient people that cannot be learned in a day. I think Baundilet is annoyed with me because I cannot stand at the base of these gigantic pillars and read them off as one reads a newspaper. Not," he continued, his assurance returning, "that anyone else can do it, either; not Champollion, not anyone."

"Perhaps even the people who made them could not all read them readily," said Madelaine, still somewhat distracted as she concentrated on the charts. "Think of the servants in Paris who know nothing more than a few words of the paper they carry for their employers."

"True enough," said Claude-Michel, obviously relieved by this notion.

Madelaine smiled as she pulled out the charts for Luxor. This was the part of Thebes she liked, the part she thought of as the most Egyptian, though she had been told that some of the most impressive ancient buildings had been pressed into use by both

Persians and Romans. "This sanctuary," she said, putting her finger
on the outline of the temple grounds. "What do you suppose it
looked like when the worshipers came here? What did they see
that we do not?" She looked out into the garden.

"Well," said Claude-Michel, considering her question, "they saw
the stones and inscriptions new, which we do not. They had the
advantage of knowing what the purpose of the temple was." He
lifted his head at the sound of footsteps. "Ah, our coffee."

"Not quite yet," said Baundilet as he came into the room, his
face glowing from his recent shave, his clothes as practical as
they were fresh. "Good morning, Claude-Michel," he said, extending his hand, and then with less enthusiasm, "Good morning,
Madame de Montalia."

"To you as well, Professor Baundilet." She did not abandon her
place at the table, thought Baundilet glared at her. "I've been
going over the Luxor charts, the new ones. I noticed that here,
in the temple precincts, there appear to be some sphynxes—at
least three haunches and paws might have been sphynxes—and
there are many sphynxes in Luxor."

"They might be lions, as well," said Baundilet shortly. "They
need not be sphynxes simply because there are others about. You
might as well find the bases of all the statues in Paris, and conclude
that all of them were equestrian because some of them were."

"Possibly," said Madelaine, determined not to be offended by
Baundilet's brusque manner. She moved away from the table and
took one of the low Turkish chairs instead. "I hope you'll include
me as you explore those old buildings in Luxor."

"You are one of us, Madame," said Baundilet, smiling determinedly. "If that is your wish, you may certainly work with us."

"Thank you, Professor," said Madelaine, reflecting that the good-
fellowship she enjoyed with most of the others did not extend
itself to Alain Baundilet.

There was the sound of the front door being pulled open, and
then the sound of Jean-Marc Paille calling a greeting to everyone,
announcing himself before he came into the drawing room. He
paused in the door and looked around. "So few; I thought we
were to be here half an hour after sunrise, Baundilet."

"That was the time I suggested," said Baundilet, motioning to his servant to bring in the tray he carried. "Good. I'm sure we're all ready for this. Please. Sit down, Jean-Marc."

Madelaine spoke at once. "I appreciate your offer, but I'm afraid that the coffee you enjoy is too strong for me. I'll wait until I'm back at my villa for refreshments, if that is suitable to you, Professor. I do not want to put your staff to any unnecessary effort."

"What is another cup of coffee, more or less?" asked Baundilet. "Jean-Marc, help yourself to these figs. They're really very good. And you, Claude-Michel. I don't suppose, Madame, that you—"

"No, thank you," said Madelaine as the men moved a little closer to the large brass tray; the servant set it on legs.

"Just as you wish, Madame," said Baundilet, but only out of concern for form. He addressed Jean-Marc as coffee was poured, thick and steaming, into small painted cups. "I saw your notes, and I must agree that there could be a hidden room beneath that floor. But I doubt the local officials would be pleased if we ripped it up without their permission and the appropriate bribes. Now that they have Europeans coming to see these ruins, they want to keep them in reasonable repair." He took a round, fluffy bread from the basket in the middle of the try and bit into it.

"But who knows what treasures we might find," said Jean-Marc as he reached for his coffee.

"That's the trouble," said Baundilet around his mouthful of bread. "If we could guarantee them treasure, they would not protest to our digging up the whole avenue to el-Karnak. But as it is, we cannot tell them what we might find, if anything." He helped himself to a sip of coffee, chewed with determination, then swallowed. "That's better," he said. "If you think we must, I'll speak to the local official, but I have to tell you that I don't hold out much hope for obtaining any digging permission."

Jean-Marc shook his head in discouragement. "We might uncover the greatest find since Egypt opened its doors to us."

"It didn't open its doors," Madelaine said gently. "Napoleon forced them open, and the Egyptians were not pleased." She met Baundilet's angry stare with a bland smile. "It's useful to recall that, for you may be certain that the Egyptians around us do." She hesitated, then went on. "A very . . . very old friend of mine has told me that Egypt has always been wary of foreigners."

"From the safety of Paris or Avignon," scoffed Baundilet.

Her faint smile did not change. "Actually, he lived here for quite a long time. He knows Egypt very well." She thought of the letter she had left in the hidden compartment of the tall secretary at her villa. How would she be able to explain to any of them how she learned about this place, or who had taught her?

"Do you find this amusing?" Claude-Michel asked, seeing something in her eyes he had not encountered before.

"Not precisely," she said, forcing herself to turn her attention to what was being said. "I did want to remind you about necessary caution, that was all. Just as Professor Baundilet warns us about scorpions and snakes and danger from too much sun." Her smile returned. "I am . . . sensitive to the sun."

"So you have said," Baundilet pointed out, helping himself to a fig. "Well, there is some merit in what you say. There are Egyptians who do not welcome Europeans. Where these are concerned, it is best that we observe the greatest decorum. Wouldn't you agree, Madame?"

Madelaine behaved as if she had not been aware of the sarcastic intent of the question. "Yes, Professor; I agree."

The door opened, this time to admit Ursin Guibert and with him Justin LaPlatte, a tall, angular Alsatian who supervised the local men hired for the digging. He spoke the local dialect tolerably well and had made himself an asset to Baundilet from the first. "Good morning," he called out, striding into the drawing room. "Where's de la Noye and the rest?"

"Haven't arrived yet," said Jean-Marc, moving so there would be room for LaPlatte at the table. "We're having coffee," he added unnecessarily.

Guibert paused in the door. "Would you like me to go to de la Noye's house and see what's detaining him?" The question was directed to Baundilet, who paused to sip more coffee.

"Wait a bit," he decided. "If they aren't here in a quarter of an hour, then it makes sense to go after them." He indicated a place on the longest sofa. "Come. Have your coffee with us."

"No," Guibert said easily, as he always did. "Perhaps another time."

Madelaine watched this exchange with covert attention. Did Baundilet realize, she asked herself, that Guibert would never agree to take breakfast with the others, that he always took his meals with the household staff? If Baundilet was aware of it, he gave no notice. She made a gesture of refusal when Claude-Michel offered her the plate of figs, saying, "I'll break my fast later," which was no more than the truth.

By the time Merlin de la Noye and Thierry Enjeu arrived, Baundilet had ordered a second pot of coffee and more of the little breads. De la Noye pulled up a stool for himself and Enjeu found a place on the longest sofa near Madelaine. He gave her a perfunctory greeting and started in on the food.

"I want all of us to be particularly alert to references to anything having to do with the river," Baundilet was saying as he finished his second cup of coffee. "I'm hoping to show something about how the cities on this side of the river dealt with the cities on the other side of the river. I think here at Thebes we have a clear chance of showing how they managed it."

"What do you want us to look for?" asked Jean-Marc. He took his notebook from his pocket and retrieved his pen from its case. As he positioned the notebook on his knee, he looked expectantly at Baundilet.

"I don't know yet," Baundilet admitted, musing at his own lack of knowledge. "There might have been a ferry of sorts. We know they didn't do much bridge-building, though it is clear they might have been able to if they had put their minds to it."

"The Nile floods every year," Madelaine said, as much to remind them she was in the room as to inform them. "It probably wasn't practical to build bridges because of the flooding."

De la Noye pulled at his short, scholarly beard. "It may be; it may also be that one god or another prohibited it. With so many temples on both sides of the river, the people of Pharaoh must have had a busy time of it, propitiating first this god and then that god."

His observation brought a chuckle from the others.

"What about the other side of the river?" asked Enjeu. "Have you ruled it out entirely, Baundilet?"

"For the time being, yes," said Baundilet. "It's a good two miles from the river to the temples there. Why put ourselves to such trouble when there are more than enough remnants of ancient Egypt right under our noses?" He reached over and clapped Thierry Enjeu on the shoulder. "A year, two years from now, it might be worth our whiles to cross the river and see what is in those barren cliffs, not that I expect much is, now that Belzoni's been over it. How many solid alabaster sarcophagi do you think there are buried in those tombs? We could dig for years and years and never stumble on anything more than plundered remnants, perhaps part of a mummy if we're lucky. The grave robbers found the important ones three thousand years ago, in any case. For the time being, we have Thebes and Luxor to occupy us, and el-Karnak after that. Look at what is standing there, and you will realize that we have no reason to cross the river, except, perhaps, to find out how the old Egyptians crossed it." He made himself laugh aloud, but there was something in his eyes that had no trace of humor in it, and Madelaine watched it with misgivings.

"What about the inscriptions we've discovered at the foot of the statue of the god with the sun on his head?" asked de la Noye. "You said three days ago that you are not certain this is the sun god, after all."

"Well, I'm still not sure. You must speak with Claude-Michel about it, for he is the language expert." Baundilet motioned his servant to bring the fresh coffee as he continued. "We are still on the threshold of knowledge. You cannot expect anyone to know beyond question what god is represented by the sun. A year ago we all assumed it was Amon or Re, or possibly Osiris, but now we have discovered that there are other gods represented with the sun on their heads, and so we must withhold our opinion for a time." He smiled, and his smile was met with the approving glance of the others.

"And if it is not Re or Amon, or even Osiris, what then?" asked Madelaine, regarding the men with curiosity, her mind casting back to Saint-Germain's letter. "Who is to say that we are correct in our assumption that there was just one god of the sun? There might be many, or the disk could mean more than just the sun."

"What, for instance?" inquired Baundilet. "Leave it to a woman to complicate things for us." He looked directly at Madelaine for the first time since de la Noye and Enjeu arrived. "Until we have reason to believe that might be the case, we should proceed on the assumption that there is one god of the sun, and that is Amon or Re, depending on which manifestation is being described. If it is not Amon or Re, then we ought to assume it is Osiris." He waited for a moment, and when she said nothing, he went on, "You are quite intelligent, Madame, and I give you credit for that. Not many members of your sex have such acute intellectual abilities. But you allow your mind to bring complications into play that have no place in our studies. We have already established that there is a sun god, called Amon and Amon-Re. That god has a son, Horus, who is represented by a hawk. There is a wife and mother goddess called Isis. There is no reason to suppose that there are others who have their attributes. You have only to look at the temples to realize how fixed these religious figures were in the minds of the Egyptians of old." His mouth approximated a smile but there was no trace of it in his eyes.

Madelaine stared down at the toe of her boot where it protruded from beneath her skirt. "You're quite certain? With all those hundreds of years, there was no change?"

Baundilet gave her his best condescending smirk, one he usually showed to undergraduate students. "Have the Apostles changed since the founding of the Church? Has the Trinity changed? What makes you think that these advanced people of the ancient world would not have gods who endured centuries, as the saints and martyrs have been remembered in Christian doctrine and tradition?" He looked to the others gathered around the brass tray that served as a table. "I don't say that Madame de Montalia's point isn't interesting: it is. But everything we have discovered thus far reveals a very limited pantheon. I think it is wisest for us to assume that is the correct view of the Egyptian religious life."

Jean-Marc seconded this opinion at once. "It's a most astute comment, Professor Baundilet." He nodded to the others as if invoking their support.

De la Noye fingered his beard. "I won't dispute what you say, Baundilet," he allowed, "but I am reluctant to decide quite yet what the beliefs of the ancient Egyptians were. You are satisfied that the gods were set and few, but I am not as sanguine as you are, for I have read much of the traditions of the old Greeks, and I am convinced that there was no unanimity of opinion among them in regard to the gods. If the Greeks brought ambiguity to their gods, why would the Egyptians not do the same?" The question was not intended to be answered, and so he was surprised when Jean-Marc took up the issue.

"The Greeks were diverse, according to what has been learned of them. They lived in separate cities and each city considered itself a country. So it is hardly amazing to find that each Greek city had its own notion of the gods. But Egypt was not cut from that cloth. Egypt had great integrity, even when the country was divided between Upper and Lower Egypt. Therefore it is appropriate to consider that unification as binding." He looked to Baundilet for endorsement.

"Most sensible," said Baundilet as he had the last of his coffee. "You express my case very clearly."

"But there is no assurance that this is the correct interpretation," said de la Noye. "It will be some time before we can be sure."

"Oh, of course, of course," said Baundilet, satisfied that he had prevailed in the dispute. "But it would not serve our purpose to divide our investigation to chase after possible variant gods." He inclined his head in Madelaine's direction. "Not that you have erred, Madame. As I have said, you make an excellent point in your way. We will have to keep it in mind as we continue our explorations." He gave a signal to the men at the table. "Well, it is nearly time that we started our labors. Enjeu, I want you to take the charts I have set out, so that we can make note of everything we find near the obelisk. I want nothing left to guesswork."

"Fine," said Enjeu.

"Are your prepared, gentlemen?" The inquiry was not deliberately exclusive, but Madelaine recognized the underlying purpose of the question. She rose as the men did.

"I am going back to my villa for a few hours. This afternoon I will join you at the exploration site." Her violet eyes lit on Baundilet. "I want to see what has been done in the last few days. I'm afraid I haven't kept up as I ought to."

Baundilet made a gracious gesture as if he were unaware of the criticism inherent in her comments. "Excellent. We will be pleased to show you what we have done."

With a sigh she capitulated for the moment. "Thank you. I'm grateful for your instruction," she said, her attitude masking the annoyance that nearly consumed her. She was nearly overcome with the desire to fight with Baundilet, using fists or knives or cannon. Her expression was bland, though all the while she was wishing she had the audacity to drub him with cudgels for his endless patronization.

Text of a letter from Professor Rainaud Benclair in Paris to the Magistrate Kareef Numair at Thebes.

My dear Magistrate Numair;

Let me assure you that the claims made by Professor Baundilet are wholly genuine. He has not misrepresented himself in any particular. His antiquarian expedition has received the sponsorship of three universities in France, and we are watching his progress with great interest and much care. You may repose complete confidence in Professor Baundilet and the antiquarians working with him, for they have been selected not only for their expertise, but for their high principles and standards of conduct. We have no desire to have any scandal disrupt this expedition, or sully the advances made in the study of the history of your splendid country.

We have agreed to this expedition because we are convinced that it is in the interest of historical understanding to learn more about the ancient people of your country, and now that the writings at last can be read, the Egyptians of old are no longer mute and we are determined to give them full opportunity to speak. We are of the opinion that all the scholarly world will benefit from what we learn of the Egyptians of Phar-

aonic times. As you are aware, we have already sponsored expeditions to measure and explore the pyramids at Giza. This
current expedition to Thebes serves to extend our degree of interest to the heart of the ancient land.

You express concern that there is a woman on the expedition.
I can only state that Madame de Montalia is known to me, and
I am certain her motives are beyond reproach. She has established herself quite satisfactorily in the academic communities
of France, and although she is not well-known, her reputation
in a small cadre of antiquarians is most enviable. You have no
reason to question her presence, or doubt her sincerity in the
study of antiquities.

If it would relieve you, I will request that Professor Baundilet
send regular reports to you, as he sends them to me and others
who have sponsored his expedition. You must wish to be kept
abreast of all Professor Baundilet is doing, so that you can better
appreciate his requests and his tasks. I am certain he will extend
every courtesy to you and will welcome your interest in what
his expedition accomplishes. He has been enjoined to keep meticulous field notes, and these will be at your disposal to inspect.
I will take the liberty of communicating your anxieties to him
in my next missive, and will urge him to call upon you to
inform you of his work. I will also be pleased to present to you
the bona fides of the other members of his expedition, with not
only their academic credentials but their character references
as well. With such documents at your disposal, surely you will
not fret as much about what this expedition is doing.

Certainly I will extend your greetings to my fellows at the
university and will strive to convey your apprehensions to them,
so that we may better co-operate with you in these endeavors.
A token of gold coins will be dispatched at the end of the year
on the first available military ship, with a messenger and guard
designated to carry it up-river to you. It is not our desire to
compromise our position with Egyptian authorities such as
yourself, and to that end, I have enclosed a bank draft for the
amount of one thousand pounds sterling, to off-set any costs
you may have in monitoring the work of this expedition, and
quite a separate matter from the gold I have already mentioned.

*I am aware that you are a busy man, and this amount should
make it possible for you to observe the work of the antiquarians
without undue strain on your resources. It was an unfortunate
oversight that the draft was not sent along before now, but a
university, like many another large organization, is a cumber-
some thing and hence is sometimes intolerably slow about these
matters. I trust you will not hold this tardiness against the
expedition. Doubtless our payments to them have been late from
time to time, as well.*

*Though we pray to God under different names, I hope that
He will bless you and show favor to you, for an honorable man
is always welcome in the sight of God. It is always a pleasure
to deal with an official who is careful of his duty and reliable
in the execution of his obligations. If there is anything else we
might do to assist you in dealing with our antiquarian expedition and Professor Baundilet, please do not hesitate to inform
us of it. I will see that any request receives the most prompt
attention.*

*With my sincere good wishes,
Professor Rainaud Benclair*

July 29th, 1825, Paris

3

Madelaine de Montalia was the last to arrive, her carriage pulling
up at Yamut Omat's lavish villa more than two hours after the
time specified in the invitation she, like the other members of
Baundilet's expedition, had received. As she stepped down from
her brougham, she looked up at her coachman. "Curtise, in two
hours, please."

The coachman touched the brim of his hat. "Bien sûr, Madame,"
he said before he whistled the three-horse team harnessed unicorn
into a brisk trot.

Servants hesitated before bowing to Madelaine, for she was a woman alone, with an uncovered face. Yet she was clearly worthy to be a guest of their master, for she was dressed at the peak of fashion in a high-waisted silk gown in a shade somewhere between lavender and lilac. There were jewels at her ears and her throat. The gauze wrap she draped around her shoulders was so fine that it might have been nothing more than a sigh. Her dark hair was done up in a knot, with three ringlets coaxed from it. She looked at the servant with the most impressive turban. "I regret I am so late," she said as if he had not failed to greet her.

"My master bids you welcome," said the servant, belatedly remembering his task. "I am sorry to inform you that you have missed the meal."

"How lamentable," said Madelaine in her best aristocratic manner. "Please be kind enough to present me to Madame Omat, and to her husband, if that is proper, and if I am not interrupting them."

The servant bowed again, his first negative impression somewhat reduced by the excellent manners the Frenchwoman showed. "If you will come this way," he said in very good French as he preceded her into the villa.

"How very grand," Madelaine said, relieved that she could offer that compliment candidly. "Your master is a most fortunate man."

"Allah has shown him favor," said the servant, indicating a small salon. "If you will wait here, I will fetch Mademoiselle Omat."

"Mademoiselle?" Madelaine repeated with surprise. "How is this?"

"It is my master's misfortune to be a widower," said the servant with a bow that was a compromise between European and Egyptian manners.

"Most unfortunate," said Madelaine, wondering just how many of the man's wives had died, for she had learned through her servants that her host had married the permitted four wives. Had they all perished, or was his being a widower nothing more than a pose or a convenience, a fiction for the benefit of his European guests? She stopped to admire a bowl inlaid with glass and polished stones which was clearly the most beautiful object in the room. As she touched it, taking great care with the splendid bowl, she marveled at the feel of it.

"They say that it comes from the tomb of a High Priest of Isis," said Rida Omat as she came through the door. She paused, surprise on her young face. "You are Madame de Montalia? I am Mademoiselle Omat."

Madelaine turned to look at her, giving her a slight, social curtsy, appropriate for a girl barely out of her teens. "I'm sorry I arrived late. I hope I do not put you out?"

"Not in the least. I trust there was no difficulty, no misfortune?" said Rida Omat, her manners so impeccable they appeared wholly wrong.

"Oh, no, nothing difficult. There were a few matters I had to attend to, and the task took longer than I anticipated." Madelaine indicated the salon. "This is a lovely room."

"My father will be pleased you like it," said Rida Omat, moving a little awkwardly. "I am not used to the shoes European women wear," she told Madelaine.

"I suppose not," said Madelaine. "You are the first Egyptian woman I have seen wearing European clothes, I believe. It is unexpected."

"Do I offend you?" Rida asked sharply.

Madelaine shook her head. "Not at all. It is a compliment to see you dressed so. I have met few Moslem men who would . . . tolerate their women in European fashions. The dress is very becoming on you."

"Is it?" Rida was genuinely delighted to hear this. "I have seen so few dresses, and most of them were not suitable for me. My father assures me that I have no reason to worry, but I cannot help it." She fingered the shawl draped around her shoulders. "This is the only part of the ensemble that is familiar to me. All the rest is strange."

"And probably not quite comfortable?" Madelaine added a canny guess.

"Not quite," Rida admitted. "I cannot rid myself of the fear that if I stepped outside the villa in these clothes, I would be stoned to death."

Madelaine raised her hand as protest, but was afraid that Rida's apprehension was not unreasonable. "Then you wear European clothes here and nowhere else?"

"I wear these fashions when my father asks it of me. He is aware of the opinion of Moslems, being one himself. But he is not a captive of his religion, as he says many are." She said the words as if repeating by rote; her large eyes revealed her confusion. "I'm sorry. I ought to see to your needs. As a guest in this villa, you should be made welcome."

"You've done so already," Madelaine said. "I feel most welcome, thanks to your candor."

Rida gestured denial. "That was an intrusion on your confidence. It would be fitting to show you the courtesy a guest of my father deserves. We can arrange for food to be brought to you—" began Rida Omat in her faultless French, ignoring the compliment.

"Oh, no, thank you. I'm afraid I have a tiresome complaint that limits what I may eat. In general, I dine privately, so I will not be tempted to have anything that is not . . . wholesome to me." She put out her hand and went to the young woman who was serving as hostess this evening. "I was delighted to receive your invitation, but I am curious, as well. I thought it was not the . . . correct thing to do, inviting women without husbands to entertainments of this sort."

Rida Omat's answer was a little breathless. "Oh, yes, it is. I mean, most households would not be . . . willing to have you as a guest without a man to escort you. Egyptian families do not often entertain as Europeans do. But you see, my father has had dealings with Europeans since Napoleon came here, and he has adopted some of the French ways." She indicated the clothes she wore. "Most girls do not have dresses like these, they go about as Moslem women have since the days of the Prophet."

"Yes; I've seen them," said Madelaine, her curiosity increasing. "I can comprehend why a man who deals with Europeans might find it convenient to accommodate European ways, but this is the first time I have encountered anyone who extended that to his family. It is most unusual—as you have said already—for a Moslem woman to dress as you do, even to please her father." She saw the consternation in the girl's face, and went

on. "I don't mean to upset you, Mademoiselle Omat. But I confess that this puzzles me. Pray don't be troubled that I mention
it, for I mean you no disrepect or mockery. And you may be
sure that many of your guests are filled with the same questions
as I am."

"As they are filled with questions about you," said Rida Omat
with sudden heat. "Oh, yes. I have heard the speculations about
you. My father has told me to pay no attention, but I know what
is being said."

Madelaine's smile was almost angelic. "And what is being said?
Will you tell me?"

Rida Omat's face darkened. "They say you have run away from
your husband, that you are here to . . . to . . . take other pleasures.
They say you look for a lover to revenge yourself on your husband." This last was said in such confusion that Madelaine laughed
in spite of herself.

"I am not married, Mademoiselle Omat," Madelaine said pleasantly. "I have never been married. I am running away from no
one. I am revenging myself on no one. I am, in fact, doing what
interests me most: studying the past." She came up to her hostess.
"My pleasures, in your meaning, are my own concern."

Now Rida was filled with embarrassment, her enormous brown
eyes brimming with distress. She moved away from Madelaine,
her restless fingers caught in the fringe of the elaborate shawl she
wore around her shoulders. "I . . . I did not mean to forget myself.
I don't know why I did. My father will be most—"

Madelaine interrupted her gently. "Your father will know nothing about it, unless you tell him yourself."

"What?" Rida turned back and stared at Madelaine.

Madelaine spoke tranquilly. "There is no reason for me to mention any of your . . . observations to your father. I realize there is
speculation about me, and it is not unreasonable to suppose you
might have heard some of it. I can find it in my heart to be grateful
to you for speaking aloud what others have only whispered." She
gave Rida a little time to consider this. "Now, if you will do me
the honor of introducing me to your father?"

Rida blinked with surprise. "My father?" Then she recovered
herself enough to say, "Yes; yes of course. I will be happy to do

that." She started toward the door, then faltered. "You truly will not tell him how badly I behaved?"

"I have said I would not," said Madelaine, in what she liked to think of as her Saint-Germain manner.

"Ordinarily I would not have spoken. It was just the shock of seeing you; you are so young. I was expecting someone older, and different," Rida said by way of excuse.

"I am not as young as you think, Mademoiselle." Madelaine fell in half a step behind Rida Omat as she led her in the direction of the ballroom.

The ballroom was large enough to comfortably accommodate more than a hundred dancers. The pillars were polished green marble, the floor a marble parquetry design that was dizzying in its complexity. Four enormous crystal chandeliers provided the illumination for the room. So overwhelming was the grandeur of the ballroom that the party of sixty seemed all but lost in it, and though a five-piece orchestra played, few were dancing.

"Father," said Rida Omat as she brought Madelaine across the ballroom, "your last guest has arrived."

Yamut Omat was wearing proper formal attire, and but for his turban, he might have been mistaken for an Italian had he attended a ball in Europe. He stood a little apart from his guests, watching them with sharp, black eyes. As Rida came up to him, he gave Madelaine a flawless bow and took her hand. "Madame de Montalia, at last," he said. "You need no introduction."

Madelaine bit back a sharp retort about gossips and dropped her host a proper curtsy. "Monsieur Omat. I thank you for your gracious invitation and ask your forgiveness for my late arrival." She watched as he kissed her hand, and knew from the possessive way he touched her she would have to be careful around this man, for she sensed he would want to bring her under his influence; he seem to regard her as a challenge. Her smile was amicable but not flirtatious.

"What is there to forgive?" asked Yamut Omat grandly. "It is more a question of gratitude than forgiveness." He indicated the rest of the guests. "You have done me the honor of attending this party without knowing me first, which is an enormous compliment."

"You have invited all the others from the Baundilet antiquarian expedition; it is appropriate that I be included as a member of that expedition." She was glad now that she could still summon up the grand courtesy of her youth. "How good of you to extend your hospitality to foreigners; too many others have trespassed on Egyptian courtesy. You might be pardoned for a degree of doubt where Europeans are concerned, Frenchmen most especially."

"Oh, you mean because of Napoleon?" Yamut Omat inquired, and followed this at once with a theatrical laugh that made several of the other guests turn their heads. "Dear Madame, I am not one of those who hid in the ruins and threw rocks at the army; I saw at once that the fighting would be short-lived, but that there were advantages to be had when the war was over. My prosperity— Allah is great!—is proof of that." He took Madelaine's hand and tucked it into his arm, and began a leisurely stroll toward the buffet table set up at the far end of the ballroom. "Permit me to offer you a glass of champagne, Madame; I do not drink myself, but I have the best that can be had for my guests. I will tell you how I came to make my fortune."

Madelaine wanted to remove her hand, but realized such a direct affront would be risky. "You may tell me your story, Monsieur Omat, but I regret I must refuse the champagne."

"Refuse?" Yamut Omat came to a halt at the word.

"I am afraid I must," said Madelaine, using this as a moment to free her hand from the curve of his arm. She gave him her most charming smile. "I do not drink wine."

"Allah be praised," said Omat, his eyes bright with speculation. In other circumstances he might have asked her more, but this was not the appropriate time, and so all he did was bow slightly. "If you will tell me what I can offer you?"

"This delightful company will suffice very nicely," said Madelaine, indicating the various Europeans who were his guests. "I do not often have an occasion to meet them, except the expedition, and then only those working with Professor Baundilet. I have never met the English party before, though, I have been told about them. They're mostly antiquarians, I understand." She moved away from him. "And I must not trespass on your hospitality; I won't ask you to dance attendance on me."

Short of insisting, there was little he could do to remain at her side. "I would be obliged if you can tell me of any service I might perform for you, Madame de Montalia," he said, bowing slightly before going to a small group of British men Madelaine did not recognize.

Left to her own devices, Madelaine looked for a place near the little orchestra; she missed hearing chamber music more than she wanted to admit, and though she played the fortepiano fairly well, she had not touched one since she left Monbussy, her recently acquired chateau on the Marne. Her thoughts were still on the chateau when she found a handsome chair in the style of her youth, and she sat down to listen to a selection of Mozart minuets. She had been listening for some little while when she became aware of someone standing close to her chair. Thinking it might be her host again, she rose suddenly, and found herself looking into a pair of arresting blue eyes.

"I did not mean to startle you, Madame," said the stranger, his French roughened by a German accent. He was dressed in full formal attire and carried an empty punch cup in his hand.

"You did not," said Madelaine, not quite truthfully, her manner reserved while she assessed the newcomer. "I thought you were one of my colleagues from Professor Baundilet's expedition."

The man smiled; strong creases formed around his eyes and at the sides of his face; Madelaine revised her estimation of his age—incorrectly—from thirty to thirty-five. There was a lick of grey in his bright brown hair, like the shine off a polished oak table. He took her hand and bowed over it. "I have been told we are neighbors. I trust that is sufficient introduction, given the circumstances. Do not be affronted if I present myself to you without an intermediary."

Her deportment changed. "You must be the physician," she said as she curtsied, adding, "I had pictured a much different fellow."

"Rotund and whiskered and smoking endlessly?" he suggested. "That was my favorite professor." Again he showed her his dis-

astrous smile. "I am Egidius Maximillian Falke; at your service.
You are Madame de Montalia, the antiquarian who owns the villa
near mine."

"Yes," she said, growing more cautious again. "How are you so
certain of my identity?"

"Look around you: how many"—he made an abrupt sweeping
gesture—"European women do you see here? Ten? Twelve? And
how many of them are under my age? Two? Three? And of them,
which of them is alone, beautiful, and apparently rich?" He looked
directly at her. "One."

"So it is nothing more than a process of elimination," said
Madelaine, feeling oddly disoriented in Falke's presence.

"And not difficult. If there had been four or five women your
age and unaccompanied, it would have been more of a challenge.
As it is, a clever schoolboy of eight could have done it." He fell
silent, listening to the music. "Oh. Good. They're off the Mozart."

"You dislike Mozart?" Madelaine asked, startled. "I thought all
Germans liked German music?"

"Mozart was Austrian," said the stranger. "And it's old-fashioned,
isn't it. I prefer something new; don't you?"

"Yes; so we have Rossini instead," Madelaine said, recognizing
the tantalizing, infectious "Di Tanti Palpiti" from *Tancredi*.
"They've passed a law against that air in Venice."

Falke grinned, the lines in his face more marked and interesting.
"Only the Italians would pass a law against a song."

"Because no one could stop singing it," Madelaine pointed out.
"And it only applies to people working for the courts."

"Something to keep the clerks from bursting out with the refrain
in the middle of a trial, I suppose," he said. He listened a short
while. "Not that it wouldn't get caught in the head, that tune. It's
like a musical disease." His good humor faded almost at once.
"I'm sorry, Madame de Montalia. That was a tasteless comment.
If I offended you—"

"You didn't, Herr Doktor Falke," she said, deliberately imitating
his formality. "In fact, I agree."

He would not allow her to release him. "But to compare music,
and excellent music at that, to disease is unacceptable." He stared

down into the punch cup he carried. "I wonder if I have had too much of this?"

"Surely not," said Madelaine, aware that he was quite sober.

"I hope not. A physician cannot afford to muddle his wits." He carefully set the cup aside on the wide lip of a tall vase that contained a profusion of large, multi-colored lilies. "There. Now I will not be tempted." He let the music account for his silence, and then he said, "Perhaps I was a trifle severe. It is my work. I am studying the diseases of this part of the world. We see things in Egypt that rarely, if ever, occur in Europe."

"A brave thing to do, Herr Doktor," said Madelaine with complete sincerity. "I trust you have taken all the precautions you can for your own protection."

He did something with his shoulders that would have been a shrug had he been French or Italian. "I have done everything that is advised. If there is anything more that will help me, and the poor wretches I treat, I would be glad to know of it."

Madelaine could not help but think of the letter she had dispatched to Saint-Germain the week before, and wondered what her cherished first lover would tell her that might be useful to this physician, and how she would explain how she came by the information. The answer to that came quickly, and she said, "Doktor Falke, the Baundilet expedition is concerned with unearthing various writings and records in Luxor and Thebes. If we should come upon anything about the medicine of the times of the Pharaohs, I will be very pleased to pass that information on to you." As she made the offer, she was relieved to think that what she would be able to tell him would indeed be medical practices from the time of the Pharaohs.

"What a fascinating notion," he said with renewed enthusiasm. "Yes. Oh, yes, if you would be kind enough, I would value all such information you can vouchsafe me."

"It will be my privilege," said Madelaine. "If it can provide treatment today as it did so long ago, then it has served its purpose twice."

"How well you understand," Falke said, looking at her with greater respect. "I will offer my thanks to Professor Baundilet."

"Professor Baundilet?" Madelaine did not give him the sharp retort that occured to her, but said, "I don't think that would be wise. Professor Baundilet is afraid that others may publish our results before he does, and in general he does not permit us to discuss anything we find until he has written his reports and sent them off. I doubt he would approve of my telling you about what we learn, because he would think that you wish to use his results to advance your own career."

"Then how can you make such an offer to me?" Falke inquired, perturbed.

"Because there is no reason for his apprehension where you are concerned, is there?" She did not give him time to answer. "Professor Baundilet is a fine antiquarian, and he seeks to enhance his position even more. To him, any inscription might hold the key to academic advancement. Your situation would have no meaning for him."

Falke was shocked. "I can appreciate his concerns. But medicine—"

"Medicine from ancient Egypt is as much the province of scholarship as any other record of the time," Madelaine said, hoping that Falke would believe what she said. She could sense his resistance to her conditions, and she went on more persuasively, "Let this be a private agreement, between you and me. I will ask that you not publish what I tell you, and you, in turn, will agree to keep our arrangement secret as long as the Baundilet expedition is at Thebes. Is that acceptable to you?"

"I don't know," he said when he had heard her out. "I will have to think it over. I do not want to compromise the work being done here."

"And you do not want any patient to die or suffer if it isn't necessary," she completed his thought for him. "We suspect that the Egyptians of long ago had the means to treat diseases that today cannot be controlled in any way. It isn't wrong of you to want to ease the patients you have."

He nodded, and smiled once more, this time with chagrin. "I must be honest. I would very much like to find a cure to some horrible ill. If the ancients had such knowledge, I would rejoice to know of it." He looked down at her, his manner attentive and serious. "I will have to think about what you have said. I don't like so covert an arrangement, but if you insist— Would it be convenient for me to call on you tomorrow evening and tell you then what I have decided?"

"Certainly." She gave him a long careful look. "I will discuss it further, if you would like that." If he would tell her what he needed to know, she would be able to include that in her next letter to Saint-Germain.

"No." He shook his head once for emphasis. "No, this I must think through for myself. I know already that your arguments are persuasive; I need time for reflection." He took her hand and bowed over it. "This has been a most unexpected pleasure, Madame. I am truly pleased to have met you at last."

"And I, Herr Doktor Falke," she said, realizing that had they met in Paris, the introduction would not have been permissible and their discussion would not have taken place at all. But then, she thought, there would have been no reason, no excuse.

"Until tomorrow, then." With that, he turned and strolled away toward the gathering of English.

Madelaine watched him briefly, then turned back to the chamber ensemble. She was not able to concentrate on the Rossini, nor on the Cimarosa suite that followed. Her thoughts continually turned toward Egidius Maximillian Falke, and she wondered why it was that smile lines and a touch of grey in the hair could so captivate her. Or was it that at all? Was it something that burned in those blue eyes?

"Bored?" Alain Baundilet asked, swaggering up to her, a half-empty champagne glass in his hand. "It's probably not up to your standards."

"It's quite delightful," said Madelaine, doing her best not to appear flustered. "I am not one who enjoys the social season as some do." In fact, she had deliberately avoided such functions for more than three decades in order to avoid those few aged ladies who had known her when she was much younger. She had twice been subjected to very unpleasant questions about her age and did not want to endure another such again.

"Given over to study?" Baundilet teased. "Permit me to say, Madame, that I find that difficult to believe."

"Nevertheless, it is true, as I have striven to convince you," Madelaine reminded him. "You have seen my credentials; you know that I am here on something more than a whim." She wanted very much to get away from him.

But he was not about to permit that. "I think you ought to plan to come to breakfast tomorrow, before the others. I have to consider your request about the inscriptions and the temples." His eyes lighted greedily on the necklace of diamonds and sapphires she wore. "I must tell you, I think you're wrong about the place, but if you realize the likelihood of failure for your theory, then we might be able to arrange something for you."

Madelaine wished she could take Saint-Germain's most recent letter and show it to Baundilet; that would lend credibility to her theories, she thought, and in the same instant, she relented, knowing that Baundilet would be convinced she was mad as well as eccentric. "All right," she said quietly. "I will arrive half an hour earlier than usual tomorrow morning. But I will not want breakfast, I will want discussion, Professor Baundilet."

"Of course, of course," said Baundilet with suspicious haste. "And let Claude-Michel find his way for himself, will you?"

"If you would prefer," said Madelaine, determined to send a message that night to Jean-Marc Paille so that she would not have to be alone with Professor Baundilet. She took a step away from him, then asked, "Pardon me, Professor, do you know the time?"

Baundilet made a show of taking his gold watch from his waist-coat pocket. "Ten fifty-three," he said.

Madelaine was able to make her relief seem to be upset. "Gracious. My driver will be waiting for me." It was not quite time for Curtise to return, but she knew he made a habit of being a trifle early. "I must go. I will plan to arrive just before dawn tomorrow." She hurried away from him and sought out her host. "Monsieur Omat," she said as she came up to him. "I have to thank you for a most delightful evening. It was so kind of you to invite me."

"You are leaving?" Omat asked as he took her hand captive in his own. "I was hoping you would join me at the midnight supper. You see how I have arranged everything in the European way."

"Yes," she said, "and you have done it remarkably well. But I must rise early and there are household duties that await me before I can retire." She curtsied and pulled her hand from his. "A very splendid occasion."

"Then you must honor me again soon," said Omat, motioning to one of his servants. "Escort Madame de Montalia to her coach and see her safely away."

It was nothing more than what a French host would do, but hearing the instructions made Madelaine want to grind her teeth. "How good of you," she made herself say as she permitted the servant to lead her through the villa. As she stepped into the courtyard, her brougham came around the corner, the distinctive unicorn hitch making the carriage stand out from the others. As Curtise drew up at the coaching entrance, Madelaine handed a silver coin to the servant with a murmur of thanks, and then stepped into her carriage.

As Curtise started the team away from Omat's villa, Madelaine sighed. The seats and floor of her carriage were lined with her native earth, and it imparted a restorative calm to her. One day, she decided, she would have to find a way to design dancing shoes that would permit her to line those thin, flexible shoes with her native earth.

Text of a letter from Kareef Numair, Magistrate of Thebes, to Professor Alain Baundilet.

Worthy Professor;

I am awaiting the verifications and credentials you assured me would be provided by your French sponsors, and will inform you when they arrive. In the meantime, I will inspect the work you are doing and see what you have done. At that time, I request an inventory of all discoveries you have made, along with a verified copy of the official notes of your antiquarian expedition. I further instruct you to require all members of your expedition to be similarly prepared for my inspection and to be on hand to answer my queries, whatever they may be. If any of your expedition must absent himself from my inspection, I will re-

quire a full, written explanation as to the cause, with signed statements vouching for the veracity of the statement.

For the last four days, I have spoken with the diggers and basket carriers you have hired, and they have given their reports to me. If your reports differ significantly, then I will have to order a formal review of your work and determine what you have done. It will go hard for you if your records are not adequate or are inaccurate.

It is my intention to watch your progress with care, for we do not wish to see more defacement of the walls and engravings in the ancient ruins you are exploring. There has been enough mischief done to these fine structures and I will not permit you to add to what has already been done. We have seen other antiquarians use their work to plunder the graves of the ancients and to disdain the laws of the Prophet. That will not be tolerated while I am magistrate at Thebes. If there is any questioning of my authority, I will request the matter be placed before the Khedive.

We are not ignorant people, Professor, and we will not permit you or any Europeans to conduct themselves in ways that disgrace us and our country. It is my intention to guard all the treasures of Thebes from exploitation, and I have sworn on the Koran to protect these stones from desecration.

Kareef Numair
Magistrate

August 16th, 1825 in Christian reckoning, at Thebes

4

Most of the work consisted of clearing away sand. Mountains, oceans of it had drifted into the ruins over the centuries, making it difficult or impossible to tell what lay beneath. Ursin Guibert and Justin LaPlatte worked side by side, calling out instructions to the diggers as they scooped up the sand, and to the basket carriers, who lugged it away.

Where the diggers had finished the members of the expedition swarmed, their notebooks out and easels set up for sketchpads. Merlin de la Noye stood on a ladder, peering upward at an enormous display of hieroglyphics cut into the stone, his pipe caught in his teeth. On the ground where a few of the paving stones were coming to light as the sand was carefully swept away, Alain Baundilet bustled from one antiquarian to another, questioning, questioning.

"What do you make of that?" Claude-Michel asked Madelaine as they worked their way around the foot of a tremendous column.

"I can't say. It looks like . . . something was changed. Just here, you see?" She pointed to a place on the column where the low relief carving was patched with a thin cement.

Claude-Michel touched the surface gingerly. "A repair, do you think?"

"A change," said Madelaine, refusing to commit herself. "Perhaps the priests ordered it."

"You mean the *Egyptians* did it?" Claude-Michel asked, dumbfounded.

"Possibly," Madelaine answered. "Make a drawing of it, in any case, and we'd better take care to get all the little notes as well —see? those figures there?—as part of it." She dropped onto her knees and looked at the decorative edge of the carving. Using a painter's brush, she cleared away the last of the sand. "Lotus border. That might be important. I don't think it says anything, but it may have significance, like laurel leaves to the Greeks and Romans."

"Oh. Yes." Claude-Michel squatted beside her. "I've read enough of Champollion to recognize some of this. That open hand is *t*. The Egyptian cross, the one with the loop on top, is—"

"*Anh*," said Madelaine. "Or *enh*." She brushed her hands together to rid them of sand. "I've studied the language a little, too."

"That's very good," said Claude-Michel. "Yes. And that hawk facing us is *m*. The horizontal jagged line is *n*." He grew flushed as he spoke, his young features glowing with excitement; he was proud of his knowledge and thrilled to have an audience. "This empty throne and eye in the seal is the name of Osiris."

"And this?" She indicated another cartouche. "What is that?"

Claude-Michel stared closely at it. "It's the name of one of the Pharaohs. Sometimes they have a double cartouche like that. I'll make a record of it. The sun disk, a kind of cup or half-circle, and part of the upper body of someone wearing a feather on his head and carrying an Egyptian cross. The other part is a feather and a rectangle with little spikes on the upper side, then the sign for *n*, then a narrower rectangle with a shape like a jar on top of it, then a crook with a plant stalk, by the look of it." As he descibed, he sketched. "There. I'm sorry I don't draw very well. I haven't the hand for it. But does that do it?"

Madelaine looked at the sketch and back at the double cartouche. "The figure with the feather on its head is holding the *anh* at an angle, slanted away from the body," she said, indicating the place on the column. "We can ask de la Noye if he's found another cartouche. I wonder which one of all the Pharaohs it is?"

"I don't know," admitted Claude-Michel. "It isn't Rameses; his cartouche is around these temples, but this isn't his." He touched the stone again. "Imagine the men who carved this stone. Sitting here in the sun for year after year, having to make a carving of equal depth. The whole temple must have rung with the sound of hammers on chisels."

"Very likely," said Madelaine, "if the carving was done here. It might have been done where the column was quarried." She rose. "When you find out which Pharaoh this is, let me know, will you?"

"Certainly," he said, scrambling to his feet. "Which part of the temple are you going to work on?"

"The shadiest," she said, only partly in jest. "I have asked if I could transcribe the hieroglyphics around the door in the central part of the temple. There are a great many of them, and they might give us some indication what the central chambers were for, and what went on in them."

"You mean rites and sacrifices?" Claude-Michel asked eagerly. "Do you think this is where they made the sacrifices?"

"I don't know," said Madelaine, her tone firm. "No one does yet. That's why I want to work on those inscriptions. The chamber is very small. It might be nothing more than a place to keep ceremonial things and vestments."

"You mean that it is nothing more than a closet?" Claude-Michel was scandalized at his own suggestion.

"It's possible," said Madelaine, amused at his alarm. "Well, there would have to be some place to store the objects and special clothes, wouldn't there?" she went on reasonably. "We know this is an important part of the temple. Over there, parts of statues are being uncovered. The chamber might be a very private place for the priests, or it could be storage, or it could be a place where certain worshipers go, like those side chapels for nobility and royalty in Europe." She tucked the brush she carried into her belt. "Whatever it is, I'm going to find out everything I can about it."

"Do you need my assistance?" Claude-Michel said wistfully.

She smiled at him. "Thank you. No. I may need it later, when I have all the inscriptions written and can read nothing more than the occasional *anh*." Her violet eyes shone with amusement. She found his devotion touching, but knew beyond doubt that if he had the least hint of her true nature, he would be horrified beyond recall. His romanticism charmed and annoyed her, and she decided it was because of her age. "Baundilet needs your help more than I do. And he is in charge here."

"Yes," said Claude-Michel, becoming very business-like. "You're right, Madame. I ought to have thought of that."

"No harm done. You've helped me a great deal." She made a gesture of encouragement, then went toward the strange small room, hoping that the diggers had got most of the sand out of the interior.

"You want to be careful in there, Madame," called Ursin Guibert after her. "Watch out for snakes and such."

"Thank you," she acknowledged the warning. "I'll try not to be distracted."

The chief digger frowned at her as he gave her a minimal bow, and called out something to his digging crew. "You want to look?" he asked, his French hard to understand.

"Yes," said Madelaine, her eyes moving over the carving that framed the door. "But I'll wait until you're finished."

"What is?" the digger asked.

"Go on," she said, gesturing for him to resume his work. "I will wait."

"Wait," he repeated with satisfaction.

Madelaine moved back from the chamber and stood in the shadow of the enormous pillars. She withdrew her notebook and with great care started to copy the figures surrounding the door. She paid little attention to the workers and was pleased that they ignored her. As she finished the figures over the top of the door, she added a note to herself to send a copy of this to Saint-Germain in her next letter. There was so much she wanted him to tell her, to explain about these vanished people. She looked from her sketch to the hieroglyphics that framed the door, thinking about the men who had put them there. "Who were you?" she whispered, willing the carvings to give up their secrets to her. With an effort she forced herself to look away, and when she did, she saw a man in a nondescript hooded robe standing a short distance away from her, watching her.

The man nodded and though his face was shadowed, Madelaine's violet eyes met his. "You are Madame de Montalia?" he asked in very good old-fashioned aristocratic French, the sort Madelaine had not heard since the Revolution.

Madelaine was startled and for a moment she wanted to call for help. But that, she thought sternly, was absurd. What was the danger of speaking to this solitary man? If he intended her harm, he had chosen a very poor place to approach her, with members of Baundilet's expedition all around them. If he intended violence, he had missed his opportunity, and he was not in a position to do anything else, now, not in so public a place. There was a single threat he might use, she knew, something that was as dangerous to her as sunlight without her native earth in the soles of her shoes: but how could this stranger know her true nature? "Yes," she said when she realized he was waiting for an answer.

"Madame," said the man coming up to her and inclining his head. His voice was warm and deep, musical. His speech was unhurried. "I am Erai Gurzin. I am a Coptic monk, a Christian."

"Yes?" she said, her reservations making her voice cool.

"Saint-Germain sent me."

She stared at him, his announcement incredible in these ruins. "What?"

"Saint-Germain sent me," he repeated, and reached into the sleeve of his habit to pull out a letter. "Here. This will explain. Read it for yourself." He watched her take the letter. "I was informed that you would expect me. Saint-Germain told you—"

"—someone would come," Madelaine finished for him as she looked at Saint-Germain's eclipse seal imprinted on the wax seal. There was the familiar, spare hand, the phrasing that was almost like hearing him speak. Just seeing his letter made her sense him, as if he were near.

"He informs me you are here to study the ancient people, the Pharaohs and the scribes," said the monk.

"Yes," she said, reading the letter again. "Yes. They have been in shadows for so long . . . they have been mute and mysterious. It is no longer necessary that we puzzle over those inscriptions. Now there is a chance to hear them speak, to discover who they were, to *know* them."

"Saint-Germain might—" the monk began.

She was caught up in the letter, and she spoke as much to Saint-Germain as to the monk beside her. "No. He answers questions when I ask, but I am not amusing myself with stories of those lost times. Learning is not the entertainment to pass a pleasant hour, it is at the core of . . . all the rest. When I ask, I want to understand my own question." Her face brightened. "I want to find the truth of these people, not learn another tale of them. I want to hear their voices over the centuries. If everything is told to me, that will not happen, and . . . " She let the words fade.

"An enormous task," said the monk.

Her smile was fleeting. "Yes, it is."

"As you see, I have been asked to aid you however I can." He glanced at the rubble from a fallen column. "I have also been told not to interfere, but to assist you."

Madelaine returned the letter reluctantly, as if parting from the writer himself. "Thank you," she said softly.

He hesitated, then said, "Before I was a monk, I was a houseboy for a Greek named Niklos Aulirios. I remember that Saint-Germain came to the First Cataract twenty-two years ago, when Aulirios was still alive. As his houseboy I learned many things."

"No doubt," said Madelaine, more curious about the monk now.

"I would have been here sooner. I had intended to leave some time ago, as the Comte requested, but there was an emergency at my monastery and I was not able to come until now. I am concerned; I have arrived at the beginning of the Inundation, for that will delay whatever work we can set out to accomplish together. With the waters rising it will be no more than a few days before your tasks here must stop." He put the letter away. "Saint-Germain has asked me, as you have read, to be your tutor in things Egyptian, and I am willing to do that for his sake and for the memory of Niklos Aulirios, if you will have me." It was not the most cordial offer, but Gurzin still found it hard to believe that this lovely young woman could be the serious scholar Saint-Germain insisted she was.

"I am . . . grateful," said Madelaine with a touch of irony. "I hope I will be an apt pupil."

Gurzin caught the tone and for the first time he smiled. "I begin to understand, and I humbly ask your pardon; I was hasty in my judgment," he said, and gave her his blessing. "Saint-Germain respects your scholarship, and I am eager to be of service to him. Perhaps we both of us ought to reserve our opinions for a few days. If my limited knowledge can be useful to you, avail yourself of it." He paused for a moment, waiting for a dismissal. "It is not so late in the afternoon that we cannot make a start. There are four hours to sunset; surely we can begin. Now, what would you like me to tell you?"

She made a gesture of helplessness. "I can't answer. Where *do* I begin? I want to know everything, and there is so much, and . . . "

"Yes," said Gurzin when she did not continue. "Where to make a start." He glanced around the temple. "I do not know everything; I was sincere when I said my knowledge is limited. Even if I did know much, much more, I would not be able to explain it all. I have some information, more than many, thanks to God's blessings, yet it is not great: Saint-Germain knows far more than I." He took a long, thoughtful breath. "Still, you have some of the language now, don't you?"

"A little, very little," she said, adding, "No one knows much. It was only a few years ago that the first translations were made. I've been studying the work Champollion has done, but I have not achieved any real skill, not of the sort I need. That will take time, and more texts to review." She indicated the inscription she had copied. "Well, since we must start somewhere, let it be here. I want to know what this chamber was for. I want to know what they did here." She put her notebook into the small satchel she carried. "I want to know whose temple it is, and when it was built, and why. I want to know what priests served here. I want to know what people came here, and how they worshiped."

Gurzin pursed his lips in sympathy. "In short, you want to know what it was to be an Egyptian, and there is no one left to tell you."

She almost reminded Gurzin of Saint-Germain's longevity, then kept silent; if Saint-Germain had not told Gurzin of his long life, it was not proper that she should do it. "You're right, I want that," she agreed. "And because I cannot be one, I want the Egyptians themselves to tell me, through their writing and their pictures."

"I will do what I can." He watched her with interest, his evaluation of her improving steadily. "I'll need to see the work you mentioned, the translations. The language of ancient Egypt was the ancestor of the one we Copts speak, and once I can see the translations you have, I will be able to assist you. If that is agreeable to you."

"It is better than what is at my disposal without your help," she said, then added, "I did not mean to insult you, if I did. But you must see that this is exasperating work, for every new discovery is another mystery, and every bit of knowledge we gather leads to a dozen new questions."

"That is the plight of scholars," said Gurzin, looking around the part of the temple that was free of sand. "How much longer do you think it will take, this digging?"

"I don't know," said Madelaine. "It will depend what we find buried under it. If this colonnade is just what it seems, possibly by the Inundation the greater part of the sand will be gone. But if there are statues or other objects, or things we have not anticipated, then it will be longer." She moved closer to the little chamber. "There's sand in the interior, and we've decided to remove it with brushes because there may be . . . oh, all sorts of things under the sand."

"Very cautious," said Gurzin.

"We're required to keep very thorough field notes. The universities sponsoring the expedition want full value for their money. In addition, the local Magistrate has been here once already and will probably return again. He is suspicious of the expedition, and watches the work we do very closely." She sighed with frustration. "I wanted to tell him about some work I am anxious to do, but he would not talk with me."

"He is a good Moslem, Madame. He is not . . . used to European women," Gurzin said, trying to imagine what the Magistrate must have thought when confronted with this young, unveiled woman. "You were fortunate he allowed you to be present when he was here. It would be more usual for him to insist that you absent yourself or veil your face at the least."

"Oh, I know that," said Madelaine. "When I ride, I tie my scarf or my neckcloth over my face in the town. But here, with the expedition, it is inconvenient to take such measures. I know that the diggers dislike me working here, with my face uncovered. I know that there are those on the expedition who would prefer I spend my time reading or purchasing trinkets instead of working here." She fell silent. After a short while, she said, "I don't want to offend them, any of them. But I intend to do my work. That is why I am here. There are other European women in this country; they can't all pretend to be Moslems."

Gurzin considered her protest. "Women in Egypt are not often educated, not as you are, certainly. Some consider it irreligious to teach women to read and write. You are flaunting an education that is not proper. That is troublesome to many. You are very young, Madame. That is more troublesome than the first; the officials would be more inclined to accept your interest in ancient things if you were more ancient yourself."

"But I am not young," said Madelaine. "Truly I am not."

"Saint-Germain said he was older than he appeared," Gurzin remarked. "If you are of his blood—"

"I am," she assured him.

"—then it may be that age has less a hold on you than it does on many others." His beautiful voice was low, soft as the pedal notes of an organ. "Saint-Germain is a man of many abilities. If he has shared some of them with you, because you are of his blood . . . " The note of speculation hung between them as his words faded.

It took her a little time to respond. "He must have told you that those who are of his blood do not show their age, if he told you so much. Be content to know that I am not as young as my face would make me appear; I have devoted decades to learning, Brother Gurzin, decades."

Gurzin pondered this, watching her narrowly. "I do not know Europeans too well, but I would say, looking at you, that you are no more than twenty or twenty-two. Perhaps twenty-five."

"I have that appearance," said Madelaine, recalling that it was just over one hundred years since her birth. "It is misleading, I fear."

One of the diggers emerged from the little chamber, carrying a basket of sand and muttering. He shot Madelaine a poisonous glance, snarled a string of words, then hurried on toward the cart where sand was put to be hauled away into the desert.

"What did he say?" Madelaine asked when the digger was out of earshot.

"It was not a compliment," Gurzin warned, then told her. "He called you a curse on the place and a demon."

Madelaine nodded. "There was also something about the spawn of toads and camel dung, wasn't there?" She gave a quick sly smile at Gurzin's surprise. "I don't know much of the language, but I've come to know some of the more common curses."

"Do they know?" Gurzin asked, intrigued by her attitude.

"The diggers? I don't think so. I've been careful not to behave as if I knew what they said. Most of the members of the expedition aren't aware of it, either, though Claude-Michel suspects, since he is the linguist for us."

Gurzin made a gesture of comprehension. "It might be wise if they do not learn of your skill, any of them," he said carefully. "There may be a time when you will find it useful to hear what they suppose you cannot understand." He touched his hands together. "In a country like this one, it is good to have a few abilities kept in reserve; a foreign woman could have more reason to hide her knowledge than a foreign man."

"It sounds as if you are concerned for my safety," said Madelaine with deliberate lightness.

"Let us agree that I am concerned," said Gurzin, then took a more scholarly manner. "Come. Let me have that notebook. This evening, if you are willing, we can compare the translation with what you have here."

She hesitated. "But why would you want it?"

"To look for similar inscriptions, of course," said Gurzin, wondering why she would question him now that she had all but won him over. "There are pillars and the obelisk and pylon to examine. By sunset, you will have more notes and I will be able to tell you what I have found. If there are writings that correspond, then it will tell us more about the entire temple."

"Yes," said Madelaine, making up her mind. She reached into her satchel and retrieved the notebook. "Here. I'll take out the pages. Don't lose them." As she spoke she tore the pages carefully from the notebook, then signed each one of them. "At sunset. I'll return to my villa then. If you are there for the evening meal, you may share it with the rest of my household, if that is permissible to your calling."

"While you, like Saint-Germain, dine in private?" ventured Gurzin.

"Something like that," said Madelaine. She handed over the pages. "I want to know what Pharaoh's name is in the cartouche, if that can be discovered. If there is a way to identify the names of the gods, I want to know that as well. Is that too much to ask of you?"

"I will not know until I have studied the pillars and other inscriptions." He held the pages up, glancing from the hieroglyphics to the page and back again. "You sketch quite well, Madame," he told her before starting away through the forest of pillars.

"Thank you," she said, her thoughts already returning to the mysterious chamber. She was quickly preoccupied with making new sketches as the diggers worked inside to brush away the sand. Her attention was now completely held by the writing in the doorway itself, which was difficult to see.

"Finding anything?" asked Alain Baundilet as his shadow blocked most of the light.

Madelaine made herself appear quite calm at his sudden arrival. "Nothing I can make sense of yet. That will come in time."

"You're a very determined woman, Madame," said Baundilet, and it was not completely a compliment. He moved a little closer to her, making it impossible for her to move by him without touching. "There's an odd fellow in a hood out there who tells me he is assisting you."

"The monk, you mean? He's Coptic." Madelaine asked, wishing Baundilet were out of the way. She heard two of the diggers inside the chamber stop work and complain that their single lantern was not enough light with people in the doorway.

"A monk, is he?" Baundilet said, moving a little closer. "Where did you find him?"

"He found me, actually," said Madelaine. "He knows French. The . . . the friend I mentioned, who had lived in Egypt for some time, recommended this monk to me, and he sought me out." She retreated a few steps, entering the confines of the chamber. "I thought, since he knows his own country so well, and has information, he could help me in my work."

"And you will pay for him, of course," said Baundilet, reaching out one hand to touch her arm. "If he is to help you, you ought to bear the expense."

"Of course," she said.

"Good." His fingers moved down her arm. "You're a very beautiful woman, Madame."

"You're kind to say so, but I'm sure your wife is more beautiful than I am," said Madelaine pointedly. She moved a little, trying to force Baundilet to give her room enough to leave, but she did not succeed.

"But she is not here. I have not seen her for months," Baundilet said softly. "Now that the flood has begun, we may be idle for many, many days. Are you never lonely?"

"That is my concern, Professor; you need not trouble yourself about it." She wondered if he would have the audacity to kiss her in this place with the diggers watching. "I am worried about my reputation, and yours, however."

Baundilet chuckled. "I can be very discreet, Madame. Give me the opportunity and I will show you."

Madelaine heard one of the diggers make a joke about whores; she looked directly at Baundilet. "If this is your notion of discretion, I am not favorably impressed." She summoned all the aristocratic manner she had been taught as a child. "I am not going to allow you to compromise me and my work, Professor, not for any whim of yours. I have too much respect for your academic standing and your marriage even if you do not. If you touch me or force any other intimacy on me, I swear I will scream, and I will leave you to explain how it happened."

For several seconds Baundilet said nothing, then he bowed. "The first point is to you, I reckon," he said, moving aside. "You did it well; I may have underestimated you." His smile was predatory. "The next point might well be mine." He reached out for her hand, but she pulled it away. "So outraged."

Madelaine did not give him the satisfaction of a retort as she left the little chamber, rushing into the shadow of the columns. Suddenly the light, the relentless heat were welcome.

As he came out of the chamber, Baundilet paused beside her. "Nothing is settled, Madame," he whispered to her, as if pronouncing a vow.

Text of a letter from Honorine Magasin in Poitiers to Jean-Marc Paille in Thebes, through the good offices of her cousin Georges in Orleans.

My darling Jean-Marc;

Georges has come for a brief stay, and has told me he will carry this and see it posted, so that my father will know nothing of it. How good Georges is, and how selflessly he has taken my part in this miserable business. He has been my comforting

*friend in your absence, and he has shown himself time and time
again to be devoted to us. You were right when you told me he
was the most reliable ally we could wish for. I am grateful for
everything he has done for you and me in this difficult time.*

*I have read with interest the letters he brought. Imagine such
places hidden in the sand. I cannot comprehend what it must
be like, to see these great buildings emerge from the dunes.
Although you are certainly correct, and I am not able to imagine
the size and majesty of the temple you are excavating, I have
tried to picture the dunes at the ocean, and have imagined a
cathedral, such as Chartres, lying buried beneath them. It is an
idea that is very hard to grasp.*

*You recall that my sister Solange was betrothed shortly before
you left for Egypt. At the time the precise date had not been
fixed. The reason that Georges has come here is for the wedding,
which will be in four days. It is going to be an enormous affair,
with three hundred people invited to attend. You cannot imagine a bride as pretty as Solange is, so fair and dainty. At eighteen,
most women are in their best looks, and it is certainly true for
Solange. Her trousseau is the envy of everyone. Our father has
been most cruel, chiding me for being a spinster while my
younger sister has her future assured: her fiancé is a widower,
thirty-eight, with two children, a boy aged twelve and a girl of
nine. He has a successful business and is a partner in a merchants' bank. The family is delighted for her, and most are
embarrassed for me, and it is useless for me to say to them, even
if I had the courage, that my hopes are fixed already, and it is
only the stubbornness of my father that keeps me unwed. All I
have heard of late have been the most subtle rebukes that Solange should be married first, and her seven years my junior. I
suppose it is useless for me to protest, to say that you and I will
one day be married. For the time being, I must put up appear-
ances, or ruin the occasion for my sister. I would not give the
family the satisfaction of showing distress or causing any sort
of uproar because I am not yet married. There is a dinner this
evening, a formal occasion, and Georges has agreed to serve as
my escort, which will make my spinsterhood less obvious.*

How I long to be with you, Jean-Marc. I have spent hours

reading over your letters and dreaming what that strange land is like. I am struck by the bravery you show by going there, and I pray that God will keep you safe in a place with so few Christians.

My Aunt Clémence has asked me to come to her home in Paris for two weeks, and my father has consented to the journey. Two weeks in Paris without my father to hinder me! She has offered to outfit me for the winter season, and who can turn down new dresses from Paris? It has been two years since I made such a journey, and then I could not indulge myself as I shall now, for my Aunt is the most generous soul alive. She is very rich, and so it is nothing to her to spend amounts that would be prohibitive to me for the best clothes. I believe that my father has asked her to introduce me to the various eligible men she knows, in the assumption that I will be turned from you, but there is no reason to fear. I have said I will accept invitations if my aunt approves, and so I shall, but I have decided that I will not entertain any man in such a way to raise hopes. I will have a delightful time choosing new gowns and frocks, and I will enjoy a concert and a play, Le Menteur Véridique *by Scribe, perhaps —which Aunt Clémence has promised me—as well as the shopping, which will make my stay very agreeable. My father is anxious to show me off this winter as something more attractive than spinsters are thought to be, and he can be certain now that I will be able to present a very good impression.*

I have read one of the books you sent me, but I fear that much of what is said in the pages in beyond my understanding. I read a few lines and I am overcome. My head aches with all the knowledge there. I am filled with awe at the descriptions of pyramids and obelisks, but much of the rest escapes me. I do not know how you are able to study so much that is foreign and ancient. When I think of your expedition, I am filled with pride that you are part of such an undertaking. One day when we are together, I hope you will be able to tell me all that you have studied and discovered.

For the occasion of Solange's wedding, my father has agreed to allow me to wear the fine pearls my mother left to me. It is part of his plan to make me wish to be married myself, so that

I will have these jewels as my own at last. There is also a gold bracelet set with emeralds, and though it is not just in the current mode, it is vastly pretty, and it is a pleasure to be permitted to wear it. In addition there is a small brooch set with diamonds and emeralds. The bracelet and the brooch must be returned to the advocate's office for trust, but my father has decided that I will be allowed to keep the pearls. I have described the necklace to you, I know: a triple strand, quite long, of pearls all the same size, separated by tiny gold beads. The clasp is gold, set with seed pearls, matching the ones on the strands. The pearls them-selves have a pink cast to them, which I am told makes them more valuable. The diamond tiara, which I have always loved, is being given to Solange as part of her marriage gifts. Her inheritance includes a choker of five strands of pearls with a cameo in a gold frame at the center; my Great-grandmother was given it by her husband when their first son was born. After the treasures you must have found in Egypt, these must seem paltry, but I am thrilled to have the pearls as my own at last. When we meet again, I will wear them, and you will tell me that I am as splendid as any wife of Pharaoh.

Every morning I think of you, and every night I speak your name in my prayers. I look forward to the time when you are vindicated in my father's eyes and received for the hero you are, when you can claim your right to my hand without any dispute. Isn't this near the time when the Nile overflows? How can you bear the thought of such a flood? I am filled with admiration for you, and it grows ever greater as you tell me of your exploits in Thebes. I would never have the courage to go to such a place, or to do the things you are doing as I put these words on paper. How brave you are, Jean-Marc, and how proud I am of your achievements. I know that once you return from Egypt and it is known that you have done so much, everyone will be as admiring as I am, and I shall probably be jealous, so famous you will become.

With a thousand kisses,
Honorine

September 5th, 1825, at Poitiers

5

There was less flooding on the east bank of the Nile than the west;
Madelaine's villa stood on a built-up foundation of rock, designed
with the Inundation in mind, and though the water rose around
it, the level was not high enough to reach the living quarters, and
now that the water was receding it was less than a foot deep
around the base of the house. The inner courtyard and stables
were also on raised ground and protected from the water, though
not from the rats that swarmed ahead of the flood. Servants had
been delegated to rid the house and stable of rats, and rewards
were offered each day for the most rats killed; at night pots of
incense said to be distasteful to rats were left all around the house
and stable.

It was well after midnight, and the scent of incense was heavy
in the air. Lanterns burned in the upper rooms, and the doors
onto the veranda that wrapped around the second floor stood
open. Most of the staff had long since retired for the night, but
the young Sardinian maid waited patiently for the owner of the
house to come to bed.

On the veranda, Madelaine paced restlessly. For all her native
earth under the floor, the water around her had made her uncomfortable and ill-at-ease. Earlier that night she had braved the
lapping Nile to visit in sleep one of the young English: a slender,
jumpy, poetic chap who welcomed her into his dreams with a
wildness he would never reveal in his waking hours.

Something brushed against her leg, and Madelaine bent down.
"Oisivite," she said as she lifted the brindled cat into her arms.
"What are you doing up here? Um?"

The cat was limp and purring, shaping himself to her hold. He
lifted his head, eyes closed, to encourage her to scratch under
his chin.

"What a creature you are," she murmured, finding his favorite
spot at the back of his ears and smiling as his purr grew louder.
"Finding many rats?" She shifted him to a more balanced position

and resumed pacing. "How do you stand it, Oisivite? Doesn't the water drive you to distraction?"

From inside her dressing room, Madelaine's maid called out, "Are you alone, Madame?"

"But for the cat, yes," Madelaine called back, adding, "For heaven's sake, Lasca, go to bed. There's no reason for you to stay up. I can manage for myself."

"It wouldn't be right, Madame, not in this household." Lasca had been complaining about the restrictions of Moslem life since she arrived in Egypt in early June. Her disdain was matched only by the great care she took in meeting all the requirements imposed upon her. "You are the mistress here, and it is my task to serve you, but I must guard you, or there will be talk. You cannot afford talk, Madame."

"There is talk already," said Madelaine, lifting the cat so that his head lay against her shoulder. "You cannot stop it."

"Nevertheless, I have my duty and I know what I must do," Lasca insisted. She stepped out of Madelaine's dressing room to the edge of the veranda. "You must not give them more reason to disapprove of you, Madame. When my husband died so shortly after our marriage, it was said that I was *strega*. I had never done anything to make anyone think so, but since my husband died only five weeks after our wedding, the whispers never stopped. You must take care, Madame, lest they whisper so about you."

"Why must I?" Madelaine asked, going on before Lasca could answer. "Because I have work to do, and I want to be permitted to do it. Yes, I am aware of that. But I have a Coptic monk in my household. Even the Moslems regard him as beyond reproach. Doesn't that count for something?" She had taken care to let it be known that Erai Gurzin was her tutor and not her spiritual instructor so that her French colleagues would not have reason to disassociate themselves from her because she had given up Catholicism. "I have you and Keila to be chaperones, if that is required. The monk has an honorable and moral reputation. I have nine servants including Renenet in the household who can testify to my conduct. What more is needed?"

Lasca stared down at her feet. "You are a young woman, very

pretty. No one doubts that men dream of you. You have beautiful eyes, and men read things in them they want to read." She raised her head. "In a place like this, you must be careful."

"All right," Madelaine said reasonably, "but that doesn't mean you have to remain awake until I retire. I'm not about to . . . jump into the flood and paddle away." There was an expression in her face that Lasca could barely see in the darkness and could not understand. "You wish to remain here until I am in bed? What is to stop me from dressing for sleep and then coming back here to walk another hour or so? Would you have to keep watch over me then?"

"It is my duty," said Lasca with determination. "You brought me here because you did not want to entrust yourself to foreigners. Well enough, but you must then allow me to do the task you have paid me to perform." She looked toward the west, where the river spread at flood. "Have you been over the river, Madame?"

Riding in the shallow, open boat had been terribly uncomfortable, with the sun above and the water below, and only the earth in the soles of her shoes to counteract the two, but it had been tremendously satisfying, poling around the feet of the statues, riding up the portals of temples; Madelaine was willing to endure worse than that to acquire knowledge. "Yesterday, not since. I hope to go again before the flood retreats. The temple statues on the west bank are impressive, rising out of the flood as they do. I wanted to go back again today but none of the expedition was willing to take another day to explore." She patted the cat. "There were statues of cats there, at the feet of the gods. And cats that are gods. At least, we assume they are gods. What else can a cat be?" She scratched him behind the ears again. "Good cat, good cat," she crooned.

"I will stay up until you are properly abed," said Lasca, who would not be distracted by Madelaine's talk with the cat. "And if I must rise at dawn because you decide to, I will also." She was not quite belligerent, but there was a rebellious edge in her voice.

"Not this coming morning," said Madelaine, hoping that she would be able to rest when she went to bed. Her mattress was filled with her native earth which would tend to reduce the enervation of the Inundation. "I was told that the floodwaters came late this year, by more than three weeks. If they are gone too soon, the whole country will fear a year of famine."

"As was described in the Bible," said Lasca with satisfaction.

"That was seven lean years, not one late Inundation," Madelaine corrected her at her most pragmatic. "Well, we hope that it will not happen. The river is falling but I am told that it is falling slowly, which they consider a good sign." In her arms the cat squirmed; with a resigned sigh she let him go, watching as he stood poised on the rail of the veranda. "If you change your mind, Oisivite, there's a place at the foot of the bed for you."

"He is going to kill rats," said Lasca doing her best not to yawn.

"Yes," agreed Madelaine, as the cat jumped down to a projection on the kitchen porch. "I ought to be grateful." She turned and went to the edge of the veranda, leaning her arms on the railing and looking out over the dark, shiny water. "It is as if I were on an island. A desert island."

"It's very late, Madame," Lasca insisted.

Madelaine did not respond at once. She recalled all the warnings Saint-Germain had given her about loneliness. Tonight it possessed her like a low, searching fever, insinuating itself into her very being, worse than the water flowing around her house. When she turned there was a distance in her eyes as if she had gone far away. "Yes, very well. Is my negligee out?" She spoke remotely and móved as if her body were under the control of another will. The river whispered and trilled as it ran by the villa, and the pull of the water was strong. She shut it out, imagining herself in another place, at another time: she was eighteen, in Paris, and Saint-Germain had ridden with her to a bridge.

"Everything is ready," said Lasca. "I will brush your hair for you, if you wish."

"No," said Madelaine quietly. "I'll tend to it. I'll ask you to dress it for me when I rise in the morning. I promise you," she said, not quite so distantly, "I will not rise too early."

Lasca curtsied. "I will put away your clothes as you undress," she said, following Madelaine into her bedroom.

"Rather set them out for washing," said Madelaine as she cast her gauze fichu aside.

It was a large chamber, the fourth-largest in the villa after the salon, the drawing room and the dining room. On two sides the French windows opened onto the veranda; on the third a door connected to the dressing room and the maid's room beyond, on the fourth there was a door leading to the hall and the rest of the villa as well as to a small alcove where Madelaine had installed her bathtub. Two large armoires flanked the dressing-room door, and the bed, between the bath alcove and the French windows, was large and curtained in sprigged muslin. A chaise longue was set up between the two sets of French windows, and covered with an embroidered throw.

Madelaine was already reaching behind her neck to start un-fastening the dozens of little buttons that closed the bodice of her dress. "This will have to be washed, Lasca. Make sure you check the flounce and mend it where it's torn. Although why I should wear a flounce in this part of the world, I can't imagine."

"It would not be fitting for you to dress poorly," Lasca reminded her.

"Who would care, here in Thebes?" she asked, giving up the unbuttoning to Lasca. "How would I get out of this if you were not here to assist me?"

"It isn't right for you to undress yourself," said Lasca in the same firm tone. "Well-born ladies do not go about without a maid."

"Of course," said Madelaine, unfastening the buttons at her cuffs. "I can understand why some of the antiquarians take up native dress, though."

"Does that include the veil?" Lasca asked sharply.

Madelaine shook her head. "No. There you have me." She helped her maid pull the dress down off her shoulders. "I do not know how sand gets everywhere, but it does. My corset is gritty with it. Have it washed very carefully, so all the sand is out. It's wearing away my skin."

"I will do it myself," said Lasca as she set the dress aside. "Let me get your peignoir."

"Never mind," said Madelaine. "Just the negligee. That is all I need." She reached to the small of her back to unfasten the laces of her corset. "How does it come about that we must wear these contraptions?"

Lasca hesitated, then explained, "It is not correct for a woman to appear without proper boning. Only depraved women go about unbound. Why do you always flaunt proper conduct?"

"I don't," said Madelaine, unfastening the bottom hook. "I only question it." She was out of her corsets now. "But how odd, that we truss ourselves up so." She reached for her negligee and pulled it on. "This is more the thing."

"I think, Madame, you like to talk scandal, to see if I will respond to your sallies. You behave with propriety." She gathered up Madelaine's frock and undergarments. "Tomorrow I'll take care of these. And I will see that the clothes set out for you have been properly cleaned."

"Thank you," said Madelaine as she drew back the curtain of her bed. "You're very patient with me, Lasca. I hope you do not have cause to regret it." As she lifted the sheets, she felt the anodyne pull of her native earth. "Don't bother to call me in the morning. I will want to sleep late."

Lasca paused in the door. "What if you have visitors? Might not Professor Baundilet or Paille want to confer with you?"

"They might, but not very early. They have their first meeting over breakfast and will not think of me until later." She drew the sheet up and leaned back against the mass of pillows. "Inform them, will you, that I want to have bath water when I rise?"

"Certainly," said Lasca, closing the dressing room door, and then the door to her own room.

Madelaine lay back, her night-tuned eyes taking in the room and the veranda beyond. Tonight Egypt felt very strange, a place she would never become accustomed to; she wished for another letter from Saint-Germain, something that would increase her understanding of the people who had lived here so long ago. They seemed so remote, she thought, that not even their stone statues held echoes of them. The House of Life: that place haunted her, the more because she had not found it yet. This god Imhotep eluded her, and with him his priests and his temples. There had to be some way to find the House of Life, to call it out of the sands and time. She sighed, looking up at the canopy of her bed. The Englishman had fed her, but she was not . . . nourished. For that more was needed, she knew, and no one drew her sufficiently for her to risk anything more than visitations in dreams. There were the men of the expedition, of course, but she had no desire to complicate an already difficult situation. If she showed preference for any man in Baundilet's expedition, there would be trouble, and the tolerance she was shown now would vanish. It was probably just as well, she told herself, that none of them interested her except as antiquarians, and that only Baundilet himself had made any attempt to approach her. As it was, she was determined to keep Baundilet himself at a distance. She had no illusions about the expedition leader: if Madelaine became his mistress, she would not be allowed to continue as an antiquarian, she was utterly convinced of that.

How long the night was. How lonely she was.

By morning, Madelaine had argued herself into a more cheerful frame of mind. She rose shortly after ten and spent the next half-hour in a tepid bath, then washed her dark brown hair; afterward she sat on the veranda and let Lasca brush it as it dried.

"Do you ever think about going home?" Lasca asked as she began to work Madelaine's hair into a neat, shiny knot on the top of her head.

"Often," said Madelaine. She was en déshabillé, and trying to choose which of her frocks she would mind wearing the least.

"Do you want to return?" Lasca busied herself with pins and a small Spanish comb as she waited for an answer.

"Sometimes. I miss Montalia—it is where I was born." She had a brief, poignant impression of the chateau; she shook the memory off. "But it is isolated. No one comes there, or not very often."

Lasca stepped back to check her handiwork. "You have lovely hair, Madame. Dark hair that shines with yellow light is not often seen."

"I suppose not," said Madelaine, who had not seen it herself in over eighty years; she was still not wholly used to having no reflection.

A sound from the courtyard below caught the attention of the two women, and Madelaine rose to look over the veranda rail, wondering who had arrived. She lingered, not recognizing the horse or the man, then realized it was her German neighbor, the physician Falke. Puzzled, she stepped back. Why had he called upon her now? He had had no contact with her since the evening they met, and Madelaine had long since decided that he had dismissed her offer for information as nothing more than small talk. "You'd best bring me my clothes," she said, brushing the front of her robe de chambre. "If Herr Doktor Falke wishes to see me, I don't want to keep him waiting too long." Why on earth had he come here? She hurried back into her room, pulling off her robe de chambre and reaching for the corset Lasca had set out on the chaise. "Will you do the laces for me? It's faster."

Lasca hastened to comply, saying as she did, "You ought to leave this task to me at all times."

"But you lace so tightly," said Madelaine. "In a climate like this, it's better not to be bound." She looked around for her dress. "Where is it?" she asked when she saw nothing set out.

"Don't you prefer to choose?" Lasca asked, puzzled by the question.

"Yes; but I don't know what's available. Is the rose-colored muslin pressed?"

"I regret, no, Madame," said Lasca.

"What about the blue gauze with the tiered ruffles?" She did not actually like the dress, but knew it was suitable for day-time callers.

"It is in your dressing room," said Lasca, her face brightening. "That is a very proper frock."

"Yes," said Madelaine without enthusiasm.

Lasca hurried into the dressing room and was coming back with the dress folded over her arm when there was a tap on the door.

"Renenet?" Madelaine called in response.

"Madame," said her houseman. "There is a visitor."

"Doktor Falke. Yes, I saw him arrive." She motioned to Lasca to hurry. "Please see that he is given something to eat and drink, in the morning room, I think, and tell him I will be with him directly." This last was muffled as Lasca lifted the frock over her head.

"As you wish, Madame," said Renenet from the other side of the door. "Shall I summon the monk?"

"Inform him that Doktor Falke is here and ask him if he wishes to speak with him," said Madelaine, tugging the dress into place and then smoothing the high-waisted sash. "Lasca, where are my lapis earrings?"

"I have them, Madame," said Lasca, and held out the pair before starting to button the frock down the back. As she made a bow with the sash, she said, "Is this the physician who has the next villa?"

"Yes. I met him some weeks ago at that strange reception Monsieur Omat held. I'm surprised that he has called." It was, she realized, a pleasant surprise. She put her earrings on, then touched her throat. "I don't need something around my neck, do I?"

"It would be better," said Lasca cautiously as she finished buttoning the back of the dress.

"But not necessary," Madelaine decided. "Just as well." She hesitated. "Did my hair get mussed?"

"A little," said Lasca. "It will take me a moment to fix it."

"Then hurry," said Madelaine as she looked about for her walking shoes. "Have you seen my black kid—"

"I have them here," said Lasca, opening the nearer armoire. "You're as nervous as a girl at her first ball."

"Nonsense," said Madelaine, though she sensed something like the excitement the first time she made her curtsy in society, so many years ago.

As Lasca knelt to put on her shoes and button them, she observed, "You are interested in this man, Madame?"

"I am curious about him, certainly," Madelaine answered, a bit too primly to be completely convincing.

He is handsome?" asked Lasca.

"Well enough, I suppose." Belatedly she recalled his smile and the creases it made in his face. "Better to ask if he is a decent man, a good man, than if he is handsome."

"And is he?" Lasca inquired with false innocence.

"I don't know," Madelaine answered blightingly, and it was no more than the truth. "I have met him only once, at the reception I mentioned. We spoke a short while, about Rossini."

"You remember the conversation?" Lasca teased.

"No one else there was paying much attention to the music unless they were dancing. No one else said anything about it; so naturally I remember," Madelaine said sharply. "For the others, we spoke of antiquities." She stood still while Lasca straightened a tendril of hair. "Pay no attention to me, Lasca," she advised as she brought her feelings once again under control. "I have had such limited society for so long, I think that I would be pleased to see Danton himself, for variety." With that, she opened the farther armoire, took out a long silk shawl and flung it over her shoulder. "I will drape it on the way downstairs," she promised as she left her bedroom and her curious maid.

At the foot of the stairs, she found Renenet waiting for her. "I have taken the visitor to the morning room; he is having coffee now. He did not give the reason for his visit."

"Thank you," said Madelaine.

"I will announce you," said Renenet in a tone that permitted no dispute.

"If you think it is necessary," said Madelaine, following her houseman to the door of the morning room.

"Madame de Montalia," said Renenet, and withdrew a discreet distance down the hall.

"Good morning, Madame," said Egidius Maximillian Falke as he rose, wiping his fingers on his handkerchief as he did. He looked directly at Madelaine and smiled, the creases around his eyes just as she remembered them.

"Good morning, Herr Doktor," she said, extending her hand. "It is an unexpected pleasure to have you in my house, at last." She sat down on one of the three chairs, leaving the settee to him.

"How kind," said Falke, a little abstractedly, his smile fading. He sat down again. "Your houseman provided me a most generous welcome here. I must compliment you on your hospitality." He indicated the tray with a selection of breads and fruit as well as coffee.

"Thank you," said Madelaine, wondering what he wanted. She folded her hands in her lap and waited.

"Will you join me?" Falke said.

"Thank you, no," said Madelaine. "I broke my fast some time earlier."

"Of course," said Falke. "Then permit me?" He picked up his

small cup and finished the coffee. "It is rather awkward," he said when he put the empty cup down. "I'm persuaded you will understand, though I almost did not come."

"I am delighted you did," said Madelaine.

Falke gestured impatiently, as if to do away with polite forms. "I don't quite know how to address the question."

"Ask it directly," Madelaine suggested. "Is there something you would like me to do for you?"

"I believe so," said Falke uncertainly. "If it can be done at all. It would be less a problem if you were not a woman, but you are the only member of Baundilet's expedition who is interested in medicine, and so, you see, I have to come to you. None of the English expedition is willing to assist me." He turned his hands palm up. "If you are not willing to assist me, I do not know how it is to be done."

"If I knew what it is, then I might be able to give an answer," said Madelaine.

"Yes; my thought precisely." He poured himself a second cup of coffee and added sugar before drinking half of it. "You see, it is important, or I would not impose on you this way."

"Since you have yet to tell me," Madelaine said with asperity, "I do not know that it is an imposition. I infer that your predicament is related to your medical practice. Is that correct?" She paused and when he said nothing, she added, "I am afraid I know little about medicine, if it is the medicine of today you mean."

Falke nodded twice. "Yes, that is it," he told her. "It's a matter of what the ancients knew, do you see? I have encountered conditions here that I never anticipated." He looked at her, meeting her eyes squarely. "You made a very generous offer when I met you; perhaps you don't remember."

She returned his look. "I do remember; very well."

"Ah." He managed a quick, quirky smile. "That makes my task a little less harrowing."

"You wish to learn more about how the Egyptians of old treated diseases? Doktor Falke, yes, we talked about this when we met." She was amused and irritated at the same time. "I was quite serious: I offered to provide you with translations of any medical material we found, and you said you would let me know if that was acceptable to you. Until now, you have said nothing. Am I to assume that you have made up your mind and wish to have whatever useful information I might come across?"

He was obviously relieved. "I should not have doubted you," he said as he visibly relaxed. "Yes. I would appreciate it deeply if you would be willing to assist me in this way."

"I have already said that I am," Madelaine said, vexed by his attitude. "What a feckless creature I should be if I were not able to abide by my word."

"I have been churlish, Madame, and you are sensibility itself." He rose and took her hand, no more than brushing it with his lips. "I cannot express how grateful I am." Once again, fatally, he smiled.

Text of a letter from Madelaine de Montalia in Thebes to le Comte de Saint-Germain in Switzerland.

Saint-Germain my love,

How much I have missed you here in this land where you lived so long ago. I look at the columns and the statues, and I think, here you were when they were put in place; in this colonnade you took shelter from the sun. Not that it is certain you did, for judging from what you have written, you rarely left the precincts of the Temple of Imhotep, wherever that was.

At other times I look at these monuments and I think of France. Egypt, whatever else it was, must have been a land at peace, for there is no evidence that I can see of violence, not the sort that overcame France in the Revolution, not the sort that brings down buildings as well as rulers. For years and years and years the Pharaohs fought no battles, or none here in Thebes. Is that correct, or am I indulging in romantic assumptions?

Were I not so lonely here, I would be content, for I have been able to do what I have wished to do for so long: rediscover that which was lost. I am happy to be digging up ruins and spending my time searching for the vanished past. I am overjoyed to have the opportunity to explore temples that have not been touched by the sun for half your lifetime.

That is one thing I have thought much about since I arrived here, dearest love. I have thought of how long you have walked the earth. Until I came here, I don't suppose I grasped the meaning of your age. It is difficult to think of all those years as an age, not for a single man to live. I am struck again by what a treasure your love is, for it has survived monuments of stone and a nation of people—many nations of peoples, no doubt. Against that, to have you love me is inestimably precious. I want to know more of how you lived here, how you changed while you were a slave in the House of Life.

I wish also to find the House of Life, but I realize now that I see the enormity of the work, that it will be a while before that is possible.

Thank you for sending Gurzin to me. He has been most helpful in making sense of the inscriptions on the temples, though some defeat him as well as Claude-Michel Hiver, our linguist. We have not yet established a dependable rapport, but for the most part, I have been fortunate indeed for his knowledge and capable aid.

Professor Baundilet is pleased with the progress we have made, or so he says. He has written several reports for the universities and for publication, which provides him great satisfaction. I suspect that he has appropriated some of the work of the other antiquarians and represented it as his own, but that is a common enough practice, or so I have been assured. I am not as sanguine about it as some of the others. Also, I am beginning to think that Baundilet's ambitions are growing, and that troubles me, for it may bode ill for the expedition. He and Jean-Marc Paille are often closeted together, Paille as loyal lieutenant, Baundilet as captain. I thought at first that I was kept away from these meetings because I am a woman, but three of the others have complained of it as well, so it may be something more than mere disdain for female scholars.

What is it about this place that makes me long for you so? Or is it the place at all? Yet I cannot look toward the Nile without thinking of you, I cannot copy an inscription, but that I wish you were with me. It may be the weight of time; it may be nothing more than loneliness, and you warned me of that. I wish you would write to me very often, but if you did that would make me miss you more than I do already. How have you managed this predicament for yourself? If you have not, tell me, so that I will be closer to you, if only in consternation.

As I was in my life, and am in yours,

Forever
your Madelaine

September 28th, 1825, at Thebes

PART II

Senhgerin
Slave

Text of a letter from le Comte de Saint-Germain in Switzerland to Madelaine de Montalia in Egypt, dated October 4th, 1825.

Madelaine, my dearest heart;

By now you should be through the worst of the Inundation; Hapy is returning to his cave at the headwaters of the Nile, which was called atur *and* atur-nir *when I was there and known as Senh and Senhgerin and Sanh-kheran. How long it has been since those names were spoken.*

You said you were going to Thebes, and it is there I am sending this letter. You will find Thebes rich beyond your imagining, if it has not been wholly plundered and ruined. There are great riches to be found in Thebes, some of gold, some of the mind and soul.

To answer your questions, as I have said I would do: I was sent from Memphis to the Temple of Imhotep at Thebes when I had been in the Black Land for little more than a century. Amenhotep III was Pharaoh then, and Thebes was his capital. He was an able man, energetic and ambitious, and he gathered an impressive court around him. He sought out those who would add to the glory of his reign, which included the High Priest of Imhotep, a sharp-faced man, Mereseh, who brought with him an enormous staff in order to establish his importance.

As a slave of the House of Life, I was given the task of tending those with the most extreme illnesses and wounds; this was

91

considered an improvement over my first work with the dying, and unusual for a slave who was also a foreigner; fortunately the priests did not know the full extent of my nature or I would have been stoned to death.

"Pharaoh is not well," said Bak, Mereseb's personal slave to Senhgerin as they were given their weekly shaving.

"Pharaoh is not young," said Senhgerin, paying little attention to the gossip Bak offered.

"He has reigned for more than thirty years, and the Black Land is flourishing," Bak marveled. "Surely the gods show him favor." He looked around, then gave Senhgerin a single, hard stare. "And what do the gods show you, foreigner?"

"I do not try to understand the gods, Bak," Senhgerin said in a tone that did not invite more conversation.

"My master has been called to Pharoah, to discover the cause of his illness." Bak took great pride in Mereseb's position at court and often found excuses to remind everyone in the House of Life of his master's importance. He regarded Senhgerin with suspicion. "He will deliver Pharaoh from all disease."

"May he succeed," said Senhgerin, knowing that Mereseb could do nothing about the inexorable toll of age. Turning toward the youthful slave who wielded the razor, he said, "I will tend to my chest."

The boy stared down at his feet. "I would, foreigner, but the scars . . ."

Absently Senhgerin put his hand to the stretched, white skin that covered his torso from the base of his ribs to his pubis, and something in his mind winced at the memory of the knives and hooks that made the scars. "Old wounds," he said.

"Severe wounds, for all that," said Bak, who considered himself a keen judge of medical conditions.

"Once; when they were new: no more." Senhgerin took the razor and completed the task for the boy. As he handed it back, he saw the little slave cringe.

* * *

*When Amenhotep III died, he left prosperity behind him, and
a son who yearned for a place among the gods, or to be num-
bered with the* newtri *or* neters—*what might best be described
as forces of nature. He also desired to be free of the machinations
of the priests who had become powerful enough to rival Pharaoh; he abolished all the gods but Aten and made himself High
Priest as well as Pharaoh, changing his name to Akhenaten, and
establishing a new capital at a place that is now called Amarna.*

*As Imhotep did not rival Aten, Mereseb was permitted to bring
himself and his priests to the House of Life at the new capital;
he was one of the few allowed to continue his worship, and
there were many who resented the favor Imhotep's priests had
been shown.*

"I hate this place," whispered Mereseb as he walked through
the courtyard out of the House of Life to make his daily inspection
of the dying. "They mock me."

Beside him, Senhgerin glanced at Mereseb in surprise. "Mock
you? How?"

"Every one of them is proof that Imhotep has failed," said Mereseb, squinting toward the sky. "There are many who are pleased
when we must send for the priests of Anubis. It is known for a
sign against Pharaoh. They say we are made weak by the gods we
have offended."

"There is only the god Aten now," Senhgerin reminded him.

Mereseb's laughter was unpleasant. "Because Pharaoh declares
it; because he is—" He stopped as he saw Bak coming forward.
"You will not repeat what I said."

Senhgerin sighed. "You are master here; I am a slave."

Though his old bones hurt him, the fifty-four-year-old Mereseb
stood a little straighter. "Yes. Yes." He lowered his voice once
more. "It's that queen of his, that Hittite woman. She's the one
who has bewitched him. Pharaoh is blinded by her beauty; it
dazzles him so that he cannot see the shadows of the gods, and
the gods will not pardon him." He waved Senhgerin away. "Go.
There are those who need your succor."

"At once," said Senhgerin, showing reverence to the old man.

He did not linger to hear more complaint, certain that it was dangerous to know too much about the affairs of priests.

How can I explain to you what I felt when they brought Hesentaton to the House of Life? The priests of Imhotep did not attempt to treat her—there was nothing they could do.

She was the daughter of a stone-cutter who had refused to marry the man who had paid for her because she preferred another. Her father tried to give back the bride-price and was refused. She, in turn, had run off with the man she had chosen. Unfortunately, her unwanted suitor pursued them, and when he caught them, he had his rival killed, but ordered her taken to the top of the high cliffs, to be suspended there from ropes until heat and thirst killed her. If her father had not found her she would have been dead before sundown, which might have been kinder. As it was, she was burned beyond recovery and blinded, so they gave her to me.

Her skin was so ruptured and blackened that it was not possible to put the soothing compresses on her without increasing her pain tenfold. She insisted on standing at first, because she could not bear to be touched.

Senhgerin came nearer to her, but took care not to get too close. "I have water for you; drink it."

"I . . . I can't," she muttered, her voice as cracked as her skin.

"I am directly in front of you," said Senhgerin. "Reach out your hand and I will give it to you."

She could not blink her sightless eyes. "Can't," she insisted, rocking a little as her strength failed her.

"If you do not, you will become light-headed and fall," said Senhgerin. "That would cause more pain than taking the cup." He waited, patient and calm.

"Where are you?" she asked a little later, the words rasping out of her.

"Still directly in front of you," he answered. "Raise your arm and I will give the cup to you."

She shrank back. "No. If I bend my arm ... " Impossible tears welled in her eyes but could not fall.

"Let me help you," said Senhgerin, unaware that he had never made such an offer before. He took a step forward and held the cup out, taking care not to let it press against her blistered mouth. "Drink," he said, tipping the cup for her.

As she swallowed, she wavered and started to collapse.

In the next instant Senhgerin had his arm around her, taking care not to give her any more pain than necessary. "I will hold you," he said as she tried to squirm away from him. "Stop. I will hold you."

She shuddered as she forced herself to stand still, and she gave one wretched sob. "No," she moaned.

Senhgerin supported her with his outstretched arm; there was no sign of effort in this, though Hesentaton was a full-grown woman. "Remain still," he told her.

She began to whimper, though she strove to make no sound. Her face was too burned to be readable, but there was something in the destruction of her eyes that reached into him. "Let me die," she whispered at last.

The shock of her words went through him like the hot wind off the desert, though he had heard them countless times before. He held out the cup to her again. "Drink," he said, his thoughts in disorder.

This time she was able to drink a little more before starting to cough. "I want to die," she insisted when she could speak again.

Before he could stop himself, he asked, "Why?"

"How can I live?" she responded.

He had no answer to give her, and no comfort but his tremendous strength and endurance which would allow him to hold her at arm's length through the night; there was nothing else he could do for her. He looked around the little alcove in the wall of the House of Life and tried to remember the number of times he had been here on just such a hopeless errand as he was now. "I have more water."

The sound she made might once have been a laugh, but the sun had burned it away as it had burned everything else. Her head lolled, her cheek brushed his arm and she righted herself with a sudden, terrible howl. *"No!"*

"Take it," said Senhgerin. He tried to hold the cup for her, but she lashed out, sending the cup flying and water splattering over her, intensifying her pain. It was all he could do to hold her as she kicked and twisted. "Don't," he repeated steadily as he held her.

Finally she went slack in his arms, her despair now more overwhelming than her agony. She whimpered when she drew breath. Then she said, very clearly, "Put me down."

"No," he told her.

"You can't keep holding me this way. Put me down."

"No," he repeated. "Don't ask again."

She set her feet more squarely on the floor. "I can stand. Look." Her whole body quivered as she strove to stay upright.

"All right," said Senhgerin, making up his mind, "I will take you to the wall, where you can brace yourself. I will bring you something to drink; it will ease the hurt, if you will drink it."

Her sightless eyes turned toward him. "I will drink it."

He guided her the few steps necessary to the door, and helped her set her hands on the frame. "I will not be long; hang on. If you call me, I will come." He stepped back from her, seeing the determination under her baked features. "Have courage." It was a foolish thing to say, he knew it, but he could think of nothing else. As he hurried toward the House of Life, he hoped that she would have strength enough to keep standing and sense enough to call for help if she needed it. As he entered the Temple of Imhotep, he clapped his hands for another slave, saying to the first who responded, "The herbs room. I must get . . . "

The slave went ahead of him, calling that Senhgerin was inside the walls.

A young priest, newly initiated to the service of Imhotep, drowsed at the door of the herbs room, his face shadowed with fatigue. As Senhgerin approached, he made himself waken and listen to what the slave from out of the House of Life wanted. "It is irregular," he said when Senhgerin was finished.

"The whole situation is irregular," answerd Senhgerin. "She cannot be saved, but she need not suffer as she does now. If you will give me the tincture I described, she will leave this life more easily."

The young priest shook his head. "Perhaps too easily?" he suggested, warily looking at the foreigner.

Senhgerin's laugh was hard. "It may speed dying by half a day or so; what does that matter, when she is past all remedy? Do you want a howling madwoman or a quiet one who passes from sleep to the care of Anubis without—"

"It is not for me to decide," said the young priest, looking around as if he expected to find other priests watching him from hiding.

"Then say I decided it," Senhgerin said. "Or come and tend to her yourself."

"I . . . " The young priest took a step back. "If there is any complaint . . . "

"I will be responsible," said Senhgerin. "I will take the flogging." In all his years in the Temple of Imhotep, Senhgerin had taken the punishment only twice; the young priest knew it.

At that the young priest capitulated. "I will provide the tincture, since you are so adamant. If the High Priest questions the use of it, I will direct him to you."

"Yes," said Senhgerin, and waited while the young priest went to fetch the earthenware jar that contained the liquid made from the roots and leaves of the Hittite dwarf apples, which were known to be deadliest poison.

As I recall, the tincture was mostly belladonna with another ingredient, probably derived from mushrooms. The priests were at pains to keep their concoctions secret, and only those who had passed the second initiation were allowed to participate in preparing them; at that time I was not privileged to know precisely how they made their medicines, or what went into them, and by the time I was one of them, their recipes had changed. That young priest, incidentally, went on to become High Priest of Imhotep twenty years later. He was the last one to have me flogged; I think he wanted to be avenged for the embarrassment he suffered from that night. He often reminded me how greatly

I had exceeded my authority, and said that had it been up to him, he would have had me flogged the next day. As it was, he had that opportunity twenty-three years later.

That was the first time I took it upon myself to go beyond my bounds, to demand something I was not entitled to have. As I look back, I cannot tell you now what it was that made me act, why it was Hesentaton more than another who awakened my pity. Or perhaps that is the answer: I did not pity Hesentaton; what I felt was far more complicated than that. I could not understand it then, and now, there are too many years separating me from what I was then for me to be certain I know what that change was, or how it came about.

She died just before morning, as the sky was starting to glow. Her poor, ruined face was composed, and she lay on her pallet without pain or trouble. She had been humming a little—the sound was dreadful but it seemed to please her—as the tincture worked its soothing magic on her ravaged flesh. There were a few bits of words, and she raised her head, called a name, then settled back, her eyes losing the last vestige of brightness, as if she could sleep at last.

Senhgerin knelt beside her pallet, so still that he might appear to be one with her in death. He thought of the fearful brevity of her life, and the waste of it, and something in his soul was blighted by Hesentaton's loss. "Poor, sad child," he said in the language of his vanished people.

Her father sought me out when she had been prepared for burial, and asked what he could give me for my care of his daughter. It was the first time anyone had offered me such thanks for my task, and I did not know what to tell him. In the end, I commissioned him to make a portrait of Nefertiti, Pharaoh's Hittite Queen, and present it to her in Hesentaton's memory. I was told that Akhenaten was pleased with the bust; I hope that assuaged her father's grief.

After that I was no longer to content to watch them die. Their anguish distressed me, eroded me. I did not change immediately, but over the next several years, I spent more time learning to treat those who had been sent out of the House of Life, and from time to time one of those I tended would recover. Had I not been a foreigner and a slave, who can know when I might have been permitted to study the texts of Imhotep?

Not that I was bitter, for I had not yet acquired my own humanity sufficiently for that. I was like a little child walking away from the front of his mother's house for the first time. If more had been available to me, I think I would have turned away in confusion and dread.

Do not judge me too harshly, my heart. I have told you many times that what I am now was hard-won. And though I wish it were otherwise, that is the wish of what I have become, not of a slave serving the dying out of the House of Life. Egypt is an anvil, and you are tempered or broken on it.

I await your letter with impatience. It is the oddest thing; I am pleased that you are there, doing the things you have wanted so long to do, as you have wanted to do them, and yet I want you with me, though that would not be wise. Your courage and determination fill me with pride in you, and at the same time I long to protect you, to guide and shelter you. How vain and contradictory. If I did not love you so completely, it might be different, and both of us would have better perspective: but not loving you would cast me into despair blacker than that I knew in Babylon.

You are the light I shine in the darkness, Madelaine; you are the fire of my soul.

Saint-Germain
(his seal, the eclipse)

November, 1825 through
October, 1826

Text of a letter from Professor Alain Baundilet in Thebes to Yamut Omat in Cairo.

My very dear Monsieur Omat;

Let me thank you again for your hospitality of last week. I could find it in my heart to feel I have imposed upon you, so frequently have I availed myself of your society. Only your continued reassurance that I do not intrude has enabled me to find increasing pleasure in your entertainments. Your villa is far and away the most splendid building in the whole area (excepting the monuments of the Pharaohs) and your style of hospitality is as fine as any that could be had in Europe. I have rarely experienced such luxury and taste in balanced combination as you have presented to me, and for which I am appreciative beyond all reckoning. Your most recent festivities have added to my high opinion of you, your daughter, and the pleasure of your society.

I am considering your recommendation of the other night, and I must say that I can fully see your point of view; your arguments are quite cogent and have been much on my mind; I am inclined to agree with you. As an Egyptian, you naturally perceive that the bounty of expeditions such as mine is surely

*more yours than the universities' I and my colleagues represent.
I am inclined to think it would be wise to regard your offer
seriously and to discuss with you upon your return what form
our contract might best take. I am willing to accommodate you
to the full limit of my capabilities but not to the point of
compromising the position of the expedition with the authorities, or endangering any of those who are participating with
me in this expedition.*

*To enlarge upon that, the local Magistrate, one Kareef Numair,
has been at pains to observe and question the activities of my
expedition, and I fear we must take into consideration his vig-
ilance if we are to reach a private understanding. This Magistrate conducts frequent inspections along with review of the
field notes of the expedition, which creates something of a problem, you will have to concur. I do not know the best way to
proceed in this instance. You must have some thoughts upon
this, and I look forward to hearing them at your earliest convenience, for I am persuaded that it would be folly to put your
plan into effect without discussing this particular Magistrate.
Our dealings cannot safely be such that Numair will be able to
identify and trace them, for that would be embarrassing for you
and for me, to say nothing of the pall it would cast on any
discoveries of my expedition.*

*A knowledgeable and experienced man such as yourself must
be familiar with the ways these obstacles can be circumvented.
I welcome your suggestions and your assistance, for you are in
a far more adaptable position than I am. It seems to me that
our dealings will be the more successful because of a little
forethought and strategic arrangements.*

*Now that the flood is over, we will be busier than ever, for
the weather is as mild as it ever can be in this land. With the
worst of the heat gone for a few months, we will be able to
redouble our efforts at the temple site, and while there to work
more expeditiously. Since the sun is not as extreme as it was in
the summer, we will have less need to avoid it. The sand, too,
is more easily handled, for it has not become gritty dust, and
will not until it is entirely dry, in a month or so. Our current
plans will speed our work, and hence, our progress. Rest assured*

that I will keep you informed of our advancements in the study of your ancient country. I have reason to hope that our discoveries might prove most worthwhile for all of us. Your curiosity will be rewarded, I am confident, as we continue the clearing of sand from the temple, for with every foot of wall, every bit of paving we bring to light, the promise of the site is reaffirmed.

It will be my honor to wait upon you when you return in order to avail myself of your advice and to establish the terms of our dealings. I cannot thank you enough for the interest you have shown in my expedition and our work in the ruins of Thebes, and I am hoping that my work on your behalf will more than justify your support and interest.

With my warmest personal wishes as well as the conviction that we will soon prosper through our endeavors, I am

Most sincerely yours,
Alain Hugues Baundilet

November 22nd, 1825, Thebes

1

"Who are these Pharaohs Saint-Germain describes?" Madelaine demanded of the letter she held as if her questions could reach Saint-Germain himself through the ink on the paper, and then rounded on Erai Gurzin. "What do you know about them?"

"Very little," said the Coptic monk as he looked up from the transcripts he had been reviewing. "Rameses I know, and a few others. Most of the names are not familiar to me. I recognize only four or five of them." He was seated at a high-backed easel in the salon, trying to puzzle out part of an inscription. "I can work my way through the first half, but this latter part here"—he tapped the sketched copy of the treacherous inscription—"is completely baffling."

"Why?" Madelaine asked, still holding the letter. "Why this more than others?"

"Well, it is something of the style. This figure here is not like the others I have seen. It may be one we have not yet translated, or it may be a different version of a marking we already know. But which?" He moved his chair back from the easel and looked toward the wide expanse of windows, as if the answer might hang in the middle distance.

In the last month the salon had been converted into a study; the sofas had been moved to the drawing room and one of the guest bedrooms; the two elegant tables were in the dining room, along with two carved chests. Now the easel and a broad trestle table dominated the salon, with two tall secretaries brought in to hold reports and supplies. Madelaine, seated on a tall chair at the trestle table, spread the letter in front of her.

"Akhenaten," she said after reading the letter again. "There are clues in that Pharaoh. If what Saint-Germain says is true, then we have a great deal to learn from him. He moved the capital, that ought to be mentioned somewhere in all the inscriptions."

"Or all mention of him has been removed," said Gurzin. "They did that."

"So you told me," Madelaine said. "Still, if I could find one mention of him, a single confirmation, we would be able to learn so much. It would help to establish the chronology, wouldn't it?" Her violet eyes brightened as she spoke. "Oh, I wish I could use this letter. Everything he tells me is fascinating, and important to our studies. But how would I explain it? How could I report on this letter and its contents without creating ... difficulties for Saint-Germain?"

"And why should anyone believe you—or him? They might say he was entirely fanciful. That would be more acceptable than actual knowledge." He continued for a short while to make notes on the large sketch spread out in front of him. "Not that Saint-Germain ever confided in me, or not to any extent," he said at last in a speculative way, "but I came to believe that his experience of the past was obtained first-hand. That letter appears to confirm my belief."

"Yes," said Madelaine slowly, on guard now. "It surely seems so."

Gurzin accepted her reticence and continued to study the sketch, but he spoke to her. "My child, anything you say to me in confidence will be bound as if you had spoke to God. I would not reveal anything that would detrimental to you or to Saint-Germain. I am aware that there is something about you, as there is something about him, that is unlike other people."

Madelaine folded the letter and slipped it into the reticule she carried. "I suppose that is a reasonable assumption," she said, her expression more circumspect than before.

"You see, I was a student of Saint-Germain's, fifteen years ago. He came here in 1803, as you would call it. He was here until 1819, and in that time, I did not see any change in him. I do not mean that in the sense we see no changes in the faces that are familiar to us because of their familiarity, but that he was remarkable because those changes did not happen. When I first met him, I guessed his age at about forty-five or so; when he left I would have guessed the same. Gurzin slid his chair back from the easel. "He explained nothing, nor did I ask."

"He is older than you suppose. So am I, for that matter." She said it flatly, and hoped that none of her servants were listening.

"Niklos Aulirios told me before Napoleon's soldiers shot him that he had lived since the time of the Roman Emperor Diocletian. He said that Saint-Germain had given him his long life." He blessed himself in the Coptic manner. "He had no reason to lie about that and every reason to dissemble."

"I never knew Niklos Aulirios," said Madelaine. "I heard of him from time to time." When her thoughts turned to Niklos Aulirios, she found it strange that Saint-Germain had provided Olivia Clemens with a bondsman and had never made such an offer to her. One day, she promised herself as she had for the last half century, she would have courage enough to ask him why.

"There was a manservant with Saint-Germain, lean and fair," said Gurzin in the same neutral manner. "I would have said he was fifty, for every year he lived here."

"Roger," said Madelaine with a nod of recognition.

"Aulirios told me that Roger was older than he was, and Saint-

Germain more aged than both of them." He rubbed his eyes. "I need a little time to rest, Madame. If you will permit?"

"Of course," said Madelaine, curious now to learn how much more Erai Gurzin knew, or had guessed. "Shall I ring for some coffee or other refreshment for you?"

"Will you join me?" Gurzin asked, his very politeness making the request a challenge.

"No; my thanks, however." She reached for the bellpull. "Well? What do you want?"

Gurzin capitulated. "Coffee would be welcome." He got up from the chair and stretched, his shoulders and wrists cracking at his effort. "When I said my prayers this morning, I thought my joints made enough noise to wake the entire household."

Madelaine heard this with concern and asked, "Do you require willow bark tea? I have some willow bark in the household supplies, and pansy too, I think." She was already summoning the servants. "Tell Renenet what it is you want and if it is here, it is yours. That includes the willow-bark tea. Don't disdain it, Brother Gurzin." This last was said with crisp sympathy.

"Perhaps I will have some later in the day," Gurzin said by way of a compromise with her.

"As you wish," Madelaine told him, and reached for a roll of sketches glued together that showed a complete frieze from the walls of the temple. As she unrolled it, she stopped at one of the figures in a column of hieroglyphics. "These two little birds, that look like songbirds of some sort." She rested her arms on the glued sheet to hold the scroll open. "They always seem to appear together." She frowned in concentration. "I wish we could persuade that young Englishman to assist us for a while." It was not the one she visited in dreams from time to time, but one of his colleagues, a clear-headed young scholar who spent all his waking hours copying friezes and inscriptions with single-minded intent.

"Would that be Wilkinson?" asked Gurzin.

"I think that's his name. He's been here about four years, I'm told." She pointed to a section of the sketch that appeared to be illustrations with captions. "See, these men are gathering reeds; there're two lines of hieroglyphics underneath. Then next to it, there are these three men pounding the reeds, and another two lines of comment underneath."

"They're making papyrus paper from the reeds," said Gurzin.

Renenet came to the door and bowed to Madelaine. "What is your wish, Madame?" he asked in a respectful manner that lacked servility.

"My wish is that you do whatever it is Brother Gurzin requires of you." She reached for the sand-filled leather pouches that served as weights for the long rolled sketches. She placed them with care, so that the glued joins would not be broken.

"Coffee, if you will, and a little wine. Cakes, but no fruit or honey." He offered Renenet a blessing, saying, "It is no offense to Allah that the follower of a prophet blesses you."

"You are people of the Book," said Renenet, with a second bow. "Your order will be filled at once." He turned away and left them alone.

Gurzin stared at the far wall, his eyes blank. "He would have disliked to see Christmas celebrated here last week, for all we are people of the Book."

Madelaine shrugged. "If he pays attention to that. Isn't it sufficient that I am a foreigner?"

"More than sufficient. No doubt that is why he keeps such close watch on you. It is very sensible of you to give him little to remark upon." Gurzin returned his attention to her. "You conduct yourself wisely, Madame." Once again he fell silent.

"Do you think he listens when we talk?" Madelaine asked when they had been alone again for several minutes.

"I think it is safe to assume that *someone* listens," he answered. "If it is not Renenet, it is another. You are a foreigner in Egypt. Of course they listen." He walked the width of the salon to one of the secretaries. "How much have you locked in here?"

"My field notes, the translations we've made," she said, concentrating on the sketches in front of her.

"Are you satisfied that your locks are secure?" Gurzin inquired as he stared at the secretary.

"I carry the key with me," she said, then looked up sharply. "Why? Do you think that they are not safe enough?"

Gurzin studied the two secretaries for a short while. "I think that anyone who could enter and rob a Pharaoh's tomb would make short work of those locks. I think that if I had these secretaries, I would keep the most valuable of my things in a safer place." He looked around at her. "But I think I would leave the field notes and a few of the reports here, so that others would not be tempted to look in other places for material you would rather not have found."

"As bait or misdirection?" Madelaine inquired with mischief in her eyes.

"Possibly as both," said Gurzin. "Have you ever seen evidence of any tampering with these locks?"

"I don't think so," said Madelaine, and then reconsidered her answer. "A week or so ago, I thought one of the locks was looser than usual when I went to open the secretary." She cocked her head to the side. "Do you think someone in the household had tried to open it?"

"Probably," Gurzin said with a long breath. "When I see evidence that servants have forgot themselves this way, I am filled with distress." He folded his hands. "They will say nothing to me, of course."

"Because you are not a Moslem but a Copt?" Madelaine guessed. "Is that reason enough for them to treat you as alien?"

"For some of them, yes. For others, it is a matter of convenience more than of faith." He closed his eyes briefly, and when he opened them, he said, "Has anyone from the expedition been here recently?"

"Professor Paille and Professor Hiver have. Five nights ago, don't you remember? They had been to Mass before they came, for Christmas." She indicated the salon. "We must have worked here until after ten. The grandmother clock in the entryway had just struck the hour when they left."

"I was thinking of a less formal occasion. Have any of them called on you in a personal capacity?" He went to the window and looked out. "You mentioned that Professor Baundilet has occasionally attempted to establish his interest with you."

"Yes, but he isn't fool enough to come here. It's difficult to seduce a woman in her own villa. He would rather I come to him, so that his servants, not mine, would be witness." She smiled with great insincerity. "He misses the comfort of his wife, and I am the only European woman, other than Lasca, easily available to him."

"Does that trouble you?" Gurzin asked, then broke off as Renenet came back into the salon with a tray.

"Where am I to put this, Madame?" Renenet asked.

Madelaine looked around. "There, I think. On that square chest. The top is large enough, and it isn't too low." She gestured to Gurzin to seat himself. "Thank you, Renenet," she said as her houseman set down the tray.

"Madame," said Renenet with a bow before he withdrew.

As Gurzin drew up a chair, he said to her, "I am apprehensive about Professor Baundilet. He has claimed your work as his own, and he wants to make you his mistress. He does not mean you well."

"Nor ill," said Madelaine. She put her mind on the sketches spread out before her. "He means to have the advantage of me, and fortunately his imagination is limited."

Gurzin made no reply to her then, but later in the day, when the sun had fallen low and the long, sharp shadows stretched out of the distant colonnades, he issued a last warning. "If your affections become fixed on another, Baundilet will not be happy. He is not a man to tolerate rivals."

Madelaine laughed, but the sound of it was sad. "All he wants is a woman to use, a convenience; how could he think of any man as his rival for that?"

"Don't dismiss him so easily," Gurzin persisted. "He is a greedy man, and that renders him dangerous."

"All right," she said, "if I find I have a suitor, I will take care." She rose from her tall chair and smoothed the rumpled front of her frock. "In the meantime, I will be at pains to keep the Professor at a distance." She remembered their encounter in the little chamber and flinched; she did not want another such incident to occur.

"I pray that will be enough," said Gurzin, moving his easel aside. "It is time for my evening devotions."

"I know," said Madelaine. "I need some time to myself; perhaps after your meal we might—" She broke off.

"What is it?" Gurzin asked as he started toward the door.

"I'd forgot this is the evening Doktor Falke is supposed to come by for a time. He is curious about the translations we have." She went to the taller secretary and stared at the front of it. Had someone really got into her records? And why? "I sent him a note that I doubt any of the material pertains to medicine, but he insists that he is curious. I expect him about eight, after he has finished with his patients for the day."

"Doktor Falke," Gurzin repeated. "Have you seen him recently?"

"Not for two weeks or so," Madelaine answered, and hoped that the tone of her voice did not reveal her quickening interest in the German physician.

"Is Baundilet aware of these visits?" Gurzin was at the door, and he turned to give her his blessing. He waited for her answer.

"I don't know. I suppose he is." She looked around the room as if her answer was part of the decor. "In a small European community like this one, there is always gossip; most of these things are known and it is no secret that Doktor Falke occasionally calls here."

"Of course," said Gurzin before leaving her alone.

Madelaine returned to the trestle table and stared down at the sketches, but her attention was elsewhere. She hated being watched, especially in her own home. She loathed having to guard herself, to consider every word she spoke, every gesture. She had had her fill of that in the dreadful days at the start of the Revolution, before Saint-Germain had come to Montalia and spirited her away to his house in Verona and safety. They had almost been caught twice in those five calamitous days, and both times due to the perfidy of servants. Although that was more than thirty years in her past, it still caused a cold fist to close inside her when she remembered how dangerous her escape had been.

"Madame?" said Renenet from the door.

Madelaine turned, and realized night had fallen.

"Would you like me to light the lamps?" Renenet asked, as if there was nothing unusual in his employer sitting alone in a dark room.

"Oh. Yes. If you would." She made herself yawn. "I must have dozed off," she said by way of explanation.

"Madame works much too hard," said Renenet as he drew flint

and steel from his sleeve; Madelaine had ceased to ask him to use a lucifer instead, though it was much quicker and more convenient. As Renenet tended to this chore, he said, "Doktor Falke has just arrived. He will be in from the stable in a short while. Where would you like me to bring him?"

The question caught her by surprise. Falke here already. She did not bother to consider her response. "Bring him here, if you will, and make sure there is a cordial for him." She touched her hair and hoped it was not too disordered. That was the trouble with having no reflection, she chided herself. She had to rely on her touch and the skill of others to keep track of her appearance. It was tempting to ask Renenet to tell her if she was presentable, but she knew that her houseman would be offended by such a question. There was not time to call for Lasca. As the last of the lamps flared alight, she resigned herself to meeting Falke just as she was.

There was the sound of his step in the hall, and then Renenet went to escort Madelaine's visitor to the salon.

"Am I intruding?" Falke asked as Renenet announced him.

"Not at all," said Madelaine, who had finally regained some of her composure. "I need an excuse to stop for the day, in any case." She moved away from the trestle table. "I thought you might prefer to speak here, so that I can show you the various inscriptions we have discovered." She turned toward Renenet. "A cordial for my guest, if you will." Then she looked back at Falke. "Is that acceptable?"

"Most welcome," said Falke, and smiled.

Why must he do that? Madelaine asked herself even as she returned his smile. The creases at his eyes and down the sides of his cheeks transformed his face in a way that captivated her. "Renenet, attend to it, please."

"As Madame orders," said her houseman, and left, full of disapproval.

"He isn't used to Europeans," said Madelaine. "He would rather I not speak to you alone." There were parts of Europe, she knew, where her actions would be met with the same disapproval that Renenet displayed.

"Do you wish to send for—" he began only to have her interrupt him.

"No, thank you. You are gentleman enough to behave as you ought," she said with a hint of regret. "This is my house, and if there is difficulty, my staff would deal with you."

"Assuredly," said Falke as he came nearer. "What is that you have been studying?"

"A sketch of a frieze, a copy." She brought one of the lamps nearer. "It's from the inner wall of the temple we are excavating."

The lamplight created a faint movement as it shone on the sketch. The figures took on the soft glow of lamplight and the subtle dance of the flame, so that they appeared almost alive. Falke stared at it in baffled fascination. "How do you account for this, Madame? What does it tell you?"

Madelaine shook her head. "Not enough," she answered after a slight hesitation. "It tells me about how papyrus was made into paper, perhaps. And here it tells me about how poultry was dressed, or so I suppose from the drawing. These illustrations here"—she pointed to another part of the sketch—"might have something to do with treating wounds, for you see in the illustrations, one of the men has a bleeding arm, and one has a broken leg, and in the next two sets of figures, the arm is bandaged and the leg is splinted."

"Good; very good," said Falke, showing genuine interest at last. "Yes, I can see how you have reached that conclusion." He leaned over the table, brushing her arm with his. He did not move his arm and made no apology for doing it. "Do you think you will find anything more of this sort?"

"Who can tell?" Madelaine said, relishing his nearness. It had been so long! She had not taken a lover, other than those she visited in dreams, in almost twenty years. Falke, with his smile and his courage, captivated her. She realized he was waiting for her to say more. "This temple has so many inscriptions and friezes that I am certain we can expect to discover much more in the next several months. The expedition is supposed to be here for another two years at least. In that time, we might find more treasure than you or anyone can envision."

"Treasure?" he said, drawing back, his face suddenly severe. "Is that your goal, Madame?"

"Yes," said Madelaine bluntly, "but not counted in gold. This" —she put her hand on the sketches—"this is treasure greater than gold, if we can learn its meaning."

His expression softened. "I understand that," he said. "Yes. This is treasure. Treasure," he repeated in a different voice. He looked from the sketches to her, about to speak again.

"I have brought the cordial," said Renenet as he carried a small silver tray into the room. A little silver cup, about double the size of a thimble, stood next to a silver decanter. Renenet held the tray as if he expected the decanter to explode.

"Put it down," said Madelaine, more brusquely than she intended. "And thank you, Renenet. I am aware that a good Moslem does not drink spirits, and that it is unpleasant for you to serve them."

Renenet nodded stiffly as he put the tray at the corner of the trestle table. "Is there anything else, Madame?"

"Not just at present. I will ring." She made a gesture of dismissal, then reached for the decanter. "May I?" she offered before she poured.

"You are having none?" Falke asked as he accepted the cup from her.

"Alas, no," said Madelaine.

"As you do not drink wine," he said. "I remember." He lifted the little cup in silent toast to her, and when he had taken a sip, he said, "Excellent." In his bright blue eyes something smoldered.

"So I understand," Madelaine told him, her words hardly above a whisper.

The grandmother clock in the entry hall chimed the half hour.

"I should leave," Falke said, his voice hushed with an emotion he did not know yet was passion.

"No," Madelaine said, her hand on his arm. "Stay."

Very slowly Egidius Maximillian Falke set the cup aside. Very slowly he reached out, cupping her face with his hands. Very slowly he kissed her.

*   *   *

Text of a note from Rida Omat to Madelaine de Montalia, both in Thebes.

The daughter of Yamut Omat, Rida Omat, requests the pleasure of the company of Madelaine de Montalia for an afternoon outing to the west bank of the Nile on Wednesday next for the purposes of looking at the ancient monuments there. Luncheon will be provided, and a buffet in the evening upon the return.

Mademoiselle Omat sends her assurance to Madame de Montalia that the proposed outing will be conducted with all propriety, with Monsieur Omat present as well as members of the Professor Baundilet expedition and other Europeans currently residing in Thebes. If Madame de Montalia would prefer, she may bring her maid or the Coptic monk who resides at her villa with her to preserve proper decorum, or designate some other appropriate person to fill that role.

If this is convenient, Rida Omat asks that Madame de Montalia send her answer and an indication of who will accompany her with the messenger who brings this invitation and Mademoiselle Omat's warmest greetings.

At Thebes, February 16th, 1826 on the European calendar.

2

That afternoon the dhow had arrived with Ursin Guibert bringing needed supplies from Cairo. In the evening, Professor Baundilet invited the men of his expedition aboard for an evening of European entertainment. The only Egyptian present was Yamut Omat, who arrived in Egyptian finery all embroidered in gold and silver thread.

"A magnificent feast," Merlin de la Noye declared at the conclusion of the meal. "I haven't had proper beef in months. And the capon stuffed with apples and raisins was truly a work of art." He raised his glass of port, and the others copied his gesture.

"I agree," said Omat, drinking along with the rest. "We do not dine in so grand a fashion in my country. I am honored to be included in this occasion." He rose to his feet, far more steadily than the others might have done. "Let me congratulate you, Professor Baundilet, on this grand occasion. I have learned today that your request for more diggers has been approved."

"How do you manage to get the news on everything first?" Jean-Marc Paille said in amazement. His head was not working very well, but he was filled with good-fellowship that usually escaped him.

"It is my country," said Omat at his most urbane.

Omat's remark was met with laughter, some of it greater than the quip merited, though Omat did not seem to mind.

"Yours and the Pharaohs'," said Claude-Michel as he peered into his glass, unable to recall how it came to be empty. He turned it over to be sure it was, and then righted it.

"Ah," said Omat. "But I am alive."

LaPlatte slapped his hard, square hand on the table and announced that Omat was as good as a Frenchman any day.

"You're drunk, Justin," said Baundilet.

"So I am, and happy for it," returned LaPlatte, giggling. "Let us have more of this superior port." He held up his glass, swaying a little. "To the mysteries of the ancients and the profit of our expedition. Tomorrow I will regret this, but tonight I am emperor of the world."

Baundilet signaled to the servants who waited on them. "You might as well open the second bottle and leave it here, along with the Moscato." He handed three silver coins to the nearest of them. "For your service."

The servant bowed for all three waiters. "May Allah show you favor."

"And you," said Baundilet before waving them out of the cabin.

"We'll have to fend for ourselves now," said Jean-Marc with a degree of satisfaction. "It's no good talking with that lot around. They might be making note of everything we say."

"Most of them don't understand above one word in ten," said Ursin Guibert as he finished the Côtes Sauvages in his glass. "The ones that do won't own up to it, not usually." He glanced around the cabin. "The captain's ashore for another hour. Seeing three of his wives."

"Three wives! Damned lot of heathens," said Thierry Enjeu with affection, as if speaking of a rambunctious pet. "Might as well keep a pack of monkeys, most of the time."

"Still, we need them," said Baundilet as the chief waiter returned with the second bottle of port and the Moscato. "We'd never be here without them, and we'd never get our work done if we didn't have their help. Those extra diggers are quite essential, don't you agree?"

LaPlatte nodded emphatically. "We need them, and we need more basket carriers. The way things are going, we're going to find another ten tons of rubble to sort through. Now's the time to push ahead with the digging. We can't count on the weather staying so clement much longer. It grows hotter and dryer every day and soon—" His expression soured. "We're being hampered now because we haven't enough help. Once the summer takes hold, we'll get even less done."

Omat gestured his sympathy. "I'll see if something might be arranged. There is no reason for you to make less progress in the summer."

"I am forever in your debt, Monsieur Omat," said Baundilet with a look that meant more than his words.

"It is a courtesy, a courtesy between friends," Omat said, sitting down again at last. "You and I, Baundilet, are very much alike, or so I flatter myself. We know what it is to make accommodation. Take this wine." He poured a little of the Moscato into his glass. "I am a Moslem and I know that Allah is God, but to say that I must not drink because of that, what foolishness! Allah understands how men must be flexible, and I praise His Wisdom." He drank half the contents of his glass. "It is said that sweet wine is a greater snare than dry. What do you think?"

"I think I would prefer champagne," said Baundilet, "but none was available, and so we settled for Moscato, at ruinous prices and with several high bribes, I might add. Not all your countrymen share your tolerance of alcohol." He poured some for himself and raised his glass to Omat. "To our mutual understanding."

"Most certainly," said Omat.

The port bottle was almost empty once it had made the rounds of the table, and Claude-Michel scowled at it as he held it up to the lamp. "I can't think how the wine disappears," he said muzzily.

"It disappears because you drink it," said LaPlatte, and seized the bottle from Claude-Michel. "Give it here, you sot."

Claude-Michel gave LaPlatte a mulish look. "Fine thing, calling me a sot," he complained, pouting.

"Well, you are a sot," said LaPlatte. "Tonight we're all sots." He laughed again and held up the bottle of port. "Two more tots. Tots for the sots. Who wants them?" He poured for the glasses held out. "Ursin, you get the last."

"Thank God fasting," said Ursin Guibert as he tasted the port.

Jean-Marc regarded Baundilet with sudden apprehension. "You do not think they'll try to harm us, do you?"

"Who?" asked Baundilet, perplexed by the question.

"The waiters," said Jean-Marc. "They could, couldn't they?"

Omat answered for Baundilet. "Do not think it, Professor Paille. They are servants. In a Moslem country, servants know their station and keep to it. We are not like France, where a rabble can overthrow anointed kings."

Enjeu shook his head. "You're out there, Omat," he said severely. "The old regime was corrupt and immoral, and without the Revolution, who knows what would have become of the people of France." He finished his wine. "It was necessary."

"Corruption?" said Omat. "It is a matter of fashion, don't you agree?"

"It was bloody," muttered Claude-Michel, ignoring Omat's remark. "The Revolutionaries were worse than the aristos."

"Not a chance. Look at the hundreds of years the aristos had to rule, and how they did it. The Revolution had to be bloody. That was the fault of the aristos and those who stood with them," declared LaPlatte. "They forced the Revolutionaries to act so harshly. The Revolutionaries were prepared to be reasonable at first, but that wasn't enough for those high-born devils. If the aristos had not behaved like martinets, the people would not have had to exact so high a price for their liberty."

"Liberty?" scoffed Jean-Marc. "There is a King in Paris today. What liberty?"

"The King is nothing more than a puppet. No King would dare be more, not after the lesson the Revolution taught," Enjeu insisted. "No matter what is said, it is the people who rule France, and tolerate a King for the sake of the rest of the world."

Baundilet tapped his wine glass with his fork. "Gentlemen, gentlemen," he admonished them. "Let's not fight the Revolution all over again. Whatever our view of it, the Revolution is in the past." He nodded to Yamut Omat. "It isn't good form to discuss our politics in front of our guest."

"Quite right," said Jean-Marc. "Very bad decorum." He gave a sudden, huge yawn. "Pardon me."

"It's the hour," said LaPlatte, drawing his watch from his waistcoat pocket and squinting at it. "I make it after eleven."

"And I," agreed de la Noye. "No wonder we're all half-asleep. It's not the wine. Or not only the wine." He drank what was left in his glass and beamed at the others. "It's time I went ashore. Dawn comes early." He snickered at his own witticism, repeating it softly to himself out of satisfaction. He pushed back his chair and on the second attempt made it to his feet. "A wonderful evening, Baundilet. No doubt I'll curse you when the sun rises, but that's another matter." He stumbled toward the door, then pulled himself erect and sauntered onto the deck. A few steps along and he called for his houseman. "It's time we left, Habib."

Taking his cue from de la Noye, Thierry Enjeu clambered to his feet. "I believe Merlin is right," he said, the words almost clear. "A fine repast, Baundilet. Wonderful food. Marvelous wine." He started to bow then thought better of it. "Tomorrow."

"Have your man watch out for you," Guibert recommended as Enjeu started out of the cabin with great care. "And take hot peppers in tea when you reach home. Your head will be less painful when you wake."

Jean-Marc started to rise only to find Baundilet's hand clamped on his wrist. "I need you here yet awhile," said Baundilet quietly in answer to Jean-Marc's startled expression.

"As you wish," said Jean-Marc as he resumed his seat, curious about Baundilet's intent.

Claude-Michel and LaPlatte helped each other out of the cabin and as they made their way uncertainly along the deck, they each gave their own version of "Le Berger et la Nubile" in incompatible harmony. Finally they summoned their housemen to aid them down the gangplank.

"First sensible thing either of them's said in the last hour," said Baundilet. "Guibert, will you see that Paille and Omat and I are not disturbed?"

Ursin Guibert rose, no trace of tipsiness about him now. His voice was steady and his words clear. "As you request, Professor." He bowed slightly and went to the door, taking care to close it behind him.

"Well," said Omat when the last clatter of hooves and wheels had faded. "How convenient to have this opportunity." He looked directly at Baundilet. "You've a deft way with your men, Baundilet. That's a good thing for a man in your position."

Baundilet tried to look modest and failed. "I'm glad you think so," he said. "If your plan is to work successfully, I must keep that influence, mustn't I?"

"Without doubt," said Omat, leaning back in his chair and taking a cigar from the humidor in the center of the table. He took a lucifer from the box and struck it, lighting the cigar with practiced care. "We are not apt to have such an opportunity as this one for some time to come. We ought to make the most of it."

"Which is one of the reasons we must have this discussion tonight," said Baundilet, speaking now to Jean-Marc more than Omat. "There is so much we must determine, and so little time to reach accord."

"True enough," said Omat. "This is not the sort of dealing one wants bruited about the world." He smiled, as if ready to bite.

"I . . . what do you mean?" Jean-Marc asked, feeling himself on uncertain footing. "What are you arranging?"

"Something to our mutual benefit," Baundilet said smoothly. "A true convenience for us and a favor for Monsieur Omat." He poured the last of the Moscato into his glass. "I cannot suppose you would object to it." This last was said amicably enough, but there was something in the set of his jaw that warned Jean-Marc that opposition would not be tolerated.

"You see," said Omat, taking up the discussion, "I have a love of rare and beautiful things. I am entranced by what I have learned of your people, and I am very much in your debt for all you are doing for my country. But I can see that some of your people do not care so much for Egypt, and wish to spirit away everything they find that they can move. I am troubled by this."

"Someone would be bound to take the Giza pyramids if they could move them," quipped Baundilet. "You can't blame informed Egyptians for being worried."

"Not everyone is equally concerned." Omat folded his hands in front of him, the gold embroidery of his robes glistening in the lamplight. "There are those who say that these ancient peoples did not know the Prophet and the law of Allah, and therefore need be of no concern to us. I do not question the importance of the Prophet—may Allah show favor to all who follow him— but I do not think that this diminishes the worth of these monuments."

"Many scholars would agree with you. We certainly do," Baundilet said as if to reinforce Omat's statement.

"I think we're in accord," said Jean-Marc carefully.

"Good. Very good," Omat approved. "So you will understand why it is that Professor Baundilet and I have come to a private understanding." He leaned forward. "Doubtless you will want to assist us."

Jean-Marc looked at Baundilet and saw only mild amusement in his eyes. "Assist you?"

"Monsieur Omat has offered his endorsement and some additional funds if we lend him our aid." Baundilet sipped his wine. "I can't manage such a venture alone."

"You're most generous," Jean-Marc said to Omat, unsure of what was expected of him.

"Naturally, he is entitled to consideration from us," Baundilet went on, his voice lowering. "That is what we must arrange tonight."

From the far side of the Nile there came the sound of sudden splashing, loud and violent in the river-softened silence.

"How do you mean, consideration?" Jean-Marc asked, this time with suspicion. He fiddled with his watchfob, all but pulling it out of his waistcoat. "What are we arranging?"

"A favor," said Omat. "A friendly gesture from Frenchmen to an Egyptian."

Jean-Marc looked about with misgivings. "Do you mean you expect us to deal privately with you about our discoveries?"

"Not all of them," Omat said. "Those that have bearing on your work are surely important enough to be shared. But there are often discoveries, very minor, that need nothing more than a mention in your work, but which I would appreciate. I have, for example, three sets of god-headed jars that were taken from tombs long ago. I bought them from someone who had stolen them from someone who had stolen them from yet another thief." He barked a single laugh. "I do not expect to receive these things as gifts. I will lend my help in getting your permission to work longer and in more places than other expeditions, and I will help defray the expenses for what you do."

"This is appalling," said Jean-Marc, his face set with disapproval.

Baundilet shook his head. "Jean-Marc, Jean-Marc, you haven't thought this through. You haven't realized what this could mean to us. To you." This last was so pointed that Jean-Marc turned and stared at him. "You are a man who is seeking to marry, and who has been refused the hand of the woman he loves because he does not have sufficient wealth to satisfy her father. I have that right, do I not? That is what you told me, isn't it?"

"Yes," said Jean-Marc, his trepidation increasing as he spoke.

"I do not expect you to give me your aid without sharing in the results. I am not so lacking in scruples as all that. You might well settle your future through what you do here." Baundilet smiled cynically. "Reflect, lad. The Egyptians would sell you the things we find without hesitation if they dug them up themselves—"

"And have, often," interjected Omat.

"—so why deny yourself when the opportunity is given so freely?" He put his elbows on the table and leaned forward. "Think a bit, Jean-Marc. In just two years it is possible that you can line your pockets so well that you will never have to work again unless you choose to work, that you will not have to teach in order to survive." He had the last of his wine and continued. "You are shocked, because you are thinking like an academic, a teacher who has never left the classroom. Well, you and I may be academics, but we are not in a classroom here. We have no students for we are students ourselves. We need the good opinion of men like Monsieur Omat if we are to accomplish the tasks our universities expect of us. We have an obligation to the universities to take full advantage of any opportunity presented us while we are here. If we are asking such advantage from Monsieur Omat, why do you think it unreasonable for us to take the contract a step or two further?"

"But you propose theft," said Jean-Marc, unable to find less damning words to express his indignation.

"From whom?" Yamut Omat asked in his most sensible tone. "What Pharaoh or High Priest is going to accuse you? They are dust, and their mummies are broken and scattered across the desert." His gesture dismissed them. "Now there is no difference between finding a stone at the seashore and taking a jar or a seal or a necklace from these ruins."

"But what of the ethics of our studies? Aren't we required to reveal all we have discovered?" Jean-Marc asked Baundilet. "How can you entertain these notions when you know they might lead to a discrediting of our work?"

"And how could that happen, pray?" Baundilet inquired with false gentleness. "If you or I reveal what we have done, then it could occur, but I will say nothing, and if you speak, I will deny what you say." He rocked back onto the rear legs of his chair. "I thought you would be the one most eager to take advantage of this unexpected turn. You are the one who has the greatest need of all those on the expedition, and the one who ought to best understand why it is that Monsieur Omat wishes to have a portion of our findings sent his way, for the sake of the integrity of this region. You have told me that you think we Europeans are stripping Egypt. Well then, here is a way to mitigate that and to profit from it."

"I . . . it did not occur to me," said Jean-Marc. "But should not our finds go to some part of the government?"

"Any official is likely to sell such finds to whoever offers him the highest prices," said Omat. "And there are many who are ready to meet the highest price." He studied Jean-Marc, staring at him with a directness that few Europeans would display. "You may be sure that anything coming to my collection will receive care and will be treasured by my family. Who knows, in time my heirs may well establish a museum for all the beautiful things I have acquired."

"A laudable notion, Monsieur Omat," said Baundilet. "Very forward-thinking."

Omat made a gesture of acquiescence. "It is as Allah wills."

"Of course," said Baundilet. "Yet you are to be commended for your idea, whether it originated with you or your god." He gave his attention to Jean-Marc. "You see? Our discoveries stand a better chance in Monsieur Omat's hands than given over to officials."

"What of the local Magistrate?" Jean-Marc asked, thinking of the stern-faced Numair who had issued several warnings about taking antiquities without the proper notification of authorities.

"I will tend to him," Omat assured him. "He does not have great understanding, but he is not completely a fool."

"Another favor?" Jean-Marc accused. "What do you expect us to find?"

"I don't know," said Omat, this time with innocent ebullience. "That is what makes it so very wonderful. No one knows what might be found by these expeditions. Every one of us would like to find a tomb that has not been robbed, or a hidden temple filled with unpillaged wealth. If there are any such to find, we do not know of them. If we do not know of them, then they are the greater find because they were unknown. Don't you think that finding a thing that is so rare that it is unknown is the greatest delight?"

Without intending to agree, Jean-Marc found himself nodding. "Yes. Nothing is finer."

"Well," said Baundilet with hearty goodwill, "there you are. We will have that chance if you and I, Jean-Marc, show a little pragmatic good sense in the cause of serendipity." He rubbed his chin. "Major items, well, they must be presented to the authorities and to our universities, but there are, as you have said, many little things, and they need not be accounted for in quite the same way. It is only sensible to share this venture."

"Do not tell me you cannot," Omat pleaded. "You do not know yet what you will find. If you do not know, how can you justify your position? How can you refuse me? Suppose you find three bags of fruit, all since turned to pebbles, and sealed with the mark of a Pharaoh whose name is unknown to us? Is that of use to your university or the officials of Egypt? How can it be? Not even the grave robbers are curious about those sacks. But I will cherish such a find because I value it."

"I don't want to see our work ... dismissed," said Jean-Marc, but with less conviction than a few minutes before. "My standing could be lost if it were ever known that I had done this."

"All you need do is say that the accusation is false. I will support you if it comes to that." Baundilet sighed. "And you will support me, of course. If neither of us impugns the other, who can compromise us?"

"Listen to Professor Baundilet," Omat recommended. "He is a reasonable man, and more experienced than you are. He has been here longer and knows the ways of Egypt." Neither of the Europeans heard the faint tone of contempt in Omat's voice. "Be guided by him, young man, as he has permitted himself to be guided by me."

"What if I say nothing but do not participate?" Jean-Marc suggested as if he had suddenly found his way out of the predicament presented him.

Omat shook his head wearily. "Do you know how many Europeans have come to grief in this country? Do you know how many of them have become invalids or perished because they did not understand how dangerous Egypt can be? Who can tell when a scorpion might find its way into your quarters? What can you do against a striking asp? And in the ruins, who can protect himself against the collapse of ancient foundations?" His smile was seraphic but there was no trace of amusement in his eyes.

Jean-Marc moved back involuntarily. "You would not dare," he said, but without conviction.

"I?" Omat exclaimed. "Most certainly I would not. I did not imply that, Professor Paille. But that is not to say that such things cannot happen, or that they would not happen to you." He looked toward Baundilet. "Your leader knows these dangers, and takes precautions. You will have to do the same yourself."

"Monsieur Omat has a very good point, Jean-Marc," said Baundilet. "I share his sentiments on that point."

Now Jean-Marc felt the first overwhelming frisson of fear. "You would support him, in fact?"

"I thought that was clear," said Baundilet. "Just as I would support your claims later if anyone spoke against you." He indicated Omat with a turn of his hand. "Both of us want nothing but good for you, Jean-Marc, but we need your promise to honor our faith in you."

"It is a most convenient arrangement," Omat told him. "For all of us."

Jean-Marc nodded several times, stopping with difficulty. He hoped he was drunk and this an addled dream that in the morning would be only a headache and queasy stomach. "You're both very good to me," he said with the sinking dread that tomorrow would bring no reprieve for him.

"Wonderful!" Omat declared.

"You're the sensible lad I knew you were," Baundilet said, holding out his hand to Jean-Marc in token of their bond.

Text of a letter from Erai Gurzin in Thebes to le Comte de Saint-Germain at Lake Como in Italy.

To my revered Teacher Saint-Germain in the name of God and the Eucharist;

I hope that this letter will reach you before you return to Switzerland, but if it does not, then do not be troubled if it does not reach you as swiftly as you would like.

Strange as it may seem, I am grateful you sent me here to Madame de Montalia. To my astonishment, she is as skilled and accomplished a student as any I have ever encountered, and I confess that I am now in agreement with you in her regard, although when I first met her, I doubted that would ever happen.

I have confessed this to God and will eventually confess it to my Brothers at the monastery when I return there. In the meantime, I have tried to find a way to ask her pardon for the assumptions I made about her that have proven to be incorrect.

We have been active in the explorations of the expedition of Professor Baundilet here in Thebes. For the most part we have been occupied with excavating the ruins that have been clogged with sand, and in recording all the inscriptions we have found thus far. It has delighted Madame de Montalia, and she has said that she is more than content with the inscriptions, but occasionally she admits that she longs to understand more. While no startling discoveries have been made, there has been real progress in gathering translations of the hieroglyphics in the temple, which may eventually lead to more dramatic finds.

Professor Baundilet has shown great interest in Madame de Montalia that is not the interest of an academic colleague, but a jealous man. She tells me that she is not concerned, but I am concerned for her; that man is not one to forgive a woman who does not bend to his will. I have tried to warn her, but she is not willing to listen to me, or if she does, she listens out of tolerance. It is her belief that Professor Baundilet's desire is nothing more than a whim and will pass. I am not as sanguine as she, for I fear that when Professor Baundilet learns that her affections are otherwise engaged, he will not retire gracefully or accept her decision without cavil.

To expand on that: Madame de Montalia has become interested in a German physician who has taken the villa next down the road from hers. This physician is not associated with the antiquarian expedition, but is often in the same company as they, due to being part of the small community of Europeans in this area. He is a man of steadfast temperament, I believe, and one who is constant in his affections; he does not view Madame de Montalia lightly, as he does not embarrass her nor does he flaunt her regard in any way.

It is my impression that this physician, Falke by name, is an honorable suitor, but when I have suggested to Madame de Montalia that Falke may wish marriage, she has informed me consistently that she does not wish to marry, that she fears the demands of being a wife would make it impossible to continue her avocation. I have not been able to persuade her from that position and I am afraid that she is determined to remain single, for she is unwilling to give up her scholarship, no matter how reasonable the purpose. She holds to the opinion that she would not be able to continue her explorations and her antiquarian expeditions if she were a wife, and nothing I have said has changed her assumptions. I have reminded her that if she does not wish for the religious life, she is obliged as a Christian to marry and have children, for that is the heritage of Eve and the glory of women, but she will not be convinced. I have striven to impress her with the spiritual consequences of her acts, but she tells me that spirituality means little to her. She is content to take a lover but she will not marry, though she says to me that Falke has not yet offered her marriage. It is my belief that he will, for he is a gentleman, but when he does I fear she will refuse him.

What do you wish me to do in this situation? I will take your advice, whatever it is, and will represent to her what your wishes are. In the meantime, I will remain as silent on this matter as I can do in good faith.

Madame de Montalia informed me three days ago that she has almost completed copying the inscriptions in a little chamber in the temple; when she is finished, she will devote her time to translating what is written there and will prepare her observations for publication. She has said that she will ask me to carry the monograph to Cairo for her, because she does not trust Baundilet to permit her to publish without usurping the credit for himself, which she cannot and will not abide, although she is aware that it is a regular practice in the antiquarian field. Baundilet, she informs me, has taken credit for more than enough of the gains of the expedition to his benefit, and she says that she is determined to salvage some small portion of her own work for herself. I have said I will do as she asks, for I agree that there is injustice in Baundilet's conduct, and she has expressed herself satisfied. I will depart for Cairo in about a month and see that Madame de Montalia's work is in the hands of one of the officials she has already designated to receive it, obtain the necessary receipts, then return to Thebes with all possible haste.

We hear news from time to time of the war between the Greeks and the Turks. It is said that a British poet died fighting with the Greeks last year or the year before, but some have told me that is fancy, a pleasant tale to give the Greeks courage and to gain the sympathy of Europe for their cause. If you know if the tale is true, I would like to hear of it; my experience of British, poets or not, suggests to me that they are not inclined to fight with Greeks against Turks. So if it is not true about this English poet, I would still wish to know of it, so that I can deny it when it is repeated. I am sometimes apprehensive about that conflict for it would take little for such a thing to spread, and if Egypt should become caught up in such a war, the devastation could be more destructive than anyone can imagine.

I pray for you, my teacher. I pray that God will protect you and will guide you in your studies and bring you at last to salvation. I pray also for the protection of Madame de Montalia, who has become dear to me for her great devotion to knowledge, for such devotion has a kind of worldly grace about it that any religious can view with sympathy. If she had that same fervor for religion she might have sanctity within her reach.

In the Name of God
Erai Gurzin, monk

By the European calendar, April 9th, 1826, at Thebes

3

At the base of the pillar Suti, the head digger for the Baundilet expedition, sat and munched pieces of chicken broiled with lemon and rosemary. He was almost finished with his meal and prepared to take a nap when he saw four Europeans approaching on horseback. Cursing them for fools and infidels, he rose and bowed, saying in poor French, "Welcome to Professor Baundilet's antiquarian expedition."

"Ye gods, what a hideous accent," said one of them in English. "How do they manage to understand him?"

"I suppose they don't have to, very often," said the tallest of the four. He dismounted and led his horse toward the temple. He addressed Suti in a passable version of the local dialect. "We wish to speak to the master here."

"Of the diggers or the whole?" countered Suti. "There is a difference."

"No doubt," said the tallest stranger as the other three dismounted. "The head of the expedition, if you will."

Suti pointed, and did not bother to use his inadequate French. "Over there. There are three men. The one who has removed his jacket and hat is the man you seek." He bowed again, all but insolently, and stood at the base of the pillar waiting for the visitors to get away from him so he could finish his meal.

"Allah protect you for your service," said the tall Englishman, his fair skin flushing. "Come," he said to the other three. "Let's go present ourselves."

"Let Masters do the talking; his French is better than yours," suggested the only one of the four who was stout, a merry, portly youth of no more than twenty. He got off his horse and patted her glossy neck. "She's a good girl," he said, as if the others were interested, "though I'm not in the way of liking strawberry roans."

"Trowbridge, will you stop about the horses?" complained the last who had been silent. "You're worse than a racing Earl, the way you carry on."

"Because you've got the hands of an ox, Halliday, is no reason to cast aspersions on those of us who're at home in the saddle. Gad, how can you not be captivated by a creature like this?" Again he patted the mare. "You pay no attention to him, girl."

Halliday clambered down from his horse, his flushed face darkening with the effort. "Fine help you are," he grumbled.

The tallest of them signaled the other two. "Stop the bickering, you two, or we'll leave."

"And have to listen to Wilkinson go on about the paintings he's found?" Halliday protested. "No, thank you. These Frenchies are better than Wilkinson. They've got a woman with them. Very practical, the French."

"Do shut up, Halliday," said Masters, dismounting last of all; he moved up beside the tallest of them. "What do you want me to say to them, Castermere?"

"Damned if I know," came the answer after brief consideration. "That we'd like to look around, I suppose; find out what they're doing."

Baundilet was already aware of their approach and was standing, arms folded as they came up to him. LaPlatte remained at his side, but Jean-Marc had moved away at Baundilet's signal. "Good afternoon," he said as the four newcomers halted a short distance from him. It was not a very promising beginning.

"Good afternoon," said Masters, his French impeccable. "I hope we are not intruding, but we are here, as you know, with a small British antiquarian expedition, and we are curious about how your work is progressing." He managed a cordial smile. "My companions and I are very new to this whole antiquarian business and are a bit lost, I'm afraid."

"So are we all," said Baundilet, more daunting than before.

"Yes, I suppose that's so," Masters persevered. "But I was hoping you'd be able to shed a little light on these monuments. We're all quite baffled. We have a few others in our party, but all they do is copy inscriptions and paintings all day. We're not in that line, if you know what I mean." This time he made a point of giving a sudden grin. "Since we met at Monsieur Omat's house, we were hoping you might extend a little courtesy to us, help us find our way around, as it were."

"That's reasonable," said Castermere, as if his opinion might carry some weight with Baundilet.

"You British have your own work to do. We have ours," said Baundilet.

"We're not here to spy, if that's what's bothering you," said Masters, more bluntly than he had intended. "We wouldn't know how to do it."

Baundilet leaned back, his chin up. "Since you will have it, yes, it is reasonable for me to assume that you are here to benefit your expedition, possibly at the expense of my own. It is not unheard of, is it?"

Masters made himself laugh, but he did not think the sound convincing. "We'd need to know more than we do to be spies."

"Or so you say," Baundilet responded. "What better disguise than the assertion that you are ignorant?" He started to turn away when Masters spoke more emphatically.

"All right, we'd tell the others in the expedition what we say if we were asked; but they wanted us out of the way. We're useless to them. None of us knows more than any other European. We came out here because we wanted to see more of the world, and Egypt isn't just in the common way, is it? We've done the Grand Tour and Russia seems too strange a place to go in safety, or China. And India is a separate issue. We're all eldest sons and we are not expected to visit India because of that." He glanced at Castermere, saw his approving nod, and went on, determined. "It's a marvelous place, Egypt, no doubt about it. Nothing quite like it anywhere. But to say it again, we're not scholars, don't you know, and we've been getting underfoot of those who are."

"And so you thought the French would entertain you?" Baundilet asked indignantly.

"Well, we thought you might like the company. Since it's time for the afternoon lie-down in any case, we hoped you might welcome society other than your own." This last was said with ingenuous candor. "Wouldn't you be glad to talk to someone other than the members of your expedition?"

Baundilet made a sound between a cough and a chuckle. "Well, there is something in that," he allowed. He regarded the four young Englishmen with a mixture of curiosity and distaste.

"It's not as if you've never seen us before," Masters pressed on, "and at Monsieur Omat's you were very accommodating."

"Parties are not the same thing as our work," Baundilet said, stern once again. "But if you are willing to stay away from where we are making new excavations, perhaps one of my expedition will take you over the parts of the ruins that were uncovered some time ago." It was a compromise and a test as well. "Is that acceptable?"

"Fine," said Masters, adding to the others in English, "We can stay."

"Good," said Trowbridge. "I don't relish riding back to our compound in this heat, I can tell you. Don't think the mare would like it much, either." He took off his hat and fanned himself with it. "How the natives stand it beats me."

"They are born here; they are used to it," said Halliday. "Look at how they live; what can you expect?"

Masters ignored this and continued in French to Baundilet, "I'm pleased you're willing to do this for us. It is beyond good manners to call this way, without preparation, but you see, our situation is so awkward, with Wilkinson and all."

"You do not want to stay with Wilkinson?" Baundilet asked, wary again. "He is a most extraordinary young man."

"Very likely," said Masters, "but he is also caught up in this obsession he has about the wall paintings, and he has no time for anything but them. If we are in his company, he is not willing to give us more than a common nod, if that much. Capital scholar is Wilkinson, but keeps to himself and his studies. I've said we aren't able to help him much—none of us can sketch well and we're all bored—and so he's washed his hands of us. Nothing nasty, you understand, but he hasn't time for us."

"I see," said Baundilet, nodding. "Well, I suppose I should find one of my expedition to attend to you, then. There are parts of this temple that will probably intrigue you." He knew there was little here that would compromise the discoveries his expedition had made.

"Even if it doesn't, it's better than tagging around after Wilkinson," said Masters, and Castermere added, his French nothing more than tolerable, "Yes; we're ready to see something new."

"This is something old," Baundilet pointed out, and then called aloud, "De la Noye! Have you a little time?"

From the far side of the colonnade, Merlin de la Noye answered, "I want to get this down before I take my afternoon rest, Professor. Can I do you that service later?"

"Of course," Baundilet called back. He started to call Jean-Marc, then smiled, pleased with himself for his new notion. "Madame de Montalia. She should be able to assist you very well." It would suit his purposes to complete satisfaction to require Madelaine to cease her own work and entertain these Englishmen. "Guibert, find Madame de Montalia, will you? She should be at the far end of those columns."

Ursin Guibert gave an Egyptian bow, muttered a few words and hurried away to do Baundilet's bidding.

"I am sure you are aware there is a female antiquarian in our numbers," Baundilet went on smoothly to Masters. "Capable in her way, of course, but like many women, not as clear in her thoughts. She has a plan to find a temple of medicine and nothing will dissuade her."

"Did the Egyptians worship Apollo?" asked Castermere, surprised at this revelation.

"There is no reason to think so, but Madame de Montalia is of the opinion that they did, or some variation on him. It is the one thing she is determined to study. She has taken the notion that those who were ill went to this physician's temple for treatment. According to what she has told me, these priests never fought with the other priests of higher gods. She claims to have found a reference to this history, but she has yet to produce it, other than to say that she knew a man who lived in Egypt for many years and believed this to be the case. You know how women are in such matters."

Although none of the young Englishmen had sufficient experience of women to agree, they all did. Castermere spoke for them all. "Wonderful creatures, women, but not very reliable."

Baundilet laughed more than the remark deserved. "Exactly. My very point. So keep that in mind while she guides you. You'll want to have a little rest during the heat of the day, but for the next half-hour, at least, I'm certain Madame de Montalia will be able to answer your questions, provided they are not too taxing."

Masters bowed a little and glanced at the other three. "We'll have the woman as our guide," he informed them in English.

"Splendid," said Trowbridge. "Very pretty woman, this Frenchwoman. I tried to talk to her at Omat's, but she kept her distance."

"Can't blame her," said Castermere. "She has a reputation to maintain."

"What kind of reputation can she have if she's on expedition here?" Halliday asked. "A woman digging in the ruins of Egypt with a group of French Professors? I'd say she's established her reputation well enough."

"Be reasonable," Trowbridge chided him. "We don't want her slapping our faces while she shows us these stones."

Masters had started to say something when Madelaine came around a nearby pillar; he motioned his companions into silence and gave her a proper bow, as if he were in his drawing room in London rather than the ruins of a temple in Thebes. "Good afternoon, Madame."

"To you, all of you," she said, her manner a bit uncertain, though not unfriendly. "Is something the matter?"

Baundilet answered her question. "Not exactly. These young men are curious about this temple; I've told them you would be happy to show them as much of it as has been studied thus far. You have been over the excavation, so you will be able to tell them what is recently discovered and what is not."

"But I'm working on—" Madelaine objected.

"It will wait," Baundilet said firmly. "We owe courtesy to these visitors. Don't you agree?"

Madelaine spoke none of the sharp retorts that rose in her thoughts. "I don't, but it would appear that means little."

"Most amusing," said Baundilet in a tone that indicated how great his displeasure was. "It is not proper of you to refuse to speak with these young men when they have come so far to avail themselves of our information. I trust you take my meaning, Madame?"

"Oh, most certainly," said Madelaine with false subservience. "And what can be more important to me than meeting your demands?" She took a few steps nearer the Englishmen. "Good afternoon," she said, her French accent making the familiar greeting seem exotic to the four visitors. "I am pleased to see you again." She glanced at Baundilet but received no help from him. "I'm sorry, but I am afraid I have not recalled your names from our brief meeting at Mister Omat's receptions. I am Madelaine de Montalia." She held out her hand, hoping one of the English would take it.

Masters did. He did his best to kiss her hand gallantly. "It is a great pleasure, Madame de Montalia. I am the Honorable Arthur Hillary St. Ives Masters." He rarely gave his name and title, but this time he took real gratification from knowing that he had some claim to nobility. "This is Horace Theodotius Peltham Caster-mere."

The tall Mister Castermere bowed but did not attempt to kiss Madelaine's hand. "At your service, Madame."

"You're very gracious, Mister Castermere," said Madelaine, looking now at Halliday. "You are the one who is a Baron, aren't you?"

"Baronet, actually," said Halliday, for the first time not offering any complaint. "How flattering of you to remember, Madame."

"Not at all," said Madelaine. "And you? Who are you?"

Trowbridge took her hand and in spite of his bulk bowed over it with a grace the others envied. "Allow me to present myself to you, Madame: I am Ferdinand Charles Montrose Algernon Trow-bridge. My uncle's the Earl of Wyncaster; your most obedient."

"Very pretty," Madelaine approved, curtsying a little to Trow-bridge. She looked over her shoulder toward Baundilet. "Profes-sor, how do you wish me to instruct these English visitors?"

"Take them around to the old material. Tell them what it means, if we know what it means, and answer their questions if you can." He made an impatient motion with his hands. "There's work to do here. Be about your tasks. In a short while I will inform you when we begin our afternoon repose." Then he turned away and shut them out as surely as if he had closed a door.

Madelaine concealed her irritation with a slight smile. "All right, gentlemen," she said in her serviceable-but-accented English, "let us begin on the far side of this colonnade." With a graceful gesture she led them through the pillars. "It isn't just the carvings that make these pillars different from the Roman and Greek pillars; they are arranged differently, with varying heights and sizes. The capitals are in plant motifs, which may be based on papyrus or lotus leaves and blossoms. No one is sure of that yet. I prefer the papyrus theory, because papyrus was so important to the lives of the ancient Egyptians." She paused at the base of one of the pillars. "This writing here"—she put her hand on a cartouche that was

as tall as she—"is the name of one of the Pharaohs. We believe
it is pronounced Baenre-hotephirma-aht, or something like that.
It is the reigning name of the Pharaoh, but some of us believe,
and I am one, that most Pharaohs had two names, one as their
personal name, and one the name they used once they became
Pharaoh." She patted the cartouche. "I'd like to know what the
old fellow was like. According to some of the inscriptions we
have found, he probably reigned about ten years."

"How do you see those words in that?" asked Halliday in obvious disbelief.

"Each of these symbols is a syllable, or sometimes a single
sound. This feather shape is *i* or *yi*. If you like, I could arrange
for one of Jean-François Champollion's works to be sent to you,
so that you can learn more. It is the same text we are using." Her
eyes met Trowbridge's and she saw a deep amusement there. "Or
does that seem too much like work?"

"It seems," said Trowbridge, "very like days at Oxford. I've
done my stint with the dons. Now I'd rather have a taste of
adventure." He nudged Masters. "Don't you agree?"

Masters smiled sheepishly. "It is more to my liking, Madame."

Madelaine turned and looked at the four young men. "Then
what brought you here? We are antiquarians, not much different
from your Mister Wilkinson. I don't suppose that anyone here can
provide you with the excitement you crave." She was about to
excuse herself when Castermere spoke.

"Actually, we were hoping we might be able to find something
. . . a little something to remember our travels by. You know how
it is. A man buys cloth in the market and half a dozen baskets,
but it isn't the same, is it? It's not as if it has anything to do with
Egypt, the way these stones do." He coughed delicately. "You
understand me?"

"Very well," Madelaine replied, and her voice was cool. "You
are proposing to steal from the dead."

"Oh, nothing so drastic as that," protested Trowbridge. "No,
no, dear lady. We have no love of those tombs. But a bit of an
inscription or a jar or a bit of jewelry, you know, that would be
sufficient."

"You are proposing to steal from the dead," Madelaine repeated.

Masters tried to smile again. "But so very long dead," he said to her. "Who among them would object, after all these centuries?"

It was an effort for Madelaine not to answer that specifically, but she made herself remain silent. "I cannot help you, gentlemen."

Castermere took up the argument. "Why not? We do not mean to take anything you scholars want. And you cannot pretend that every antiquarian turns over everything he finds to the patrons and universities who sponsor these expeditions. Why, not three years ago that Italian made off with hundreds of pounds of such trinkets."

"It was a despicable act," said Madelaine, doing all she could to hold her temper.

"Why should he not take them?" Halliday inquired, less diplomatically. "You cannot tell me that these Egyptians would not steal the things themselves and sell them to the next European with ready money for them." He looked up at the column. "If someone could find a way to move this, it would be in Paris or Rome or London, and the Egyptians would be glad of the gold."

"That does not make the act less despicable." Once again she was about to leave.

"We have the permission of the local Magistrate to take something," said Trowbridge. "Send word to him if you would like to confirm it. The man is Kareef Num—"

"Numair," Madelaine finished for him. "I have met him."

"Well, then you know. He is willing to permit us to purchase minor items, as long as they are not already claimed by those on antiquarian expeditions. You know which of your discoveries you wish to keep. We're not opposed to that. We only want the little things that are left over." Trowbridge put his hand over his heart. "Madame, we are not dishonorable smugglers who want to make off with the goods, as some do. We have permission."

Madelaine closed her eyes, wanting to scream at them, wanting to revile them for their callowness as much as their innocent rapacity. "How much did you have to pay Magistrate Numair?"

Masters cleared his throat. "He sets a high price on men like us. We each laid down twelve guineas. Your Professor Baundilet paid less than a hundred guineas and he is entitled to remove far more than we are."

"Damned robbery if you ask me," said Halliday.

"What do you mean, Professor Baundilet paid less than a hundred guineas?" Madelaine asked in a still voice. "Was that his fee to excavate?"

Trowbridge laughed. "Of course not. The university paid for that, and to Numair, of course."

"Numair likes the Frenchies," said Castermere. "No offense to you, Madame," he amended hastily.

But the minor slight meant nothing to Madelaine. "Let me understand you clearly: you think that Professor Baundilet has bribed the Magistrate so that he can collect antiquities for his own purposes?"

"Naturally," said Halliday. "They all do."

Madelaine ignored this. "What proof do you have?"

"What proof is there ever of such things?" Masters asked with cynicism that was startling in so young a man. "You know how these things are done—quietly, without fanfare. They have made their arrangements and there's an end to it."

"That's your assumption," Madelaine said quickly, hating what she heard, looking from Masters to Trowbridge.

"We all assume," said Trowbridge, his tone gentle. "It is the usual thing, like needing your hostess' permission to dance the waltz with an unmarried girl."

"Numair has made quite a tidy sum over the years doing this," said Halliday. "My uncle was here twenty years ago, and he said all the Magistrates and local authorities had their hands out. It's no different now. Unless it's worse because there are so many more Europeans here."

"That's for fortune-seekers, not for antiquarians," said Madelaine, her manner uncertain now that she had listened to the Englishmen. "No antiquarian wants to compromise an expedition."

"How can this compromise it?" Castermere asked her politely. "It assures your Professor that he will have something to show for his efforts beyond monographs and a few pieces in a university museum. It is sensible of him to find the means to continue his work, and what better way than this, for it will enhance his reputation." He leaned on the pillar, his long body blocking the cartouche of Baenre-hotephirma-aht. "Why are you shocked, Madame? Professor Baundilet is merely exercising good sense. He's a reasonable man, not like some of these antiquarians who only care for what the ancients left behind and can think of nothing else."

"Is that what it seems to be? Pragmatic?" Madelaine challenged, then shook her head. "I do not mean to question you, gentlemen." She paced away from them, wishing for several strides that she had not sent Brother Gurzin down river to Cairo just now; she collected herself, then came back. "If you want to exercise your right to take something, you will of course do as you wish. But pray do not attempt it when I am about, for I will stop you, no matter what the Magistrate has promised, or what Professor Baundilet has done." She knew she was speaking too quickly and that her anger was too apparent. Her violet eyes remained irate and bright, but she was able to calm herself. "You must excuse me. I come from an old family and we treasure ancient things."

"My family goes back quite a way," said Trowbridge. "My grandfather used to say we came over with the Conqueror, but there's nothing to prove that. Besides, from what I can tell, that's not the sort of connection a man should boast of. Still, the house was around when Stephen and Mathilda were chasing each other up and down the country. I don't suppose I'd like it above half if someone started taking bits away from the old place." He bowed to Madelaine.

Her smile captivated him. "Thank you, Mister Trowbridge." She began to think she had made a mistake in choosing the willowy, poetic young Englishman who tagged after Wilkinson; Ferdinand Charles Montrose Algernon Trowbridge with his inquisitive eyes and engaging smile now seemed a much more interesting dreamer than Magnus Oberon Daedalus Hearne, Lord Mailliard.

"Pleasure's all mine," Trowbridge assured her with a twinkle in his eyes. "I'll see to it that we don't make off with any of these antiquities. No fear we'll renege. But what you'll do about Professor Baundilet is a more difficult problem, isn't it?"

"Yes, I'm afraid it is," she said slowly, aware for the first time that Suti was not far away, and listening. For the first time she wondered if the head digger understood English.

Masters laughed, his voice ringing off the pillars. "A vastly improving discussion, Madame. We'll be very careful about what we take with us. Can't make Trowbridge a liar, after all." He signaled to the other three. "Let's find someplace cool. It's almost time for work to stop, in any case." He tipped his hat to Madelaine. "I must wish you success in your endeavor, Madame, though I won't say I hold much hope for you to persuade others as easily as you have convinced us: we have so little to lose, compared to your Professor Baundilet." With that, he strolled away to where their horses waited, not pausing to look if the others were following.

Trowbridge was the last to leave. He bowed deeply to Madelaine. "I won't say I think you'll manage to change Professor Baundilet's mind, but I pray, for your sake, that you do not turn him against you." He looked directly at her. "If I can ever be of service to you?" Then he turned on his heel and toddled after the others.

Watching him go, Madelaine could not stop the cold that crept through her in spite of the inexorable heat of the day.

Text of a letter from Yamut Omat, currently at San el-Hagar on the Delta, to the Magistrate Kareef Numair in Thebes.

May Allah show you favor and advancement, may he shower you with blessings and thriving sons, may he fill you with wisdom and the desire to know the secrets of the innermost heart of men, may he welcome your praise from now until the end of eternity.

How unfortunate that I should be away just at the time you seek me out. I cannot express my regret sufficiently to show how great it is. Allah knows—he is all greatness!—that I am grateful that you, with your great responsibility and position, should be willing to seek me out and request such assistance from me. It is an honor that surely I do not deserve, but one I welcome as I would greet the birth of handsome twin sons.

It is surprising to me that you have not been received well by

Professor Baundilet, for I have assumed when you have met at my villa, in spite of the fact that he and his party are Infidels, there was nonetheless a cordiality established between you, which undoubtedly might work to your mutual benefit. Yet now word comes that you have been rebuffed by Professor Baundilet, and in such a way that he has insulted you beyond tolerance. I can only say that I do not suppose Professor Baundilet is aware that he has transgressed so greatly. In his society, or so I have been informed by him and others, the presence of a woman, while not usual, is not intended to insult those attending meetings. For some, because Madame de Montalia comes from an old line of power and title, she might be seen as an asset.

It is not acceptable that men should speak of business in the presence of unveiled women. That much is certain. It is a dreadful error they made, though it was from ignorance. I vow on the swords of my ancestors, I will do all that I can to explain to Professor Baundilet the reason for your displeasure and the greatness of the offense his thoughtless action has created. I cannot be certain he will wholly understand this, nor can I promise he will make amends as he should, but if he does not, it will not be because he misunderstands. Let me ask you for my sake and your own, to permit him to expiate his error in some acceptable way so that we need not have to end the dealings on which we are currently embarked. I must urge you to think of the waywardness of children and the ignorance of Professor Baundilet, who is without the consolation of Islam and the wisdom of the Koran to guide him in all that he does.

While I am here, at the place once called Tanis and Djianhnet, I will learn what I can of how these officials have come to terms with the Europeans, and I will be pleased to report to you in full what they have to tell me. This place, like Thebes, is the subject of exploration and speculation, and the Europeans swarm over the land like locusts in search of something to eat. It is unwise to hope what they devour will be deadly poison, for that would only bring misfortune on all of us: rather, let us hope that it is for us to decide what they will be allowed to sate themselves upon.

Surely you have been given greater knowledge of these for-

*eigners than most have, and you have been shown by Allah—
may everything in creation praise him!—the way that they may
be dealt with so that they are no longer the ones at an advantage.
It was a sad time when Napoleon brought his men, and surely
many true followers of the Prophet suffered then, but now we
see that we are vindicated, and it is fitting that we use what we
have learned of the Europeans against them and to our advantage. You are in the vanguard of the faith now, and who can
doubt that you will be one who shows others the way to best
these sacrilegious foreigners without sacrificing what they have
to give us: weapons, marketplaces, and gold. Think how well
your position suits those purposes, and when you are minded
to be rid of the Infidels, think that we will make better use of
their gold than they are able to.*

*I am pleased you have mentioned these apprehensions to me,
and have allowed me the honor of telling you my thoughts. It
is truly a great honor to be asked to guide so eminent a Magistrate as yourself in dealing with the Europeans. If Allah—
glorious is his name!—wills, we will emerge from this time
triumphant and strong, with the Europeans willing to accommodate us in our dealings. In the next several months, I will
be greatly pleased to show you how easily these Frenchmen are
to be led. Then I will do the same where the English are concerned. You will discover that they are not mysterious and unreasonable: they have accepted only part of the truth and have
turned from the wisdom of Allah—nothing is greater than he!
—and embraced the prophet Jesu, who foretold the coming of
Mohammed. If you can accept that, and their notions of law,
then the rest is simplicity itself.*

*Your concern over the German physician is another question
we ought to discuss at length. I cannot see that his presence is
a difficulty, for he is willing to treat our people for ills we have
yet to cure. If Allah wills—all eternity resounds with his
praise!—this Infidel might be an instrument, however unworthy, of the people of Egypt who have borne such burdens from
the time of the Pharaohs until this day. I would not limit him
more than is absolutely required, for his skills are most valuable, in their way. One can think that in part he is able to return*

to us some of what the other Europeans have callously taken away. If this is not agreeable to you, let us decide how best to approach him before you refuse him the right to treat our people, for we do not wish those in his care to endure more anguish through any misunderstanding.

Last, I petition you in this note to be allowed to speak with Madame de Montalia. There is no reason for you to subject yourself to further offense by sending for her. I will, myself, call upon her when I return to Thebes, and I will make it plain to her why it is she must never again appear in your presence unveiled. I am not certain I can persuade her never to approach you again, for she is used to a degree of independence I have been told is most unusual among European women, and were she not of a distinguished house and great fortune, her actions would not be tolerated by Frenchmen any more than they are accepted by us.

What more can I say to you, Magistrate, that will ease your thoughts at this difficult time? Should you have any task you wish me to perform, you need only request it and then repose complete satisfaction in knowing it is done. I am your willing servant and the servant of Allah—who is exalted above all things—and the dutiful son of Egypt.

May Allah give you guidance and favor, may you have a hundred sons, may every female in your household grow big with your seed, may your strength never fail you.

Yamut Omat

4

As Erai Gurzin rose from his prayers, he saw the ship's carpenter approaching, an awl in one hand and an unlit lamp in the other. With a last, murmured blessing, he made his hand into a fist and prepared to lash out.

The attack came only half a breath later. One instant the carpenter was unconcerned, the next he was swinging his lantern
with all his force at Gurzin's head, a whispered oath coming with
the blow, and then an abrupt cry as Gurzin slammed his arm
across the carpenter's abdomen with all his strength.

As the carpenter staggered backward, Gurzin got to his feet
and launched himself at his attacker, his hands up and extended
to seize the man's throat. He shouted as he bore down on the
carpenter.

For half a minute they grappled, the carpenter falling ever backward, his arms attempting to shield him from Gurzin's wrath.
Then, as they reached the aft deck, the carpenter struck the rail,
shrieking once before overbalancing and falling into the dhow's
wake. He thrashed on the surface briefly then disappeared.

Gurzin braced himself against the rail, panting. He stared at the
wake and muttered a blessing for the man who had attacked him;
as he straightened up, he heard the sound of voices behind him,
and hid behind a cluster of barrels lashed to the aft deck. He
opened his mouth wide to breathe so that he would make less
sound, and listened intently.

"They say the river is rising early this year," remarked the
captain's eldest son.

"Better than last year; it rose late." The man with him spoke
with an accent Gurzin did not recognize. "They say there was
heavy rainfall to the south, which will bring a good Inundation."

"It is Allah who brings the water," said the captain's eldest son.

The other man with him laughed once. "And before that, it was
Osiris or someone. They say that one of the old gods was a
hippopotamus. A hippopotamus." He paused, and when he went
on, he was musing. "Well, whether or not gods brought the rain,
the rain is what causes it. If it is dry in the south, where the Nile
begins, then it is dry in Egypt." He hesitated. "It could be more
severe, being early."

Gurzin sniffed, the odor of burning leaves reaching him and
almost making him sneeze. He pinched his nose, waiting.

"A blessing for Egypt, for there will be more grain," said the
young man.

"We will hope so," the stranger responded. He and the captain's eldest son had reached the aft rail, and they stood there in the last of the fading light of day. "A splendid sight, the Nile."

"Of course, Excellency," said the captain's eldest son.

"None of that. I am only a humble trader bound for the First Cataract. I am looking for jewelry and cloth for trading." His laughter was low and comfortable, like a loud purr.

"Yes, Excel— sir."

"Better, much better," said the titled man. "But you must take care. I do not want it known that I am in this part of the country." He paused, then started back toward the forward part of the dhow. "I want it understood, youngster, that I must not be found out. If I am, it will go badly for all of us."

"I will be careful, sir. I will," the young man said, hurrying after the stranger.

Gurzin waited until he was certain they were gone, until all he heard was the thrum of the sails and the endless song of the Nile; the last of sunset had faded to a tarnished line above the western hills. Shakily he rose from his hiding place, hoping that none of the crew was aware of what he had done. He smoothed the front of his habit and rubbed his hair where it was clubbed at the back of his neck. What on earth was that about? he asked himself as he reviewed what he had heard. The titled man was unknown to him, that much was certain. Which meant that he came aboard in secret and might well continue that way while the dhow sailed south, up the river toward the half-buried monuments of Abu Simbel. Gurzin whispered a prayer for his own safety and asked God to aid him in his thoughts. It was a perfunctory sort of plea, but it was sufficient to allow him to retire two hours later with hope that by morning he would have some sort of plan.

Yet the next day and the next brought him no wisdom, though he was careful to observe the men on the ship. He listened to the crew talk, and aside from an occasional cryptic reference, found nothing of importance in what he overheard. Who was the man, and what did he want? For a short while Gurzin entertained the idea of remaining aboard ship until it reached his monastery at Edfu, but quickly changed his mind, knowing that his community might not grant him permission to leave a second time.

Finally the dhow reached Thebes and Erai Gurzin reluctantly

left the ship, no more aware of the identity of the man known only as "Excellency" than when he had overheard him speak. He supervised the unloading of the various items Madelaine had requested, and rode with the two laden carts to her villa.

Although it was just before sunset, Madelaine's villa was already well-lit and the servants busy. Now that the Inundation was beginning, the courtyard walls were being shored up, and the foodstuffs that were stored in cellars for most of the year were being moved to insulated chambers near the stables. Gurzin entered the courtyard to be greeted by half the household, each one of the servants with a tale to tell. He listened briefly, then entered the villa by the side door and sought out Renenet.

"Madame is waiting to speak with you," Renenet said in his austere manner. "Was your passage safe?" He made it apparent that this was an afterthought, hardly worthy of consideration since Gurzin was an Infidel.

"For the most part," Gurzin replied as he followed Renenet to the salon, where Madelaine pored over another large sketch of wall friezes. He waited until she looked up, then offered her his blessing as he came into the room.

"Well," said Madelaine when she had curtsied and kissed his monk's ring, "I was beginning to wonder if you had forgot the way home."

"There's only one river," said Gurzin, looking around at all the large sheets of paper scattered through the room. "You have been busy in my absence, I see."

"Don't chide me," she said at once. "I've been trying to get down as much as I can, but it is no easy thing. Our demand is pressing everyone in Professor Baundilet's expedition, and all of us reflect that. The Nile's rising three weeks ahead of schedule, and none of us is prepared." She indicated the chaos. "There will be time to straighten this out while the floodwaters are high. For the time being, I want to be certain I will have enough to keep me occupied until the water goes down." She motioned toward one of two chairs that was not heaped with books and sketches. "There. Sit down and tell me all about Cairo. Did you give my monograph to Monsieur Sauvin, as I asked?"

"Yes," said Gurzin, reluctant to tell her too much while they might be overheard. "I presented your letter of introduction and was granted an interview two days later." It was much less delay than he had anticipated and it convinced him of the position Madelaine's family held in France. "He asked many questions about you, taking some pains to assure himself that you are well and in good hands here, and when he concluded our discussion, he desired that I carry his compliments to you. I have a letter in the case I carry." He saw her nod. "A very superior man, this Monsieur Sauvin."

Madelaine chuckled. "A man with a wife and six children, Brother Gurzin, so do not imagine connections there. He is a fine fellow in his way, and it is useful to know he is in Cairo, but don't assume anything more."

"I made no such assumptions," said Gurzin a bit too hastily.

"Naturally not," said Madelaine mendaciously, then explained. "You always get that anticipatory look when the subject of an accessible man arises. You cannot help wanting me to live the way you believe is correct. Unfortunately I cannot oblige you."

"Because you do not want to," said Gurzin, pleased to have this familiar argument to keep him from speaking of the stranger on the dhow. "You have said you are not going to marry, and if anyone mentions that possibility, you turn away from it as you would turn from the Antichrist."

"Possibly," said Madelaine, her manner polite but her attitude making further discussion ineludible. "Ring the bell and have Renenet bring you something. You ought to have arranged for that as soon as you arrived." She leaned back in her tall chair. "There should have been three large cases of earth?" she asked as if the question were not important.

"In the stable, above the stalls," Gurzin replied. "Their seals give France as the place of origin, and they were shipped from Marseilles. I supervised the loading and unloading myself, and no harm came to them." He reached out to tug the bellpull when Renenet presented himself in the doorway.

"What would you want to welcome you back, Gurzin?" he asked with as much a show of fellow-feeling as he ever demonstrated.

"Whatever you can spare without difficulty, so long as there is some wine and some honey in it." Gurzin realized as he spoke that he was famished. "And some of those breads."

"Of course," said Renenet, and left them alone.

"How has it been?" Gurzin inquired when he was certain that Renenet was in another part of the villa.

Madelaine shook her head, hardly moving at all but warning Gurzin as surely as if she had clapped a hand over his mouth. "It has been a busy time for the expedition, with the flood starting early and the diggers all wanting to tend to their families and prepare for planting as soon as the Nile recedes." Her frown deepened but her voice was light and pleasant. "We've attracted some attention—a few of the English expedition and half a dozen of the Italians have come to see what progress we are making. I think some of them believe we are fools to devote our time to the temples here on the eastern bank when there are so much greater possibilities on the western bank, where the sands continue to yield treasure every time you lift a spade."

"But you do not agree with them," said Gurzin.

"Of course not. Nor does Professor Baundilet. He is determined to show that the temple we are digging up is as remarkable as any in that ... that great cemetery across the river. So much of what was on the western bank was for the dead; this bank was for the living, at least here at Thebes; sunrise for living, sunset for death." Madelaine's eyes flicked toward the door, and in a moment, Renenet returned with a large tray laden with almost all of Gurzin's favorite delicacies: dates, raisins, figs in syrup, three kinds of bread, honey still in the comb, wine, a dish of sugared almonds, and a tall pot of sweet mint tea.

"Wonderful," enthused Gurzin as he looked over the bounty on the tray. "I was beginning to despair of good food, but here you have shown me my fears were needless." He took the single heavy cup and filled it with steaming mint tea. "May God bless you, Renenet."

"There is no God but Allah," said the houseman deliberately.

"As you wish." Gurzin tasted the tea. "Like nectar," he said, though his impatience had caused him to scald his tongue. "I will ring when I am finished," he added when Madelaine said nothing.

"As you wish," said Renenet, echoing him deliberately, then bowing deeply and departing.

When the hallway was empty, Gurzin repeated a blessing over his meal and then gave a quick look at Madelaine. "More spies, Madame?"

"Sadly it would appear so," she answered as she again stopped her painstaking work copying the symbols on her sketch. "I don't know whose they are or what they are supposed to discover, but Lasca tells me that everyone on the staff is suspicious of her and of me."

"That's most aggravating," said Gurzin as he ate. "I did not think matters were so far out of hand when I left."

"I don't think they were," said Madelaine. "But ... there have been incidents. Professor Baundilet's chief digger, a lean fellow called Suti, though I understand he has another name, has been seen around my villa several times in the last few weeks. When I asked Baundilet about it, he claimed ignorance, but I could not believe him." She leaned her elbows on the table and stared toward the windows. "He's keeping more to himself, Baundilet is."

"With the others as well?" Gurzin asked as he broke one of the little breads into three pieces.

"Well, he has not included Claude-Michel in his morning gathering, and de la Noye has said that Baundilet does not consult him as he did at first. It may be due to the progress of the expedition, but I am afraid that isn't the case." She paused to sweep a strand of dark hair back from her brow. "I think he'd be happier if half of us were to depart."

"And will you?" asked Gurzin, thinking that a woman like Madelaine de Montalia did not belong amid ruins and floods.

"Of course not," she said with some indignation. "What a poor creature you must think I am. Why would I leave when we have only begun to learn the riddles of this place?"

"Because it is not safe to be here, Madame," said Gurzin with feeling. "You may learn these riddles at too great a cost."

Her smile was quick and enigmatic. "I have already sought the answer to one great riddle: Saint-Germain will confirm that." She shivered once, as if the night had turned cold for an instant. "There is nothing here that frightens me enough to force me to leave."

"It is very dangerous, I fear," Gurzin said quietly.

"Breathing is dangerous if you do it in the wrong place," Madelaine declared. "I have wanted to be here since"—she stopped herself from saying "since before Napoleon came here," for that was a quarter of a century ago—"I could read about the place." That much was accurate; she had been reading about Egypt fifty years before Napoleon set out for it.

"Then you will be able to read more, and discover that—" Gurzin began, only to be cut off.

"I ask your pardon, Brother Gurzin, for speaking before you finished, but I know you do not wish to say anything that would be truly offensive to me. And I wish you to know that what you are proposing is that. I might as well tell you to confine your study of religion to reading comments on it written by those like Voltaire, who advocated doubt." It startled Gurzin to realize that so beautiful a woman could suddenly become so imposing, and he stopped himself from protesting, though she saw this and her face softened. "Did you remember to ask how many of my letter packets have arrived at Cairo, and how many have been sent on?"

"The monograph and letters I carried were the first they have received in six months, or so I was told. Professor Baundilet or—"

"—Magistrate Numair, or one of the other antiquarians, English or French, or a servant in Baundilet's house, or someone on the boats, or one of the men in Cairo, or one of Monsieur Sauvin's staff, though probably not Monsieur Sauvin himself," Madelaine listed, exasperated. "Allies or enemies. How to discover which is which without increasing our danger?"

Gurzin shook his head. "Another indication this is not a safe place."

"Perhaps." She put her hand to her lips and fell into a stillness that hardly seemed natural in so animated a woman. "Did you hear anyone?"

"In the courtyard," said Gurzin after a brief silence. "They're unloading the carts."

She cocked her head. "So they are. Your hearing is remarkable, Brother Gurzin." Her expression was less guarded as she went on, "That is the trouble with wondering if one is being watched;

it is impossible to get the assumption wholly out of your mind. Something as minor as the sound of unloading a cart becomes a terrible noise, a proof of treachery."

"A regrettable thing, Madame," said Gurzin, his voice still low.

Madelaine set her pens aside and moved her copied inscriptions where she would not smudge them. "What is troubling you?" She clicked her tongue in disapproval as he started to protest. "You have been on edge since you arrived, probably since you were on the boat. What is the cause, Brother Gurzin? What makes you fret as you do?"

Gurzin licked his fingers and sighed. "This isn't the time, Madame. Tomorrow, perhaps, if we can find privacy, I will be able—"

"Now," Madelaine said, making it the gentlest of orders.

"It isn't safe," Gurzin objected, but with reduced force.

"All the more reason for you to tell me," Madelaine said, her violet eyes fixed on his. "Couch your terms as you wish, but tell me what I need to know."

Slowly at first, with many digressions and detours, Gurzin told her about his voyage up the Nile, about the attack by the ship's carpenter, and the stranger with the unrecognizable accent. As he went on, he became bolder, and by the time he described how three of the crew had made the sign against the Evil Eye when he left the boat, he was no longer being as cautious as he had sworn he had to be. "So," he finished at last, "I paid the men with the carts, with a generous—what do you call it?"

"Doucement," Madelaine supplied.

"Yes; they were given half again as much as they charged for carrying your cargo here. A bit excessive but not enough for them to think it significant. With the river rising, the carters always charge more, and expect something for their service." Gurzin ate a little more, but now the savor had gone out of the food. He licked his fingers a last time and said, "Monsieur Sauvin said he is always ready to assist you in getting from Thebes to Cairo, if that is required. He has ships—a felucca and a dhow—at his disposal and they can be sent here on very short notice."

"Brother Gurzin, I know what you wish I would do, but I am not going to leave. I have just started to discover a few things that are exciting and new. There is another small chamber in the temple we have located, and I am certain the paintings in the interior will be a triumph for antiquarian scholarship." She smiled a little at his dismayed expression. "What do you think I am, a capricious child who has come here on a whim?"

"Not now," said Gurzin. "I was worried at first that you did not have the temperament for this work, but I have learned otherwise."

"How tactful," said Madelaine with an irrepressible grin. "You know very well that you wish I would leave because you don't think I can deal with the rigors of life here." She paced a short distance. "And it is true that I do not fare well in the sun, but I am not the only one to have such difficulties, am I?" She had come across the room to where he sat and now dropped into the chair across from the monk. "This is important to me."

"Important enough to risk your life?" he asked gravely. "That might well be the stake demanded of you."

A strange, unreadable emotion passed over her face; her violet eyes clouded with it. Then she shook it off. "The risk of my life," she mused. "Well, I have done it before."

"Not in the hunting field or in other sport," said Gurzin impatiently, suddenly uncertain how to proceed with her.

"The hunting field." She thought back to that autumn in 1743, when she had gone hunting at Sans Désespoir, and had become the quarry of Saint Sebastien and his coven. "You can lose more than life and limb hunting, Brother Gurzin. Ask Saint-Germain."

"I am more apprehensive about your welfare just now," said Gurzin with great formality. "I was asked to assist you and guard you. Thus far you have been willing to accept only a little of my assistance and none of my protection." He folded his arms. "How am I to face our teacher if you will not permit me to do the thing expected of me?"

Madelaine leaned back in the chair. "Oh, Brother Gurzin, I am sorry you find me such a trial, and immoral into the bargain. If it is too much of an imposition on your and your calling, then you must return to your monastery and leave me to fend for myself. I am certain Saint-Germain would tell you the same thing. He might even say that you ought to have left before now." She looked directly at him. "I would like you to stay, but I will be no different than I am now. I am not making a bargain with you. I am not offering to change in return for your presence, but I would appreciate it if you wouldn't leave." Her eyes were cool now, but not angry or uncaring as he thought they might be.

"I will pray tonight," said Gurzin. "In the morning I will give you my decision." He looked down at the food still on the tray.

"Why not take it to your room," Madelaine suggested. "You might want to have a bit more of it in the night, and Renenet will not feel offended."

Gurzin nodded. "I will." He started to rise, then said, "I am not trying to force you out of Egypt, Madame de Montalia. I feel I have an obligation to keep you from harm, and you do not make that an easy task."

"I don't require that of you," said Madelaine, getting up and returning to her table with the sketches. "All my life I have wanted this, Brother Gurzin. Everything I have studied since I was a child has pointed me toward this. How can I turn away just when I am starting to achieve something?"

"It is not wise, Madame." He wiped his mouth with the French serviette provided, then got to his feet. "Will you retire now, Madame?"

Madelaine drew one of the sketches nearer. "No, I don't think quite yet," she answered. "Take the tray and go, Brother. Sleep well." She did not look up from the table as he started out of the salon. "I will need your assistance tomorrow, if you decide to remain."

"Yes?" Gurzin paused in the door with his tray balanced precariously on one hand.

"I have to copy these paintings I have found before the floodwaters reach them. If the Nile gets too high, the paintings could be ruined. As it is, they might become mildewed or stained or faded." She set one of the sketches atop the rest. "I would value your help."

Gurzin stared thoughtfully at the sketches, though he made no move toward her. "I will pray for wisdom," he assured her at last.

"For all of us, if you will," said Madelaine, between jest and seriousness. She heard Gurzin's tread in the hall, but paid him little mind. The sketches held her imagination the way nothing else had for more than two decades, and she welcomed the chance to work on them far into the night. In spite of everything, she told herself as she continued to make a precise copy of the inscriptions, I am here. I am here.

Text of a letter from Honorine Magasin in Paris to Jean-Marc Paille in Thebes.

My cherished Jean-Marc;

As you can see, my father has once again permitted me out of his house, and though he begrudges me the right to marry the man of my choice, he has been willing to allow me to come here so long as I am under the protection and social aegis provided by my Aunt, and thus I have returned to my Aunt Clémence, who has received me with every show of welcome and affection. She is truly a very worthy woman, and my father believes she sets an excellent example for me.

While I am here, Aunt Clémence has said she will keep guard over my correspondence, but she is the greatest darling and has made no objections to allowing me to have any letters Georges brings to me, and so our communication is made simplicity itself. Georges is willing to continue as intermediary and as long as he does that, Aunt Clémence will not insist that I give my mail to her for first reading.

My Cousin Georges accompanied me from Poitiers to Paris, and brought me your most recent letters when he came to Poitiers. He informed me that it was not wise to bring them to Poitiers, though he did it, for he knows that my father is a most intolerant wretch and does not approve of our continued exchange of letters, as if there was damage to be done at so great a distance. My father has chided me for my clandestine interests and has told my Aunt that I am not to be trusted, nor allowed to have strangers visit without his prior approval. Luckily both my Aunt Clémence and Cousin Georges—she is his aunt as well—are agreed that my father is behaving as if this were still the time of monarchic despotism, and that is fortunate for us.

I cannot tell you how good it is to be in Paris once more. It must be the most wonderful city in the world. The chestnut trees are splendid now, and everywhere one sees the most elegant carriages tooling along the boulevards Napoleon caused to be made. How dreadful it must have been before, with those cramped, narrow streets. My Aunt Clémence has a gorgeous berliner carriage for special occasions, and yesterday she ordered her matched chestnuts harnessed to it to carry us to our first social event together, which was a most interesting concert, for I saw a great many persons I met during my previous stay who remembered me most kindly. There was quite a crush in my aunt's box during the intermission, and afterward, we were escorted to her carriage by no less than five gentlemen. My Aunt has said that this is a very promising beginning. The music was something German: perhaps Beethoven or Schubert or one of those other lugubrious ones. I paid it little mind, having so much else to do.

When you return (and I long every hour for that time, my dearest Jean-Marc), you will be astonished to see how much the fashions have changed. I was quite agog at the new gowns, for they are quite different than they were just two years ago. No one who wishes to be thought a person of taste dare be seen in a gown that does not expose a portion of the shoulders. Balloon sleeves edged in lace are also the coming thing. Aunt Clémence has ordered just such a gown for me, in the most enchanting shade of soft pink called "whispered sigh," and I know you will find it ravishing. They say that the waists are dropping a little, which will certainly be enchanting, though the waists are also being nipped in more tightly, and occasionally belted as well.

You may imagine how enthralled I was to read your letters. How can you bear to be in such a place, my darling? Every night as I pray I try not to dwell on fears for you, but I cannot keep them wholly from me, for it is true that everyone who has any knowledge of that place is full of dire tales. I tell myself, as you have instructed me to do, that this is fancy, and my

Cousin Georges has warned me that I ought not to entertain such morbid reflections. He said that such contemplation should be left to Italian and English novelists, who are temperamentally inclined for it. You can guess how we all laughed at his jest, but later I was still cast down to know that you were in so distant and hazardous a place.

I was told three days ago that camels are bad-tempered beasts, who kick and spit and are afflicted with wind. I think it would not be possible to ride such an unpleasant animal, and you have said that they are not often used to pull carriages. Crocodiles in the water and camels on the land, with all sorts of deadly vermin. Oh, Jean-Marc, you must take care, for I could not stand it if you were to come to harm while you are away.

Word came from my father yesterday that my sister, Solange, may be in an interesting condition. It is early to be certain, but the indications are there, and my father has said to her husband that he will pay a thousand golden Louis from before the Revolution if he will permit his name to have "Magasin" added to it in a court of law, so that the name does not die out. That is contingent, of course, upon the birth of a son. I fear that my brother-in-law did not look upon his offer well, and my father is distressed that even Solange shares in her husband's sentiments, though if she truly is in an interesting condition, her behavior can be understood.

My Aunt Clémence informs me that Georges has arrived. He is escorting us to a ball tonight. I have still to finish letting my maid dress my hair. I have on a rose-colored gown, jewels on the corsage, and though the sleeves are not really full enough for fashion, they are not too dowdy. Best of all, I have a pair of stockings. I know I should not mention them to you, but they are so pretty, a pale jonquil silk embroidered with roses entwined with vines, that I could not resist mentioning them. My shoes are satin; a gift from my Aunt. I have put on my pearls, and poor Volette is about to run distracted because I have taken so much time to write to you. I must close, my beloved. I miss you every hour of every day, and you are always in my thoughts. When we at last are united, all the suffering we have endured will seem sweet because of our triumph.

May God protect you and keep you from harm.

With endless love,
Honorine

August 13th, 1826, at Paris

5

For a few seconds after he ducked into the sanctuary, Claude-Michel was all but blinded by the darkness. Then, as his eyes became accustomed, he could make out the splendid figures on the walls and ceiling of the stone room.

"Something like a crypt," he said with a nervous titter. "God, it's so dark in here; how do you stand it?"

"It's not too bad," said Madelaine from where she held her lantern, taking care that none of the smoke escaping from it was allowed to drift toward the white-washed and painted portions of the wall. "You get used to the dark, in time."

Claude-Michel made a sound that indicated he did not agree; he narrowed his eyes as he tried to make out the figures on the ceiling. "Night and day?" he ventured when he had studied it a short while.

"That's part of it, I think," said Madelaine. She used the blunt end of her pencil to point out sections of the ceiling. "That portion, with the gods in such a strange configuration, I suspect is their zodiac. See where the figures are marked with large dots? I believe those represent the stars. I want to get a complete copy of this ceiling, so I can try to match the marks to the stars." Her voice was hushed with excitement and she could not keep from smiling as she spoke. "This figure here seems to be what divides the day and night portions," she went on, using her pencil as a pointer, though its shadow became more distorted and indistinct as she moved away from her lantern. "You see, there are phases of activity here, in the day portions. It could represent what was done for the god, or the seasons," she said. "There's the Inundation, and there's planting and there's harvest."

"That's only three seasons," said Claude-Michel, his first dread of the enclosed dark giving away to a sense of awe. "Is this a burial chamber?"

"I don't think so," said Madelaine. "No mummy, and no place for one. There's no funeral offerings and nothing that looks like any were ever here." She indicated the sand still to be cleared away. "There might be something under there, I guess, but it doesn't seem likely."

"Could it have been robbed?" Claude-Michel asked as he peered around the gloom.

"Probably, but I don't think it was recent." She looked at her sketch pad, suddenly almost shy. "Will you help me? If I try to copy the ceiling will you do the inscriptions? We'll have to abandon this place soon, when the Inundation reaches it, and I don't want to lose any of this."

"No, I can understand that," said Claude-Michel. "All right." He pulled off his jacket without apology and tugged a leather notebook from his pocket. "I've pen and pencil; which do you recommend?"

"Whichever you are best with," said Madelaine with a wide smile. "Thank you, thank you, thank you, Claude-Michel."

In the dark it was hard to know if he blushed or if there was only a bashful hesitation in his response. "We're part of the same expedition. We're supposed to share the work." He pulled out his pencil. "Probably more reliable. I have a knife in my pocket, if the point should break." He found a place where he could sit and see most of the inscription under the night frieze. As he squinted upward he said, "It's times like these that I wish we had that English fellow Wilkinson here. He does better drawing and copying than I do."

"Probably better than most of us," said Madelaine, her attitude now slightly remote as she concentrated on the ceiling. "What constellation do you suppose that is?" she asked as she started to sketch the one that seemed to her the most improbable: a crocodile climbing up the back of a hippopotamus.

"If it is a constellation, it might not be part of one we know.

It might be a little bit of Taurus and a little bit of ... oh, I don't know, Draco, perhaps." He was talking to make noise, for the dark was still too near for his taste. "Look at this inscription. The hieroglyphics are painted over as well as carved."

"We're finding more and more of that," said Madelaine, aware of Claude-Michel's discomfort. "Professor Baundilet found that section of wall, if you remember, with flecks of paint sticking on the sides of the raised relief."

"I wonder why they started painting the writing?" Claude-Michel inquired of the chamber as he continued to work.

"Or why they stopped," said Madelaine, and in the next moment bit back a curse as ink spread over her hand.

"What's the matter?" Claude-Michel asked, starting to struggle to his feet.

She shook her head. "I seem to have broken my inkwell," she said. "I think I'd better stick to charcoal, no matter how messy it is." She moved carefully so as not to overset the inkwell more than it already was. "Ah. I've got it." She turned to Claude-Michel. "I have my supplies just outside. It won't take more than ten minutes for me to clean this and come back. Will that be all right with you?"

Claude-Michel blushed again, but this time for shame. "You may take as long as you wish, Madame," he said, determined not to embarrass himself further. "It's true I dislike the dark, but this is Egypt, the land of tombs, and I am an antiquarian."

"You're a linguist," said Madelaine gently. "If you'd rather come with me?" She let the question hang between them. "If you're certain."

"Go ahead. I've been childish and at my age it's time I was over such fears." He did not quite believe himself, and knew that he was not convincing Madelaine either.

"All right," she capitulated. "But if you change your mind, I will not think the less of you." With that she ducked out the door and went toward the white donkey tied up at the edge of the excavation. Her easels and sketching supplies were covered in oiled cloth and strapped to the pack-saddle. Madelaine looked down at the bitter green of her skirt and shook her head at the enormous inkstain that marked most of the right side of the front.

"Oh, what an inconvenience," she sighed. That was something she had not anticipated when she came to Egypt: the toll the desert and her explorations would take on her clothes. Little as she liked it, she would have to ask Lasca to arrange to have more dresses made, for she had now only four day frocks to work in that were not stained or worn past all use. She tugged at the pannier on the pack-saddle and found another inkwell, which she passed by. Tucked into a small tube were her charcoal sticks, and she pulled out the tube and untied another large sketch pad before patting the donkey and starting back toward the heart of the temple.

She was less than ten paces away when she heard Claude-Michel scream; she dropped all she was carrying, lifted her ink-stained skirts and ran for the sanctuary. As she ducked inside, she thought she saw out of the corner of her eye the hem of a workman's robe. There was no time to puzzle about it. Madelaine paused in the darkness, for the lantern was out, and heard a moan. "Claude-Michel?" she called, glad her voice was steady.

Her answer was a soft sound between a cough and a moan.

"Are you where you were?" Now her night-seeing eyes were adjusted, and she swept the chamber, finding him at last sprawled on the remaining hillock of sand, face down. She sighed and started toward him.

"Stay back," Claude-Michel muttered, his breath thready as his voice. "Scorpion."

She did not hesitate, but continued to his side. "Where are you stung?"

"Thigh," he said, so faintly that she almost could not hear him. "Left."

Madelaine put her fingers on his neck and felt the pulse; there was no time to call for help, to send for Doktor Falke. She took hold of the cuff of his trouser leg and pulled, satisfied as the fabric tore all the way to the belt. "I have a knife," she lied, not only to account for the ruin of his trousers but to have an explanation of what she had to do next.

"Watch for . . . scorpion." He was barely able to whisper now, but Madelaine made herself concentrate on his injury.

"I squashed it," she said, knowing that while the poison of the scorpion might make her ill for some while, it could not cause her any lasting harm. "I'm going to suck the poison out," she told him as she found the swollen welt just above his knee. "Hold still."

"Don't," he protested, his voice so faint that it was less than a distant echo. Feebly he tried to pull away from her.

Madelaine dropped to her knees and wrapped one arm around his leg, drawing it toward her. As she started to put her mouth to the sting she could not keep from an ironic realization: that she, of all people, should tend to Claude-Michel. When she spat the first mouthful of poison and blood onto the sand, she thought of the men she visited in dreams. She gave them pleasure with what she did, with words and her kisses, but Claude-Michel could have something else from her; he could have life. At least for his allotted span of days.

She had sucked mouthfuls of blood from Claude-Michel when a shadow appeared in the door. "Is anyone in here?"

"Jean-Marc," said Madelaine, knowing by the taste of Claude-Michel's blood that she had done all she could for him. "Get help."

Jean-Marc stared, his face going white, his eyes suddenly dark in his head. It took two deep breaths for him to blurt out, "What happened?"

"Scorpion," said Madelaine. "I've tried to get the poison out."

"Jésu et Mère Marie," whispered Jean-Marc, still too shocked to move.

Madelaine deliberately jarred him out of it. "Are you going to watch him die, then? Hurry."

Claude-Michel groaned, and his mottled face was lit by the sliver of light that spilled in the door. He tried to speak, a thin foam on his lips, then lapsed into semi-consciousness.

Jean-Marc fled.

Madelaine sat in the dark, holding Claude-Michel's hand and occasionally laying her fingers on the pulse in his neck. She knew it would be a close fight, whichever way it went. "Hang on, Claude-Michel, it won't be much longer. You will have help soon; hang on," she told him, her voice soft and confident. "Courage, mon brave."

There was a scuffling at the entrance to the sanctuary, and Alain Baundilet rushed in. "What the devil happened?" His tone all but accused Madelaine of causing the trouble, whatever it was.

She did not protest, giving her answer as if Baundilet had been civil. "Claude-Michel was helping me copy the ceiling here"— she indicated the day and night friezes, which were almost invisible in the dark—"and while I was fetching some charcoal and paper, he was stung by a scorpion."

"In here!" Baundilet burst out.

"Apparently." Her mouth was set.

"But where?" he commanded, as if the scorpion would march forth for its punishment.

"I don't know. I haven't found it." She indicated Claude-Michel. "Bring a hurdle or a stretcher. Take him to Doktor Falke. He needs help now. We can discuss the scorpion later."

"Of course," said Baundilet, his brusqueness greater than usual. "Here! Suti! Bring your men." He bustled out the door and continued to issue orders. "A stretcher! At once!" He repeated his commands in the local dialect, which he spoke badly, then added, "Notify Magistrate Numair. Tell him that one of my expedition has been stung by a scorpion. You. De la Noye, you tend to it."

From some distance away, Merlin de la Noye called back, "The Magistrate can do nothing about the scorpion, Professor." His voice echoed off the pillars, fading eerily.

"Do it!" Baundilet shouted. "Be quick!"

Claude-Michel thrashed suddenly, almost knocking Madelaine aside with the force of it, then subsided back into stupor.

"What was that?" Baundilet demanded, blocking the doorway as if he expected Claude-Michel or Madelaine to escape.

"He's getting worse," said Madelaine calmly, promising herself that when this was over she would smash crockery or tear a bolt of cloth to tatters, because she could no longer weep.

Then Suti arrived with four or five men, a make-shift stretcher between them, and Baundilet stood aside to permit them to bring Claude-Michel out.

"Christ and the Devil, look at him," Baundilet whispered, crossing himself and shuddering at the same time. "Poor man." He started to touch Claude-Michel, but drew back. "You. Suti! He must go to the German Doktor, the physician." His voice got higher and louder. "Now. Do you understand."

Madelaine put her hand on Baundilet's arm. "I'll go with them. I may be only a woman, but I know where to find the German physician," she said, with a shrug in the direction of the diggers. "Unless you want to send one of the others with me? Or with Claude-Michel."

"No. Good. You go with them." Baundilet seemed to gather his wits once more. "Suti. You do what Madame de Montalia says. She is my deputy, for she is a neighbor of this physician."

Suti spat. "A unveiled woman is a disgrace."

"Very likely," said Baundilet drily. "But you will do as she says or you will be taken before the Magistrate. I myself will accuse you. You don't have enough to bribe him, not compared to what I can pay, so you will be punished." This struck home with Suti, and he said something to his men in a quick undertone.

"We will hasten, Excellency," he said to Baundilet, bowing before he set off, signaling his men as he went.

"It is a good place for scorpions to be, that chamber; dark, and protected. We're probably lucky this hasn't happened before now." Madelaine started after them, then turned back to Baundilet. "Have someone bring my donkey to my villa, will you?"

Baundilet glared at her. "Very well," he said, and went back toward the sanctuary, walking cautiously, as if he expected to find more scorpions with every step. He stopped to swab his handkerchief across his brow, but whether this was due to the heat or his own nervousness was impossible to tell.

The sun was obdurate, giving no quarter and offering no relief. In the more than three miles between the temple ruins and Falke's villa, Madelaine knew that her earth-lined boots were not truly adequate against the overwhelming sun. After the first quarter-mile Madelaine felt light-headed; her disorientation increased as she followed the men carrying the stretcher. She tried to concentrate on Claude-Michel, fixing her attention on his mottled and pasty face, but found it increasingly difficult to pay attention to him. Once she thought she stumbled and was cursed by Suti; she made herself move more quickly, though moving was torment. She had to resist the urge to throw away her hat, for now it

seemed to be an iron band clamped around her head. A feeling
that would have been nausea if she were still living came over
her, and her eyes seemed dry as old leather.

Two servants met them at the gate to Doktor Falke's villa. With
them was a nurse, a Dutch woman, middle-aged and stalwart.
"Professor de Montalia," she said, and earned Madelaine's undying
gratitude for calling her Professor.

"Jantje," Madelaine answered, her arm out to brace herself
against the gate so that she would not fall. "Professor Hiver"—
she nodded toward Claude-Michel—"has been stung by a scorpion. I sucked out what poison I could, but as you see ..."

"Yes, indeed," said Jantje, all business. She spoke sharply to the
servants, called for assistance and then signaled to one of the
Egyptian boys who were at the villa recovering from fever.
"You. Gameel. You bring Doktor Falke at once." Her command
of the local dialect was very good and her manner left no room
for argument; she turned to Suti, and continued. "Put him down.
We will tend to him from here. There is food in the villa. Ask
one of the servants to guide you and they will be certain you
are fed."

Suti muttered something and did not quite bow as he motioned
to the men with him.

"We'll have none of that here," said Jantje, and added a few
pithy phrases to make her point. "Your Allah will not thank you
for defaming those who care for others, women or not." She knelt
down beside the stretcher. "Well, you certainly were stung,
weren't you?" she said to Claude-Michel in French. "How long
ago?"

The sun had made the time interminable. "Less than an hour,"
Madelaine said, though that seemed ridiculous to her. She leaned
against the wall and watched, thinking of how Claude-Michel had
deserved better than this. She was half-aware of everything Jantje
did, but exhaustion caused her attention to wander, and so she
did not know exactly when it was that Egidius Maximillian Falke
strode up.

"Madame!" said Falke after he had assured himself that Claude-
Michel was still alive. He got up and came to her side. "God in
heaven! You are pale as flour. What is the matter?"

"The sun," said Madelaine.

Falke cursed. "You ought to be indoors. Europeans don't tolerate the sun as Egyptians do," he said. He touched her face. "You are cold, Madame."

She tried to think of something witty to answer, but nothing came to mind. "Professor Hiver. Is he all right?"

"Not yet, but he may be," said Falke, his piercing blue eyes searching her face. "I am more concerned for you."

"She tells me she sucked out the poison," Jantje informed the Doktor as she readied Claude-Michel for being moved once more. "If she hadn't, he'd probably be dead this half-hour and more."

"Sucked the poison!" Falke took her hands in his. "Are you mad?"

"I spat it out," she said. "Poison and blood together."

"But ..." He put his hand on her forehead. "Has it afflicted you?"

How could she explain, she wondered. What could she tell him that he would believe? Was she supposed to meet his incendiary blue eyes and tell him she was a vampire, and had already died once? The very thought made her come close to laughter. "I don't ... think it can," she answered when she saw the distress in his eyes.

"If you swallowed any of the poison ... The venom of scorpions is as potent as that of the adders. What have you done, Madelaine?" He took her shoulders as if to shake her, then drew her close to him. He was not aware he had used her first name. "Please. Tell me you did not swallow any, for the love of God."

"I don't think I did," said Madelaine. "It's not venom, Falke. It is just the sun, Falke. It has sucked the strength from me as I sucked poison from Claude-Michel." She had wanted to say this lightly, but as Falke's eyes turned hotter, she knew she had said the wrong thing. "I am very tired. Will you let me lie down? You can tend to Claude-Michel without having to trouble yourself about me."

"Yes, of course," said Falke. "Jantje, let us trade places. You find Madame de Montalia a room where she can rest—the little sitting room behind my office would be best—and then give me a hand with this poor fellow." He kept his arm around Madelaine until his nurse got to her feet. "Try not to let her convince you that she is all right."

"You need have no fear on that head, Doktor," said Jantje, letting Madelaine's arm rest on her shoulder. "What sort of nurse would I be if I let every little tale convince me?"

As they left Doktor Falke bending over Claude-Michel, Madelaine said, "I won't try to change your mind, Jantje. I need rest."

"Well, any sensible person can see that," said Jantje as they passed the stable which had been turned into an infirmary. "And I know that no matter what Doktor Falke says, he is proud of you for caring for Professor . . ."

"Hiver," Madelaine supplied.

"Hiver," repeated Jantje, adding, "How is it that men with names like Hiver and Neige and Glace want to come to places like this?"

"I don't know that they do," said Madelaine as she allowed Jantje to lead her into the house, "but perhaps we notice them more in places like this because winter and snow and ice are so far away."

"I suppose you have the answer," said Jantje, very comfortable with what Madelaine said. "Now, up the stairs. You needn't hurry."

"I will manage." Now that she was out of the sun, Madelaine was not quite as weak as she had been. "You're being very kind to me." As soon as she said it, she wished she had not.

"What did you expect?" Jantje asked with a chuckle. "Doktor Falke would have baked the hide off anyone who tried to harm you. And I think he is very right to feel so. I don't mean to give offense, but I noticed he used your Christian name, Madame." She indicated a door a short way along the hall. "This is the sitting room. There is a chaise for relaxing. I can arrange for water or coffee or tea, if you like."

As Madelaine stood in the open door, she looked at Jantje and smiled. "No need. You are very good to me, whether it is for Doktor Falke's sake or not."

This time Jantje gave her a wider smile. "Well, it's easier with you than with some. When that swine Numair comes here, I want to scour my skin off when he is gone, to be clean of him. One must be polite to the Magistrate, but his eyes leave a scum behind them like pus on a wound."

Madelaine, who had met Magistrate Numair only twice, nodded somberly. "He reminds me of . . . a man I knew once." It was strange to sense the same convoluted and implacable menace in the soft-faced, pudgy Magistrate Numair as she had known in the elegant, corrupt Baron Clotaire Saint Sebastien. "A very bad man, who killed my father."

Jantje stopped and raised her chin a little. "What a terrible thing. I hope he received just punishment."

"Yes," said Madelaine, remembering the conflagration at the Hôtel Transylvania.

There was a brief silence between them, then Jantje said, "You have your rest now, Professor, and when Doktor Falke is finished with your colleague, I'll send someone to fetch you. It's likely to be a while; scorpion stings are uncertain wounds. It will take a while to know if you removed enough of the poison for him to overpower the rest."

Madelaine nodded, then went into the little sitting room. It was simply and prettily decorated, with a chaise, two chairs, a writing table and two large chests. She went to the windows and closed the shutters, blocking out more of the enervating sunlight. As she lay down on the chaise, she decided that she would have to speak to Baundilet about the scorpion, for although it was true that such creatures hid in dark places, Madelaine could not rid herself of the nagging suspicion that the scorpion did not come there by chance. As she dozed through the afternoon, Madelaine wondered who could wish harm on the Baundilet expedition, and was not comforted with her conclusions.

Falke came into the sitting room near sunset, looking haggard. On the threshold he paused, as if unwilling to interrupt Madelaine's rest; then he made up his mind, stepped inside and closed the door. He sat down on the chair nearest the chaise. "He will live," he said when Madelaine had opened her eyes. "He must return to France, he will need much care, and his recovery will be slow, but he will live."

"How soon will he have to leave?" Madelaine asked.

"A week, perhaps two, when he has strength enough to make the voyage. He will need some help, as well. He cannot travel by himself." He leaned back and put the tips of his fingers against his eyes. "You saved him, Madelaine. Without you, he would be dead."

Madelaine shook her head. "I was there. Anyone else would have tried to do the same."

"Would they?" He took a long, slow breath. "I am not so sanguine as you. I think he was blessed to have you there."

She did not say anything at first, but then spoke, revealing what her afternoon reverie had suggested to her. "Unless the scorpion was intended for me, in which case he is suffering on my behalf, and it is I who owe him and not the reverse."

Falke dropped his hands and stared at her. "What do you mean?" he asked, though understanding was already brightening his blue eyes.

"There are many who do not ... welcome me on this expedition," she said carefully. "Some are more dissatisfied with my presence than others." She looked away from him. "It isn't impossible that someone wanted to be rid of me, and what more convenient way than the sting of a scorpion, which might happen to anyone?" She held out her hands to him. "Falke, don't you see? I was the only one supposed to be working in that sanctuary. No one else was especially interested. I dragooned Claude-Michel into it shortly before he was stung. So far as anyone knew, no one else was with me."

"This is ridiculous. You're suggesting something completely monstrous." But as he indignantly denied her allegations, he took her hands in his and held on tightly. "No one could want to hurt you. No one."

"Because you don't?" she asked gently, wishing now that she had tasted his blood when he was awake, instead of sharing only kisses.

"It's more than that," said Falke, dropping onto his knees beside her. "You are like no other woman." He put his arms around her, looking up at her. "Madelaine, don't risk yourself. I beg you."

"Don't risk myself?" she echoed, her voice not entirely steady, "Falke, you're a fine one to suggest that, coming here to treat rare diseases. My risk is nothing compared to yours."

"But I am prepared; it is what any physician in my place would experience. What you are suggesting is not what all antiquarians anticipate, is it?" He did not permit her to answer; with sudden passion he drew her down to him, their kiss tumultuous, giving way to more, their lips meeting again and again as if in mortal combat. "I love you; I adore you," he whispered, when he had breath enough. He fitted his hands over the corsage of her dress, seeking to touch her breasts at last, then drawing back, aghast at the liberty he had taken. He made himself kiss her cheek instead of her mouth.

Finally Madelaine freed herself from his arms enough to look at him directly. For once she made no attempt to conceal her exasperation. "Falke, how can you do this to us both? Why do you persist in—"

He released her at once. "I . . . I'm sorry. God, I never intended to compromise you thi—"

"I'm not compromised," said Madelaine bluntly. "I've told you before: nothing you have done could compromise me, nothing. You wouldn't do that, would you? No matter how much I might want you to, or need you." She leaned forward deliberately and kissed him once more.

"No," he whispered, taking her by the shoulders and moving her back. "If you knew how I dream of you, it would appall you. I won't impose my—"

"You impose nothing." She looked at him. "I have dreams, Falke. Let me tell you how my dreams go."

"Not like mine," he insisted.

"Of loving you. Of how you love me," she kept on, and saw him wince.

"You're no trollop, to bed a man she has not honorably married," he told her, putting even more distance between them. "And I am not in a position to marry, and you are not willing to marry, so what is left to us, honorably?"

"Falke!" Her outburst was both irate and sad. "I am a woman who loves you, and seeks you. How many times must I tell you? Your honor has nothing to do with that, not the way you think it does. I would not seek you if I did not honor you. My chastity is not in question." She flung herself back against the chaise, wishing she could convince him of her desire. "Don't you realize that I value your love? Won't you let me come to you? Can't you accept my desire as well as your own? Don't you know that I am not a child or a fool?"

He could not trust himself to reach out to comfort her, for fear of what else he might do, things he had already done in his dreams. "I know that you tell me you want me, but you don't know what it would mean. Kisses are all we have, and they are ... nothing. You tell me you know my dreams, but how can you?"

Madelaine thought of the dreams—sweet, joyous dreams—she induced in him when she visited him in sleep, knowing she could describe them in detail, wishing that she could have them as more than dreams; but she remained silent about them, saying only, "You think because I am unmarried I am ignorant. I'm not."

"You're innocent," said Falke. "I know."

She slid off the chaise and moved near to where he sat on the floor attempting to put his clothing into better order. "Falke, listen to me. I know what you want of me. I am happy you desire my love. I want to give it to you. For both our sakes, will you take it?"

He put his hands over hers, though it seemed to him that her skin was hot as molten steel. "We'll talk of this again, when we're both ... calmer."

"I don't want to be calmer," she said softly. "I am afraid, Falke, and I seek the comfort of love. Why do you deny me?"

He kissed her forehead. "Because you are afraid," said Falke, his passion subdued now. "When you are not afraid, we will talk again, and I will not hold you to anything you have said."

Madelaine met his eyes with hers. "I will not change, Falke."

"I pray so," Falke responded, the burning still in his eyes.

Text of a letter from Karl Molter, physician to the French embassy at Cairo, to Professor Alain Baundilet at Thebes.

My very dear Professor Baundilet;

This is to inform you that your colleague, the young Professor Claude-Michel Hiver, has departed today for Europe. As you requested, I examined him myself to determine if he was well enough for such a sea voyage, and I am satisfied that while he is not strong, he is not so weak that he cannot endure passage. Thus, he was put aboard Le Roi d'Est, *which is bound for Greece, Trieste, and Venice. I have discussed Professor Hiver's condition with the ship's surgeon and he is in agreement that there ought to be as little disruption as possible for Professor Hiver. I have also provided copies of the records you supplied to us, including the treatment by Doktor Falke. This has made my work more successful, I am certain, and our reports together ought to be useful to Dottore Togliero.*

Professor Hiver has told me that were it not for the prompt action of one of your expedition, he might not have survived at all. How fortunate that someone was prepared to deal with so dangerous a situation. You must be pleased that you have one of your number who is so competent during such an emergency. While I do not advocate the methods this Madame de Montalia employed, for there are tremendous risks in such action, I can only applaud the presence of mind such action displays. I hope you will extend to this most capable female my congratulations on her timely response.

I have requested a full report be supplied to me by Dottore Togliero, and upon receiving it, I will take the liberty of informing you of its contents as well. I have every confidence that in time this young man will be restored to health, but I am aware that it is going to be some while before that occurs. I hope he does not decide to make an invalid of himself, but I also hope he will not try to abbreviate the necessary time for recovery, for that would lessen the degree to which he is restored to health. When I examined him, I took advantage of our discussion to warn him of the various risks he might encounter during his recovery, and I am sure that Professor Hiver took what I said very much to heart.

Because I have been informed that not all letters carried up and down the river arrive safely, I am sending this with the Reverend Jasper Ryerston of Berkshire, who is visiting the English antiquarians and is said to be utterly reliable. It is distressing to have to rely on such tactics, but one must accommodate, especially among foreigners.

With the wish that I may be of service to you in future, in less grave circumstances,

Karl Hector Molter
physician

October 9th, 1826, at Cairo

PART III

Sanh-kheran

Servant

Text of a letter from le Comte de Saint-Germain on the Dalmatian coast to Madelaine de Montalia in Egypt, dated January 4th, 1827.

Beloved Madelaine, my heart;

I was growing apprehensive when I had no word from you for so long. When your associate Claude-Michel arrived, he explained to me how difficult it has been for you to get messages out of Thebes. If your circumstances should become more hazardous, I hope you will do the prudent thing and arrange to come down-river at once. Though it is hard to leave Luxor, isn't it? Of all the cities where the House of Life was raised, Luxor was the most beautiful; it is the one I remember most clearly even now.

How absurd, to advise you so: I know even as I write the words that they are foreign to you. You faced Saint Sebastien and all his howling pack, you have made a place for yourself among scholars, and you accepted me wholly and unreservedly from the first. Why should you forget yourself so utterly?

Your questions about proper pronunciation are not easily answered. Each city, every district had a dialect, and the priests did not speak the same way as slaves, nor donkey-drivers the same as Pharaoh; and from century to century the tongue

175

changed: the French of your youth is not quite the French they speak in Paris today, and it was the same in Egypt. And just as in France, the further away from cities the people lived, the more their dialects diverged from standard city speech. Remember also that it was the priests who tended to the temples, and to the inscriptions on the temples; what you read there is what they wished you to read. There have been deliberate alterations in some of the texts, and others have been defaced by sand and time. The inscription you sent me is probably best translated "Rameses II, the ever-living and favored by Ptah, with a glad heart has finished his father's temple in Abydos." The figures that follow show the number of men who worked on the project during Rameses' reign. To know the exact number, you have only to count them: the Egyptians were meticulous about that.

Erai Gurzin can help you, if you ask him. His language is related to that of Pharoahnic Egypt; he has made something of a study of the old inscriptions, and he has access to many you have not seen. You say in your letter than you find his Christianity baffling; the Copts are closer to the first teachings of your Christ than the Catholic Church. Listen to what he says.

Yes, you are right; for the most part the reign of Rameses II was peaceful. But he was Pharaoh a long time, and not every year was fortunate. There were years of famine and years of plague while he ruled, and he was unable to change those things.

Sanh-kheran sat in the passage that led out of the House of Life, his arms resting on the low table in front of him, his dark eyes turned toward the courtyard where those too far gone in hunger waited for the release of death. The slave who attended him was his scribe Kephnet, who recorded all Sanh-kheran's comments on behalf of the High Priest Hapthep-twu; the High Priest had served in the House of Life for seventeen years and regarded Sanh-kheran as a great and unwelcome puzzle.

"They say the famine is worse in Memphis," Kephnet remarked

when Sanh-kheran had been silent for some time. "I heard a man from the docks report there had been riots."

"Very possibly," said Sanh-kheran. "I fear there will be riots here if we cannot find grain for bread." He leaned back, his linen headdress brushing the wall. "It's happened before, but not recently."

Kephnet looked ashamed, as he often did at any reference to Sanh-kheran's age. "There are records in the House of Life. None of them tell of a famine that has lasted so long."

"Three years is not the worst I can recall," said Sanh-kheran. "Five would be very dangerous, but three is not too uncommon." He got up and went to the open door, staring out of the House of Life. "And if we feed them today, what do we do tomorrow? We have a little for today, but less for tomorrow, and tomorrow there will be more of them, and our stores will be that much more depleted. Do we give these another day of false hope, or do we turn away from them because we cannot help them? And what are our few handfuls of grain once hunger has ruined the body beyond repair?" He was thinking aloud; as he turned back he was startled to see that Kephnet was writing down his words. "There's no need for—"

"I have been commanded," said Kephnet, and went on writing.

Sanh-kheran sighed. "Does Hapthep-twu insist on having every syllable I speak? Never mind," he went on as he watched Kephnet's brush move. It was not more than a century ago that he had been a slave, and he remembered the burden of serving his master. "Do whatever you must, Kephnet. But let me see what you have recorded before you give it to Hapthep-twu."

"It is not permitted," said Kephnet.

"Will you read back what you have put down?" he asked, anticipating the answer.

The scribe looked away. "It is forbidden."

"Ah." Sanh-kheran nodded.

It was not only I who had changed; the priests of Imhotep were not the magicians of old, though they were hardly physi-

cians as you understand the word. Those who served in the House of Life had learned that wounds and infections and disease and tumors and broken bones were not the will of the gods or the work of malignant spirits or the result of curses; they had established sensible treatments, performed basic surgery and dentistry, and had reliable herbal preparations to treat many ailments. True, they also offered prayers and sacrifices, but then, so does any good French physician today, though the prayer may be only a Paternoster and the sacrifice a candle. At the House of Life, those who came for treatment received the best care that was to be had. But as the quality of the treatment increased, so did the cost. By the time Rameses II ruled, the Temple of Imhotep, which had been a haven to those in need, became a sanctuary for those with riches.

"We have no right to turn him away," said Sanh-kheran for the second time as he faced the High Priest; his expression and posture were respectful, but the tone of his words was abrupt. "He came to us in good faith."

"In good faith, perhaps, but without adequate funds," said Hapthep-twu, his eyes bright and hard. "It is disrespectful to Imhotep to come to the House of Life with no offering beyond a goat and a length of linen."

"It is all he has, and his children are ill; his wife is already dead." Sanh-kheran gestured impatiently at the colonnaded front of the Temple of Imhotep, newly expanded and decorated. Beyond the door Luxor rose gloriously around them. "What is the use of this show if we cannot follow the precepts of the god?"

Something furtive slipped over Hapthep-twu's features and was gone almost at once. He gave Sanh-kheran his best stare and said in a deliberate way, "You are a servant here; the records say you were once a slave."

"Seventy years ago," Sanh-kheran agreed, seeing the High Priest flinch at the number.

"You were a slave," Hapthep-twu insisted. "As a foreigner, you can be a slave again."

"At the will of Pharaoh," said Sanh-kheran pleasantly, his dark eyes fixed directly on the High Priest's, though it was an insult to Hapthep-twu. "What has that to do with the teachings of Imhotep? He admonished all his priests to serve those who came to the House of Life in the name of life."

Hapthep-twu turned away to avoid further contamination by the infuriating foreign servant. "You have your task to do—you decide who will be treated and who will be sent out of the House of Life. You are not to treat those who cannot bring sufficient offering to the god. Is that clear?"

"I understand your words," said Sanh-kheran bluntly. "I do not understand why you refuse to do as Imhotep instructed you."

The High Priest took his rod of office and swung it in Sanh-kheran's direction, not quite a threat but not without force. "It is not for you to interpret the teachings of Imhotep. You have been at the House of Life for many years, and there are those who say you are an agent of the god—though Imhotep would never employ a foreigner for that task—and they put stock in what you say."

So there it was, Sanh-kheran thought. Hapthep-twu was jealous of his reputation and offended at the respect the servant was accorded. He made a gesture of proper submission. "Such rumors are not my doing, High Priest; those who are ill seek for the aid and wisdom of the god, and they fasten on whatever instrument they can. It is because I work at the door out of the House of Life that some think such things of me."

It was not enough, but Hapthep-twu appeared mollified. "It is regrettable that such ridiculous things are believed."

"Truly," said Sanh-kheran with feeling.

"I wish you to deny any association with the god." He looked at Sanh-kheran warily, with a glint of fear in his eyes.

"Certainly." He decided to ignore the risk and continue. "When I was among my own people, I was given to another god: how can I be one with Imhotep?"

The fear gave way to contempt. "And your god is so mighty that you were a slave in the Black Land and now you are a servant."

"Yes," said Sanh-kheran, thinking of the eight hundred years that had passed since the god had tasted his blood in that dark, sacred grove.

Satisfied, Hapthep-twu turned on his heel and strode away.

When the plague came to Thebes and Luxor, five years after the famine, the High Priest was one of the first to fall to it. He had been ailing for over a year, troubled by a cough that would not cease, and the plague—cholera—was more than he could endure. The House of Life was thrown into disorder, for many of the physicians and priests fell ill with the disease and were as much in need of help as those who came to the House of Life for succor.

At the height of the plague, when there were more corpses than the priests of Anubis could tend and the scent of death was everywhere, word came from the Temple of Thoth that all the priests and scribes were suffering from the plague and must perish. There was as yet no new High Priest, but the most senior of the priests and physicians consulted—a cautious and frightened man called Sehet-ptenh—and it was decided that it was safest and most prudent if I should go to the Temple of Thoth and determine how serious their condition was. That was a sophistry, of course, for there was no hope held for those in the Temple of Thoth. It was regarded as a very ill omen, and none of the priests wanted to leave the dubious protection of the House of Life for what was certainly a House of Death.

As he crossed the threshold of the inner temple, Sanh-kheran smelled the ripe scent of the dying. He hesitated, and for the first time since he awakened from death he had to suppress a shudder at what lay beyond this door. It was an effort of will to go on.

Inside the door, huddled together in an alcove, three temple slaves lay, heaped like trash, their bodies grey-green and distended. Sanh-kheran paused beside them, trying to quell the horror rising in him. He leaned down and started to dispose the bodies properly, on their backs with their arms at their sides, so that the priests of Anubis would not find them defiled and unacceptable to their god. At the touch of the cold, waxen flesh, his throat tightened, and he had to wait to master himself. It was absurd, he told himself sternly. He had no gorge to rise, and yet a sensation like nausea—a thing he had not felt since his death —quivered in his throat. He took a long breath; he could not be distracted from his task. There have been dead by the thousands since your death, and you have not flinched—or not often, he told himself. He wanted to harden his eyes and close his heart, but the more he strove to do this, the greater his distress became.

In the outer sanctuary where the gifts to Thoth were received there were four temple slaves guarding the doors so that no supplicants could enter. One of them was very ill, the odor that enveloped him heralding his approaching death; another, younger, was lost in febrile dreams, muttering to the phantoms of his mind. The third, the tallest of the three, leaned against the wall, his skin already showing the greenish shade that was mortal. Even as Sanh-kheran watched, the fourth sagged and slid down the wall, his spear falling from his hands. At the center of the outer sanctuary a single novice initiate sat, a scroll open on his lap. He read the sacred invocations in a failing voice, and broke off as he caught sight of Sanh-kheran.

"Who are you?" the novice asked. His face shone with sweat and his eyes were bright as glass.

"Sanh-kheran," he answered. "I was sent by the House of Life." He moved carefully as he came nearer. "We were told that the plague is here."

"As you see," the novice answered, his face composed. "I have not entered the inner sanctuary—it isn't permitted—but all the priests have gathered there." He coughed and spat blood. "The rest have been sent away."

"The sanctuary: where is it?" Sanh-kheran asked, wondering how much longer the novice would be able to survive.

The novice was startled. "No. You cannot enter, either. You are not of this temple, you do not serve Thoth."

"I have been told to learn how many are ill; I must go there; the priests of Imhotep require it. If you will not tell me, I will have to search for myself, and that will take time." He was standing at the novice's shoulder now, and was certain that the fever had its hooks deep in the man.

"It is forbidden for you to enter," insisted the novice. "I would fail in my duty if I—" This time his coughing did not stop for some little time, and when it was over, the man listed to one side, like a sinking ship.

Sanh-kheran stepped back. "I will return," he said, not wanting to abandon the novice to the tightening embrace of the fever. He left the outer sanctuary and went toward the heart of the temple, to the place where the priests communed with their god. He knew it had to be one of three or four chambers at the heart of the temple, as with other temples.

The second door he opened was the place he sought, and he drew back as soon as he had crossed the threshold into the darkness, for his night-seeing eyes discerned the corpses as clearly as he breathed the stench of their deaths. For a brief time he remained in the door; then, his thoughts deliberately blank, he closed the doors again and left the priests alone before their most sacred mysteries.

Another one of the guards was on the floor when Sanh-kheran returned to the outer sanctuary. The novice continued to read from his scroll, but his voice was thready now, and the words came without sense, mere sounds repeated by habit. As Sanh-kheran approached, he faltered, then continued to read.

"You have to leave here," said Sanh-kheran to the novice, surprised at himself for what he had said.

The novice stared at him, his words silenced at last. Finally he framed a response. "This is my temple. I am initiate here."

"You are dead here," Sanh-kheran corrected him. "You must leave or you will be as dead as the others."

"I am sworn to Thoth." He put his hand on the scroll as if it were his protector.

"Thoth has no priests here any more," said Sanh-kheran as bluntly as he could. "Only Anubis and Osiris remain here."

"*I* have vowed to remain," the other persisted, stubbornly clinging to the one thing that filled his thoughts.

"That is vowing to die," said Sanh-kheran, wondering if he would be able to carry the man away without much of a battle.

"It is the fate of men to die, and to enter into the House of the Gods." His voice was singsong, the words losing their meaning as he spoke. The scroll fell from his hands.

Sanh-kheran came to the novice's side. "You will enter into the House of the Gods in good time, never fear, but not yet. For the moment, I am taking you to the House of Life." Before the novice could object, Sanh-kheran reached down, lifted him from the floor as he might lift a half-grown child, and slung him over his shoulder.

"I will be sick," muttered the novice.

"Better than dead," said Sanh-kheran as he set out for the House of Life, rehearsing in his mind how he would explain his actions to the priests of Imhotep.

You never knew Aumtehoutep, of course. He was my bonds-man before Roger and he died for the second time in the Flavian Circus; he was the first I ever restored to life, and at the time I did not know if I would be able to do it. The living I could infect with my nature, given time and knowledge and blood, but for those dead, my blood could make no difference; I needed the ultimate skills of the Black Land for that. I counted on the confusion in the House of Life to permit me the chance to restore the novice from the Temple of Thoth. Since it was certain he would die, I thought it might be possible to attempt the resto-ration on him without serious objections being raised. Given the plague, I hoped that they might welcome the procedure if it succeeded.

In fact, the priests watched with fascination, seeing their own restoration in what I did for Aumtehoutep.

Sehet-ptenh had been High Priest of Imhotep for less than a year and he was already showing signs of failing health; he was thinner and his skin seemed too tightly stretched for his bones.

Occasionally he complained of a gnawing in his gut, but for the most part he bore his ills with the dignity his high position required, for it was thought to be a bad omen when the High Priest in the House of Life was touched by disease.

"Tell me, Sanh-kheran, how you—" He gestured to the man on the other side of the small chamber.

"You were there, High Priest," Sanh-kheran said, no longer enjoying the constant repetition Sehet-ptenh demanded. "I followed the teachings in the old scrolls."

"From the time of Djoser," said Sehet-ptenh, as if he were determined to catch his foreign servant in a lie.

"That is what is written on the scroll," said Sanh-kheran quietly. "It may have been another, but the cartouche was Djoser's, and the writing was in the manner of his time."

"A difficult thing to read, that old writing. How is it you are certain you have done it properly?" He leaned on his staff, his breath coming more sharply.

"I'm not," was Sanh-kheran's curt answer. "But Aumtehoutep lives now and he was dead by the time I got him here. You were the one who declared him dead." He rose from the low desk where he had been putting down his daily report from those who had been sent out of the House of Life.

"When I am dead, once the priests of Anubis are finished with me, you will restore me. You have the knowledge of it." This was the first time Sehet-ptenh had given so clear an order.

"I am not certain that it can be done once you are embalmed," said Sanh-kheran, his face showing little emotion beyond curiosity. "The organs are needed in the body, and once the priests of Anubis have removed them, I do not know if—"

"It is sacrilege to fail to embalm a priest," said Sehet-ptenh, putting an end to the discussion.

Sehet-ptenh died three years later, wasted away to a husk of a man, and he was embalmed and wrapped in fine linen; his heart was placed in an alabaster jar and there was no resurrection for him. His successor was Imensris, a portly, political knave with a yen for power and the honor of an asp. He

insisted that the reanimation of Aumtehoutep be kept secret,
so that he could exercise his judgment and gain influence. He
was eager to be the companion of Pharaoh; he assumed that
he could use my skill for his own advancement, and made
that clear to me.

"What do you mean, no?" Imensris demanded when Sanh-
kheran refused his request.

Sanh-kheran looked up from his scroll a second time. "I mean
that I cannot guarantee what may happen if I undertake such a
venture again," he said patiently. It was almost sunset and he was
starting to feel the annealing touch of oncoming night.

"I am the one who is responsible," said Imensris, putting his
hand over the huge pectoral he had taken to wearing. "I am
the one who will have to answer to Pharaoh if you do not
succeed."

This assurance was given so glibly that Sanh-kheran was more
certain than before that the High Priest of Imhotep had no intention of accepting anything but praise for bringing Pharaoh's
daughter back to life. "I have not restored a female, only a male.
I do not know if the procedure will work for a female," he told
Imensris. "You do not want to have the first mistake be at the
cost of one of Pharaoh's family."

"The child has been dead only half a day. If she is brought here
now, before the priests of Anubis get to her, you will have all
night to work on her." His eyes shone with avidity, the only
sustained emotion Sanh-kheran had ever seen in him.

"It does not matter how long she has been dead; I am sure it
is not safe to attempt to reanimate her. Things are not now as
they were when Aumtehoutep woke from death." He stared down
at his scroll, at the personal sigil that marked his portions of the
temple records. "You seek to gain the notice of Pharaoh through
the life of his daughter—how would you explain when she remained forever a child of twelve?"

For the first time there was doubt in Imensris' face. "How do
you mean?"

"Look at Aumtehoutep," said Sanh-kheran at his most reasonable. "He is the same as the day he came here from the Temple of Thoth. He is not one day older in his appearance, and there is no change in his body that I can detect that would reveal his age." He set his pen aside and put a cover on his ink cake. "It would be the same with Pharaoh's daughter."

"How can that be?" Imensris demanded, leaning over the low desk where Sanh-kheran sat.

"I do not know," admitted the servant from out of the House of Life. "But I see it, and it is stated in the old scrolls—read them for yourself, High Priest—that those who are brought back to life do not age." He waited while Imensris considered this. "Pharaoh might come to curse you for what you have done, as some of the priests here have cursed me."

Imensris grew ruddy. "Are you saying that I have spoken against you?"

"I am saying that someone has," answered Sanh-kheran with every appearance of respect.

There was an uncomfortable silence between the High Priest and the foreign servant; then the High Priest turned away and never spoke to Sanh-kheran again for the remaining evening, the next week, the nineteen years more of his life.

For many years, decades, I did not attempt another restoration, and the next time I did, it was not successful; the man did not reanimate. After that, I waited three centuries before I tried again.

You will find a record of this in the House of Life at Luxor, if the inner sanctuary is still intact, and nothing has faded the writing. I do not recall the precise wording, but there is a report of that reanimation, for by then I was a physician, and the priests kept records of all that transpired in the House of Life. The inscription, read from right to left, tells of the reanimation; read from left to right, it is an invocation to the gods for the protection of the people of Luxor.

Shortly after the death of Rameses II, Libyans invaded Egypt. Mernaptah, Rameses' son, defeated them, but it was a minor victory, and a dear one, and the succession was no longer secure. After his death, there followed twenty years of jostling for the throne of the Black Land.

To answer your questions about the Sphynx; it is a statue to Hapy, god of the Nile, the only hermaphroditic god in the entire Egyptian pantheon; the Great Sphynx, as you will discover, is both male and female. For a time, it was the fashion to cut the face of Pharaoh on the annual Sphynx, but after Amasis, who ruled before I came to the Black Land, this practice ended, though the Sphynx continued. Each year a Sphynx was constructed at the high-water mark of the Inundation, with a cistern beneath it, against drought. Most of these statues did not last long, and in a matter of centuries were reduced to shapelessness by the Nile itself. Not that the current course of the Nile is as it was in the time of the Pharaohs; each year it cuts a slightly new path after the Inundation; today it would be impossible to locate and identify most of the Sphynxes built so long ago. As I understand it, the Great Sphynx was erected so that it would last longer, and be a tribute to Hapy that would not erode. There is an enormous cistern beneath the figure by the pyramids, as there is beneath all Sphynxes.

Remember, my heart, that Egypt is an ancient land. You know how long I have lived; a quarter of my life was passed in Egypt, at the House of Life, and that time was not the totality of the history of the Black Land, which was old when I came to it. You see its monuments and marvel at them, but they are nothing more than inscriptions and stone—treasures, to be sure, and holding a wealth of gold and knowledge. The existence of Egypt was its greatest achievement; only China has proved more durable.

Is there a vertigo of time, I wonder. For if there is, then I have sensed it as I write this to you. I have sensed, also, the danger around you, and I ask you again to be prudent. You are all the joy of life to me, Madelaine; without you there is no savor or merit or beauty. Once I believed it was not possible to have what we hold between us; I yearned to be known for all that I am, and loved for all that I am. I did not know that as you loved me, so would I love you, but so it is, and I am still caught in the wonder of it. I could not endure knowing you were out of the House of Life.

> *Saint-Germain*
> *(his seal, the eclipse)*

February through September, 1827

Text of a letter from Ferdinand Charles Montrose Algernon Trowbridge to Madelaine de Montalia, both in Thebes.

My dear Madame;

You doubtless recall the discussion we had last month at that dreadful evening at Omat's villa. I have done as you requested, and I have tried to learn of any actual trading of antiquities in our expedition. To be frank, I have not found much but the occasional rumor, which means nothing. Yet the other day I had occasion to go with Halliday to the west side of the Nile, where Wilkinson and his crew are working, and I happened to see Sevenage with one of the local headmen—a rogue of a fellow with one eye and the first finger gone from his left hand; he's the brother or cousin to your head digger—off behind one of those enormous walls. Sevenage was handing over a small basket, which is what caught my attention. The headman is a digger himself, and if he wanted to purloin something, he would not have to use Sevenage to do it. Therefore, thought I, it follows that there is something odd in the transaction. Sevenage has found a number of those little alabaster jars with the gods on them. They have something to do with burial, or so I've been told. That basket could easily have held a set of those jars. Mind,

I'm not saying it did, because I don't know what was in the basket, but it isn't beyond possibility. I don't know what to make of it myself, but perhaps you will be able to gather some sense from it. It's a bit disquieting to think that one of my own chums could be caught up in that business.

I've been told by Castermere that we have to come up with some money again or Magistrate Numair will see us thrown out of Thebes. This is the third time he's demanded money since we've arrived, and that's beyond what the expedition is giving. Who knows what the university is sending along. He's a greedy man, there's no doubt of it, and his greed increases as more parties come here. It's vastly dissatisfying. I've sent word off to Pater, asking for that and an extra hundred, but it's anyone's guess if he'll send it. Mater's got it into her head that I ought to be casting about for a bride, and wants me home so that some native wench does not snare me while I'm here. I've assured them that the only woman in Egypt I've met who could capture my heart is a French antiquarian, a lovely girl with eyes like violets and rich dark hair shot with gold. I've mentioned you have estates in France, and a title when politics permit. That ought to satisfy Mater, at least for another six months. After that, I may have to find other excuses to offer. When you consider I never dreamed I'd be here more than half a year, and now it looks as if I will be here two years at least; I suppose their concern is reasonable, given the circumstances.

That part about you is true enough. It's not right to say this to you, but better to put it on paper than make a mull of it trying to tell you face to face. You are a most captivating woman, and I am overwhelmed at your kindness to me. I won't embarrass you telling you what I have dreamed, but I wish you to know that I am truly honored by your friendship; occasionally I am puzzled as well, for I know I am not the most handsome fellow about, and though I'm well-enough off, I'm not made of money the way some of us are. The name's old, of course, but you can't eat a name.

Now that makes it appear I am ungrateful, and it is nothing of the sort. I wish you to believe that I freely admit being cap-

tivated by you, and that captivation is most delightful. I'm content with your company at parties and in my dreams, and you may rely on me: I will not importune you now or any other time. Unlike some men I've met, I'm not one to disdain the honest friendship of women, or to regard your affections as fancies and whim. You are valuable to me, Madame. You are easily the most remarkable woman it has been my pleasure to meet, and I can hope nothing for you but what is best and most joyous. I can even find it in my heart to wish that odd monk comes back to work with you. It troubles me that you are there at your villa without some protection more than servants, and while a monk may not be much, he is an improvement over nothing at all.

I apologize for any distress this may cause you. I offer in recompense an invitation to meet with John Gardner Wilkinson, who is curious about this sanctuary you have done so much work to uncover and document. I showed him that long inscription you gave me and he said he is very curious about the rest. He asks that you call at the villa where the English expedition is staying at half after four on Wednesday next. I'm to give him your response, if you will be obliging enough to send it with the messenger who carries this to you. If you are permitted to bring more of your sketches, Wilkinson would like to examine those, as well.

Will you be at the reception Magistrate Numair is giving, or does he not include women in his invitation? Hard to tell with him, you know, if he's going to be Egyptian or European at any one time. If you are there, let me have the pleasure of your company when you are not with the German physician. An excellent fellow in his way, but on occasions such as this, I find him a trifle de trop. *You must pardon me for that.*

Yr. most obt. svt,
F.C.M.A. Trowbridge

February 19th, 1827, at Thebes

1

Madelaine rose from her place at the table in her salon, extending her hand, not surprised when he did not take it. "Monsieur Omat," she said to her unexpected visitor, "what a pleasure to have you visit me at last. Do come in." She curtsied and gestured to Renenet. "Refreshments for my guest."

"At once," said Renenet, moving away from her more quickly than he usually did.

Yamut Omat looked around the salon, nodding a little. He seemed to be measuring everything she possessed. At last he turned back to her, giving her a spectacular smile that was all the more interesting for its falsity. "It is strange for a man of my faith to visit a woman this way. I trust you will make allowances. It is my understanding that afternoon calls are permissible in French society. I did not mean to give offense for not doing this sooner." Although he was dressed in proper European clothes, his superfine blue jacket good enough to be seen in Paris, his inexpressibles perfectly cut, his boots as shiny as fashion demanded, his turban and demeanor identified him; he bowed to her as if he were in Egyptian robes.

"I know that it is a hard thing for you to be here," said Madelaine as cordially as she could as she wondered what prompted Omat to come at all, "but I hope my staff will provide the hospitality you . . . deserve."

"Most gracious," said Omat, standing uncomfortably in the center of the room. "Yes, most gracious."

Madelaine realized how awkward he felt. "Sit down, Monsieur Omat. Please." She indicated one of the chairs. "I think you'll find this comfortable. If you won't mind, I'll remain here at the table. We can converse easily and I will not have to abandon the work I've just begun." She also hoped that having the table between them might make Omat less distressed.

"I did not mean to interrupt you," said Omat, his tone perfunctory at best. "I thought that since it was late in the day, you would not still be working, or—"

"I am glad to have occasion to stop briefly." She rested her elbows on the table and looked directly at him. "Has there been a difficulty or a misunderstanding of some sort? Do you require my assistance? Is there something I can do for you, Monsieur Omat?"

He studied his hands. "I was hoping, actually, that you would be willing to ... speak with my daughter."

"I?" Madelaine asked, quite unprepared. "Your daughter? Monsieur Omat, why would you ask this of me? Surely your daughter has a mother, or ..." She bit back "one of your other wives" and said instead, "... grandmother who might be more suited for—"

"Not in this instance," said Omat, interrupting her. "In this instance, all the women in my household are against what I am doing, and nothing I have done has changed their minds yet. So if Rida is to learn anything, she cannot learn it from any of them." He took a fine linen handkerchief from his pocket and patted his brow, taking care to replace it so that the elegant arrangement of folds and creases would not be disturbed.

What an absurd dandy he is, Madelaine thought, trying not to smile at his fastidiousness. "What is it that your female relatives so oppose?" she asked politely, then looked up as Renenet came into the room with a full meal laid out on a brass tray, as if Yamut Omat were a guest for supper and not an impromptu afternoon caller. "Your daughter is quite charming."

"The lamb grilled with herbs and onions is especially good," said Renenet to Omat as he put down the tray, bowing deeply as he did. "The sherbet was made with special grapes." This was Renenet's way of telling Omat that he had been served wine, which the Koran forbade.

"Thank you," said Omat. "May Allah—glorious forever!—bring you fortune and many sons."

Again Renenet bowed with more respect than Madelaine had ever seen him display, and withdrew.

"Enjoy the meal," said Madelaine, glad that Moslem law did not permit men and women to eat together often, so her abstinence would not seem peculiar to Omat. "I have a good staff in the kitchen."

"Very gracious, Madame," said Omat, and tore one of the fragrant breads in half as he reached for the grilled lamb. He ate quickly and noisily, helping himself to some of everything on the tray, as good manners demanded. Only when he was through did their conversation resume. "An excellent repast," he told her when he had wiped his hands on the damp towel provided. "You have a treasure in your cook."

"So I have been told," said Madelaine. "I will convey your compliments."

"A thousand thanks," said Omat, and at last got back to the reason for his visit. "But to explain my presence: my daughter . . . she cannot be just another Egyptian girl, do you see?"

"Well, she's not like any other Egyptian girl I've ever met, but I have had the opportunity to meet very few of them," said Madelaine, cautious but amiable. "She indicated when we met that there are Egyptians who would not approve of her European clothes or attitudes." In fact, as she recalled, Rida Omat feared Egyptians would stone her to death for uncovering her face.

"Sadly, there is reason for her fear. This is a very ancient country and our ways are set. At the same time our nature is impulsive. We are a volatile people, Madame, and some of us are more easily offended than others. A girl like my Rida, not many understand why I want her to move in the European world. In many ways she likes the Europeans she has met, but the rest of the family is often shocked. While you were with us the other evening, I could not help comparing her to you, and seeing that she has more to learn than I had supposed." He shook his head slowly.

"And why *do* you want her to move in the European world?" Madelaine asked, softening her bluntness with a smile.

"Because the European world is coming here, and we are not prepared for it. Because business is European now, and if we are not to become little more than slaves, we must acquire knowledge of the ways of the European world, and teach our children how to go on." He moved the tray aside and shifted in his chair so that he faced Madelaine directly. "You can understand that, can't you? We Egyptians are being thrust into progress as Europe was thirty years ago. If we wish to escape the violence, then there are things we must learn, and learn quickly, for there is no turning the tide now it has started. You see how many Europeans are here for the privilege of digging sand out of ruins. There are others who want cotton and wheat and hemp and the rest of it." He waved his hand to show how complicated it was.

"Europeans do not often do business with girls, no matter how pretty," said Madelaine, remembering how often she had found just such barriers in her own life.

"But they will pay more heed to a young woman who wears pretty frocks and drinks tea and goes to the theater and concerts than they will to a girl who is veiled and speaks to no men but her husband, her father and her sons." He saw the agreement in her eyes. "All four of my sons died before they were twelve. My daughter is the only child to live longer. Her sisters are less than five, and so it falls to Rida to serve our interests. A daughter's first alliance must be to her family. You know this. She has known this from childhood. You know this for yourself."

"Yes," said Madelaine after a short pause. "I know the dictum."

"So. You must come and tell Rida how it is to go on in European society. How she ought to speak. Her French is good, and her English is tolerable, but that is not to say she can converse. How she is to present herself to others. How she is to act at the theater. Whom she is allowed to dance with, and whom she is to shun. She has to learn the way women use fans—do they still use fans?"

"Some do," said Madelaine, watching Omat in appalled fascination.

"But young or old?" Omat pressed. "Ought she to use a fan?"

Madelaine opened her hands. "Monsieur Omat, I haven't been in Paris in over three years." That was something of a mendacity, for she had not been to Paris in more than two decades. "I don't know what the mode is today. When I left, a girl like your daughter might carry a fan to a ball, but would probably not bring one to the theater. Fashions change so quickly, though, that by now it may be the reverse."

Omat nodded heavily. "The mercurial nature of Europeans," he said. "We do not comprehend it. I have learned to enjoy it, but that's not the same as understanding. The clothes Egyptians wear today"—he looked at his own fine outfit—"who keep to the old ways, not those like me, are almost the same as garments worn a century ago, or two centuries. It's the desert; it makes demands."

"So does winter in Switzerland," said Madelaine pleasantly. "Still, you do understand I cannot be certain that the advice I might give your daughter would be correct. If she would be willing to accept it."

"She will be willing," said Omat. "If she is not, I will beat her until she is."

Madelaine straightened. "I'd rather you didn't beat her. She will not be a willing student if you beat her."

Omat laughed. "I am a man with a family. The law requires me to discipline my family. If any of them are not properly behaved, it is my duty to chastise them." He looked squarely at Madelaine. "European law gives fathers rights over their children."

"Yes, it does," said Madelaine. "But I do not like sullen children, as those who are beaten so often are." She recalled the times her father had taken a cane to her, or her mother had slapped her, and how adamant she had been in her hatred, until she learned what her father dreaded, and how he was striving to protect her. "The longer I live," she said, "the more I am certain that beating does not improve a person."

"Another radical notion. Wait until you have children of your own, and you will understand. How can a person improve if he is not beaten? The pain is a reminder, an instructor more persuasive than any other teacher. Let a child know that misbehavior will bring certain pain, and the child will not misbehave. What will happen if there is no pain to give authority? You will have anarchy. Europe is seething with it just now." Omat rose. "Tell me you will do this, and I will give you my word that I will not beat my daughter unless she is very stubborn. I will even tell her why she is not to be beaten unless it is necessary. Is that acceptable to you?"

"Perforce," said Madelaine, once again offering her hand, and this time perplexed when Yamut Omat shook it.

"Then I will consider this settled. I will have my servants call on you . . . shall we say day after tomorrow?"

"Day after tomorrow?" Madelaine asked, curious why Omat demanded the lessons begin so soon. "Three days later is preferable." The day actually made little difference to her, but she wanted to know how willing Omat was to accommodate her.

"All right, three days." He nodded once. "Very fine, Madame de Montalia. I will inform Rida she is to be prepared to receive you at—"

"I think it would be a good idea," said Madelaine, knowing that the interruption would annoy Omat, "if Rida came here instead. She would be less restricted here, I think. Your villa, for all its treasures and your European furniture, is still an Egyptian household. Here, I have a European household. In fact," she added in sudden inspiration, "I will have my maid serve us tea, and show Rida the patternbooks she has brought from Paris and Rome."

Omat listened carefully. "A most telling point. Very well, in three days, my daughter will come here ... when?"

"Three in the afternoon?" Madelaine suggested, choosing a time that was immediately after the midday rest time. "I will have my sitting room prepared for her, very European, I promise you." She waited for Omat to agree. "Though I confess I do not know how much I can help her."

"That you will instruct her is more than enough to place me in your debt. I cannot tell you how much this means to me, Madame," Omat responded, with a lavish bow. "My daughter, too, will thank you in time."

Madelaine caught the angry note in his voice but chose to ignore it. She favored him with a pleasant smile. "I hope she will gain from our meeting," she said, and added, "Tell her I hope she will have many questions."

"Ah, she is a female, and what are females if not curious?" He paused, as if testing the waters before going on. "I am certain you would agree, Madame, since you have more than enough curiosity for ten women." His smile was wide, bright and superficial, and Madelaine returned it in kind.

When Yamut Omat was gone, Madelaine went up to her own suite of rooms, calling for Lasca as she went. "I think we may have something of a problem," she said when her maid emerged from Madelaine's dressing room, where she had been repairing the sleeve of Madelaine's second-best riding habit. "It is apparent to me that Monsieur Omat is more determined for his daughter than she is; he is prepared to beat her into submission in order to have his way. I want no part of such tutelage."

"Then why agree at all?" Lasca asked reasonably.

"Because it is not safe to anger Omat. He is one of the most powerful men here, and he is not above using his position and wealth to my disadvantage." She hesitated. "And I'm sorry for the girl. She is being made into something that is neither Egyptian or European, and she is not going to be wholly part of either ever again." She went to the armoire that contained her gowns and formal clothes. "I think it would be best if we show her these first. She's seen enough European women in these ghastly traveling ensembles that I don't think another one would catch her interest, do you?"

Lasca pursed her lips. "Who knows?" she said when she had considered it.

"She has three ball gowns I have seen," Madelaine went on as if Lasca had not spoken. "One is the most gorgeous sea-green satin with a slip of ruched Belgian lace that must have cost the earth. The waist is high, the sash very narrow, of satin gold braid. The bodice is edged in lace and overembroidered with tourmalines, about a dozen of them. It is a very pretty toilette." She stared at her own clothes. "That one. The wine-red one in velvet. I doubt I'll ever put it on in this climate, but it will serve its purpose: nothing she has seen will be like it."

"Red velvet is too old for you, Madame," said Lasca as she gave the gown in question a critical perusal.

"You think so?" Madelaine asked, her voice suddenly wistful. "Well, I will consider that, but put it out for Mademoiselle Omat, in any case."

"Certainly." She was about to close the door when a soft yowl caught her attention.

"Oisivite," Madelaine cried softly and bent to pick up the cat. "Where have you been?"

The cat did not deign to answer, but purred as Madelaine found the right place to scratch.

"He's been in the stable, or so I was told," said Lasca, trying to be severe. "He catches rats there, but the cooks are afraid of him."

"What are the cooks doing in the stable?" Madelaine asked,

shifting the cat as he tried to stabilize his place by hooking his dewclaw into her upper arm. "Stop that," she admonished him gently.

"They keep some of their supplies in the room between the garden and the stables. They say he shrieks like a demon." Lasca reached out and patted the cat once.

"He probably does," Madelaine said as she considered it. "Most cats can sound like babies being roasted over a slow fire." As Oisivite suddenly reached satiation, she let him go. "If he's too unpleasant, I suppose I'll have to think of some way to keep him out of the stable, though how to keep a cat from going where he wants to be I don't know." It was getting harder to have pets, she thought as she watched the cat sprint across the room. When she had first come into her new life, into the life Saint-Germain had given her with his blood, she had surrounded herself with cats and dogs, knowing that they would accept her as people would not: they would not notice or care if she did not eat, or have a reflection; they would not question her nighttime excursions. But their lives were so very short, and nothing she could do would change that.

"Is something the matter, Madame?" Lasca asked, breaking their silence.

"I . . . what is the expression: a goose walked over my grave." She could not pull off the laugh she wanted, but her smile worked well enough.

Lasca shook her head. "It was something else, wasn't it?" She busied herself lighting the lamps in the room. "Do you think you will be here tonight?"

"Most of the night," she said distantly.

"I meant no disrespect, Madame," said Lasca. "But I sleep lightly, and I have noticed from time to time you leave, sometimes for an hour, sometimes for longer. You are always back before sunrise." She looked directly at Madelaine. "If you have a lover, I can be discreet."

Madelaine did not know how best to answer. "I don't have a lover, not the way you mean, and I am not a loose woman. But I am a restless one, and there are times I cannot sleep." She decided not to accuse Lasca of insolence, though she might have succeeded in turning Lasca away from the matter. But then the questions would remain, she knew, and next time her maid would not bother to inquire, but would seek information on her own.

"Where do you go?" Lasca asked, her tone dubious.

"Usually, I go toward the ruins. Sometimes, late at night, you can sense things that elude you during the day. Sometimes the ghosts of the past are present when it is late, and there is little of today to interfere." She looked at her maid. "And sometimes, I leave because while I am surrounded by those ancient, ancient things, I feel less lonely."

"Ah, Madame," said Lasca with a sympathetic nod.

"There are echoes in places like Thebes. All the past sighs through them with the wind. I want to hear them." She touched the old-fashioned necklace of pearls and one pear-shaped garnet that Saint-Germain had given her over eighty years ago. "It is like remembering the voices of old friends."

This time Lasca lowered her eyes. "I am sorry, Madame. I didn't think that it was so hard for you here. I thought you . . . you were meeting Doktor Falke. Gurzin certainly thought you were."

"Doktor Falke—no," said Madelaine sadly. "He is an honorable man. Oh, he is not above long embraces, but he is not willing to do anything that would—"

"Dishonor you," Lasca finished for her. "I am relieved to hear it. I told Brother Gurzin that he was wrong, that you had no clandestine lover in Doktor Falke."

"Only dreams," said Madelaine, knowing that Lasca would misunderstand. Two nights ago she had sought out Falke, and while he slept, she had called forth all his passion, all the ardor in his soul. For him it was nothing but a dream and a little blood; for her, it was life itself.

Lasca was finished with the lamps. "Can you let him know that you wish for more?"

This was more than Madelaine was willing to confide to her servant. "Lasca, how I deal with Doktor Falke is none of your concern unless you believe that my behavior has compromised you. If you do not fear that, then do not pry." The words were sharp but she said them kindly, without any ire.

"It was not my intention to pry," Lasca said stiffly.

"I know. But it is tempting, isn't it, being so far away from the world we know?" She did not require an answer, but reached up to her glossy knot of dark hair. As she tugged the pins out, she said, "Come; bring the brushes and shampoo. I feel as if I have a bushel of sand on my scalp."

"Small wonder," said Lasca, accepting Madelaine's rebuke with little more than an inward shrug. It was not proper for her to ask such questions, and she knew it. There was a line between servant and mistress, and it was not wise to cross it, even here in this foreign place. Curious as she was, Lasca knew that the confidence of her employer had limits; going beyond them could lead to regret. She opened the door to the dressing room. "Do you want the basin brought here, or—"

"On the veranda, I think," said Madelaine, looking out through the filmy curtains. "It is a pleasant night."

"A beautiful night." She busied herself with gathering her brushes and the large ewer and basin. "A night when you might not stop at home."

"No, I might not," said Madelaine serenely, refusing to be goaded into any more harsh answers. "Come; now that I've noticed it needs washing, I must get my hair clean." She opened the french doors onto the veranda and walked out. "There are days I think the desert is very clean. But then I feel the sand chafe, and I know that it is sterile, not clean." She glanced over her shoulder. "I want the wool-fat dressing for my hair. It is getting too dry in the heat."

"Wool-fat is what peasants use," Lasca said, using that bit of information as a small rebellion.

"Wool-fat is what sensible people use," Madelaine corrected her. "And the oil of violets: I want that, too."

"We don't have much left," said Lasca as she carried the basin stand onto the veranda. Her brushes and the cake of shampoo were in it. "I'll bring the water. I must send to the kitchen for more."

"Do that," said Madelaine, her attention fixed on the distant, faded shapes of the ruins. As she looked at the temples, she reached up and unclasped her necklace, gathering the pearls into her hand, fixing it so that the pear-shaped garnet was at the center.

Only then did she look down, and her smile was blighted with an ache she could not deny. She thought of Saint-Germain, and wished that he were not far away. As much pain as she felt being near him and unable to be his lover no matter how much they loved, she felt more when they were separated. And yet she had been the one to insist they part, for she could not bring herself to look for anything more than the ephemeral satisfaction of the dreams she induced in men while he was with her. She was content to be here, but she missed him more than she thought possible, and she yearned for touching with something more than dreams.

"Madame?" Lasca said. She had returned with two ewers. "Shall I fetch a chair?"

Madelaine shut her thought away as she hid her necklace in her reticule. "Yes, if you will," she said, and went to get her peignoir.

"Is Brother Gurzin going to be back soon?" Lasca asked as she brought the dressing room chair onto the veranda.

"That is my understanding," said Madelaine as she sat down next to the basin and prepared to have her hair washed, her mind now determinedly fixed on practical matters, her longings successfully shut away.

Text of a letter from Erai Gurzin in Thebes to the Brothers of the monastery of Saint Pontius Pilate at Edfu.

To my beloved Brothers in the Name of Christ, my prayers are with you;

I have considered your counsel and I am prepared to leave if it is your final judgment that I imperil my soul here, for my sake as well as for the honor of the monastery. But I wish to say that I can see no cogent reason to think that I am at risk. How can that be? She is virtuous and I am sworn to God. It is true that the woman is unwidowed and unwed, but you have known that from the first. You were willing to accept what Saint-

Germain said of her then, but you question his recommendation now, and this troubles me.

This woman's safety has been entrusted to me by Saint-Germain, and her instruction in our language and history have been mandated to me. I have sworn to serve as Saint-Germain's deputy as we vowed to be his students so many years ago. As we profited by his instruction, so she may profit from mine. Whatever the case, you do not show yourselves the faithful friends you vowed to Saint-Germain you are. For over a decade he instructed you, and you were glad to have it so. You permitted him to teach you and to help increase your learning. You accepted his benefice without question, though he never told any of us that he would never have requests of us: he said often that the day would come when he would ask our assistance on his behalf. He has required nothing of us until now, and what he wishes is less than many anticipated. There is no sacrifice asked, no burden placed on the monastery. His request was to me, not to the entire monastery, and you were willing to abide by my decision. I have seen my way, and after two months of retreat, I am still certain that I wish to serve as mentor to this young woman. She has done me no ill and I am a very poor Christian if I suppose she will. If there are those who talk scandal, it will not be the first time that virtue has been doubted and reviled.

I have sought answers in prayer, I have searched my soul for sin, for deceit and lies, but those I found were not the lies of Madame de Montalia, who has been guileless as Saint-Germain was to all of us. She has informed me that it would be best if I did not question certain of her activities, but beyond that she has given me her word that she is chaste and honorable, and I believe her. She has done nothing at any time that could remotely cast her honor into question. These aspersions are the more outrageous because I have seen her take pains to remain beyond reproach.

It is true that she has a suitor. It would be most remarkable if an unmarried woman of her fortune and appearance did not have suitors. If it was her desire to taunt men or demand pleasures from them, she could do it easily. But she permits but one suitor, and maintains propriety at all times. She declares it is not her intention to marry, and has conducted herself properly for that determination. The suitor is an honorable man, who would not offer false coin to Madame de Montalia.

Her household staff will say what I have said if you wish to send anyone to question them, though such questioning would surely be offensive to me and to Madame de Montalia. Still, if that is what you require to be certain that the tenets of our vows are upheld, then by all means, come and question the staff, and those members of her expedition as will speak with you. I do not wish to think that our monastery brings calumny on those who live virtuously. Your complaint that she is in the world and there-fore subjected to its temptations and wiles I can only answer by saying that for Madame de Montalia, an antiquarian expedition is as out of the world as a nun in her country is likely to be.

I await your reply, and pray that the wisdom we have gained is still in your hearts and faith, and as the earth is renewed, so will your souls once again flower in the love of Christ that is the legacy of His Blood.

> *In the Name of God*
> *Erai Gurzin, monk*

The eve of the Glorious Resurrection of Our Lord, at Thebes

2

"What do you make of it?" Jean-Marc Paille asked as he held up the little statue for Madelaine to inspect. He removed his hat and wiped his handkerchief over his face. "I hate sweat in my eyes."

She turned into the light spilling through the door, holding his find with great care. "Where did you discover it?" The little ala-baster hawk with the Pharaohnic crown on its head gleamed where the sunlight struck it.

"Just here," said Jean-Marc as he shoved aside more of the sand. They were at the back of the sanctuary where two little windows let in brilliant shards of light. He moved on his knees. "Here. You see? There is some kind of a depression. It appears that something must have fitted in."

Madelaine bent nearer. "Whatever it was, it's gone now," she said sadly.

"Probably centuries and centuries ago," said Jean-Marc, his shoulders getting tense. "But under this"—he used the handle of his brush to lever up what seemed a loose bit of flooring at the wall—"there is something else, a hiding place, I think. That was in it. I couldn't get it high enough to find out if there was anything else."

"Sensible precaution to get some help, Jean-Marc, considering what happened to Claude-Michel," said Madelaine.

In spite of the heat, Jean-Marc shivered. "Scorpions, snakes, no, I can't abide those things. Don't say anything to Baundilet. He doesn't pay any attention to vermin like that, but they make me ill, the way they move."

"They will certainly make you ill if you get stung," said Madelaine quietly. "Still, we ought to see what's in there."

"I'll call Suti," said Jean-Marc, starting to get to his feet.

Madelaine put her hand on his shoulder before he could rise. "No. No. For the moment, let's see what we can discover for ourselves. Let this be our find, a thing we can claim as ours."

Jean-Marc hesitated. "As ours?"

Madelaine chuckled. "Not as booty, Jean-Marc. I did not mean we should keep these things. I only meant that if we call the diggers now, it is the find of the entire expedition, which is to say Professor Alain Baundilet's; this way, we can secure some recognition for it." She watched him as he considered what she said. "I can understand why you might want to enhance your own reputation as well as his." She said it deliberately, hoping to gain a little time for both of them.

"Well," said Jean-Marc at last, "since this might be a single artifact, and it could be there is nothing in the hole but . . . vermin, then we might as well determine it for ourselves first, so that we won't raise hopes for no reason." He dropped back on his knees. "The stone is heavy."

"I'm no weakling," said Madelaine, wondering how much of her tremendous vampire strength she could use without causing Jean-Marc to question her. "Let me get my prybar and perhaps together we can raise the stone." She went to her satchel and took out the short steel bar with the spatulated tip. "If I can get this under one side, and you have your brush handle under the other, then we can try to get it up." She held out one easel wedge. "We can use this for a shim."

It was very hot in the little stone chamber, and the air was close. Overhead the heavens of ancient Egypt paraded along the ceiling. As Madelaine knelt, she grasped the prybar, wondering if Jean-Marc would notice that she was not sweating. With care she traced the edge of the stone, then found an irregularity in the stone beside it that allowed her purchase to move it. "I think this will do it," she told Jean-Marc as she tested the prybar.

"I'm ready," said Jean-Marc. He took a firm grip. "In three?"

"Fine," said Madelaine, all her attention directed at the flooring stone.

"One," said Jean-Marc, a little breathlessly. "Two. *Three*." He forced his brush downward and heard the ominous sound of cracking wood. But at the same time he felt the stone move.

"The shim!" Madelaine cried out, as if she were using all her strength to press the prybar.

Nodding automatically, Jean-Marc reached out for the wedge, hoping that his brush handle would hold long enough for him to get the wedge into place. He grunted with effort.

As his brush handle broke, the shim slid into place.

"Got it," said Madelaine, easing off the prybar. "That's the beginning."

Jean-Marc stared at the displaced stone, his eyes wide with equal parts of fascination and fear. "Is anything coming out?"

She held up the trowel she had been using to clear away the last of the sand. "If there is, I'm armed."

"Don't make light of it," protested Jean-Marc. "Mère Marie, what if a cobra should come out?"

"One won't," said Madelaine, who had already sensed that nothing more dangerous than beetles lurked in the concealed place. She watched Jean-Marc, seeing how pale he was. "Is something the matter?" she asked suddenly.

His shrug both denied trouble and feigned indifference to it. "Nothing having to do with our work." His tone said he did not want to discuss it.

"But it worries you, whatever it is," Madelaine persisted, unwilling to ignore his distress. She sank back on her heels. "I will need a few minutes before I try to move the stone again," she said, though it was a lie.

"Bien sûr."

"And in that time, you might—" she began, and it was sufficient.

"A small thing, Madame." He stared at her. "Something I do not wish to discuss." It was as blunt as he could be with a woman.

Madelaine gave him a swift smile. "I am an antiquarian, Jean-Marc, and we are both a very long way from our native earth. We must depend on one another, and therefore, I cannot pretend unconcern, for your well-being may be the key to mine." She went and fetched her satchel. "Tell me what is bothering you while I try to find something to take the place of your brush. Two more attempts and we should have that stone up."

While she rummaged in her satchel, Jean-Marc leaned back against the wall, his mouth set in petulant lines. "I am concerned for my fiancée. Her father will not recognize our betrothal, you see, and he is attempting, I think, to find ways to sway her. She tells me this has not happened, but now that she is in Paris with her Aunt, I cannot help but worry."

"Why is that?" Madelaine asked, remembering her own first days in Paris with her Aunt Claudia. Aunt Claudia, who had been so much her friend, who had welcomed her into her house like a daughter, who had introduced her to Saint-Germain at that fête in October of 1743; Aunt Claudia, who had cared for her until she died, and who had died herself of an inflammation of the lungs fourteen years later without knowing that Madelaine survived that first death. Madelaine's unexpected reverie had such a hold on her that she did not hear the beginning of Jean-Marc's explanation of his unhappy engagement.

"—and even with her Cousin Georges' help, we haven't been

able to correspond easily. Her father does not allow her to have letters from me, nor to send them, and that is repugnant to me, for I dislike anything that is not honorable." He wiped his forehead again. "So I must do what I may to present myself as an acceptable son-in-law before he can develop a scheme to force her to marry another. He has already compelled his younger daughter Solange to marry a widower with children, and she is hardly more than a child herself."

"But Cousin Georges helps you?" Madelaine asked. "Why is that?"

"He sees the unfairness of it all. He and Honorine have always been great friends, and he is not one to let a lack of fortune stand between those who truly love." He picked up a pebble and shied it across the little room. "I don't know how we could have managed without him."

"Truly?" Madelaine said, keeping her voice neutral.

"Oh, yes." He gave a short, hard sigh. "It's been over two years since I've seen her. In her letters she says her affections are unchanged, but with the joys of Paris around her, and the flattery of distinguished men, how long can she remain true to our private vows, especially since her father is determined that we will not marry."

"And you are hoping that if you succeed here in Egypt, you will be able to change his mind?" Madelaine asked.

"Yes. I want to show him that he was wrong in assuming that a man who makes his way in the world exploring ruins is not as worthy as a fellow with enough money to have a manufactory in Arles." His expression was so sullen that he looked more like an angry child than an adult. "Her father is a rich man who wishes to advance himself. He calls himself a son of the Revolution, which means he learned slogans to gain favor."

"France has her full share of those," said Madelaine with more harshness than she intended.

Jean-Marc looked at her sharply. "You're an aristo," he said, making it an excuse and an accusation at once.

"My family certainly has such claims," said Madelaine carefully. She pulled a smaller prybar from her satchel. "Here. This should do better than your brush." She held it out to Jean-Marc. "I am sorry that your fiancée should be in so awkward a position. It is very difficult when families oppose a match."

"It is," agreed Jean-Marc, his face hard. He took the prybar and put it near the shim. "Do you think you can try again?"

"Certainly," said Madelaine, knowing that if she were alone she could easily lift the stone with her hands. "I may be an aristo, Jean-Marc, but I know something about working with my hands."

He gave no sign that he heard her remark. "I've got this into position," he said.

"I'm ready. Shall we press on three again?"

This time the stone moved more easily, and there was almost enough room to put a hand into the space. A second wedge was in place.

"If there is anything important in there," said Jean-Marc as he leaned back, panting a little, "it could be my fortune."

Madelaine turned to him. "What do you mean?"

He flushed. "I mean that it would give me the reputation I need to establish myself well. I want to be an endowed Fellow at a good university, not just a lecturer on antiquities who may or may not find employment at any given time. I want to have expeditions of my own, and—" He broke off guiltily. "I do not mean to speak against Professor Baundilet."

"Of course not," said Madelaine.

"But I have a future to consider. Professor Baundilet is already established, and has no reason for anxiety about where he will teach, or who will sponsor another expedition. And there are the other arrangements, as well, in case he should prefer not to teach again at all." He rubbed his forearm. "That block is very heavy."

"Yes, it is," Madelaine agreed, wondering what other arrangements Jean-Marc meant, and what those arrangements could do to their discovery. For the discovery was tantalizing to her. Whatever lay in that concealed place, though it was nothing more than a few figures in stone, might well prove the most respectable find of the entire expedition. She held her excitement in check, though her violet eyes glowed.

"Do you think we could call this an important discovery?" Jean-Marc asked, still rubbing his arm.

"We haven't made it yet," Madelaine reminded him, amused

that he was more anxious than she was. "There is no point in anticipating."

"Well, we need one more try, don't we?" He coughed once, delicately. "I don't wish to ask it of you. I could send for one of the others, not the diggers, but perhaps Professor Enjeu?"

"I can manage," said Madelaine. "Unless you want to bring others into the discovery?" It was a ploy.

"Oh. I see." He rubbed his hands together. "All right. Yes. I am sure you're right. This ought to be just between us, oughtn't it? There's no reason to bring in the others." He wiped his hands against his shirt, saying, "I ought not to do this. Look away, if you wish."

"It doesn't bother me," said Madelaine. "Not after two years in this infernal heat." She touched her prybar. "Well?"

Once more Jean-Marc counted to three, and this time the stone shifted several inches. As he let go of his prybar, his arms were trembling, but not entirely from exertion. "It's open."

"Open enough for our purposes," said Madelaine. "We ought to make a sketch of this, for the records."

"Be damned to the records," said Jean-Marc. "I want to see what is in there. We can sketch it later, if we must." He moved nearer to the revealed compartment. "How large is it?"

"Not terribly large, I should think," said Madelaine bending over the opening.

"Empty?" Jean-Marc asked, suddenly quite breathless.

Madelaine peered, then turned to him, an odd smile on her lovely mouth. "No." Very carefully she reached in, her fingers moving as lightly as dust motes among the unknown treasures. She gathered several of the smaller items into her hand and brought them out, opening her hand very slowly where the shaft of light from the window would illume what she held.

"Jésu et Marie!" whispered Jean-Marc.

There were half a dozen faience amulets in her hand, none of them longer than her fingers. The largest was a winged beetle, the smallest a tubular case of gold inscribed with minute hieroglyphics. "There is more," said Madelaine in a voice she hardly recognized as her own.

"What are these?" Jean-Marc picked up a small green figure of a jackal-headed mummy. "Whose was this?" He turned it over in his fingers. "Which god? Osiris?"

"Anubis," Madelaine corrected him. "The jackal's head is Anubis." She looked at the others: a squatting dwarf sticking out his tongue; a bull with elaborate designs inscribed on his sides and back, and with a disk between his horns; and a tiny figure of a standing ibis holding a scale.

One by one Jean-Marc took them and laid them out on the floor in the slice of sunlight. "Look at them," he breathed. "What have we found. What have we found." There was so much excitement in his voice that although he was whispering, his tone was more intense than shouting.

"Let me bring out the rest," said Madelaine, forcing herself to look away from what she had found. Once again she slid her hand into the hole and felt carefully for what was there. "There is more."

This time she brought out a statue as long as her hand; the figure was of a man with the head of a crocodile wearing a crown of stylized feathers. It was carved from a hard, rosy stone, and when she set it down with the rest, Jean-Marc swallowed hard.

By the time the compartment was empty, Madelaine had added four more figures—a seated woman with the head of a lion; a bronze figure of a cat; a painted wooden figure of a cross-legged scribe with his writing implements at the ready; and gold tablet about the size of Madelaine's palm that looked to be some kind of temple or sanctuary plan, surmounted by a pair of upraised arms.

Madelaine held this last to the light. "Is it too much to hope that the plan is for this temple?" she asked of the walls.

"It's gold," said Jean-Marc.

"So is the inscribed tube," said Madelaine, trying to discourage his too-obvious greed. "It isn't the materials that give these value; the things themselves are valuable, if they were made of nothing more than mud." She turned the tablet in the light. "According to this, there ought to be another sanctuary just outside the walls in that direction." She pointed off to her left. "We haven't cleared that yet."

"Assuming the ground plan is for this temple and you are reading the scheme correctly." Jean-Marc picked up the little ibis amulet. "What do you suppose this was for?"

"Someone probably wore it," said Madelaine. "See? There's that little ring on it, and you could thread a chain or a thong through it." She put the tablet with the rest. "Jean-Marc," she said, "I believe we have solved your problem with your future father-in-law."

Jean-Marc looked up sharply. "What do you mean?"

"I mean that once we have made sketches of these and prepared our reports, your reputation will be made. I will have Brother Gurzin carry the reports and the artifacts down-river for us, so that there can be no question of who has made the discovery, nor who prepared the material." She reached for her satchel again. "I have small paper sacks. They will protect these finds until we can finish our monograph on them."

"What?" Jean-Marc looked up, his expression dismayed. "What are you talking about."

Madelaine regarded him patiently. "Do you want credit for this discovery? Are you willing to share it with me?"

"Yes," said Jean-Marc uncertainly.

"And you are aware that Professor Baundilet is not above selling small antiquities like these to finance this expedition and to cultivate those who can do him favors?" She saw the wariness come back into his face.

"I have heard something of this," said Jean-Marc carefully.

"And you know that if Professor Baundilet sends these on to the university for their collections, he will award credit for the discovery to the Baundilet expedition—that is to say, to himself." She waited a moment while Jean-Marc considered this. "Therefore, why not take the time to protect your own interest, since you say it is necessary for you to do this if you are to marry honorably."

Jean-Marc scowled as his gaze rested on the little figures. He picked up the ibis, holding it by the ring. "Think of this around the neck of some graceful Egyptian girl, all in white, her hair smelling of fine oil and her eyes outlined in kohl. Or did girls wear these as necklaces? Perhaps it was fixed to a bracelet or a belt." He fingered the wings. "What god does this represent?"

"It might just be a bird," said Madelaine as she resolved to ask Saint-Germain in her next letter what the significance of the ibis was. "They made trinkets, too. And toys, I wouldn't wonder."

He looked up at her in patent disbelief. "Toys?"

"Of course," said Madelaine. "They had children, so they must have had toys." Her look grew more acute. "Well, what are you going to do—throw in your lot with me, or hope that Baundilet will let you profit from this discovery? We haven't much time if I'm to get these to my villa without comment."

Jean-Marc caught his lower lip between his teeth. "Very well," he said after a moment. "I will take half and you will take half. That's fair. I will let Professor Baundilet know what I have found, but not what you have. If he does not send these to the university or takes the credit for himself, you will still have your antiquities to show, and if you will permit me to share your—"

"You found the hiding place, of course you will share," said Madelaine, her chin rising a bit. "I will give you my word on it in writing if you would like."

"No!" said Jean-Marc, suddenly worried. "Nothing in writing. It is too dangerous. If anyone learned of it, it would make it seem that we did not trust Professor Baundilet, and if he ever learned of our agreement and the reason for it, such knowledge would not go well for him."

"You are prepared to protect him?" she inquired.

"He brought me here. He has given me this chance, and I could not repay him so shabbily." Once more he touched the little figures.

Madelaine made a gesture of acceptance and looked down at the figures. "All right, I agree: which do you want?"

Now that he had the choice, Jean-Marc hesitated. "I have it in mind to select those I would want to show to my fiancée. I would never be able to do that, except visiting the university, but I am imagining which of these would delight her the most. Those are the ones I will choose." He claimed the ibis, the tubular gold case, the winged beetle, the seated woman with the lion's head, and the bull with the disk between his horns. The squatting dwarf, the tablet, the figure of Anubis, the bronze cat, and the feather-crowned crocodile-headed man he left to Madelaine. "There." His expression was dubious. "That is reasonable."

Madelaine said nothing in disagreement. "I would appreciate it if you would write up a description of what you found, so that I can add it to the whole. Do sketches, too, if you're able. I want to have as complete a record as I can for our monograph. I can find some reason—perhaps terms of sponsorship—why we divided the discovery. I will not make it appear to be your decision, but my own, so that if Baundilet later questions what you did, you may say it was at my insistence."

"That's hardly necessary—" Jean-Marc could not help blustering as he thought of what Baundilet might say.

"Yes, it is. We wouldn't be dividing these figures if it weren't," said Madelaine. She picked up the ibis again. "That's a beautiful piece of workmanship. They all are, but this is . . . more whole, wouldn't you agree?"

"How do you mean 'whole'?" Jean-Marc asked as he began very carefully to gather up the figures, placing them in his handkerchief, taking care to wrap each one so that it would not directly rub against the others.

She gave a small shake to her head. "The artist who made it had only one thought in his head: this ibis. You can . . . see it." Her face lightened. "It doesn't matter, Jean-Marc. The find is wonderful whether the figures are great art or poor craft. Their existence is what matters." She reached into her satchel for soft papers to wrap her pieces.

Jean-Marc gathered up his handkerchief, holding it as if there were something alive within it. "It is a wonderful find, yes. You're very generous, Madame. I . . . I am surprised."

Madelaine paused in wrapping the crocodile-headed man. "Surprised? You? Why?"

"I never supposed you would . . ." He trailed off in confusion. "You are wealthy and young and pretty. Why should you bother to consider me when there is no reason?"

Madelaine went on with her work. "What a paltry excuse for a woman you must think I am, Jean-Marc," she said in a tone that was light and brittle. "I'm astonished that you are willing to take my word on anything, that being the case."

"I've offended you," he said contritely. "I had not intended—"

"All the worse," said Madelaine in exasperation. "You are not aware that your doubts might be demeaning or—" She made herself stop. "You have my word that I will keep our pact, and as for the rest, we will declare it unsaid; if you bring up the subject again, that will be another matter entirely."

"You're most . . . gracious, Madame. Most gracious." He put his laden handkerchief into the most capacious pocket of his jacket. "You will have the sketches by the end of the week," he promised as a peace offering.

"I look forward to receiving them," said Madelaine, her manner polite but unforthcoming.

"Yes," said Jean-Marc as he made his way to the door, still trying to find some way to undo the damage. "Yes. Glad to be of service, Madame." Then he was gone and Madelaine was facing the glare of sun in the doorway.

As she finished putting her share of their unlikely spoils into her satchel, she had a single apprehensive frisson, and then it was gone. "He is not one to bring in others," she said aloud, as if hearing the words would make them more convincing. She waited for a short while, uncertain why she was waiting; then left the shelter of the sanctuary for the unshielded onslaught of the sun.

Text of a letter from Professor Alain Baundilet to Yamut Omat, both at Thebes.

My dear Omat;

I have arranged with my university for another payment to be made to Magistrate Numair, at double the amount of the previous donation, and that ought to settle the matter for a time. I do not know how we are to resolve our differences with the Magistrate; I am depending on you to learn how this can be done in such a way that there is no embarrassment for any-

*one, yourself included. It is hardly fitting that you should have
to bear any discomfort for the efforts you extend on our behalf.*

*The small jar I am sending with this was found at the foot
of one of those ram's-headed sphynxes being uncovered. The
surface is damaged, but it appears to be painted in a pattern
of papyrus stalks, and it has the look of something quite old.
Since I cannot place a time on it, there is no reason to include
it with the discoveries of my expedition. It would give me great
pleasure if you would be willing to accept it as a token of our
friendship.*

*Yes, I have thought over everything we discussed, and I cannot
contradict you: your observations about Madame de Montalia
are well-taken. I agree that she is a most attractive young
woman, and I share your bafflement that she is here at all. This
is hardly the place one would think she would like to be, and
I begin to share your suspicion that there is a mystery about
her. I can understand why you have not wanted to discuss her
situation, for it is a curious one; at the same time I must confess
that I know relatively little about her but that she is willing to
pay handsomely for the opportunity of being part of this expedition and thus far has conducted herself in a manner almost
above reproach. I must confess I was certain she would be gone
by now. When she remained through the Inundation our first
year in this site, I was startled. I would be less than candid if I
did not tell you that you are correct: I find her a most disturbing
woman. She has so much about her to attract a sensible man,
yet being married myself, she has made it plain to me that I
can hold no hope she will forget my wife even if I will. It is
galling to know she hankers after that damned German and
will give no thought to me. She is more attentive to that plump
English lordling who all but drools at the sight of her.*

*You see how great her capacity is to upset me, and this is not
to the good. I must arrange for some alteration in my dealings
with her so that there need be no trouble between Madame de
Montalia and myself. Perhaps I ought to assign Guibert to keep
covert watch on her. He seems enough the native to be invisible,
and I can then know more of her. It might be best if he simply
spoke to her servants: they know everything. Her intentions seem*

clear enough and I suppose it is not unreasonable of her to decide to set her sights on a man who can give her an honorable establishment, which the German is in a position to do. And in regard to the other—Heaven knows that the Englishman is harmless, what I have heard other English call "fat as a flawn," and while he has position, I cannot think there is anything in him other than his childish adoration to claim her attention. She is sure to tire of him. It is the physician who is the greater barrier to my purpose, yet I can think of nothing that would serve to dissuade her from her attachment. Perhaps I should become a Moslem like you, and allow myself another wife; for I fear she will not accept a less regular contract.

I have recently had word from Paille that he has come upon a few small figures that he wishes to show me. He will not tell me where he found them, saying that he has all there are to be found in that place; he implied that he found them in an area he was not allowed to explore. He has offered to show me three of the pieces, the ones that are the best, he assures me. I have already told him that I expect to be given everything he finds. I suspect he may save out a piece for himself to gain a little with the university, which I shall not begrudge him.

Your gratitude for the pieces I have sent to you is unnecessary: I am the one who ought to express gratitude, for without your intervention with the authorities, I fear I would not have made the discoveries in which you share. I am wholly convinced you are entitled to equal shares with me, and I hope you will not forbid me to continue with the arrangements which have become so much a part of my life here in Thebes. You have aided me without recompense; this is my way of expressing appreciation.

In that regard, let me say that I would welcome the entertainment you have proposed for the start of the Inundation. Those weeks have proved to be difficult for my expedition, and I think that such a diversion as the three days you have outlined would be more than acceptable to all of us. Certainly we would be pleased to see the English antiquarians and any other Europeans of note who are here when the river starts to rise.

In answer to your questions regarding Mademoiselle Omat,

let me assure you that your daughter has made great progress. The more she applies herself to the task, the greater her success will be. As she is now, I am sure you could introduce her in any salon in Paris and not see her snubbed. In that regard, Madame de Montalia has proven to be an excellent teacher. Your daughter has profited by her instruction. You can be at ease on that head.

Will you do me the honor of visiting me the day after to-morrow between mid-afternoon and sunset? I will be at my house, not at the expedition site, where we will be able to speak in complete confidence and without interruption. You and I can settle our plans as well as discuss the question of Magistrate Numair and his insistence on higher payments.

With my true affection and continuing regard,

Most sincerely,
Professor Alain Hugues Baundilet

May 16th, 1827, at Thebes

3

His smock was bloody from neck to hem, and the sleeves, rolled up above the elbows, were also red with blood. His hands looked like those of an iron statue gone to rust. He leaned back against the wall in the lengthening shadow, his face drained of expression, his eyes dull; he paid no heed to the others who sought his help, nor to the gentle spread of night.

"Herr Doktor," said Jantje when she found him a little later.

"What?" he asked, his voice so remote that he might have been a mile away.

"I was concerned." She did not appear troubled; her manner was as pragmatically cordial as it always was. "You left your infirmary so quickly."

"The fellow died," said Falke, very flat.

"He was badly hurt," said Jantje, not allowing herself to be drawn into his state of mind. "No one could have saved him."

"With proper facilities, I might have," he protested, though he knew it was foolish.

"His ribs were broken and his lungs were punctured," said Jantje calmly. "Saving him would not have been a kindness, not if he would have been an invalid. This is not a place where invalids thrive." She waited a moment. "Madame de Montalia is here," she said in the same tone.

Falke turned his head away.

"She asked to see you," Jantje persisted. "I have told her I would find you."

"I can't see her. Not this way." It was too dark to make out the color of the stains on his clothes and hands, but he could not bring himself to look at them in any case.

"Shall I tell her so?" Jantje asked.

"Yes." He moved away from her, toward a niche in the wall where there was enough shelter to hide.

When Jantje reported this to Madelaine a few minutes later, she added, "The death of that digger was hard for him to bear. He has lost fourteen of his patients in the last five days. This was the hardest." She nodded toward the door to the infirmary. "Now that they know there is help to be had here, more and more of them come; Doktor Falke needed more help than he had a year ago; now it is twice as demanding and he is still working alone with just myself and Erlinda." She straightened herself. "Not that I wish to complain, for that was not my intent."

"You have good reason for complaint," said Madelaine, her eyes hardening. "How is it that there have been no others come to join him?"

Jantje pressed her hands together. "There were supposed to have been two more physicians and three nurses. It was agreed when we came that we would have these to assist us in the next year. But it is one thing to say you will come to a place like this and another thing to do it. The others read what Doktor Falke says of the diseases he treats, and the suffering he sees, and they cannot summon the courage to follow his example. A few weeks ago a letter came from one who said that his family had made him prom-

ise to remain in Tübingen because of the danger of infection."
She flung up her hands. "What are we to do, if they are cowards?"

"And the other physician?" prompted Madelaine. "And the
nurses?"

"We have heard nothing, and no one is here." She shook her
head impatiently. "We have tried to help them. We have done
everything we know to do, but it is not enough. It will never be
enough."

Was this how Saint-Germain had felt all those centuries he
served out of the House of Life? Madelaine wondered. She touched
the nurse's wrist. "Find one of your servants to relieve you and
see you have a meal and the chance to lie down. You're as exhausted as he is."

"But there isn't time." Jantje took a step away from her.

"There never will be. You will have to claim it for yourself,"
Madelaine told her, then added, "I'm going to find Falke."

"In the old garden. By the wall," said Jantje, her manner distracted. "If you wish someone to rest, let it be him. He is worn
to the bone, poor man."

"Perhaps he might be willing to talk a walk with me," Madelaine
said. "Do you think it would help?"

Jantje cocked her head. "Better than hiding in the garden. He
needs to have more time to himself." She looked narrowly at
Madelaine. "He is a very good man, Madame."

"Yes," Madelaine said. "And I am concerned about him. I am
concerned about all of you."

"Would that others with more cause would show themselves
half so willing as you do, Madame," said Jantje, as if satisfied by
what Madelaine had told her. "I know you will not trouble him,
Madame."

"Thank you," she said, then added, "See that you care for yourself as well as those who seek your help. Otherwise no one will
benefit."

"When I have finished with the two children," Jantje said with
some purpose. "I'll have a little time then." She hurried away from
Madelaine toward the far end of the infirmary, arranging her cap
as she went.

As Madelaine stepped into the garden, she located Falke at once; her dark vision was not hampered by night and shadows, but, more, she felt the blood drying on him, breathing it on the jasmine-laden air. Slowly she made her way toward him, all the while wishing she had the temerity to run to him, sure that his arms would open to her.

"Who's there?" he demanded from where he sat, his back to her.

"Madelaine," she answered, stopping.

"Oh, God," he whispered, his misery so profound that against all his intentions he began to weep.

She came up behind him and rested her arms on his shoulders, her hands lying on the bloodstains on his smock. "Falke."

His words were uneven, muffled. "Go away. Go away."

"No."

He swore, softly and vehemently.

"You can't save them all," she said quietly after a short while, when she was certain he was listening. "It isn't possible." She smoothed her hand over his hair. "No one can save them all."

"They come to me. They rely on me." He tried—without success—to move away from her. "I have an obligation to them."

"You've accepted an obligation," she said with care. "They did not force it on you, and they would not blame you if you did not help them forever." This time she spoke more loudly. Then she dropped onto the bench, facing him. "Listen to me, Falke. You are not the Angel of Mercy. No one is."

He looked at her, his blue eyes luminous with despair. "I am a physician. I have taken an oath to heal."

"And you have healed many, and at terrible risk to yourself," she said. Now that she could see the extent of the blood on him, she found it hard to concentrate. So much blood, she thought, dazed by it. And so useless.

Falke saw the turmoil in her face and drew back. "I didn't intend you to see this," he said, folding his arms over the front of his smock.

"If there was this much blood," Madelaine heard herself say with a composure that she did not feel, "then nothing you could have done would have kept him alive. The poor man; his veins must be completely empty."

"Almost," said Falke with difficulty. "It was the ribs. They were in the lungs. One of them . . . I wasn't aware until I tried to relieve the pressure. It . . . the rib . . . was against a large blood vessel. I didn't know . . ." He pressed his hand to his mouth. "I didn't know—I swear before God!—that the rib had punctured the vessel. I would never have removed it, had I known that."

"But you did," Madelaine said, making it sound more of a question than a statement. "You moved it and then could not stop the bleeding?"

"No: no. There was blood everywhere. If he hadn't bled so much already, there would have been blood on the ceiling. As it was . . ." He looked down at his smock again and had to swallow hard to keep from vomiting.

"Falke," Madelaine said, putting her arms around him, unmindful of the gore on him.

"Your dress . . ."

"The blood is almost dry," she said kindly. "Even if it weren't, it would mean nothing." Gently she wiped his face with her fingers, taking care to remove the smudges. "Falke," she said before she kissed him.

For once he did not hesitate. He locked his arms around her as if he were drowning; his mouth was insistent. Only when he released her did Madelaine move against him. "I should not have done that." He started to move back and was amazed when he realized she would not let go of him.

"Why not?" she asked, kissing his temple where his smile lines were. If only he would smile more often, she thought. "I've wanted you this way for over a year."

He stared at her in revulsion. "This way?" he repeated, aghast.

"Not bloody and exhausted, no," she said, a little amusement in the sound of her words. "And not despondent either, or filled with remorse," she added. "But I have hoped that you desired me as I desire you. I have wanted you to show me your passion as well as your affection."

"How do you mean?" He regarded her in fascination that was not entirely proper. Never before had he permitted himself to think of her as he did now, except in his dreams. He chided himself for taking advantage of friendship, for dishonoring virtue by what he felt now, but the rebuke was nothing compared to the need for her that filled him. How could he tolerate such craving when it was so reprehensible? He pulled her closer. "How, Madelaine?"

She could not tell him the whole of it, she knew: not now. In time, perhaps, if there was need, she would explain her nature and his risks. "I mean," she told him, "that when I say I love you, it is not enough. When you kiss me, it is not enough."

"Madame—"

"Madelaine," she corrected. "I want to touch you. I want you touching me, flesh and spirit." She kissed him, and this time her lips were open to his. She felt his urgency increase as their kiss deepened.

"It's ... I can't offer you ... You are ..." He looked down at her face as he made a last, desperate, inconclusive attempt to get away from her.

"I don't want your name or your fortune, Falke. I want you." She let him have time to consider this. "I am not a loose woman or a fallen one. I have no other man I desire." It was not quite the truth, but Saint-Germain was not accessible to her, and would not have been even if she had been in his embrace and not Falke's.

"A woman of your position," he started, faltering. "You have ... your reputation."

"Who will you tell?" Madelaine asked softly, kissing the corner of his mouth, the lobe of his ear, the place where his neck and jaw met.

He shook his head once in strong denial. "I will tell no one." It would be as much shame for him as for her—greater shame if he should boast of it. "No one, Madelaine."

"Nor will I," she said, and took his hand in hers, bringing it to her lips to be kissed before guiding his fingers to the corsage of her dress.

"My hands are—"

"I don't care," she said softly. "I wouldn't care if they were muddy or burned or any of the rest of it. They are your hands." Her eyes were on his, violet on blue. Then she said, "On the other side of the western wall there is an old building. Gurzin tells me it used to be a place for pilgrims. Whatever it was, it is vacant now and no one goes there. We would not be disturbed."

Falke nodded once, his hand sliding so that his fingers curved around her breast. "A pilgrims' station. It may be sacred ground. We can't go there if we are . . ." He could not make himself speak the words.

"If we are to be lovers, what better place than a shrine? Besides," she went on when she realized how much the notion distressed him, "I am certain it has been many, many years since pilgrims used it." She rose, signaling him to rise with her. "I have wanted this for so long."

Once on his feet he gathered her into his arms. "It isn't fitting for you to say this to me. I have no right to hear it." All his resolution faded as he watched her in the first pale light of the moon. He had no words for the emotion that seized him, that rocked him as much as an avalanche would, though he sensed lust and desire and tenderness in it. He strove for some objectivity and failed. "If you will have me," he said at last, unable to release her.

"Oh, yes," she said, one hand closing over his. "There's a gate near the new stable, isn't there?" she asked, knowing the answer already. "No one uses it." She could not make herself look at him, in case she saw something in his eyes that would not accept her.

He put his arm around her shoulder so he would not have to let go of her as they walked. Once he bent and kissed her forehead, admitting, "I'm . . . apprehensive."

She smiled a little. "So am I," she told him.

He frowned. "No, not that way. Not yet." He stopped her and looked down at her, thinking how beautiful she was, how well and sweetly she fit within the curve of his arm. The pressure of her body made him ache with longing. "It's later that bothers me. If you say later that I forced you . . ."

"I won't say that," she promised him. Her eyes softened and a hint of a smile curved her mouth. "You didn't force me. If anything, I have . . . forced you."

"Not forced, never forced," he said, resuming their progress toward the door, loving the way her hip moved against him.

"Persuaded," she corrected, and though she made light of it, that amusement concealed her fear that he would not want the whole of her, that he would have reservations when he knew her nature.

"What is it?" They were at the door, and he had reached for the heavy iron latch when he sensed her hesitation. He drew his hand back. "What's wrong? Why do you hold back now?"

She looked up at him, wanting to keep no secret from him, but aware that for a time she must. "What if I am not what you seek?" she said seriously.

"Impossible." He had kissed her many times before, but always with caution, knowing that they could exchange only kisses and the kisses must end. Tonight he did not curb his passion, wanting her to have some notion of the burgeoning desire beyond his devotion to her.

The most difficult thing for Madelaine was not appearing too light-hearted, for Falke would not believe that her light-heartedness was born of the joy he gave her; he would think her labile, she was convinced of that. Perhaps later he would understand. Perhaps they would laugh together. Perhaps there would be a time when what she was mattered to neither of them. And yet she felt a reserve in herself, a place in her soul that was filled with loneliness and Saint-Germain; she wanted no other to come there. Saint-Germain had told her she could not lose him now or ever, but she was not convinced of this, and she was terrified that in learning to love Falke more she would have to love Saint-Germain less: that was intolerable, no matter how Falke moved her, no matter what he evoked in her, no matter how great her need.

The orchard between the wall and the abandoned pilgrims' hostel was small; the trees offered concealment, the moonlight leaving a dappled pattern under the trees, a place to stop for kisses and tentative caresses.

At the door of the deserted building, Falke stopped short, trying to look at the hostel as he would look at any other deserted place. "Are you sure it's empty?"

"No beggars sleep here, so Brother Gurzin informs me. The worst we might encounter is rats." She hoped this would not be enough to discourage him. "If there are other vermin, I am not aware of them."

At this practical observation, his stance altered. "You truly are prepared to bed me, aren't you?" He spoke as if he had wakened from sleep.

"Yes," said Madelaine.

He considered her response as if there had been much more to it than a single word, which there was. "There are risks," he said, trying to discover how much this woman knew about the dangers of what she was doing.

"I know," she said, aware that they were referring to different hazards.

He learned her face with the tips of his fingers, his touch lighter than a petal dropping. "I . . ." Whatever he was going to say was suddenly replaced with his captivating smile, the deep lines around his eyes and down his cheeks sharpened by moon-shadows. His smile widened.

It was what Madelaine had waited for, the sign she had been searching for without knowing it, and it reached to that closed place she had wanted to hold inviolate, moving the wards of the lock on her heart so that she was no longer protected by her barrier of memories. She went into his arms with a freedom she had not known she sought, and it ignited her soul. Her violet eyes were alight with ardor.

Her beauty, her esurience dazzled him. Suddenly he could not breathe deeply enough; he was drowning in his hunger for her, and resurrecting his soul. All his life Falke had been warned about the caprice and unsteady temperament of women, how they were creatures of extremes, given to irrational appetites and ungovernable obsessions that required the careful guidance of a man if women were not to be the victims of their own tempestuous emotions. Until he flung open the door to the abandoned pilgrims' station, he still believed some part of it. He had always been at pains to be sure he could retain control where it was needed, for he must not leave any woman at the mercy of her impulses. But once inside the ancient structure, his certainty fled and was replaced by a wildness he thought he could not possess. He held out his hands and grinned happily as Madelaine dropped her hands into them. "This is your last opportunity to walk away."

She chuckled. "Oh, Falke. If I were going to walk away, I would have done it long since," she pointed out, pleased as he led her inside. "There are trundle beds on the far side of this room. Not very trustworthy, I'm afraid. There are four rolled mattresses against the wall. You may choose which you think would be most ... suitable."

He glared at her in mock annoyance. "You make it sound as if I were buying poultry."

"Not that," she said, chuckling again. "Tell me which you want. I'll help you get ready."

"We'd better use the mattresses," he said, trying to feel his way toward them. "Two mattresses side by side ought to permit us ..." His face was reddening.

"They surely should," said Madelaine, starting toward the mattresses rolled and standing against the wall. She was relieved now that she had ordered a smoke pot set off in this ancient hostel, for she was no longer afraid of what might be found when the mattresses were unrolled. As she moved one of the mattresses toward the center of the room, she said, "If tonight goes well, we will be prepared. I hope there will be other times."

"Please," Falke protested. "No, do not mention such things, Madame, for they are disgraceful for such as—"

Madelaine dropped the first of two mattresses to the floor. "I am not ashamed of loving you, Falke. I am not ashamed to be your lover. I don't suppose that will change unless you conduct yourself as if I am chattel or a whore." Or something worse, she added to herself: something undead. The second mattress landed beside the first. "Help me to cut the thongs holding these closed, wont' you?"

Distracted, he nonetheless lifted his smock and took a penknife from his waistcoat pocket. "Is this serviceable?"

"Try it," she suggested, thinking that some of the fervor she felt was fading in the face of all these mundane requirements. "And kiss me. I want you to kiss me."

Falke paused in severing the thongs holding the mattresses rolled. He rocked back on his heels. "Kiss you?"

"I am not a ewe, to be tupped by a ram. I am a woman, and I seek loving caresses and gentle words as well as the rest of it. I want something more of you than a little time and sweat. If this is to be anything more than a diversion, I will seek your soul." The words were deliberately chosen to shock him. She laced her fingers behind his neck and raised herself in order to press her lips to his. "Did you think this was nothing more than a brief amusement?"

"I . . . no." The incredulity faded from his eyes to be replaced by something more enduring and frenzied. He slashed the thongs on the mattresses with swift, fierce strokes, and as the mattresses flopped open, he flung his penknife away and all but dragged Madelaine into his arms.

Clumsily, joyously, they tugged and pulled their clothes off one another, tossing them aside so that they could discover and marvel over the treasures that lay beneath. There was no understanding between them yet, for their passion was beyond learning and reason and words, their bodies coming together like magnets, moving as one, as if they could fuse as well as join. Release came abruptly at the end of welling need, shaking both of them like a sudden tempest so that they clung more closely to each other, his face in the glorious tangle of her hair, her lips to his throat.

Some time after, as the moon rode over enormous temples on the western side of the Nile, Falke stirred from the languor that was not quite sleep. He brushed curled dark tendrils back from her cheek, loving the fine texture of her hair. "Madelaine?"

"Um?" she responded, turning her head to kiss the palm of his hand.

"Do you know who I am?" he asked in serene confusion.

She smiled and would have answered with a quip, but she saw the serious question in his blue eyes. "Egidius Maximillian Falke, physician, German scholar. Brave man."

"Your lover. That is who I am." He stared up at the roof, noticing for the first time that it was nothing more than interlaced palm branches. "All the rest . . . I don't know. I thought I did, but now . . ."

"Hush." She moved closer to him, her leg over his, her arm across his chest, hand on his shoulder, her head in the curve of his neck. She wished she had courage enough to tell him all of it. Next time, she promised herself, she would explain it all, and hoped he would not shun her after.

He gathered her closer, no longer in delirium; yet the depth of his longing for her remained unknown. Though he expected no answer, he asked softly, "Who have you made me, Madelaine de Montalia? Who have you made me?"

Text of a letter from Claude-Michel Hiver in Vienna to Jean-Marc Paille in Thebes.

To my respected colleague Jean-Marc Paille;

I do not know if this will reach you before the Inundation begins this summer, but I have made arrangements for it to be carried on the fastest ship leaving Venice, which may get it to you before the Nile rises again.

First let me tell you that I am very much recovered. If I had not been tended to so well by Madame de Montalia's relative, then I fear it would be otherwise. This fellow Saint-Germain took excellent care of me, and put his manservant at my disposal during my recuperation. I suspect, although we did not actually discuss the matter, that this Saint-Germain escaped the tumbrels and la guillotine *through good fortune and at great cost. I would think the same of Madame de Montalia were she thirty years older than she is. This Saint-Germain has an air about him, as if he were in exile. There is something about the man that reminds me of an excommunicant priest I knew once, though I cannot tell you why. He does not speak much of his past.*

He has, however, been most curious about our work in Egypt and has assured me that if finances become difficult, he is prepared to underwrite our continued work there as long as Madame de Montalia remains a member of the expedition. I confess that startled me, but I suspect now that he has been her support all along. He asked me to tell you this in case Professor Baundilet encounters some resistance. He has lived in Egypt himself, and has done studies of his own there. I questioned him, and I will say that he does have some knowledge, though I must add that the theories he expressed are quite ludicrous, and the number of gods he claims for the Pharaohs is ridiculous. Still, he is rich and he has applied himself to learning more of Egypt; he is in a position to be useful to all of us, and has declared himself willing.

In that regard, I have another thing to tell you, something that I fear you will not be pleased to know, yet better to know it now than discover it later for yourself. I have now seen three of Baundilet's monographs from our expedition, and there has been no singling out any member of the expedition for individual approbation of any kind. He has named the members of the expedition—he can hardly refuse to do that—but he has not assigned credit to discoveries and work as he stated he would when we joined the expedition. I am aware that this is not uncommon, and we are not likely to receive much sympathy in the sponsoring universities if we lodge any protest for this treatment. In fact, I have been warned that it is possible for such complaint to have an adverse response from many of those in antiquarian disciplines. Therefore I cannot suggest to you that you express your protest, but at the same time, I am of the opinion that you have a just complaint against the way in which Professor Baundilet has appropriated your work and the work of the others as his own. Let me suggest that you find someone to advise you before too much time passes, for you may want to end these questions before you actually return to Paris. I will keep copies of the monographs for you, and if you wish to see them, let me know of it and I will see they are sent to you at once. Saint-Germain will probably also have the monographs, if you would prefer not to involve me.

I will remain here in Vienna for another three months. The physician who has been treating me here is much pleased with my progress but he does not want me to undertake a long journey until I am stronger than I am now. How strange to have to guard myself this way, when not so long ago I thought nothing of laboring most of the day in sun that would broil a lobster. I pray that with a little more care, the day will come when I will not have to be as careful and I will have enough strength to resume some of my work. You cannot imagine how I would welcome that day.

Upon my return to Paris, I will have to arrange lodgings of some kind. I don't know yet what my financial prospects will be, and so I am reluctant to plan. When I have an address where I may be reached, I will send word to you. I hope you will let me know of the progress of the expedition, and the discoveries you have made, as much to satisfy my curiosity as well as to have an unofficial record of what you have done.

Incidentally, if Madame de Montalia has any more of those inscriptions copied, I would appreciate seeing her sketches, for those are where my most abiding interest lies. As I recall she was preparing another series of sketches of a frieze that was most promising. If she has completed it, ask her if she will have a copy made for me. It is a great deal of work, of course, but I hope she will be inclined to do this for the sake of our studies as well as the success of the expedition. She has been diligent in her search for inscriptions, hasn't she? Her relative was enthusiastic about the various inscriptions she had found, though I believe he has misunderstood the nature of what the inscriptions say. A pity he does not have a better education in these matters, for he is a most dedicated student.

While I have been recovering, I've had an opportunity to catch up on my reading; I had almost forgot what a pleasure it can be to read for amusement and recreation. In another month or two I should be well enough to be permitted to attend the theater and go to concerts without fear of overexhaustion; in the meantime, books have filled my hours and nourished my spirit. One of the most interesting novels I have delved into is an historical one by de Vigny called Cinq-Mars; *another treasure Saint-Germain has provided is Pushkin's* Boris Godunov, *which has permitted me to return to my studies of Russian. I am sad to say that I am badly out of practice and I fear it will be some time before I am able to get through the entire work. Another fascinating work, which I confess I did not completely understand, is Nicholas Carnot's* Puissance motrice du feu. *I must read it again when I am more able to wrestle with his ideas.*

I have already written to Professor Baundilet and assured him of my returning health. I have said nothing of these other matters, in case you would want me to assist you. I feel under some obligation to you, Paille, for I am quite aware that it would have been only a matter of time before Baundilet assumed the title to my work as he has already done with yours. You may count me your friend in this, and I give you my word I will speak on your behalf whenever you require it.

With my thoughts and prayers,

Most sincerely,
Claude-Michel Hiver

June 21st, 1827, in Vienna

4

At the back of Yamut Omat's luxurious villa there were three gardens, each terraced and partially enclosed, each in a different style. The largest of the three was reserved for the use of Omat's wives, but the other two were available to his guests at his elaborate entertainment.

"It is quite wonderful, isn't it?" Baundilet asked Madelaine as he escorted her between the perfectly trimmed beds of roses. Their scent was almost palpable in its intensity.

"Yes," said Madelaine, trying to get a little more distance between herself and the Professor.

"We're truly honored to be allowed to come here," Baundilet went on as he indicated another path inlaid with colored stones. "It's strange, isn't it, to be in this place with all these grand statues and bas reliefs on the walls of the ruins, but to see that there are no modern statues, no contemporary illustrations because they are Moslems now." He smiled, his eyes glittering.

"The Pharaohnic Egyptians were not Moslems," said Madelaine, as if speaking to a precocious child.

"True enough, true enough," Baundilet said, laughing as if she had said something truly original. He took a firmer hold of her elbow and started her toward a small bower. "Perhaps we should be grateful that the Egyptians of old made their monuments so large: otherwise the Moslems might have pulled them down for religious reasons."

"Possibly," said Madelaine. "I understand that has happened before." She looked about the garden, hoping to see others from their gathering, but discovered to her displeasure that they were wholly alone. "Professor Baundilet, we will be missed."

"Ah, no," he said, smiling at her as he might at an elegant meal. "Who knows we have gone? And if they have, what is there to think, but that we wish a few words in private, as colleagues will do."

"And is that what you intend? A few words in private?" Madelaine imagined how he would bellow if she brought her foot down along his shin.

"Naturally." Again his predatory smile. He guided her toward one of two stone benches. "Here. You will find this very pleasant."

"I'd rather be with the others," she said, making sure there was no flattery in her voice that he might take as flirtation.

"Don't trouble yourself." He nudged her a second time. "Sit, Madelaine. Go on. No one will know we're here."

"Then I would prefer to be somewhere else. This is not suitable conduct. I do not like indulging in clandestine meetings." She kept her voice steady, but she was starting to be afraid of Professor Baundilet.

"Hardly clandestine, in the garden of our host, the sun shining, the air still and pleasant." He sat down at her side. "You must be aware that I hold you in high regard, Madelaine."

"As you hold your wife?" she challenged. "It is not fitting for me to listen to you, Professor."

"My name is Alain, Madelaine."

"I don't recall giving you permission to use my name, Professor Baundilet." She moved as far from him as the bench would allow.

"Oh, after so long, it is an understood thing, is it not?" His eyes traveled from her face to the corsage of her dress. "We have been here over two years. Soon it will be three. We cannot pretend that these days have not left their mark on us."

Slowly Madelaine rose. "Professor Baundilet," she said with

great deliberation, "I must return to the villa. I don't think it is correct for me to be here with you, nor is it correct for you to bring me here."

His face darkened. "You only want secret meetings with German physicians, is that it?" He was on his feet suddenly, menacing. "Is it correct to meet Falke as you do?"

Her expression grew more remote, though she was appalled at what she heard. "What makes you believe that I have any meetings with Doktor Falke?"

Baundilet's laughter was harsh. "I've had Guibert following you for months. He has seen where you go and what you do."

This information horrified her, but she did not reveal that outwardly. "Then he has told you tales."

Baundilet came two steps closer to her, his smile now turned to a grimace of anger. "Impossible." He took her by the shoulders. "You have met him twice in a deserted building between your villa and his. You have lain on mattresses there and conducted yourselves in ways that a proper man should not speak of, let alone do. What do you say now? Madelaine?"

She was trembling and she hated her body for this betrayal. "I say that Guibert has embroidered the truth." She looked directly into his eyes. "I owe no explanation to you, Professor Baundilet. I have not taken one sou from your expedition; I have my own means. How I conduct myself is my concern, not yours."

"You are here at my pleasure, Madelaine," he said, emphasizing her name. "If I request it, you will be instructed to leave Thebes, and I will ensure that your stay here is most awkward and expensive. What if your servants could no longer purchase food? What if no one would carry your goods on the river? Do you think I cannot do this?"

"I suspect anyone can, if they can afford the bribes," said Madelaine with utter contempt. "Since you meddle in my affairs, and threaten me, I will give you some account of what I have been doing. You are not entitled to it. You are demanding it against my will. Is that clear?"

His face flushed, and his expression changed, this time to a greedy eagerness. "Tell me."

She attempted to step back, but he would not release her. "I have met Doktor Falke there, yes, because to go to his villa interrupts his work. He does not come to mine because his presence offends Brother Gurzin. So we have compromised, and I have said it is satisfactory to me if he wishes to speak to me from time to time in that place."

"At night." His hands tightened.

"Once at night, once in the early morning, as you know from Guibert, if he is truly following me." She was pleased now that the second meeting had not led to more than a few hurried kisses, for it gave her a chance to convince Baundilet he was mistaken about her private times with Falke.

"He follows you. And he will continue to follow you." Again he smiled, but this time there was no warmth in it, not even the heat of lust.

"Is it wise to tell me?" she asked, wondering if she dared slap Baundilet for his impertinence. "If I were engaged in clandestine meetings, I would be warned."

"Oh, I want you to know. I want you to think about it wherever you are, so you will always know that if you do not do what I wish, I will deal with you as you deserve." He clutched at her breast through the satin of her corsage. "It's been so long since I had a European woman."

"And Egyptian?" Madelaine countered, breaking away from him and stepping back. "You have obviously forgotten how to conduct yourself." She knew it was folly to turn her back on him, so she pointed at him. "If you attempt to force your attentions on me, I will see you regret it."

He laughed. "How?" He waited, then continued. "How many times have we been alone? Dozens of times, isn't it? What man could doubt that you and I have achieved an understanding already? If I told the others you are my mistress, who is to deny it?"

"I will," said Madelaine, her voice strong though she was caught up in growing despair.

"And who would believe you? You're compromised just being here." He gave her a slight, ironic bow. "Come, my dear. Consider. If I inform the others of your little . . . well, whatever it is, with Doktor Falke, your reputation and his will be irremediably damaged. That need not happen. If you will end your dealings with him, we can—"

An outburst of applause from the villa caught them both by surprise.

"What I do, and with whom, is my concern," Madelaine said, her eyes shiny with anger. "You have no authority—"

"This is my expedition. I am in charge of what we do, and I have responsibility to the Magistrate and other officials. You are here at my sufferance. Mine. You need my protection. This is a Moslem country, and women are not permitted liberties. The officials do not approve of European women. They don't like you being here in the first place, Madelaine. I repeat: you need my protection. If I told them you were becoming a difficulty, they would rescind your permission to work with us at once, and you would not be able to buy your way back into my expedition, or any other." He essayed another smile and took a step toward her.

"You cannot be sure of that," said Madelaine, still moving away from him. "If you touch me again, I warn you I will scream."

"Who would think you had cause?" Baundilet inquired, mocking her with a slight bow. "Who would believe that any man had to force himself on you? Who would believe I would have to?"

"Mademoiselle Omat might; as I understand it, you are interested in an arrangement there, if her father can be persuaded. Do you think it would help you if I spoke against you?" She felt the sprigged muslin of her skirt catch on one of the rose vines, and she pulled it away, wincing as the fabric tore. "I am leaving here, Professor Baundilet, and if you insist on pursuing me, I will not hesitate to denounce you."

"As if that would frighten me," said Baundilet, though he made no attempt to get closer to her now. "You're very short-sighted, Madame. I forgive you for that. You haven't had time to assess your situation. Take a few days to consider your position. We'll talk again in a few days, when we're both . . . cooler. You'll realize the wisdom in this, if you listen. Your dealings here could be very pleasant, if you are willing to make a few sensible accommodations."

"I will never accommodate you." Madelaine turned on her heel and walked away, leaving him in the bower. She was so furious that she was trembling, and she did not trust herself to do anything more than walk, for anger made her reckless, unguarded. Her feet were hot, as if the good Savoie earth that lined the soles of her shoes were burning lava. How she wanted to turn on Baundilet for the satisfaction of seeing him afraid. That was the most senseless impulse of all, for it would betray both herself and Falke. And more than anything she wanted to seek out Falke, to warn him of the threats Baundilet had made, but that would certainly be what the Professor was expecting, had anticipated. It would be folly to risk contacting Falke now. It would have to be later, when she could be cautious. As she climbed the steps to the garden courtyard, she forced herself to go slowly, to think, preparing herself for any unpleasantness that might follow. She had almost reached the top when a voice stopped her.

"Madame de Montalia," said Ferdinand Trowbridge as he strolled around the side of an elaborate fountain.

"Mister Trowbridge," she answered, grateful that it was the portly young Englishman who found her and not one of the others.

He came up with the unexpected grace of the stout and kissed her hand. "I noticed a while ago you and that professor chap had come into the garden."

"Yes," she said, trying not to succumb to a rush of irrational laughter. Dear God, she thought, is the entire gathering following me? First Baundilet admits he assigned Guibert to spy on her and now this. Is everyone keeping watch? "He wanted a word in private."

"None of my business of course," said Trowbridge, studiously unconcerned, "but I notice your corsage is ripped. Didn't know if you—"

She looked down, shock dizzying her for an instant. "Oh, Jesus fasting!" she burst out, and for once was glad she could no longer weep.

"I didn't think you knew," said Trowbridge as if he were discussing the weather. "Decided I'd better mention it before you went any farther. Not the sort of thing you want seen about, I shouldn't think."

"No," she said, wondering how she would be able to deal with this. "I don't know how I can leave without being noticed."

Trowbridge made a sympathetic gesture. "Don't want to intrude where I'm not wanted, Madame, but it seems to me I might lend a hand. The thing is, I have a notion how to handle this, if you wouldn't mind." He looked at her, gave her a quick, impish smile, then once again resorted to his more aloof manner. "I wondered if perhaps you might like it if I cut a little rose vine. Not much, you see, but enough. I'd be happy to snag it in your corsage and make it appear that you caught yourself inadvertently on one of the vines, don't you know, as you did your skirt. A pity. It's a vastly pretty dress, Madame."

The dread that had taken hold of her evaporated. "Trowbridge, you are the perfect cavalier servant. I must have taken leave of my senses to let this happen, and you are my champion."

He turned quite scarlet with incoherent pleasure. "Not at all," he said at last, each word spoken with difficulty.

"I may be forever in your debt," said Madelaine, her relief now making her feel weak. "Trowbridge, you are . . . well, a hero."

"No such thing," he said at once. "Not at all. A man's not a hero if he does his duty to . . . someone like you, Madame. Pleasure to be of service; anyone would. Be a cad if he thought otherwise." Again he kissed her hand. "Come inside, and I'll tend to getting the rose vine."

She permitted him to take her away from the steps, and remained patiently in a stone nook at the base of the fountain. As she waited, she decided she would have to visit Falke herself, but much later that night, when the household was asleep and even her guards nodded.

"Here." Trowbridge was back, a little breathless and pink, a length of rose vine in his hand like a sharp trophy. "Now, I think if you'll snag it there, where the . . . fabric is torn . . ."

"Of course," said Madelaine, following his instructions. "Fine." Now that she was doing something, she felt better. She was a bit surprised that she had not seen Professor Baundilet returning to the villa yet, but she assumed she would deal with that later. With the thorns set, she took the vine and tugged so that the rips widened. "There," she said in satisfaction.

"Most credible," said Trowbridge, then added in another voice. "I wasn't spying on you, Madame. I swear by my sainted grandmother I wasn't. But I did hear a little of what he said. I didn't mean to, but ... well, he wasn't trying to keep his voice down, was he?"

"I suppose not," said Madelaine, wishing now she had scratched Baundilet's eyes out no matter what the consequences.

"It was a dreadful lie, wasn't it? What sort of man would attempt to compromise you? I'd never believe you are his mistress, no matter what he claimed," said Trowbridge softly. "I know you love that German physician. I can see it whenever you look at him."

Madelaine stared. "I must have been less circumspect than I assumed I was," she sad, trying to soften the blow to Trowbridge. "I never intended to offend you."

"Nothing of the sort; I ain't offended. And you ain't indiscreet. But there is something in your eyes, no matter how impeccable your conduct. I suspect you are not reserved with him." He held up his hands to silence her. "There's also that fellow you write to, the one who used to live here. You told Wilkinson about him, if you recall. It's not that important to me. I don't aspire to more than your friendship. But I don't want to see you slandered by Baundilet; I'll keep my assumptions about Falke to myself. And I won't discuss what happened here unless you authorize it." His eyes twinkled suddenly. "It is delightful to have a secret between us, isn't it?"

"I suppose it is," said Madelaine, fascinated by Trowbridge.

"You can rely on me, Madame. I would never speak against you, and I will not say anything that is not to the physician's credit." He offered his arm. "Do you think you can walk as if you have twisted your ankle? It might make the whole more convincing." He winked at her. "Do you know, I think it will be interesting to see what comes of this. If we tell it properly, any claim Baundilet makes will seem ridiculous." He rocked back on his heels.

"How do you propose to achieve that?" Madelaine asked, now caught up in Trowbridge's schemes. "It will be your word against his."

"Precisely. And what interest have I in any of this? I found you sitting on a bench, your ankle turned, your dress snagged by rose vines, and we have needed extra time to return to the villa, where we will ask for cold cloths for your ankle and sweet oil to rub on the little scratches the vines have left. Or better yet, you will request leave to depart, so as not to cause an uproar over a minor injury. For a man to claim that he was ... using a woman while she was clearly ... unavailable is not believable. Is it?"

"I suppose not," said Madelaine, her eyes narrowing with amusement.

"Thus, we will assume that everyone will doubt the Professor's word, and tend to believe yours, which will be to your benefit." He bowed, his arm still at the ready. "If you lean on me, Madame, I will endeavor to help you up these steps. It is a pity about your ankle."

Madelaine shook her head in rueful amazement. "Where did you get such a fertile imagination?"

"Oh, it's not that. Nothing in my skull but Latin and Greek, or so I've always been told. Not the type to cut capers, though I was something of a madcap boy, of course; but this, this is nothing more than an improvisation." He patted her hand as she slipped it through the bend of his arm. "It's most incorrect of me to say this, Madame, and you must surely think I'm a looby to mention it at all, but we must have something to discuss, and recent events will not do: how did you come to be an antiquarian? I have wondered how a woman as young as you are acquired the scholarship you have. And why you wanted to come here?"

She made sure to limp as the continued up the steps. "I'm not as young as you think I am, Trowbridge. Those of my blood do not age as quickly as some do." She glanced back over her shoulder; she saw no one behind them. It was dreadful being followed, or thinking you were.

He gave a single, accepting nod. "I supposed it might be something like that." He reached the courtyard and climbed up ahead of her, reaching back to assist her. "Be careful. The last step is higher than the others. It's probably a device to keep people from skulking about in the dark."

"No doubt," said Madelaine as she contrived to limp up. "I hope it isn't going to be an imposition on Monsieur Omat to get compresses for my foot. I feel a bit of a—"

"Ninny," Trowbridge supplied for her as he cocked his head in warning toward the door. "Well, anyone getting so badly snagged by nothing more than a plant might well feel that."

"Yes; a ninny," she said, noticing Jean-Marc Paille coming toward them.

"Jésu et Marie," exclaimed Jean-Marc as he rushed into the courtyard. "What has happened to you?"

"You might well ask," said Trowbridge with asperity. "I am shocked that Madame de Montalia should be left without escort."

"Without escort?" echoed Jean-Marc.

Madelaine cast a single quick look at Trowbridge and launched into what she hoped was the right tale. "It was the greatest mischance. If I had not been so unwise ... I was wandering in the rose garden; Professor Baundilet had recommended it to me, but did not linger. I was not paying close attention, making my way along the paths, and I stupidly caught my skirt on a rose vine"— she held up the ripped section of muslin—"and while trying to pull it free, I stumbled, twisted my ankle and ruined the corsage of my dress."

"Bon Dieu!" He looked more upset than such a story ought to have made him. "You were alone when this happened?"

"Yes," said Madelaine, doing her best to conceal the suspicions she felt. "And if it weren't for Trowbridge coming upon me accidentally, I should probably still be where I was."

"Most fortuitous," said Trowbridge with his best cherubic smile. "I have a great fondness for flowers and gardens. Suppose it's being English. I'd taken a notion that I might learn a trick or two from how Omat has laid out his roses, and so I was meandering about, looking. You know how it is." He gave a blithe wave of his hand.

"I am not much interested in flowers," said Jean-Marc as he came a few steps closer to Madelaine. "Madame, are you all right? How badly are you hurt?"

"I have turned my ankle, nothing more. It is a silly complaint and a ridiculous accident." She turned to Trowbridge. "I am grateful for all you've done for me."

Once again Trowbridge flushed. "Dear me, no. Nothing to thank me for. The merest token, Madame. Your most obedient servant always, believe me." He started to bow, then changed his mind, removing her hand from the curve of his arm. "Let me find Mister Omat and tell him what's happened. There's the dandy." He moved away from her with alacrity, leaving her standing off balance beside Jean-Marc.

"Something like being rescued by Don Quixote," said Jean-Marc with a half-smile. "Or perhaps Sancho Panza."

Madelaine shook her head. "You do him an injustice," she said thoughtfully. "He was kindness itself; he might not be a beautiful man, but he is a good one, and goodness lasts longer than beauty for most of us." She limped over to the wall and leaned against it. "A very foolish thing to do," she said, this time her words hard and crisp.

"It seems unlike you," Jean-Marc said uncertainly.

"I suppose it was. I was not thinking about roses." She wondered if she could use this supposed accident as an excuse to leave the festivities early.

"I'm surprised Professor Baundilet left you alone," said Jean-Marc, his eyes hardening. "How did that come about?"

"It seemed the more discreet thing to do, since we would have been alone in the garden, and that would not be wise. What sort of man would choose to put a woman in a compromising position?" Madelaine said, striving to keep the bitterness out of her question.

"Yes. I can understand that," said Jean-Marc. "Still, if he had been there this might not have happened." He looked at her with some confusion. How often he had heard Professor Baundilet declare he intended to make Madelaine de Montalia his mistress, and yet it had not happened. He stared down at the toes of his shoes. "Did you send him away, Madame?"

Madelaine answered with great care. "If I did, I would not say so in any case. But why should I?"

Jean-Marc nodded several times and looked at her with some relief. "Yes. I can see that. Yes." He came to her side, his manner now solicitous. "You are a very sensible woman, Madame. I have said so many times before. You confirm again my good opinion."

"How gracious," said Madelaine drily.

Trowbridge appeared in the open door again. "Miss Omat is coming directly," he said.

Jean-Marc paid no attention to this announcement. "It's the way of aristos, isn't it?" he asked, catching Madelaine's tone and bristling. "When they're not abusing everyone in sight and demanding more of the rest of us than flesh can bear, then the aristos are the most pleasant company in the world. Aristos learn how to make others oblige them, don't they? They are taught ways to be assured of the assistance of others."

"I say," Trowbridge said politely, though there was high color in his cheeks, "that's outside of enough. No way to talk to a lady."

"And lady she certainly is," said Jean-Marc at once. "No one doubts that, Madame. You are charming—everyone agrees." He was about to go on when there was a commotion at the door and Rida Omat hurried out, her pretty French frock fluttering the ribbons of two dozen tiny bows framing the corsage of her dress.

She paused as she glimpsed Madelaine. "Are you hurt, Madame?"

"My ankle and a few little scratches," said Madelaine, feeling embarrassed by the attention she had attracted. "And my pride."

"Mister Trowbridge told me how you were caught on a rose vine." In spite of her intentions she giggled.

"So I was, twice," said Madelaine, indicating the snags in her dress. "I should have paid more attention."

"Dear me," said Rida Omat, glancing around in pretty confusion. "I am afraid, Madame, that there is little I can do to assist you. I cannot admit you to the women's quarters—they will not allow European Infidels to enter. If the servants can be of assistance, tell me what you wish them to do." Her confusion was at once genuine and contrived. "How badly is your ankle hurt?"

"Not very badly," said Madelaine. "I suppose that if my phaeton were brought around, I could return to my villa where my maid could dress the ankle. I do not want to disdain your assistance— be certain that I do not."

"I quite understand," said Rida, and was about to say more when her father came into the courtyard.

"My goodness, Madame de Montalia. I am shocked that you

should suffer a mishap here." This was in his usual elegant, smooth manner, but Madelaine still felt a cold finger on her spine when Yamut Omat spoke.

"It is nothing; truly nothing." She looked from Trowbridge to Jean-Marc. "If it is agreeable to the rest of you, I'd like my phaeton harnessed and brought around, and no fuss made. I feel I have caused more than enough trouble already. I am very grateful for your assistance, all of you." She sighed. "This is most embarrassing."

"Send for Madame's carriage," said Yamut Omat to one of the servants near the door. "It will be ready directly."

"I'll escort you back to your villa, Madame," said Trowbridge. "Your driver won't have to be concerned on that head." He looked toward Yamut Omat. "I'll come back here as soon Madame de Montalia is at her home."

"Never one to miss a chance," Jean-Marc said, one eyebrow lifting.

"Because it occurred to me before you thought of it?" Trowbridge responded with a good-natured wink. "That will teach you to be more beforehand with the world." His bow was slight but very to the point.

Rida Omat watched this exchange with interest. Finally she turned to Madelaine. "Don't you find this exciting? I know I should."

"Actually, no; I do not," said Madelaine, feeling suddenly weary. "At another time it might be otherwise," she added when she saw the disappointment in Rida's eyes. "But I have had a shock, and that is uppermost in my thoughts." She inclined her head. "You've been most helpful. I am grateful you and your father understand the difficulty of my position."

Yamut Omat came to her side and kissed her hand. "I am devastated that such an ... accident should occur at my villa. I hope you will not hold it against me, or regard this place with disfavor."

"Of course not," said Madelaine, wishing she could take a few steps back from Omat. "My misfortune is not of your doing." It was an effort to smile.

"How kind," said Omat, with every appearance of sincerity.

Once again Ferdinand Trowbridge intervened. "Here, Madame de Montalia. Take my arm. I'll escort you to the porte cochere. We'll wait for your carriage and I'll borrow a horse."

"Most certainly," said Omat, but there was something under the cordial offer that almost made Madelaine wince.

"I am sorry I must leave this way," said Madelaine to her host. "I thank you for the splendid entertainment you've offered and I regret I cannot stay for all of it."

Rida Omat giggled in her discomfort. "It will be much less amusing with you gone."

"My daughter," warned Omat.

"Well, it will," said Rida with unusual defiance. "I know it is correct for Madame de Montalia to leave, but I wish she did not have to, that's all." She dropped a little curtsy to Madelaine. "I look forward to our next lesson, Madame."

"Thank you," said Madelaine, now grateful that she had Trowbridge to lean on. "We will arrange the time shortly."

"Good," said Rida, glancing once at her father to make sure her enthusiasm earned no reprimand. "I hope it will be soon."

"Permit me," said Trowbridge to Madelaine as he made a general bow to the rest. "Can't have you hurting yourself more, Madame." He nodded in the direction of the coaching gate. "Come."

As they started away from the courtyard, Madelaine nodded her thanks. "You're most astute, Mister Trowbridge."

Because they were safely out of earshot, Trowbridge chuckled. "I am, ain't I?"

Text of a letter from Honorine Magasin in Paris to Jean-Marc Paille in Thebes.

My dearest Jean-Marc;

I have received the necklace you sent me, and I cannot tell you how much it overwhelms me to think that this beautiful, ancient ornament once hung around the neck of a great Egyptian Queen. What a magnificent work this is, and how unlike anything I have ever seen. I have already told my Aunt Clémence that I wish to wear it at our next afternoon salon. She has yet to give her permission, but I am certain she will be persuaded by me.

You will be delighted to learn that these salons have become something of a vogue: many people seek invitations to these afternoons when my Aunt entertains. She has given the time to letters, so we have poets and professors rubbing elbows here, each taking turns in presenting to the gathering the most recent work they have produced. At the last salon an historian presented his theory that the Norsemen who ravaged the coast of England also came as far up the Seine as Paris. It is generally thought that the people living along the river were able to fight these marauders back, but this one man believes that the defenses were less extensive than has been assumed. It is a very curious notion, but he speaks of it persuasively and many of those attending listened to him with care, though very few agreed.

My Cousin Georges attended that salon and pronounced himself pleased to be in such elegant company. Georges may not be bookish, but he finds the world of letters most intriguing, and he took our Aunt Clémence aside to compliment her on her success. He is of the opinion that in time these salons will become a center for the most advanced intellects in Paris. While that is not the same as attracting those with titles and lands, it is much safer, if one is to take a lesson from the past. How you would laugh at Georges, for he is truly witty when he has been among the learned and gifted men of letters. He told me that you ought to make your appearance here upon your return, when you could instruct us all in the life of those vanished Egyptians. You have seen so many fascinating things, and there are many who would hang on your every word. I would wear the necklace you've sent me and between us we would be a sensation.

My sister Solange has been unfortunate enough to miscarry. My father has told her that he is disappointed in her, and has discussed with her husband the necessity of having another child at once. My father is convinced that Solange was lax in her behavior while she was increasing and that was the reason she could not bring the infant into the world. It is shocking to say these things, I know, but you are a man of science, and you know about such things. My father is beside himself with apprehension, for if there is no heir, then he will have to look to me once more to provide him with heirs. I had hoped he would not press me in that matter, but he has decided that I have not sought a husband as diligently as I said I would.

I did try to remind him that I regard myself as affianced to you, but he will hear nothing of it. If Georges had not intervened, I cannot guess what would have become of our meeting, for my father was quite consumed with rage. Georges told my father that he himself would take on the task of finding the appropriate suitor for me, and then told me in private that he knows I am devoted to you, and will not trouble me about the threats my father has made.

That was most unpleasant, and my Aunt Clémence decided that we needed a time to clear the air, and so we went to the country for a week. We had a most delightful time at the estate of her friends, Monsieur Caillou and his family. Madame Caillou is the most amiable woman imaginable, a superb hostess and cordial companion who has been at pains to make me welcome. She told me that she, too, was hectored by her father, but that she maintained her determination to have Monsieur Caillou, and eventually her father came to the realization that she would not be bullied. I confess that Monsieur Caillou, with his ruddy hair and overbearing ways, would not be the man I would want, but I know that Madame Caillou is wholly devoted to him and believes that she has made an excellent match. I have taken much strength from my dealing with her. She is all sympathy for our situation and tells me that she is certain all will be for the best.

My father has been reluctant to extend my stay here in Paris, but he has not actually ordered me back to Poitiers. He is still occupied with my sister and her husband, and does not truly wish to have to put up with what he calls my sulking, which I would surely do, deprived of you and Paris as well. So long as Georges is willing to remain here, I believe my father will be tractable in his demands. He does not like to see any woman without the support of a man, or so he tells me, though he continues to deprive me of your support, which is the one thing I want most in the world. I have said this to him often, but he will pay no heed, telling me that I do not know my own mind, that marriage to an antiquarian would be a life of tedium and poverty. Have you ever heard of anything more ridiculous! He will have to recant when I show him the necklace you sent, for that will keep his attention.

I wish I could be there with you. Every day I imagine what is must be like, the great ruins all around, the servants bringing fruit in the heat of the day, the boats on the Nile with their sails set to catch the breeze off the desert. I want a folly on the banks of the Nile where I can watch the river and ruins, so I will know everything as it happens: you at your work in the ruins, supervising the men and taking their respect as your due, unearthing beautiful things and making drawings of the old writings. In the evening we could hold a little salon ourselves, so that all the antiquarians could gather to discuss what they have found. You have said something like that has happened already, but I know we could be more splendid. Your mention of Monsieur Omat tells me that it is possible to have proper entertainment in even so remote a place as Thebes. I suppose I could arrange for a small piano to be sent, and we could have glees or other musical evenings.

You will be delighted to know, I am certain, that my Aunt has ordered four new dresses for me for my birthday, including the most ravishing gown in fawn-colored silk embroidered with pearls and little gold beads. It has very wide sleeves, and you might be shocked at how much shoulder it reveals. Your necklace will be stunning with it. I know it would not be acceptable to everyone, but here in Paris, it is very much at the first stare of fashion. I wish I could show you this gown at once, for I know you will find it superb. I cannot bring myself to tell you how much it cost, but all the other dresses together are not the half of that gown.

This afternoon I am going with Georges to a display of new paintings. I shall wear my peach dress with the lace trim, and my most fetching hat, the one with the two ostrich feathers. They say that Ingres and Delacroix are supposed to have work exhibited there, but it hardly seems possible that two such disparate artists would show their work in the same place. I am still awed by Dante and Virgil Crossing the Styx, *which was first shown five years ago. My heart was quite in my throat at the sight of it. There are those who prefer Ingres, but I do not think his work has the same intensity as of Delacroix. When you are in Paris again, you will have to tell me if I have perceived the merits of these two correctly. Georges is a strong admirer of Delacroix and tells me that he has actually met the artist on two occasions.*

How much I look forward to being together once more, when we can go together to the salons and exhibits, when you can tell me of all the wonders you have seen in Egypt and how they compare to the world of art today. I am certain we will both enjoy this tremendously. Perhaps I will be able to purchase a few small paintings. Then when we go to Egypt, I can bring them with me, to see for myself how they compare with the work of the ancients. I am certain that the Egyptians will be amazed at new paintings. I would like to hear what your friend Monsieur Omat would say if he could hang a Delacroix on his walls.

I know I ought not to suggest this, but if you discover any other treasures in the tombs that you are able to send to me, I would be thrilled beyond measure. It is the most wonderful thing to be able to say that my fiancé sent this to me from the ruins of Egypt. As soon as Aunt Clémence permits it, I will wear the necklace at every opportunity, and I will tell everyone that it is your gift to me.

Every night I pray for you and every day I miss you.

Your adoring
Honorine

August 7th, 1827, in Paris

5

With a tiny shake of his head, Erai Gurzin turned away from the bed where Jantje tossed, burning with fever. "I'm afraid I cannot do more for her," he said to Doktor Falke.

"Oh, God," whispered Falke, his face stricken, the lines that usually framed his smile now sunken into his cheeks as if hewn. "I brought her to this place. If she had not come, she would not be dying. I am responsible."

"She came here because it was her duty," Gurzin corrected him. "That is what she said last night when she spoke with me. She knew how dangerous it was—you told her all the hazards of being in this place—and she decided that she would work with you." He put his hand on Falke's arm. "Don't brood on it, Doktor. It will only serve to hurt you; it cannot save her. Nothing but God will save her now."

"You know this fever?" Falke asked, dreading his answer.

"Yes. It is known to anyone who lives in Egypt. You see the way she picks at her cover? that restless plucking? Everyone who takes this fever does that." He blessed the delirious woman, hoping that she could understand enough to find some comfort in what he did. "She will worsen for two days at most, and then she will recover or she will die."

"How many recover?" Falke kept his voice level though tears stood in his eyes.

"Very few," said Gurzin. "If you wish to contain the fever, close this villa, and permit no one in or out until you know how many are suffering from it." He looked up at the ceiling. "I know that some of the diggers from Baundilet's expedition have told him about the fever. He has given orders forbidding members of his expedition to expose themselves to the fever for any reason whatsoever."

"Did he say so officially?" Falke marveled, amazed and shocked that Baundilet would be so blatant.

"Officially, certainly not. He does not want any shame attached to his expedition, and such actions are shameful. He has let it be known, and for the most part, his party has followed his tacit orders."

"For the most part. There has been an exception?" Falke asked, his thoughts still on the enormity of Baundilet's actions. How could any man turn away from the suffering brought on with fever?

Gurzin hesitated before he replied. "Madelaine de Montalia was here with me yesterday. She visited your nurse and read to her for a while."

"I told her not to come here," Falke said, his face more stark than before. "I was tending to patients. I never saw her."

Gurzin made a gesture of philosophical resignation. "Have you ever known Madame de Montalia to accept orders?" he inquired. "She will smile and say something polite and then do as she wishes. Still, I can warn her." He waited for the Doktor to nod, then drew Falke away from Jantje's bed. "I will carry word to her myself, if you wish. She will listen to me, though she might not obey me. I will see that her villa is closed, in case the disease has spread there."

"All right," said Falke, trying to keep his thoughts from racing desperately and uselessly. "I thank you."

"I understand it is necessary." said Gurzin, then added, "I will also notify the Magistrate Numair, if you like. He may prefer having word from me than from you."

"You mean it will cost less," Falke said bitterly. He rubbed his hands through his bright brown hair. "I don't know. I think I am useless, impotent. When I came here I told myself that it was worth the risks to help these people. But I have made so little difference. I feel I have saved them from one thing so that they will die of another."

"Eventually that will happen to all of us," said Gurzin quietly. "At least you have been concerned. How many can say that? And how many have been willing to put their lives at stake as you have?" He sighed. "I am worried on your behalf, Doktor Falke. If anyone is likely to take disease from this woman, it is you."

Falke shook his head impatiently. "How can you be troubled by that? It is bad enough that I am so listless when I am needed the most." He looked back toward the bed. "What kind of physician would I be if I let such considerations restrain me?"

"A more usual one, I suspect," said Gurzin. He put his hand to the front of his habit. "I will return this evening. Try to rest a while, if you can, until I return. If you like, I will remain here with you. Since your nurse is ill, you will need some assistance, I believe."

From outside the window came a sudden cry, and an Egyptian voice was lifted in lament.

"Not you, Brother Gurzin," said Falke with a sigh. "It's not your place. I will find a way."

"Forgive me, but it is," said Gurzin. "I am sworn to God and to do the work of Christ. He did not hesitate to go among the crippled and the sick; neither should I, or I profane my vows." He nodded once. "Besides, I am not a young man. One year more or less, well, it is foolish to begrudge a few days at my age." He cocked his head toward the window. "There will be more like that unfortunate woman in your courtyard. Do not disdain my help."

Falke did not answer, and the hitch he gave to his shoulders might be interpreted in any number of ways.

From where she lay, Jantje began to make a low whine back in her throat, her eyes blank as she stared around the room.

"I must attend to her," said Falke, doing his best to shake off the lethargy he had been feeling.

"Until this evening," said Gurzin. He was almost at the door of Jantje's chamber when something more occurred to him. "The Inundation has many legacies, Doktor, and fever is one of them. As the water recedes, you will find illness in its path. Farther up the river it is less so, and on the Delta there is more." He touched his hands together and then blessed Falke. "This evening, Doktor."

"This evening," Falke capitulated, more grateful for the monk's persistence than he could admit even to himself.

Gurzin made his way back through the orchard toward Madelaine's villa, his thoughts profoundly troubled. He was certain that if there was fever in the village, it might reach out to all of them. It was necessary to warn Madame de Montalia at once, and to assist her in passing the warning to others. There were the antiquarians, French and English, who would have to be told of the fever; they needed to be informed, for their diggers would not do it, and it was not certain that the Magistrate would bother. Omat could not be depended upon, for Gurzin knew the wealthy man would flee down-river at the first suggestion of danger. He was trying to decide how best to issue warnings without giving rise to panic when he entered the side door of her villa and made his way to the salon where Madelaine was working.

Renenet was in the hall and bowed a greeting to Gurzin, though he said nothing as he passed on his way toward the kitchen.

"There you are," said Madelaine, looking up from the trestle table as Gurzin came toward her. "I've been wondering where you were."

"At Falke's villa," said Gurzin, the words coming more sharply than he had intended.

Madelaine hear something in his words that caught her attention. "Falke's villa? What's the matter?"

Gurzin shook his head and sat down. "There is fever," he said at last. He looked up and saw her leaning forward across the table, for once paying no heed to the sketches there. "His nurse has taken it."

"Jantje has fever? Badly?" This last was harsh.

"Yes. She is failing." Gurzin found it difficult to look at Madelaine.

"And Falke?" Madelaine's voice was low but the words cut.

"Exhausted but not ill, not so far." He leaned back. "That will change. His fatigue is not good. It will lead to worse."

"You mean he will become ill?" Madelaine asked, making no excuse for the anxiety in her question.

"I fear so, though I pray I am wrong: I know these fevers. He is not one to resist the fever." He started to pray, then broke off. "Unless you have the same skills in medicaments that Saint-Germain has," he said, as if the idea were new to him, instead of his last, desperate hope.

"Skills? How do you mean?" She was too worried about Falke to be alarmed at what Gurzin said.

He made his case very carefully. "When Saint-Germain was with us all those years, the fever came to our monastery twice. Both times it did not touch him at all. He made a preparation which he insisted we consume; those who did were alive when the fever had run its course. Those who did not take what he offered were in the walls." He cleared his throat. "I was wondering if you, being of his blood, might know his secrets as well."

Madelaine looked away in confusion. She was certain that Saint-Germain had not shared blood with an entire monastery. This would have to be another secret, an alchemical one. "I . . . don't know. Falke needs this medicine?" It was a foolish question, but it would gain her a little time to think.

"If he is to save his nurse and himself and any other unfortunates with the fever, yes." He placed his hands together again. "Saint-Germain knew a way. He did not teach us; he said it was not wise."

"And I can hear him say it," said Madelaine in sudden fond exasperation. "For once his wisdom was short-sighted, it seems." Then she leaned back, aware of how unlike Saint-Germain short-sightedness was. "Unless . . ."

When she did not continue, Gurzin stared at her. "Unless what?"

She gave a little shake to her head. "When I left to come here, he sent me certain papers and materials, things he recommended for this climate." She had paid little attention to the material, but now it struck her that it would be like him to protect her in this way. "I will have to search through them. As soon as I write a note to Professor Baundilet. The least I can do is inform him of what I intend." She reached out for a blank sheet of paper and the inkstand. "One of the servants will take it to him," she said as she wrote. "See that Renenet chooses one of the servants who understands French, will you, Gurzin? I must go and examine . . ." With decision she rose from the chair. "Excuse me, Brother Gurzin. I must attend to . . . something." As she left the salon, she tried to think which of the six chests Saint-Germain had sent her might contain what she wanted. She had avoided them since her arrival at Egypt, wanting to succeed on her own merit, and to keep from being haunted by his absence. Now she began to fear she had placed her independence above prudence.

"Madame! Let me help you," Gurzin called after her.

"Thank you, no," she replied, not wanting the monk to see some of the things Saint-Germain had entrusted to her.

The sun had set and she had put lamps in the lumber room where she searched. Three of the chests had been examined carefully, and while Madelaine had taken certain of their contents, she had yet to find the thing she sought. The fourth chest was more promising, holding two leather-bound books closed with silver hasps, each labeled as medical. Beneath the books were twenty-one sealed bottles, every one wrapped in a sheet of vellum covered in Saint-Germain's familiar, meticulous hand.

Madelaine drew the largest of these out, and took the wrapping off, spreading the sheet with care so that she could read what was written there: *For the treatment of burns*, it said in Latin. *To be used only after administering syrup of poppies*. There was a second note, in red ink, appended to this: *not efficacious to those of our blood*. She considered the bottle. There might be sufficient to sponge two bodies with the contents. The next bottle was for treatment of swollen knuckles. The third was for shortness of breath and pain in the chest. A preparation for the treatment of scars and lesions was next, and after that a pungent salve for all manner of scrapes and abrasions, with the added notation, *be certain that skin is free of sand and other matter before application*. The eighth bottle was almost as large as that for the treatment of burns. *For fever*, said the vellum. Madelaine had to restrain herself from shouting with relief as she began to read the instructions for dispensing it, and the description of how it was made. The information set out there was the first welcome news she had had that day.

By the time Madelaine left the lumber room, Gurzin had left the villa for Falke's, but he had informed Renenet where he was bound.

"He wishes me to tell you that it is not safe to come there," said Renenet, frowning to make the words more important.

Madelaine dismissed the idea. "It will be safer once I deliver this," she said, indicating the bottle she had put into her satchel. "This is a medication; certainly Doktor Falke wants it."

Renenet shook his head. "It is not appropriate for you to take it to him, not with fever there. One of the servants will—"

"The servants do not know how to dispense this. I do." She was growing impatient. "Appoint one of the grooms to come with me, if you think it is necessary, and I will leave for the Doktor's villa at once. The longer we delay the greater the chance that people will die."

It was not proper for a servant to detain his master, but it was equally improper for a woman to go about alone. To Renenet's mind, Madelaine did far too much of that already. He had no wish to expose himself to fever, but if Madame de Montalia had a medicine that would stop fever ... He made up his mind. "I will bring the lamp and accompany you myself. That way no man can question how you have come there."

"Oh, certainly," said Madelaine, relieved that there was no more objection. "Hurry. They are waiting for us."

Renenet was pained to be urged. It was not fitting for a man in his position to hasten at the word of a woman. He lowered his eyes. "I will prepare," he said, and turned back to the kitchen, where he issued orders to the cook and the rest of the staff before coming back to Madelaine. "They will look after the villa."

"I should think so," said Madelaine with asperity. "You lead the way. But remember that the orchard is faster."

"Of course," said Renenet, taking the lamp by the door and setting out for Doktor Falke's.

As they made their way through the orchard, Madelaine did her best to come up with some explanation for the medication she was about to offer Falke. She had already decided she would not bring Saint-Germain's name into it, nor his studies. Falke knew she was fascinated by the physicians of the Pharaohs, and that was a starting place: her recent discoveries had included what might be part of a temple of medicine, what Saint-Germain called the House of Life. She had yet to receive his answer to her letters about it, but she supposed she could convince Falke that she had found some medical information from these ancient days. As she passed the pilgrims' station, she felt a pang of desire and loneliness; she banished it, but not before she felt her esurience renewed. It had been more than a month since she and Falke met there for the second time, and dreams were not sufficient to nourish her.

"We are almost to the villa, Madame," said Renenet, clearly disapproving of her visit. "I will go the rest of the way, if you would prefer."

"Pray don't be so protective," said Madelaine. "I have a task to do, and you are good enough to aid me." She motioned in the direction of the villa's walls. "Go on."

"Yes, Madame," said Renenet, his neck stiff as he bowed.

As they reached the door, one of the servants ordered them away.

"You see," said Renenet, prepared to leave at once.

"Open the door," said Madelaine, ignoring Renenet's defection. "I have something for Doktor Falke, something that is needed here."

"No one is to come in," said the servant.

"Tell him I have a medicament for him," said Madelaine, then added, "It can save many lives, yours included."

"We ought to leave before they open the doors," Renenet said.

"You are free to depart if you wish," said Madelaine smoothly. "But if you do, you are no more servant of mine."

Again Renenet bowed, this time in acquiescence.

"What medicament?" demanded the servant from the other side of the door.

"I cannot explain it to you. Open the door and fetch Doktor Falke." She pitched her voice louder than usual in the hope that Falke would hear her and let her in.

There was a scuffling, and then Erai Gurzin called out to her, "Why are you here, Madame?"

"The same reason you are, Brother Gurzin: to help." She paused. "I've brought medication."

"What medication?" he asked, too tired to mock her but reluctant to admit her. As much as he longed to see her, he wanted to drive her away to safety.

"It is a treatment for fever," she said at once, speaking more rapidly as Falke approached. "It is prepared from a formula of an ancient Egyptian physician." She consoled herself with the knowledge that what she said was true.

Falke, who had just arrived, laughed once, then sighed. "Discovered the other day, and translated by you? How can you know if it is—"

She interrupted him. "How can you be sure it isn't?" She did not give him time to answer. "I had the help of . . . another antiquarian. It is made according to the specifications set down. It is supposed to relieve all but the most advanced cases." She hesitated. "Falke, please. Let me do something. How can you condemn me to wait for my servants to start dying? How can you ask me to do nothing while you die?"

"I don't want you to take hurt from this, Madelaine," he said, and there was anguish in the words that made her ache.

"Then let me in where I can help you," she said, then dropped her voice as she turned to Renenet. "If you would rather leave, do it. But remain at my villa or know that I will enter a complaint against you with the Magistrate."

"He hears no complaints from women," Renenet said, not quite sneering.

"He hears the sound of gold coins clinking together, never fear." She permitted him a short time to consider this. "Do you remain or leave?"

Renenet made a gesture of abdication. "If there is fever in the air, then it does not matter what I do, for it is written on my forehead when I will die. If they let you in, I will come with you."

"Very good," said Madelaine, and raised her voice once more. "You need working hands, Doktor. You cannot turn away those willing to help."

Falke's voice was ragged now. "I can't bear to have you die, Madelaine."

"You will not have to," she said with sad certainty.

"Because of the remedy you're bringing?" Behind his incredulity there was a forlorn hope.

"Yes," she lied.

At last the door opened. Egidius Maximillian Falke leaned in the opening, his face haggard, his blue eyes faded almost to ice. "Very well. If you are willing to gamble, so am I."

Madelaine dropped him a small curtsy. "Danke, Herr Doktor," she said, using half the German words she knew. As she walked through the gate, she reached out and took his hand in hers, much to Renenet's disapproval. "Here." She held up her satchel with her free hand. "Take me to your dispensary and I will start preparing this for you."

He stopped her, making her turn to face him. "What if it is useless?"

She met his eyes squarely, with compassion. "You will be no worse off than you are now, will you?" It was no effort to break away from him, but the act of letting go of his hand was arduous. "Where is Brother Gurzin working? I'd like him to join me, if you can spare him. You may have Renenet in his place, if you require him."

Renenet stared at her, aghast, but had sufficient self-possession to bow to Falke. "An honor to serve," he muttered.

Gurzin, who had moved to one side, took a step forward. "If you require me to assist you, Madame, I am prepared to do it."

"Good," she said, motioning him to come with her. "The dispensary. And Falke, make sure your staff is treated first."

He turned even paler than he was. "And if the medicine sickens them as well, what then?"

Madelaine sighed. "If you'd rather, you can send half your staff, to see how they respond. Then the other half, if you are satisfied that there is no danger in this remedy." It was tempting to castigate him for doubts, but she could not do that without revealing more of the nature of the medication than she intended to. She looked away from him so that her mendacity would be less apparent. "The Egyptians of old were famous for the skill of their physicians. This is what they used for fever. You need not fear that their medicaments will fail you."

"I pray God you are right," said Falke with so much emotion that neither Gurzin nor Madelaine could find words to second his outburst.

* * *

Text of a letter from Professor Alain Baundilet to Magistrate Kareef Numair, both in Thebes.

Most revered Magistrate Numair;

It is an honor to be of service to you and your people; what I authorized my fellow-antiquarians to do during the recent outbreak of fever is what any man of learning would be compelled to do. I am convinced that Doktor Falke would agree; while I am grateful for your thanks, I am of the opinion that in such emergencies the man who does nothing is worse than a devil, so you will realize it was no effort to place our various talents at the service of those who suffered.

On the second matter, I must confess I have no notion how the golden scarab discovered last month came to vanish. During the fever I know my fellow-antiquarians were less diligent about guarding our finds, being preoccupied with those with the fever rather than the treasures of so long ago. I am shocked that you think one of my expedition would take the scarab, though it is as valuable for its age as for the precious metal of which it is made. I fear that one of the diggers who saw it might have decided it was more his than ours, and taken it, being Egyptian and believing himself entitled to have it. Surely there are some Egyptians who feel this way. I will make inquiry among my expedition to discover if any of these antiquarians have any information about the scarab. Whatever I learn, even though it is nothing, I will report to you at once. It is offensive to my honor to think that any of my expedition could be suspected of such rapacity. And in any case, what would any of them do with the scarab if they had it? How would they transport it without notice? We are scholars, not smugglers, worthy Magistrate.

Your praise of Madame de Montalia is most flattering to her, and I am almost afraid to tell her of your many kind words, knowing how easily women are led into vanity. If you will not be offended, I will limit what I say to informing her that you

*were aware of the work she did at the villa of Doktor Falke,
who must deserve the greatest part of the credit, for it is he who
is the physician and who has ability to heal. The gentle hand
of a woman is truly wonderful succor in hard times, but to
praise her for what is little more than women's nature is to
encourage willfulness, which is not attractive in females. Her
work must be the doing of Falke, whose instructions she was
sensible enough to carry out.*

*Along with my sincere good wishes, I send you this small
purse in token of my respect and esteem, which I ask you to
accept for the high regard we share. I assure you that your good
opinion means as much to me as the bounty of the Pharaohs.*

*With utmost esteem,
Professor Alain Hugues Baundilet*

September 15th, 1827, at Thebes

PART IV

Sanh Djerman Ragoshzki
Physician

Test of a letter from le Comte de Saint-Germain in Switzerland to Madelaine de Montalia in Egypt, dated November 8th, 1827.

My cherished Madelaine;

The more you tell me of Baundilet the less I like him. I want to tell you to warn the authorities, but, sadly, they do not care; more sadly, they would not listen to a complaint from a woman, especially a foreign woman. This is not the way Egypt was when I was there, for such theft as you describe would have brought a nasty, prolonged death to anyone caught perpetrating that act. But then, the people of the Black Land stoned to death anyone who killed a cat.

You say that Gurzin has offered to bring you down-river, and again you hesitate. I hope you will listen to him; he knows Egypt better than either one of us, my heart, and his warnings are not to be taken lightly. Do not despise his advice, for me if not for yourself.

The inscriptions you sent me are not forgeries, they are examples of other misrepresentations: four of the inscriptions were altered, in the case of the second inscription, just after the Pharaoh died. The third inscription is a report about the fall of Troy, from the Egyptian diplomat who had just come back from there because he knew that the Trojans would not prevail against the Greeks. Oh, yes, the Trojan War took place, for all you think that Troy was myth. In regard to these inscriptions, I will in-

265

dicate what has been changed on those which have been altered, as far as I am able. Perhaps that will aid you.

Remember that the Egyptians were in awe of words, and that for them, the written words themselves had potency. It was thought that in changing an inscription, events were influenced so that the person claiming credit, in some magical way, became the person who performed the recorded deed. It was one of the reasons that priests had so much power, because they were the custodians of so many inscriptions.

Part of the courtyard out of the House of Life needed repair, though the priests could not agree what ought to be done.

"The place is too large; if we make the courtyard smaller, we can enlarge the temple sanctuary," said Kepfra Tebeset, who had recently been made High Priest. "We will show our respect to Imhotep if we do this." In the last hundred years the fashion for wearing perfumed cones of fat on the head had been replaced by tinted salves spread on the face and chest. Kepfra Tebeset's visage and upper torso were as gold as a Pharaoh's funerary mask.

"If we have another plague, we will need more space here than we have now," remarked Sanh Djerman Raghoshzki, who was only a physician and therefore of little importance. His long years of service to Imhotep gave him certain privileges, though he was a foreigner. "When the last plague struck, we had to turn the people away, and even then we had not room enough for those who were admitted here."

"A disgrace," said Menpaht Resten, who made no secret of his rivalry with Kepfra Tebeset. "If we are not to bring more shame on our god, then we must be prepared for the worst that the gods and neters bring us." He rubbed at his face, smearing kohl so that streaks ran under his eyes and mixed with the alabaster tint of the salve he wore.

"Flies and sand," muttered Omethophis Kuyi. At twenty-three, he was the youngest physician to be elevated to priest, a distinction accorded him more because he was cousin to Pharaoh than because of his aptitude. He squinted where the wall had fallen. "How did it happen?"

"It was from the Inundation," said Sanh Djerman Ragoshzki before Menpaht Resten could answer. "Every year it has come up almost to our gates, and every year the water has eaten away at the rock under the wall." He met the hard stare of Kepfra Tebeset. "It has happened to other structures, hasn't it? Think of all the fallen sphynxes: how many thousands of them were there, and how many are still standing?" He expected no answer to this last question, and got none.

"It was the will of Imhotep that the wall be changed," said Menpaht Resten. "It was Imhotep who raised the Great Pyramids; the wall of his temple would not fall unless it was his will that it fall."

The wind off the desert was gritty with dust and sand, sure promise of a storm to come before the next sunrise.

"Perhaps Imhotep wishes us to make the courtyard larger, not smaller," suggested Omethophis Kuyi. "If Sanh Djerman Ragoshzki is correct, Imhotep wishes us to prepare for the dying, and makes us aware that many will sicken." He was small and wiry, his head was long, but his voice was more beautiful than the deep notes of Pharaoh's gongs. When he spoke, others listened for the pleasure of hearing him.

"It is not for us to know the will of the gods," said Kepfra Tebeset. "We are here to offer sacrifices for those who are ill and to tend to those who come to us." He strode along the wall. "We will have to inquire of the god what is to be done. If we act without the guidance of Imhotep—"

"How do we know that Imhotep guides us?" asked Omethophis Kuyi, uncaring that he interrupted a superior. "Would it not be wiser to consult with Pharaoh to receive his instruction than to pray for guidance that might not be the will of the god?"

"Pharaoh cannot tell us all we wish to know, for he is partly a man. We seek the wisdom of the god." So far as Kepfra Tebeset was concerned, that was the end of the matter.

But Menpaht Resten was not satisfied. "And the wall remains broken, so that any disreputable person might come into the courtyard? What do we do to stop those who cannot afford to pay the donation Imhotep requires? Are we to permit them to come here, and climb through the break in the wall?"

"It might be better than dying in the streets," said Sanh Djerman Ragoshzki, but no one paid any attention to him.

"I want an inscription painted on the wall at once," said Kepfra Tebeset with decision. "I wish it to say that Imhotep curses all those who enter his temple through the break in the wall, and I want it written there that the curse was made at my order." He gestured his satisfaction. "That will protect us until we have learned the will of the god." He signaled for the rest to follow him as he started back toward the temple sanctuary.

"It isn't fitting," murmured Omethophis Kuyi, the timbre of his voice filling his complaint with meaning. "It isn't for priests to—" He did not finish, afraid of speaking blasphemy or treason.

During the night the wind rose higher, bringing sand that scoured all it touched. Some of Pharaoh's columns were obliterated on the side where the sand blasted them, and this was seen as a dire omen. The storm lasted for three days; the sound of the wind, the feel of it was inescapable. Horses, asses and cattle went mad with it, and so, I think, did many of the people. I had seen severe desert winds before, but I can recall none that were fierce as this storm, in the fifteenth year of the reign of Rameses III. When it was over, there was devastation from the Third Cataract at the edge of the Nubian Desert to Tanis on the Delta. In the remaining sixteen years of Pharaoh's reign, from his capital at Memphis, not even his successful opposition to the loosely confederated Sea Peoples had such impact on the Black Land. For those of us at Thebes, the storm brought other disasters in its wake.

When the wind at last died down, the temple of Imhotep began to fill. Some were suffering from abraded skin already turning puffy and red with infection. Others had broken limbs and gaping wounds incurred while trying to salvage something from the voracious wind. All but the most infirm slaves were pressed into service, tending those who arrived and assessing the worth of the offerings they brought. Everyone worried that the wells were contaminated, though no one spoke of it.

"I think it would be better if we informed Pharaoh," said Omethophis Kuyi as the priests gathered to decide what to do about the crowding of the temple. Because he was related to Pharaoh, his opinion was regarded with suspicion. "If more come, we could have a riot here, and we are not prepared for that."

"No one will riot," said Menpaht Resten contemptuously. "They need our help; how would they dare riot?"

"For that reason," said Kepfra Tebeset, hoping some of the others would agree with him. "The temple and all within it are in my care. We have room for another twenty, twenty-five at most, and then we must turn them away. Sanh Djerman Raghoshzki, what do you say? You have been here longer than any of us." This last was admitted uneasily, for the foreigner showed little signs of age, yet if the records of the temple could be believed, he had been there for two, possibly three centuries. Perhaps longer than that.

"I fear you will have to fight if you try to close the doors, and if you admit too many more you will not be able to tend them. And Pharaoh is a long way down-river from us." He said it calmly, as if he discussed nothing more urgent than the ripeness of figs.

"You cannot be certain of the riot," declared Menpaht Resten. "It may be that nothing will happen; you cannot decide for the people."

"No," Sanh Djerman Ragoshzki allowed. "Neither can you."

"If we seek assistance, we will be telling the priests of Osiris and Amun-Re that our god is not as powerful as theirs," said the High Priest petulantly. "We will be seen as servants of a—"

"We are servants of Imhotep, who is not like Osiris and Amun-Re," said Sanh Djerman Ragoshzki. "We sing praise to Amun-Re each morning and do not think Imhotep is compromised by our worship. We leave offering for Osiris so that the work of Imhotep will flourish. We have shown honor to the gods and the neters, and it is no disgrace that we seek their help and favor now. We would be lax in our care of those who come to us for aid if we did not do all that we must for their benefit, as long as that is possible."

The High Priest folded his arms across his chest. "You are a physician, not a priest."

"Because I am a foreigner," Sanh Djerman Ragoshzki reminded him unnecessarily. "In my own country, I am a priest," he added, which was no more than the truth.

As Kepfra Tebeset glared at Sanh Djerman Ragoshzki, Menpaht Resten said, "We must be strict, and take in those who are in the greatest need. The others will have to be content to wait. We will send out the servants, to explain to them why this must be. We need not call on Pharaoh for this. After such a storm, it will be days before we can sail to Memphis, in any case." He knew that the other priests would rally behind him if he became more insistent.

"I say that we must send word to Pharaoh, at least," said Omethophis Kuyi. "It is required that he know how much his people are suffering. He is their access to the gods when the gods are not in their temples."

A few of the priests added their support to Omethophis Kuyi's demand. "It is fitting that Pharoah know," said the oldest of these, a man with a bent spine and a keen eye. "If Pharoah decides that we must close our doors, we will be informed of it."

"His messenger would not arrive here for many days: we will not close our doors," insisted Kepfra Tebeset. "It is not right that we close our doors."

"But you will accept the protection of Pharoah's army," said Menpaht Resten with visible relief.

"If Pharoah deems it the will of the gods, then it is for us to be thankful. Troops will not come quickly, in any case. If Pharoah does not send us his troops, then we will know that the gods wish the doors to remain open." Omethophis Kuyi looked around the small chamber. "It will be my honor to inform Pharaoh of what transpires here."

"Honor?" said one of the priests, making no apology for his mockery.

Omethophis Kuyi gave the priest a truculent stare. "Honor," he said again, more loudly.

* * *

There was a riot, the first of many; Pharoah never sent troops to us because they were busy guarding the storage depots from those who were set on looting them. Five of the priests of Imhotep were killed that day, and another three died because of injuries received then.

The trouble was that Egypt was weakening and those around her were gaining strength. If Egypt had taken the path of China, and learned acceptance of all peoples, the Black Land might still be flourishing instead of filled with vacant ruins and tombs.

Certainly there were foreigners in the Black Land, but they were required to live apart from Egyptians, in enclaves, where they were governed by Egyptian restrictions. The laws of Egypt, even in decline, were strict and preferential, so that no one who was not Egyptian could count himself safe from Egyptian whim. It was folly. Had the Egyptians permitted greater tolerance for foreigners who lived in Egypt, they might have found friends and allies in their need. As it was, they found foes.

By Egyptian standards his dress was outrageous, a bright blue color, made of cotton and gathered at the waist with a studded leather belt. He held a hand to his forehead; blood ran through his fingers. "I need to see one of your physicians," he informed the slave who monitored the door of the House of Life.

"You are a foreigner," said the slave as if that was the only consideration worthy of mention.

"I was born here, I speak the language better than you do," said the Phoenician. "I need a physician. I have money." The last was added with contempt.

The slave straightened. "How much money?"

"Phoenician and Babylonian gold," said the bleeding man. "Hurry up. My head is bursting."

"It may have burst already," said the slave judiciously. He moved away from his post at the door and went down the long hallway in search of a physician, making no haste with this task.

A short while later, Aumtehoutep stepped up to the door and

signaled the warder. When the slave did not respond, Aumtehoutep started to ring the gong again.

"He's off searching for a physician," said the Phoenician. He was sitting on the wide, shallow steps, his back to a granite pillar. "I'm waiting for a physician."

Aumtehoutep gave the man a long, speculative look. "It appears you require one."

"The slave didn't think so," said the Phoenician, ending on a groan.

"I will find you a physician," said Aumtehoutep; he moved to unfasten the lock. "Come with me."

The Phoenician stammered out an objection, ending, "You are a servant; they will not allow it."

"That is my concern. My master is a physician here, and he will tend to you, no matter what the slave at the door has decreed. Come with me, or can you walk on your own?" Aumtehoutep approached the Phoenician. "Do you need my assistance?"

The Phoenician was trying—with little success—to lever himself to his feet, working his back against the pillar. "No. I'll manage," he said with effort.

Aumtehoutep reached out and brought the man upright. "There. It is not wise to strain so much when you are bleeding, especially from the head."

The Phoenician merely grunted, suddenly sweating very heavily. "I . . . I must have . . . gotten a harder knock than I thought." He wobbled in Aumtehoutep's hold, then did his best to get his feet walking properly.

The warder slave was outraged at Aumtehoutep's action, but said nothing as the servant approached him. "I am taking this unfortunate to my master."

"He is a foreigner," said the slave, turning the word into the basest condemnation.

"This man or my master?" asked Aumtehoutep quietly, and made his way toward the courtyard out of the House of Life where Sanh Djerman Ragoshzki still tended those beyond recovery.

The Phoenician paled as he saw the man in the black kalasiris standing amid a crowd of lepers. "I . . . I am no leper," he croaked.

"Neither is my master," said Aumtehoutep. "Do not fear him; you will take no hurt from him."

The Phoenician shuddered. "How can he bear to touch them? Look at them, so white, and with ... fingers and toes ... gone."

"It is the disease," said Aumtehoutep reasonably. "If you are distressed, I will take you to the infirmary and we can wait for him there."

"Yes," the Phoenician panted. "Yes."

Aumtehoutep signaled his master, then half-carried the Phoenician back into the House of Life. "He would not permit you to become infected," said the Eygptian confidentially. "He is not so callous." As he led the Phoenician down a narrow hall, he went on, "I will bathe the wound and prepare the salves my master uses. He will know which is best for your hurt."

The Phoenician was breathing irregularly now, and his color was more like clay than flesh. He bobbed his head convulsively, and all but collapsed onto the bench where Aumtehoutep escorted him. Muttering the name of his gods, he dropped his chin on his chest and lost track of time.

When he opened his eyes, the other foreigner stood beside him, his small hands gently probing the Phoenician's head near the wound. "It's swollen a great deal," he said without excitement when the Phoenician looked at him. "My first worry is infection and fever."

"Will I sicken?" The question was anxious.

"I hope not," said Sanh Djerman Ragoshzki as he reached for a pail of water. "I will want to save a little of the blood, so that I will have it ... for rituals." He smiled once, quickly. "Blood can tell a great deal."

Until they permitted me to become a physician in the House of Life, few of the priests of Imhotep were curious about how I determined treatment. When I was admitted to the ranks of the physicians, that changed; my life was more closely scrutinized. I had to tell them something, and so I said that I used the blood for rituals and that the nature of the rituals showed me how to proceed. It was not far from the truth, for those of our blood can tell much from what we taste, though it be only a drop. I had become wise enough that I did not seek nourishment except from those who were far gone in their illnesses and would not question anything I did. Their delirium gave me sustenance of a sort, and eventually I developed the skill to bring about pleasant sleep; you know the technique—it is very like the things I taught Mesmer almost a century ago.

As I rose in the House of Life, the Black Land continued its decline. There were occasional regenerations of the old grandeur, but the inescapable truth was that other nations were growing and the advances that had given Kheme, the Black Land, its preeminence in the world were now shared by the others. The rise of Judea, Tyre and Assyria did much to shift the power in those ancient Mediterranean lands. The descendants of my people had drifted far to the west by that time, some of them reaching as far as the Italian peninsula; I doubt you'll find any mention of them in the writings you are examining, for the wanderings of barbarians were of little interest to the Egyptians.

I had made a kind of peace with myself by then. I had a place in the House of Life, I had turned away from the terror and the destruction and the hunger. All in all, I was as content as my foreignness and my nature would permit, but I had shut away passion except for my love of music. Men have rarely held a physical fascination for me, and priests, no matter what their stripe, are not safe with secrets like ours. I continued to take what I required from those out of the House of Life, never more than three times so that they would come to no harm from me. Do not condemn me for what I tell you now, my heart, for it was the beginning of the long journey that led to you: the House of Life was a place without women except those who came to be helped; I let myself be lulled into the certainty that I could not be subject to desires beyond the simple gratification of my needs. What folly.

It was during David of Hebron's campaign against Jerusalem that the number of Judeans in Egypt increased; those who could afford to escape the fighting paid handsomely to purchase as much farm-land as the Egyptians would permit these foreigners to own. So it was that from time to time we would have Judeans

*at the House of Life, and depending on the disposition of the
High Priest, we physicians were or were not allowed to treat
them.*

There were tassels on his clothes, which marked him as a man
of some importance in Judea. He stood at the entrance to the
House of Life, his daughter borne on a pallet by his slaves. Another
slave held the offerings he brought. "I beg you," he said to Sanh
Djerman Ragoshzki. "The High Priest will not give his permission
for anyone but you to treat her, because you are a foreigner."
There was a quick, speculative light in his eyes; then it was gone
and he was saying, "No one in my household has been able to
help her. We have consulted others, and they can do nothing for
her. She . . . she fails and we do not know why. Please. You must."
Sanh Djerman Ragoshzki studied the man, his expression revealing nothing of his thoughts. He knew his black kalasiris and
headdress as well as his height made him imposing, and he often
took advantage of both. "How long has she been ill?" he asked
finally.
"Ten days, good physician," said the girl's father. "She complained that her head was sore, and that her ligaments were
stretched too tight. Her mother said it was women's uncleanness
that caused it. Then she had a fever and this swoon. I am afraid
she will die."
There was nothing Sanh Djerman Ragoshzki could say in hon-
esty that would put the fear to rest. "How have you been treating
her?"
The Judean shrugged. "We have made her swallow water and
honey. It is all she will take." He came a step closer. "Say you
will receive her. Look at her. She is turning into a dry husk. If
you will not take her in, then she is completely lost. Our God
has not protected her, though we sent four young goats to His
altar."
"I cannot offer you hope," said Sanh Djerman Ragoshzki. "Children who take this fever do not recover. I have not seen the fever
in anyone her age. If I treat her, it may well be for naught."

"We have no hope now," said the Judean. He waited, his eyes shiny with tears.

Sanh Djerman Ragoshzki hesitated, then spoke as if against his will, "If I can save her life—and I am not convinced that I can— she might well be unable to walk or care for herself. I tell you again, I have seen this fever before, and often it is kinder to let those who have it leave this life. If she lives, she may come to curse her salvation."

"I am rich," said the Judean. "I am Elquanah ben Illah, and I possess forty-four oxen and sixty . . . sixty-three goats. I have three concubines, one of whom is a Hittite. My wife is related to the old King Saul. We have position in Hebron and Judea and here in Egypt. I have told the High Priest we will bring an offering to this place every day that my daughter lives."

"All right," said Sanh Djerman Ragoshzki against his better judgment. "My servant will show you where to take her. There is a courtyard at the back of the temple. He will escort you." With that he went into the temple and clapped his hands twice for Aumtehoutep.

To be candid, I did not expect her to last the night, but she did. There was something stubborn in her that would not surrender to the fever. Eloine strove for life, and in time I took up her cause, working beyond the limits I had accepted for so long.

"Are you sure you want to try?" Sanh Djerman Ragoshzki asked as he saw how wasted her legs were.

Eloine could not speak clearly, and every breath was an effort, but she answered with a motion that once would have been a toss of her head, "Yes. I have to."

"All right," he said dubiously, coming to her side. "If that is what you want, I will help you."

Her smile was more of a grimace but her defiance made it beautiful. "Ready?"

"If it is what you want," he said, preparing to help her to her feet and knowing it would be useless. Her disappointment would be bitter as gall to him, but he hoped that his emotion would not be visible to her as he lifted her.

She hung in his arms like a sack of grain, her efforts to control her limbs making her plight more distressing to him. Her eyes were hard as glass. "I will do it, Sanh Djerman. I swear on the blood of Hebron I will do it."

"Oaths taken in blood are binding," he said, unable to tell her of his increasing certainty that she would not walk or regain much control of her arms and legs. That she was alive startled him, and provided the comforting kernel of doubt that kept him from despair for her.

"Then you will have to help me fulfill my oath," she said, and fell back, exhausted, her withered limbs shaking. Her eyes remained fixed on his. "You will help me, physician."

"If it is in my power to do it," he answered obliquely. "You are . . ." He took her hand in his, searching for the right words. "You are so fragile, and you are made of strength."

She was about to answer, then sighed a little and remained silent.

That was the first time I experimented with making braces, and my designs were clumsy. Until then, I had confined my healing to medications and better methods for surgery; for the priests of Imhotep were permitted to perform surgery, and though they were not the mystical adepts so many would like to think them today, they did far better than most in those distant times. They could set broken limbs, care for many illnesses, reduce pain and suffering, relieve infections, and perform basic surgical procedures. The braces were different, unlike anything I had done before, or anything the priests and physicians of Imhotep had done. I did not offer them to Eloine for some while because I feared they would be no help to her. It drove me wild, to be so little use. Oh, yes; I provided her with salves to keep her skin supple, and Aumtehoutep massaged her twice a day. I would have done that myself, but I could not trust myself to touch her so. I devoted myself to trying to make braces, and thought that was enough.

* * *

"The archers gave me the idea," said Sanh Djerman Ragoshzki as he presented the braces to Eloine. "Their bows are flexible and yet hold their shape." He faltered. "They are not pleasing to look on, but I think they will give you the support you seek."

She looked at the braces, her face unreadable. "You made these?"

His pride was stung; suddenly and irrationally he wanted her to know what he had done for her. "I am the only foreign physician in the House of Life, and I am regarded as the most capable. Of course I made them. Who else here knows enough?" And who else would want to? he added to himself.

Her laughter was puzzled. "Will they work?" Her speech was clearer and she did not tire as rapidly as she had a month before, which made her continuing weakness particularly frustrating to her.

"I don't know," he admitted. "They are better than dragging yourself around on a child's cart."

She winced at his words. "Yes, they are," she agreed promptly, sitting up with her customary effort. "Death is better than a child's cart."

"Don't say that." His voice was low and even, but they both heard the pain in him.

For a long moment she stared at him. "I am crippled. I am worse than those who have fits. I cannot move without help. I am useless."

"Flowers cannot move without help, yet they are not useless." He moved closer to her. "If these work, then you will be able to move."

"Or so you hope," she countered brightly, blinking rapidly twice, but unable to stop the tears that slid down her face.

He hated to see her cry; without thinking, he reached forward and drew her into his arms, holding her close to him as if to lend her all his preternatural strength. When he kissed her, he could not conceal the tremor that passed through him, nor did he want to.

* * *

She lived almost two years, and I fought for her life every day she was with me, just as she resisted her weakness until she no longer had the strength to breathe. I never tasted her blood, for she was too weak to give up a single drop of it, but I did give her what pleasure I could, and found a kind of fulfillment in that which I had not expected. Because we were both foreigners, the priests of Imhotep ignored us; I could not interest them in the braces, though Eloine was able to walk after a fashion when she wore them.

When she was dead, I felt nothing, so great was my pain at her loss. The day her father came for her, I almost refused to give her to him, though I knew there could be no reanimation for her, not into so damaged a body.

In the following years, for decades, I gave myself to study and experiments, anything that would be a barrier between me and the grief I felt for her. I learned a great deal, and slowly I acquired the reputation of being favored by Imhotep, something that puzzled the priests, since it was understood that no foreigner could be so favored. It was then that I was given the privilege of bringing in shipments of my native earth, and for the first time, I did not need to fear sunlight, or travel over water. The priests believed that the earth increased my strength, which in a sense was true enough.

You say that you have found part of a temple in Luxor you think was the House of Life. From your description, it is part of the later temple, since the walls are fortified. For many, many centuries the temple of Imhotep had enclosing walls without fortification, because there was no need of them. That part of the temple was built at right angles to the older temple, and it was not as large as the older, yet another sign of the gradual fall of the Black Land.

You ask me to advise you about the German physician: I do not know what to say. If you want to make him one of our blood, it is your decision. But do you think he would want to be a vampire? All the qualities you mention do not easily accept the lives that we are required to lead, assuming he did not think you were deceiving him. You tell me he takes pride in his prag-

matism and rationality, and certainly those are admirable traits in a man of medicine; would his rationality reject your nature as being part of folklore?

I hope that it will be as you wish it to be, Madelaine. I fear that in spite of the impossibility of our situation, I can find it in my heart to envy your Doktor Falke, who can have the riches of your love if he is not so rational that he cannot welcome what you offer, and value the gift you give.

In four days I leave for Buda-Pest; your messages will find me at the Empress Elizabeth Hotel. I will be arranging for more shipments of good Carpathian earth, and should remain there through most of the winter. If you have need of me, send word and I will leave for Egypt at once. You need not be concerned; I can set my memories aside in Egypt or any other place, especially when you are there.

Strange: as I write this, I hope you will send for me, yet I do not want any danger to touch you, but an end to danger would obviate the need for my presence. It is a dilemma I have lived with since I first saw you; be certain I will always long for you until the true death. Nothing will change that, my heart, no matter how much other things may change.

Saint-Germain
(his seal, the eclipse)

December, 1827 through March, 1828

Text of a letter from Rida Omat to an unknown person at Thebes, delivered in secret.

My dearest light of my soul, rose of my love;

Do forgive how badly I write in French. In spite of Madame de Montalia's instruction, I have not yet mastered your beautiful words. I do not know the language well enough to say to you all the things I would wish to say. My heart is full of you and resounds to your love, but I am mute in this tongue, or I prattle like a child.

It is a very wrong thing we are doing, meeting in secret, without the consent of my father, and it troubles me that it must be so, for we are both risking so much. I could not do otherwise than come to you when you sent for me, but I wish you to understand how much we could both lose: you are not a Moslem and if you were apprehended with me, though you offered me honorable marriage, they would still geld you. I would be sewn in a sack with a cat and thrown in the Nile to drown, for I would dishonor my father, and there is no recourse for a daughter who does that. I tell you these things not to frighten you or drive you away, but to make it clear why I have said we must be careful, always careful.

I am afraid that we will have to trust one of your colleagues, for I cannot rely on anyone in this household, and if you send a servant, there will be talk, no matter who that servant is. You said that your man Guibert would be wholly reliable, and that may be, but he is known as your servant and could not protect himself or you if there was trouble.

Let me beg you to convince one of your men to serve as an escort for me, a man who will not betray you or me, who will not decide to make his silence dependent on my compliance with his desires. I could not bear that. It would be likely to destroy my passion for you if I had to bargain with another man to have it. I have to ask you to be very careful whom you pick, but I beseech you to pick someone, or we will not be safe. I have no dread of my own fate, for without you there is no point in living. But you, I would not ask you to endure that humiliation and loss for me. I know already, though my father does not, that I have become a woman only a European will have, for no Egyptian man, no true Moslem, would have me now that I dress without modesty and conduct myself more blatantly than the most degraded women in this country. I have nothing to give to anyone but you. But you cannot be made to pay that price for loving me. It would be too cruel for them to make a woman of you.

How am I to find a way to see you? You tell me that your wife need know nothing of our union, that you are willing to marry me here under Moslem law and say nothing to your wife in France, who is a Christian. You have said you will provide for me while you are in France and will live with me while you are here. I can imagine nothing more wonderful, nothing that would make me happier. Yet I fear that my father would oppose such a match, for he is eager to act in accordance with Europeans, and therefore would not look favorably on such an alliance as the one you wish with me.

Oh, my most dear one, my sunlight, my source of love, do not stay away from me too long. Already my legs tremble and open, ready for you to lie between them. Your one-eyed head has seen into me, and wept copious tears of joy. My belly aches to be full of you. Every moment you are gone from me I begrudge you. Every look you bestow on other women, even the aged and the deformed, consumes me with jealousy. You cannot know how great my love for you is: Allah alone—glorious forever—knows that.

I will wait at the entrance to the herb garden tonight, and if your messenger should come, he will find me there. I can reach the place without making myself known to others, and I will do it. But I cannot remain there very long, for there is a chance the servants will see me. Therefore, three hours after sunset will be the time I go there. Tell your man to bring a cloak for me, and to take care not to pass the east side of the house, for that is where the poultry is kept, and they will set up more noise than a pack of wild dogs.

Until I am with you again, I only breathe to taste the air that was yours. Until I am with you, I will have my women servants massage me with sweet oil and pretend that you are with me already.

In adoration,
Rida

1

As she drew her horse up in the shadow of the wall, Madelaine turned to her companion. "Who were these gods, Trowbridge? If they were gods." She indicated the enormous figures carved in low relief into the stone. They were outside the walls of the recently discovered small temple that stood adjacent to the precinct they had been excavating for over two years. Madelaine was certain that this was the House of Life, the temple of Imhotep, though no one else thought so.

"Must be gods," said Trowbridge after a brief scrutiny. "Animal heads, all of them but the ones that look like mummies. Well, it stands to reason they're gods." He squinched his eyes as he looked toward the east, watching the sun rise. "Christmas morning," he said at last. "And it will be hot as a smithy in two hours. Where's the snow and the rest of it?"

"There is some snow in the mountains," said Madelaine. "Not here in the desert." She swung out of the saddle and brought her mare's reins over her head, preparing to lead her as she walked.

"But Christmas without snow. Or at least rain," he modified, shaking his head in disapproval.

"You'll find them in Europe, Trowbridge." She chuckled, looking up at the wall once more. "What do you think? Was this the place they sent the sick and the dying?"

"A temple?" Trowbridge considered the question as he dismounted. "Shouldn't think they'd send sick people to a temple. Odd thing to do." He led his horse up beside Madelaine and hers. "But those Egyptians were odd coves all around. Come to think of it, they might have brought people to the temple when they were doing poorly."

"They did," said Madelaine confidently. "They brought them here." She indicated the sand that was being cleared away. "We don't know how large this place was, not yet, but I don't think it could be as huge as the main temple. The walls aren't as tall, and so far there's no colonnade, just what might be a series of court-yards. We'll know more when the sand's gone. Professor Baundilet still believes this is merely another part of the main temple. He does not give much credence to my theory."

Trowbridge cleared his throat. "Not to say anything against the Professor, but he's something of a rum go, isn't he?"

"If that means what I suppose it means, I'm afraid he is," said Madelaine, her manner serious. "I am . . . concerned about how he is conducting himself."

"Shouldn't wonder. That episode in the garden: not at all the thing. And one hears rumors. Not the sort of tales a gentleman can repeat," said Trowbridge, falling silent as they continued along the wall. He paused by a partially eroded figure of an ibis-headed man holding a tablet and writing on it. "A fellow wouldn't like something of that sort going on around him, would he? Can't see how the Egyptians liked it, but still." He frowned at the next frieze, which was half-covered in sand. "What's that scale got in it?"

"I'm told it's a feather. On the other side, once we unearth it, there ought to be a jar." She stood back a few steps and studied it, as she had studied it every morning for two months. "I don't know why a jar and a feather, if that is what you're going to ask."

Trowbridge grinned. "It was." He turned around, not wanting to climb over the drifted sand. "How much longer do you think it will take, clearing away this place?" He gestured in the general direction of the small temple.

"Oh, I don't know. Years, I suspect." She followed him. "The work takes forever, and there are always officials to deal with as well."

"Years," he said, pursing his lips thoughtfully. "They won't permit that."

"Who won't?" Madelaine asked, baffled.

"Mater and Pater. They'll want me home before summer, I fear. They're worried, don't you know. I've been gone too long and that doesn't suit their purposes." He stopped and looked at her. "I'd hate to leave you here."

Her eyes softened. "Trowbridge . . ."

"Oh, I'm not declaring myself. Your most devoted, and all that, but not more than that. Told you that months ago, and I haven't changed. Not in a position to be a suitor, and not up to it, either. Truth to tell, I'd as soon not marry at all, but I'd never be able to get Pater to approve. Besides, you said you aren't going to marry, and I believe you." He gave her a long look. "It's more than wanting to keep your independence, isn't it?"

Madelaine looked at the wall so that she would not have to see his eyes. "Yes."

"Thought so," said Trowbridge in his comfortable manner. "Just wanted to be sure." He started walking again. "The thing is, I've had a chance to watch you. I notice things."

She hated to ask. "What things?"

"Little things. You eat alone, or so I hear. I know you don't eat in company. I noticed you don't have mirrors. I thought, well, Moslem country, mirrors frowned on. But it's more than that, isn't it?" When she said nothing, he said, "Nuns don't have mirrors, I'm told. Has to do with modesty or some such thing. They don't go in for haute cuisine, either. With everything that's happened in France with religion, well, I can see how a nun wouldn't want to admit being in Orders. There could be repercussions, even now. The Terror was over thirty years ago, but it might be the danger isn't over for nuns. Especially if one came from a good family." He looked down at the reins laced through his fingers. "You don't have to tell me if you don't wish to, but . . ."

It would be so easy to lie to him, thought Madelaine. He had made a case for her that was almost perfect. He would be content with the lie: she would not. She shook her head. "I'm not a nun, Trowbridge, not even a run-away one."

"They sent nuns to the guillotine, didn't they?" he persisted.

"They sent many, many people to the guillotine; nuns weren't the only ones to lose their heads," said Madelaine, her voice low.

He went beside her in silence for several minutes; when he spoke again, he said, "It's time I took you to that meeting you attend every morning. The antiquarians will be expecting you."

She nodded, relieved to have her thoughts interrupted. "Yes, you're right. Professor Baundilet said that after Mass we're still to review our projects with him."

"Have you been to Mass?" Trowbridge asked, a bit surprised.

"I have a monk in my household. He holds Coptic service every morning," she said, not adding that she did not attend.

Trowbridge nodded. "Must seem strange."

"What must seem strange?" she asked, preparing to mount her horse once more.

"The Coptic monk. They're not Christians the way we are, are they? Not to say anything against them, you understand, but it's hard going to think of them as Christians sometimes." He patted his horse's neck. "Let me give you a lift up," he offered.

Madelaine was already in the saddle, adjusting the fall of her skirts over the curved horn. "Don't trouble yourself, Trowbridge," she said with a smile. "I've been climbing onto horses longer than you can imagine."

"No doubt," said Trowbridge as he got onto his horse. "There's some festivities this evening, if you'd care to come to the house we've taken. Punch and carols and similar fare, I reckon." He grinned at her. "I'd be pleased of your company."

She shook her head. "I had best not," she said. "Professor Baundilet does not like his antiquarians to be too sociable with other expeditions if he is not included in the occasion. He wants us to keep to ourselves. I know he is spending this evening with Monsieur Omat." She made an impatient gesture. "But if you wish to ride morning after next, I would be glad of your company."

"I will present myself at dawn," said Trowbridge with alacrity.

"Fine," she declared, and turned her mare away from the ruins. As they trotted along the dusty road, Madelaine suddenly gave a rueful smile. "It struck me just now: why it does not seem like Christmas morning."

"Because it is hot as a bakeshop and dry as old bones," Trowbridge said.

"No. Because there are no bells," said Madelaine. It had been more than four years since she heard church bells. Her expression grew distant. "I miss the bells."

Trowbridge pulled his horse to a walk. "You're right." His round face was suddenly quite serious and Madelaine realized that when he got old he would no longer look like a cherub; he would become a bulldog. "A cousin of mine—I've got dozens of them —is a parson, the kind who likes port and hunting more than he likes reading Scripture. Wonder what he'd make of this?" He indicated the ruins and the low village buildings that were the same dust-color as the distant cliffs.

Madelaine reined in her mare as well. "The hunting here is quite poor."

He greeted this observation with laughter. "Egad, I must remember that. When I'm back in England, I'll tell him." He scowled. "I'd rather not go. Some days I think I would like to walk into the desert and disappear. But then I remember," he went on lightly, "how atrocious the heat is, and how desolate the desert is, and I know I prefer England."

Madelaine laughed, as much because it was expected of her as for genuine amusement. They were almost to Professor Baundilet's house and she was reluctant to give up this pleasant morning for another round of antiquarian bickering. "Of the two, England is more pleasant," she said.

"So I think," said Trowbridge. He pulled his horse aside to avoid a collision with a donkey pulling a cart.

They had almost reached Baundilet's house and had slowed again. "You were very good to ride with me this morning, Trowbridge."

"Pleasure's all mine," said Trowbridge as he bowed in the saddle.

They were at the gate now, and Madelaine rang to have the gate opened. "Not entirely; I enjoy these rides, too." She slipped out of the saddle, looking up at Trowbridge from where she stood. "Day after tomorrow, then."

"At dawn," he agreed, and swung his horse away as Baundilet's servant opened the gate.

Baundilet was waiting in the door as Madelaine handed her horse to a groom. He had dressed in a loose Egyptian robe and worn sandals instead of shoes. Only the crucifix around his neck served as a reminder of the day and his religion. "There you are. You're the first."

"Happy Christmas," said Madelaine as she came toward him, thinking as she did that he did not appear as ridiculous in Egyptian garments as most Europeans did.

"To you as well. And a joyous New Year to begin soon." His smile was possessive, more predatory than cordial. "Come in, come in. I've had a breakfast set out. Perhaps you'll abandon your austerity this one time, Madame?" He stood aside to bow her into the house.

"Thank you, but I do not take food at this hour," she said, as she had said so often in the past.

"When *do* you take food, I wonder?" he asked, his tone a bit caustic. "De la Noye and Enjeu will be here directly. Jean-Marc sent word that he won't arrive for a while; he's gone to Mass with LaPlatte." He indicated the main salon, which had recently been done over in Egyptian style. "We'll have the servants bring the notes if we require them."

"I'd like to see the sketches Enjeu did of the wall we discovered. I had another look at it as I came here, and I think he may have left out some details." She saw that there were still two French chairs in the room, and selected one of them as her own. "I'm not dressed for reclining, Professor Baundilet," she said as explanation.

"Surely here you may call me Alain." He went to pour himself coffee, asking as he did, "Is there any point in offering a cup to you?"

"Only the point of good manners," said Madelaine. "Otherwise I thank you and decline." She sat down, her hands folded in her lap.

"I have had little time to go over your latest notes and sketches. I see you persist in claiming that the decorative borders are actually inscriptions. Quite an interesting supposition; I'd like to know how you came by it. Perhaps one evening this week it would be possible for us to discuss what you have been working on?" He showed his teeth. "You may choose where we meet."

"Wherever you are meeting with the others, that is satisfactory to me," said Madelaine in her most unconcerned manner.

"But you know how controversial your work is just now, and there might be discussions and arguments that would not clarify anything. You persist in these unorthodox notions, and that serves only to aggravate the others; there is no reason they should be part of our discussion, not if I am to get a better grasp on your work and your ideas. If you and I were to have a talk without the disruption of others, we might make more progress, gain more understanding." He let the word hang in the air as if it had body and form. "You have not explained why you entertain the theories you do. I want to know more, so that I can evaluate what you are doing." This time his smile was practiced and easy. "An hour or two should be sufficient, Madame. You and I can reach an excellent understanding."

Madelaine resisted the urge to rise and leave the salon. "I doubt I am prepared to do as you suggest," she informed him.

"Then you are not confident about your theory?" There was mockery in his eyes now, and something hard and unforgiving.

She changed the subject. "What have you heard from the university? You said you expected some word before the end of the year."

"And so I do; we have a week yet of 1827. They have been receiving regular reports and shipments from me all year long. I assume that word will come and we will be able to determine how the expedition will go on for the year. I don't know how much money will be granted this time. They're losing interest in what we're doing, I'm afraid." He gave a short sigh as he found a hassock and sank onto it, coffee cup balanced expertly. "If I cannot obtain the money we require to continue . . ."

Madelaine looked toward the window and the courtyard, where a small fountain splashed. "You say you will require more money from me if there is to be an expedition here." Her voice was without emotion and that deception satisfied her.

"It may come to that, yes," said Baundilet heavily. "I regret, Madame, that I must make such a request of you."

"I doubt that," she responded, her tone not quite so cool. "You have never hesitated before; why should you do so now?"

"Why?" He drank a little of the thick, sweet coffee. "It is hardly fitting for an academic of my standing to require so much assistance from someone like you. Oh, I am not adverse to finding a patron, but it is not appropriate to intrude on you in this way." He looked up as the bell sounded in the courtyard. "De la Noye, I suppose." His eyes flicked in annoyance. "He's early."

"He and Enjeu," said Madelaine, relieved that she and Baundilet would not be alone any longer.

The two men were escorted to the room by Baundilet's houseman, who did not linger to perform needless introductions.

De la Noye came across the room and kissed Baundilet's cheeks as he wished him a Happy Christmas. "I had almost forgotten what day it was when Thierry reminded me. How can one think it is Christmas?" He laughed and went to help himself to coffee, pausing only to nod in Madelaine's direction.

Thierry Enjeu was more courteous. "God send you a Happy Christmas, Madame," he said to Madelaine as he came to get his coffee. "I hope your endeavors will prosper in the New Year."

"Thank you," said Madelaine. "I hope the New Year will be

successful for you, as well." She noticed as he poured coffee that he had grown even thinner in the last few months. Where before he had been lanky he was now gaunt, the bones of his face showing through the muscles like a carnival mask. It crossed her mind once more that Enjeu was ill.

"I trust that the next shipment we have from Cairo will include my pipe tobacco," complained de la Noye in good-natured gruffness. "If I have to smoke anything more of what they offer us here, I will go off of an inflammation of the lungs." He sat on the divan, resting his feet on one of the enormous pillows. "This is the way for a man to relax."

"My servants will be bringing breakfast soon," said Baundilet, adding, "You're excused as a matter of course, Madame."

"You're most gracious," said Madelaine, trying to estimate how much longer she might be expected to remain. She already regretted accepting the invitation. "If you'll let me review the sketches and notes while you have your meal? I would appreciate that."

"Always working," said de la Noye, not unkindly. "How industrious you are." He put his hand to his chest. "Now I do not have your dedication, especially not today, when I am expected to celebrate."

"Don't fence with her, Merlin," said Enjeu, his voice weary. "If she wants to see the sketches, let her. She can always go make her own sketches if she does not like ours." He drank his coffee quickly and poured himself another cup.

"You were out last night, Alain," said de la Noye as he settled more deeply into the cushions.

"What makes you say that?" asked Baundilet in some surprise.

"A few of us came to the gate and were told you were not in," said de la Noye, drinking his coffee.

"Oh, pay no attention to that. I told my servants that I wanted some time to myself. You know what they're like when you give them such instructions." He glanced up as his houseman returned. "What is it, Ahzim?"

"They are ready for you in the dining room," said Ahzim, bowing with more respect than anyone in the room deserved.

"One day you will take your insolence too far," said Baundilet, his attempt at the local dialect wrongly accented.

"As you say, Professor," Ahzim said, bowing a second time before departing the room.

"What's the matter with your houseman?" Enjeu asked, curious about what he had just seen. "It's not the same fellow you had six months ago."

"No. This one was recommended because he has some command of French, but he has his audacity as well," said Baundilet. He rose. "But I suppose we might as well go and have breakfast. He's a high-handed scoundrel, but he does not announce breakfast if it isn't ready." His laughter was a trifle forced, but the rest echoed it dutifully, leaving the room empty but for Madelaine, who rose as soon as the men were gone.

She was debating whether she could risk going to Baundilet's study when she heard the door open again, this time to admit LaPlatte and Jean-Marc Paille. She stood still and listened, hoping the new arrivals would go directly to the dining room; she was certain the houseman would take them there. If they all were at breakfast, she would be able to explore.

"I'll be along directly," said Jean-Marc, near the salon door, and a moment later he stepped through the door. "Madame de Montalia," he said, adding as an afterthought, "Happy Christmas."

"To you as well," said Madelaine, irritated by his good wishes. "You have come from Mass?"

"Yes. A makeshift affair, but better than passing Christmas with only a feast this evening." He came and kissed her hand, striving for an ease of manner he did not feel. "I was hoping you would be here."

"For what reason?" Madelaine asked, sensing turmoil in Jean-Marc now that she could look at him closely. His eyes, she saw, were sunken and bruised; he had cut himself shaving, and when he went to pour himself coffee, his hands shook. "What troubles you, Jean-Marc?"

He did not answer her directly. "It is nothing to concern you. I . . . I am probably mistaken in any case."

"Mistaken about what?" she said, noticing that he was not only distraught, he was frightened. "What is it?"

He shook his head. "There is no reason to trouble yourself."

"Then why did you make a point of speaking to me now?" she

inquired in her most reasonable manner. "You want to tell me something. What do you want to know?"

He gave his head a single shake, as if to rid himself of his thoughts, and then he said in quick, hushed words, "You remember the items we found in that hidden compartment? We divided them between us?" He downed the coffee in one swallow and poured more.

"Of course I do," she said quietly.

"There was the figure of an ibis. You recall it?" He finished the second cup and poured himself a third, saying, "There's no more coffee."

"I recall the ibis. There was a ring on it, so that it could be worn, or so we thought." She came a little closer to him. "What is it?"

"I am certain I have seen the ibis," he said. "It must have been that one. There have been no others. But I gave it to Professor Baundilet, as I ought to have done. I gave him my report as well." He stared down into the little cup, at the dregs of coffee in the bottom. "I thought it was the right thing to do."

Madelaine could find nothing to say. She did not want to make assumptions, for she guessed that Jean-Marc would shy away from such speculation. She indicated the divan. "Why don't you sit down?"

"I mustn't," he said, his nervousness increasing. "I must go in to breakfast. But I wanted you to know I've seen the ibis again. After I gave it to Professor Baundilet."

"In his report, or his shipments?" Madelaine was already certain that his answer would be no.

"Mademoiselle Omat was wearing it. She had it threaded through a gold chain around her neck. I saw her at a gathering last night. She said it was a gift from her father." He put the cup aside and stared up at the ceiling. "How can it be a gift from her father? How can her father have it at all? I gave it to Professor Baundilet."

"You have given other things to Professor Baundilet that were not sent to the university," said Madelaine, her tone no longer sympathetic and her manner strict. "You have aided him in his dealing in antiquities, and he does deal in antiquities, no matter what he tells the rest of us." She folded her arms. "Haven't you."

He could not look at her. "I've needed the money, Madame. You do not know what it is to need money. But I never consented to a sale of this sort. I was told that my finds would be sent to the university, and I would be given the credit for the discovery." He sat up abruptly. "But he didn't send it."

"It seems not," said Madelaine.

"It was my discovery, mine! It was supposed to go to the university. I was told it had been sent." His voice had risen and now he looked around quickly, guiltily. "If anyone recognizes it, they will say that I sold it. If the university hears of it, they will not—" He broke off as Ahzim appeared in the door.

"Professor Baundilet and the rest are waiting for you, Monsieur Paille," he said with extravagant courtesy.

"Oh, God," whispered Jean-Marc, almost dropping his cup. He turned to face Ahzim as if he had been apprehended in a crime. "I . . . wanted a word with Madame de Montalia," he stammered as he put his cup aside with shaking hands. "Nothing important, really. It can wait. It's just a minor matter. We'll clear it up another time. I'm coming now." He glanced once at Madelaine. "I don't know what to do." With that he gave her a slight bow and left her alone.

Madelaine picked up Jean-Marc's cup and put it on the table where the other cups were; all the while she could not banish the image of a bauble in the shape of an ibis from her mind. More than Christmas, more than the inscriptions at the newly discovered temple, the ibis haunted her, driving all other thoughts from her attention.

Text of a letter from Claude-Michel Hiver in Arles to Merlin de la Noye in Thebes.

My dear friend and colleague de la Noye;

I thank you for your concern: indeed, I continue to improve, going from strength to strength. As I told Jean-Marc, I am one of the lucky ones. In fact, the physician here has told me that the treatment afforded me by Saint-Germain was most benefi-

cial. He informed me that such stings as I had have been known to result in the withering of limbs or a failure of sensation, which has not been the case with me, as it turns out. There were weeks when I feared it would be so; now I am pleased to tell you that I am almost as strong as ever I was, and the results of the sting have turned out to be minimal. If all goes well for this year, it may be possible for me to return to Egypt at some future date.

As I write this, I cannot describe to you the delight I feel in that prediction. Here I have been preparing myself to lead a life of study without exploration, forever condemned to examine the prizes others have found. That was surely the most egregious fate I could suffer. Now I am told that it may be possible for me to venture to Egypt again. I could feel no better than if I had been granted a pardon from a lifelong condemnation to the prison of scholarship without expedition. I do not intend to cast aspersions on the academic life, but for those of us who have gone into the field to pursue our studies, libraries and lecture halls are poor substitutes.

I confess I read your letter eagerly, wolfing down every scrap of information you proffered, envying you for being there to share in these revelations. Your description of the smaller temple you have unearthed has so fired my imagination that it is all I can do to keep from writing to Professor Baundilet or Madame de Montalia to request them to provide me with sketches and other information on the place. You must be excited beyond measure to make such a discovery. To find a temple that was previously unknown, perhaps for centuries! I wish I had been with you when the discovery was made. I cannot understand why more has not been done to excavate it, but I suppose it must be done with prudence, taking care to make note of everything along the way.

Because my recovery is greater than had been hoped, I have requested the opportunity to lecture on the antiquarian discoveries in Egypt at several universities. It will improve my chance to have a teaching post in the autumn, and it will also stand me in good stead if and when I am ready to come back to Egypt for more studies. I intend to devote some of my lecture to the work you are continuing to do in Egypt. I believe it will serve your purposes well, and be useful to me. If there is anything you wish me to discuss, you have only to inform me of it, and if there are discoveries that are in dispute, then warn me so that I will not compromise the studies that are continuing even as I put pen to paper. You may regard this as my request for your assistance in preparing my lectures, and I beg you to accept my thanks in advance of receiving your response.

The concerns I expressed to Jean-Marc Paille several months ago remain unchanged. I mentioned to him that Professor Baundilet has presented his monographs on the studies of his expedition as if all the work were his own. I supposed after I had brought this to Jean-Marc's attention that Baundilet might relent, but I fear it is not so. A man of your experience and years of antiquarian studies ought to know of this, and take what measures you may to prevent the whole of your current work from being appropriated by Baundilet. Let me tell you now that I am disappointed in what Professor Baundilet has done, and the more I see of his monographs, the more I am inclined to think that in some ways that scorpion's sting was a happy escape.

I am sending along a copy of Victor Hugo's new novel, Cromwell, *which has received much attention. Are you an admirer of Hugo's? I've tried to call to mind what you've said of him, but haven't been able to. In any case, I think you will find this an interesting work. I recall you often expressed dissatisfaction in being so far behind the times in regard to new books, and so I have taken the liberty of obtaining this copy for you. I have not finished reading it yet, and so I cannot comment on it. When you write again, as I hope you will do soon, let me know your thoughts about this book. I think Hugo is a most persuasive writer, but I know that not everyone shares my opinion.*

I have heard that there was a great battle between the fleet of Egypt and Turkey against French, British and Russian forces. Has that occurrence made any difference to your work in Thebes, or do you continue much as before? It is difficult to imagine that there is a war going on when one is busy excavating ruins as ancient as those temples. Whatever the case, I trust that you will not be treated badly because of a battle that took place far away.

Be good enough to extend my greetings to all those in the expedition, especially Madame de Montalia. Without her good offices I fear I should be a good deal worse off than I am now. When I think of the risk she took on my behalf, I am astonished anew, and I ask myself if I would have her courage if the circumstances were reversed. Not all my recollections are so dire, or so filled with emotion. I think of all of you often, and with great kindness. When I am at last permitted to return to Egypt, I hope I will be fortunate enough to work with you, Merlin, or with those among you who remain in Egypt, for I am convinced that the Baundilet expedition—without Baundilet—has proven to be one of the most accomplished ever sent to that distant land. Heaven smiled on me once; it may be that it will show me favor once more. In any case, leave a few mysteries unsolved for when I come back, if you please.

> *With sincerest regard,*
> *Claude-Michel Hiver*

January 22nd, 1828, at Arles

2

Lasca's shriek was still echoing in the hall when Erai Gurzin came rushing from his room, his habit in disarray as he hastened to her aid. His hood was thrown back, revealing his greying fringe of hair.

"God protect me!" Lasca whimpered as she backed out of the dressing room, very nearly colliding with the monk.

"What is it?" he demanded, forcing her to turn toward him.

She required three deep breaths to reply. "An asp. Christ! *An asp!* It is enormous." She was quivering, breathing quickly; she was quite pale.

"An asp!" Gurzin was alarmed. "Here?"

"I opened the chest. I opened it, and the asp was there." She crossed herself and then covered her face with her hands. "It is so enormous."

"Is it still there?" Gurzin asked, holding her shoulders tightly to keep her attention. "Tell me!" He looked toward the open door of the dressing room. "Did you close the chest?" When she did not answer, his voice rose. "Think, woman! Did you close the chest?"

"Yes!" Then she stared at him. "No. I don't remember."

"Which chest?" Gurzin asked, trying to be calm.

From halfway up the stairs Renenet called out, "What is the trouble?"

"I will attend to it," Gurzin assured the houseman, hoping Renenet would not insist in coming the rest of the way, for he did not want news of the serpent to spread through the household. "A mishap." He shook Lasca once, not too hard. "Which chest?"

"The Russian one, on legs. By the linen press." Her voice was not quite so shrill, but her eyes were glassy with terror. "I . . . I cannot go back in that room. Do not make me."

"What is in the chest?" Gurzin demanded.

Lasca keened her answer. "The serpent!"

"Other than that." Gurzin knew he had asked a foolish thing. "What does it hold? Not the snake; what else."

"Fichus, scarves, hoods, wraps," Lasca told him, each word hard, shaking her head for emphasis. "I won't go near that asp."

"Of course not," Gurzin soothed. He could think of few things he would less want with him when he was hunting a deadly snake than an hysterical woman. "How did you know it is an asp?"

"It rose up, and there was a hood." She started to cry. "Oh, please. Kill it. Kill it."

"Yes; I'll do that." He moved her aside, deliberately pushing her away from the door to the dressing room. "I'll need an urn to put it in when it's dead," he said to her. "Can you get one for me?" That would force her to act and remove her from where he was at the same time.

"Yes," she said, nodding as if her head was on a string. "Oh, yes." She started away from Madelaine's suite of rooms. "There's an urn in the second bedroom." She stopped suddenly. "I don't want to go in there alone."

"Then bring the urn from the entryway. There are three of them, and they have water in them. One of those will do." His voice was brusque from worry. He looked around for something he could use as a weapon against the snake. "Is there a sword in the second bedroom?" he called out to Lasca, who was making her way down the stairs, tottering as if she were very old.

"On the wall." She stopped and looked back to where Gurzin stood. "It isn't very sharp."

"It doesn't have to be," said Gurzin, steeling himself to go into the second bedroom. He was glad to have this delay, though he was afraid that if the chest were still open, the snake would be gone, hidden somewhere in the house if he waited too long. He made himself move quickly, and opened the door with care, looking at the places where a serpent might be hidden. On the wall there were two ceremonial swords, crossed over the de Montalia arms. He hurried to take one, then made his way toward the dressing room, the sword held awkwardly, for he was unfamiliar with weapons.

Lasca had closed the chest: Gurzin sighed with relief. The serpent was still inside. An asp, Lasca had said, though the hood meant a cobra. He swallowed against the tightness in his throat and chest, coughing a little at the effort. He knew he had to position himself with care, so that the snake could not easily strike at him. Very carefully he pulled the chest away from the wall, sliding it as easily as he could over the uneven planking of the floor. He did not want to warn the snake or frighten it. Once he had the chest in the center of the room, he moved back, rubbing his chin repeatedly as he mastered his fear.

Finally he reached out and pulled up the lid, standing so that the open chest provided him a shield.

The cobra slithered and coiled and rose to strike, and as it did, Gurzin swung his sword with a prayer to Christ to make his aim true. The impact of the sword was more jarring than he expected and he almost dropped the sword. His hand tightened convulsively, and he pulled the sword back to use it again.

The snake writhed and whipped about, but it was not able to rise.

Gurzin stepped from behind the raised lid and hacked the blade down repeatedly, praying with every blow, until he was certain the cobra was dead. Then he let the sword drop from this hands. Aghast at his actions, he dropped to his knees and begged God's forgiveness for his ferocity.

"Is it dead?" Lasca stood in the doorway, holding the urn awkwardly, her face not quite as pale as it had been.

"I think so," said Gurzin, getting to his feet. "I think so." He peered into the chest and saw the remains of the cobra. He decided he ought to be sickened by the carnage, but could not make himself ashamed.

"God guided your hand," said Lasca. "May God be praised forever."

"Not for killing snakes," said Gurzin with feeling.

"For killing this one," Lasca insisted, setting the urn down. "What are you going to do now?"

"Put the serpent in the urn, so that we can show it to Madame de Montalia when she returns." He desperately wanted to sit down, to have a glass of wine, not for honoring God but to restore his nerves.

"Why not leave it where it is?" Lasca asked, flinching at the monk's suggestion.

"Because the longer it remains there, the likelier it is that the household will learn of it," said Gurzin, drawing up the upholstered stool where Madelaine sat to have her hair coiffed.

"And so they should," said Lasca with heat. "That such a thing could happen in this villa."

But Gurzin shook his head. "You have not considered," he said as he breathed deeply, helping the nausea rising in him to fade a little. "You are amazed that a cobra was in this chest. So am I."

"And we ought to—" Lasca began only to be cut off. She held up her hands as if to ward off blows instead of words.

"Because," he said in a voice that was deliberately rough, "because I do not know how it came to be here, in a closed chest. It could not get there on its own." He turned toward Lasca and made her meet his eyes. "Someone had to put it there."

Lasca blanched. "No."

"Yes," Gurzin said. "Someone had to put it there. It could be there no other way." He made a gesture to ward off evil. "Accept this, Lasca. Someone put that serpent in this chest. It could not be there any other way." He hated how he felt saying those words, and he hated the sickened look in Lasca's eyes. "Therefore, we must say nothing, or we warn whoever is responsible for the cobra being here." He rubbed his hand over his forehead. "Come. I will need you to hold the urn for me."

"No. Please." Lasca shrank back. "Don't ask it."

"I can ask no one else but Madame de Montalia, and she is not here." He got up and walked the few steps to the chest. "It was a good-sized snake; almost as long as I am tall." He was able to quell the distress he felt. "I cannot imagine who would do this. But I must."

"I don't want to look at it," Lasca whispered.

"It's dead," said Gurzin as he picked up a comb and prodded the dead snake with it. "I cut it in several pieces." He said it distantly, as if he had done the killing long ago.

Lasca crossed herself. "I do not like to look at the serpent."

"Then look at the urn instead," said Gurzin. Whoever had brought the snake had probably carried it in one of Madelaine's scarves, which meant that the person who put the cobra in the chest was probably part of the household. He took the corners of the silken scarf and drew them together, holding the dead snake inside. "Look away," he told Lasca as he carried the cobra to the urn, fitting it in the wide mouth with care. "It's done."

"Oh, Saints protect me," she whispered, crossing herself again. "How could anyone want to bring such a monster into the house?"

"I don't know," said Gurzin, admitting to himself now that the shaking in his hands was the aftermath of moving the snake. "And that worries me."

Lasca moved away from the urn. "It is deadly, the asp."

"The cobra," Gurzin corrected gently. "Yes, it is deadly." In spite of his best intentions, he went on, "And someone put it here deliberately."

"Truly," Lasca answered. She paced the length of the dressing room, taking care to avoid the urn. "How will we find out who has done this?"

"I don't know," said Gurzin candidly. He wondered if it would be wrong to ask Renenet to bring him a cordial.

"But we must," said Lasca with feeling. "If we do not, there may be another."

"Or something worse," said Gurzin, continuing slowly as he made sense of his thoughts. "This was a warning, not a threat. The cobra was in a chest, enclosed. It could not escape. We did not have to hunt for it to kill it. So they intended us to find it and kill it." He stared down at his hands as if they were unfamiliar. "It was a warning."

"Of what?" Lasca asked wildly. "How could anyone do this?"

"Someone wishes Madame de Montalia to know that she is suspect." He saw the dismay in Lasca's eyes. "Serpents are used by witches," he explained. "By leaving this cobra here, someone is telling Madame that she is a witch."

"*Dio proteggemi,*" whispered Lasca.

Gurzin kept on as if Lasca had not spoken. "Madame does not cover her face. Madame spends her time in the ruins, copying the writings of ancient priests. Madame is very young, yet she is an acclaimed student. Madame has given medicines to the Doktor which came from the writings of the old priests, who were little more than magicians, or so the Moslems believe. Madame has no husband or father or brother. Madame does not eat where others can see her." He ticked off these oddities on his fingers. "It is not surprising that someone in this household is suspicious." He folded his hands. "Madame will have to be much more circumspect if she does not wish these rumors to continue."

"And she's at the ruins now," said Lasca in alarm. "She is gathering more drawings and inscriptions. She ought not to do that." She looked at Gurzin. "We must persuade her to abandon the ruins."

"Do you think you could?" Gurzin inquired. "She came here against opposition and she remains here in spite of the disapproval of many. Do you actually think that she would give up her studies because there are those who disapprove? It has not deterred her until now."

"I think we must make her understand how great her risk is," said Lasca after considering the question. "This is not the same as whispers. The asp might have killed her."

"Do you think so? With all the medicaments she has from that chest she found, do you think the venom of a cobra would be deadly to her?" He got up and lifted the small bell from the table, ringing it once before saying, "I want Renenet to know of this. We will learn from how he responds, not what he says." He motioned to Lasca to sit down. "Let me deal with the man."

"Gladly," she assured him, taking his place on the stool. "I would not know what to do; he does not speak with any woman but Madame."

"Yes," said Gurzin, signaling her to silence as he heard Renenet approaching. "Houseman," he said with a respectful bow as Renenet paused warily in the doorway. "We require your assistance and silence."

"If I am able," said Renenet as he came into the dressing room, his eyes filled with doubt.

"We have found a cobra in one of Madame de Montalia's chests. I have killed it"—he gestured toward the urn—"and I will show it to Madame when she returns from the ruins. What I wish to determine is how the cobra came to be in the chest." He bowed again, his deference now slightly insulting.

"A cobra?" Renenet echoed, his brows rising. "Are you certain it is a cobra? There are many other serpents in Egypt, and it might be one of those, perhaps quite harmless."

"I know a cobra when I see one," said Gurzin. "It is hooded."

"Merciful, all-wise Allah!" His voice rose with distress.

"It would not be able to get into the chest without being placed there," Gurzin said, noticing how Renenet fretted. "Therefore, someone put the cobra in the chest." He waited for the houseman's next response.

There was a slight pause before Renenet achieved a short, blustering laugh. "Who would put a snake in Madame de Montalia's things? Who would be so foolish?"

"That is what I am determined to find out," said Gurzin.

"It is absurd that someone should do such a thing," said Renenet as a frown deepened on his brow.

"Nevertheless, there are the remains of the snake in that urn, and when Madame de Montalia returns, I will show them to her." He folded his arms. "Who in the household has raised questions about Madame?"

"No one," said Renenet, much too quickly. He realized his mistake and went on with a nervous laugh, "No one has been serious in that regard. Everyone is aware that she is . . . remarkable. But aside from occasional idle speculation, no one says anything against her."

"Yet the serpent was here," said Gurzin.

"And there have been visitors to the villa," said Renenet, his tone more confident now that he was on safer ground. "There have been the scholars and that physician and Omat's daughter, all in the last two days. Do you know when that chest was last opened?" It was a clever ploy, and it worked.

"Four days ago," said Lasca in answer to the question and the gesture from Gurzin. "I was putting some of the scarves away. I haven't opened it since."

"So you see," Renenet said, shrugging to show that he could not be responsible for the presence of the serpent.

"I see that there are more possible enemies," said Gurzin bluntly. "I see, as well, that you are more willing to protect the servants than your mistress."

Renenet bowed. "Madame is here for a short time. The servants are Egyptians and will abide here all their days."

Gurzin sighed in acquiescence. "And what am I to tell Madame, then?"

Renenet paused, and the polite mask that was his usual expression slipped a little. "Tell her that she would do well to be gone from here before worse happens to her than a cobra in her chest."

"Is that a message?" Gurzin asked in some surprise. He had expected a formal neutrality from Renenet, not open challenge. "Who has made you his messenger?"

"I am no messenger," said Renenet, polite once again. "I am only telling you what I fear. The presence of the snake is a message, and you know it as well as I do. Someone accuses Madame of witchcraft, and that is a grave charge. If she is not prepared to defend herself, then there are those who will take her silence for an admission of guilt."

"Yes," said Gurzin softly. He pointed toward the urn. "That serpent might have killed Madame's servant, or one of the household who opened the chest on request. If someone inquires about the cobra, you might tell them this, and warn them that we will be at pains to protect Madame." He indicated the door, nodding dismissal. "You have been most helpful, Renenet. I will inform Madame of that when I report the rest."

Renenet paled. "How have I been helpful?"

"By your answers, of course," said Gurzin. "You have told me much, and I am grateful. Madame will be as well." Having planted the barb to his satisfaction, Gurzin waved Renenet out the door.

"Why didn't you force him to tell us what he knows?" Lasca demanded after she heard Renenet descending the stairs.

"Because he would lie," said Gurzin. "We have no copy of the Koran here, and therefore we could not compel him to tell the truth." He took a turn about the dressing room. "Oh, he would be willing to tell us he *would* so swear, but unless he actually had his hand on the Koran when he said this, his word would mean nothing." He saw disbelief in her face. "Moslems are not the same as Christians in the giving of their testimony."

"But to lie, and about such a thing as this." She brought her hands to her face again, though they could not stop her tears. "We will be murdered, all of us, won't we?"

Gurzin did not give her an easy answer. "It may come to that, if we are not careful. We must convince Madame that there is greater danger than we thought there was." He touched Lasca's shoulder. "Come. We will retire to the withdrawing room and wait for Madame there. She ought to return within the hour, and in that time, we will be able to form a plan."

"I hate this," Lasca said, following after him.

"Make sure you lock the doors to the dressing room. I do not want that urn to vanish while we are gone from the room," Gurzin recommended. He waited while Lasca locked the dressing-room door, the door to her own room and the door to Madelaine's bedchamber. "Excellent," he said. "If she should ask, we can tell her that we know these doors are locked."

"And if they aren't? Locked?" Her look was disturbed, as if each new possibility made her more apprehensive than the last.

"When Madame de Montalia returns?" Gurzin asked, though he was sure of her answer.

"Yes. What if these doors are open? What if the urn has vanished, and the snake with it? What then?" The pitch of her voice rose sharply.

Gurzin did his best to appear calm. "Then we know the culprit is in the household, not an outsider who has taken advantage of a lack of attentiveness, which simplifies our search." He indicated she should speak more softly. "But we do not want to alert the guilty one, do we?"

"No," she said, but with less determination than he showed. "But how can we find out? I want to know who is doing this."

"As do we all," said Gurzin. "And if we are fortunate, we will be able to discover who has done this before anyone in this villa has any more misfortune." He was at the door of the withdrawing room. "I will ask for a little food to be brought to us, for Madame is not expected for more than an hour, and it is not strange that we would take refreshment now."

"I don't think I can swallow, let alone eat," Lasca warned, her lips turning pale. "I'm afraid I'd be sick."

"That would be a warning, as well, and it would say that you are weak like all women. You must defy the guilty ones, and take strength and purpose from your—"

Lasca threw up her hands. "All right. I'll eat. If you think it wise," she said with feeling, her face set in lines that were new to it.

"I think it prudent; that may be the same thing." He opened the door for her and passed inside when she was seated on the divan.

For the next hour and a half Gurzin directed their conversation, making certain that they did not dwell on the growing certainty that they would have to be much more careful if they were to avoid any other trap set for them or for Madelaine.

Renenet brought them a platter of spiced meats and honeyed fruits. He was so polite that Gurzin and Lasca might have been strangers and Moslems visiting the household instead of Christian

servants within it. He told them he would come when they rang
for him, and made a show of departing quickly, not lingering
where he might overhear anything they said.

"He's afraid he's gone too far," said Gurzin when Renenet had
left them alone. "He knows that he has overstepped his position."

"By refusing to assist Madame?" Lasca wondered as she tasted
the lamb cooked with cinnamon and onions. "Do you think it
worries him?"

"Yes, I do," said Gurzin unexpectedly. "He may disapprove of
her entirely, but he is in her employ, and that creates certain
requirements he must meet or show himself unworthy of the
trust of his place in the household. If he wishes to work for
Europeans again, he cannot be found lacking in his conduct now."
He murmured a blessing over the food, then went on, "If he knows
anything, he will have to inform Madame if she requires it."

"Do you think she will?" Lasca asked, not yet as confident as
Gurzin that the servants would take their employer's cause.

"I think she must," said Gurzin, and changed the subject to less
awkward matters.

When Madelaine was escorted to the withdrawing room, she
found Gurzin and Lasca deep in a debate about the Gospels, Gurzin
defending the books of the New Testament identified as the Apoc-
rypha, especially the Books of Infancy.

"Well," she said when Gurzin broke off his staunch defense of
these texts, "I expected something out of the ordinary, but the-
ology was not part of it," she told them with amusement. "Renenet
told me you wanted to speak with me, that it is urgent: I understand there was something of a problem here while I was gone.
Such a vague description: 'something of a problem.' Would either
of you like to tell me what it was?"

Lasca looked to Gurzin. "Tell her," she pleaded.

Gurzin contemplated his folded hands. "Anything I tell you now
is little more than speculation, and as such has no meaning."

"I understand that, and I know as well that you do not want
to have to speak against anyone without acceptable reason." She
sat down in a saddle-maker's chair, waiting for Gurzin to tell her.

"There was a cobra," said Gurzin, watching as Madelaine sat
bolt upright in the chair. "In a chest." As concisely as he could,

Gurzin reported everything that had happened from the time the cobra was discovered until they came to the withdrawing room to await her. As he went on, he studied Madelaine, noticing how guarded she became, though little of her outward demeanor changed. "I have the cobra, or what's left of it, in an urn in your dressing room."

"If it is still there," Lasca added darkly.

"It would be a great mistake not to leave it there," said Madelaine. "I don't think we will be fortunate enough to have stupid enemies." She leaned back in the chair, but this time she was not relaxed. "I will want to see the cobra, of course. And I will want to interview Renenet, for what little good it will do. I will also need to find a way to register a complaint with the Magistrate without having it originate with me." She glanced at Gurzin. "Are you able to do that, or should I find another?"

"Yamut Omat would be the best one to do it," said Gurzin. "He is a crony of the Magistrate and they have a long understanding between them."

"And they're both Moslems," said Madelaine. "Very well, when next I tutor Rida Omat, I will try to have a word or two with her father. If Omat is not the one who arranged for the cobra, then he may take my part." She tapped the tips of her fingers together. "The accusation of witchcraft: how serious is that?"

"Serious enough, if it continues," said Gurzin. "These people stone witches to death."

"Stone them," Madelaine repeated, knowing how deadly that would be to her. If her spine were broken, her skull crushed, it would be the true death for her as it would be for any living creature. "I see."

"It is a very bad taint," Gurzin persisted. "And there are many questions about you that lend credence to the accusation. Perhaps we ought to discuss—"

"Not just at present," she interrupted. "I want to see the cobra. Then I want to notify Professor Baundilet, in case Europeans are the target. I'd better send word to the Englishmen, and to Doktor Falke, as well."

"There are some who would take that as a bad sign," Gurzin

cautioned her. "They would view the warning as complicity or guilt."

"Possibly," said Madelaine, getting to her feet with purpose. "But I warrant none of them are Europeans." She gave them a very slight curtsy. "The cobra?"

Gurzin made a gesture of protection as he let out a long breath. "Of course," he agreed.

Text of a letter from Professor Rainaud Benclair in Paris to Jean-Marc Paille in Thebes.

My dear Professor Paille;

I am in receipt of your letter of 10 January this year and I must tell you I am very much shocked to have it, and from so honorable a man as you have been represented to be. The tone and nature of your letter are most distressing. How can you accuse your expedition leader of the kind of perfidy you do is more than I can comprehend. You say that he has claimed the credit for the discoveries of his expedition when he had promised that they would be shared with those of you who are part of his expedition, yet you cannot offer anything specific in proof other than your field notes, which, you must forgive me for saying, are not the best source of unbiased evidence. You say also that the Professor has been selling the antiquities he has found to wealthy patrons. That, if it is so, is regrettable, but scarcely reason for the accusations you make. It is generally understood that a few trinkets will be offered to such persons as local Magistrates and other dignitaries so that the work you do will be able to go on without hinderance. To suggest that Professor Baundilet would be so short-sighted as to sell off the most important of his discoveries because they fetch the most money assumes a cynicism and avarice that cannot be present in so distinguished an antiquarian as Professor Baundilet.

We have reviewed your letter here, and we have decided that for the time being we will take no action against you, for we have reason to believe that the pressures of the expedition can bring about certain mental aberrations, of which your outburst is typical. If another such diatribe should come from you, we will be forced to require you to return to France at once, and we will make public the reason for our decision to take such action against you. It would not be to your advantage to have such a turn of events be visited on you at this stage of your career. Let me urge you to consider the ramifications of this act before you force us to demand you leave the Baundilet expeditions. Upon mature reflection I am certain you will see the wisdom in what I recommend. On the other hand, if we receive similar complaints, we will review what you have written to us and decide what measures, if any, are to be used. We cannot be more fair than that.

Over the last three years we have made sure generous donations were offered to Magistrate Numair, who has assured us that as long as these donations continue, the work of the expedition may proceed unhampered. However lamentable this process may seem to you, it is worthwhile and it does provide the opportunities for antiquarian scholarship that would not be possible if the Magistrate were to forbid you to excavate the ruins. Your indignation has much to recommend it, but I fear we are not in a position to change our policy toward the Magistrate at this point without hopelessly compromising your expedition. We have been told by others that this practice is to be encountered all over the Eastern world, and whether we pay these donations to Moslems in Egypt or Mandarins in China, they are part of the price of learning.

Let me suggest to you that you examine your conscience diligently, Professor Paille. You have set yourself above your expedition leader in making the complaint you have sent us; it is hardly appropriate for us to hold such accusations in confidence, yet because of the circumstances, we will do that for the time being. We are going to take your suggestion and speak privately with Claude-Michel Hiver, to discover if he has any similar experiences to report. If he does not, then reluctantly we will have to address Professor Baundilet himself and ask him to respond to your charges. Doubtless that will be the end of your affiliation with the Baundilet expedition, but it will also serve to give an example, either to you or to Professor Baundilet.

It is distressing to have to deal with so distasteful an incident as this one. It is my hope that the matter can be settled quickly and with minimal inconvenience to everyone concerned.

Most sincerely,
Professor Rainaud Benclair

February 28th, 1828, Paris

3

Falke's smile used his whole face, from the lines at the edge of his eyes and cheeks, to the folds from the corners of his nose to the ends of his lips, to the lines on his brow. He held open the side gate and bowed Madelaine through. "More decoctions from that old temple?" he asked, indicating the basket she carried. He did not wait for an answer before he bent to kiss her. Lamplight and moonlight both gilded and silvered his features.

When she could answer, she replied, "In a manner of speaking," for these were more of the medicaments from the chest Saint-Germain had provided her. She turned in his embrace without breaking away from him. "They spring from the days of the Pharaohs, certainly. This one is for abrasions, and this one is for insect bites and rashes caused by them. This third bottle has a solution that can be used to treat swollen gums. This last is for boils and other eruptions of the skin, but is not to be used around the eyes." She held out the basket to him. She was dressed in gauze embroidered with gold thread, suitable for a supper at home but not for entertaining. There was a fichu around her neck, and beneath it a choker of pearls and a ruby.

"They're prepared from the inscriptions at the physician's temple?" he asked, already knowing what her answer would be. Over the last six months she had been able to convince him that the small temple was also some kind of infirmary, and though her colleagues laughed at the notion, Falke now decided that she had proved her point, and he was satisfied that the ancients were accomplished apothecaries. As had become a pattern with him, he was both relieved and apprehensive by Madelaine's donations, for he had not yet conceived an explanation that would not make it seem he was experimenting with the lives of his patients, and though many would applaud his efforts, there would be others who would discount everything he had accomplished because his methods had been so uncertain. "Will you," he said, making the request for the twentieth time, "provide me with the formulas for these remedies?"

Madelaine took a deep breath. "Why do you keep insisting?"

"Because how can I regard my patients as healed if I do not know how it was brought about?" He held up one of the containers. "What is in this salve?"

She sighed. "They are very ancient remedies."

He took the basket from her. "I thank you most heartily. Truly, Madelaine, I do. Everything you have provided me so far has been quite useful, and so I assume that these will be, too. But I would like to know what they are. Don't you understand that?"

"Yes, I can understand it," she said quietly, and capitulated. She would explain to Saint-Germain, she decided, and he would not protest her decision. "All right. I will do what I can to provide you the formulae, but remember that . . . the medicines are from long ago. It may take time to—"

"I'll try to be patient."

"The measurements are . . . not very precise." It was as much of a warning as she wanted to give.

"They still heal," said Falke. With a smile he indicated the door into his private wing of the villa. "I've missed you, Madelaine."

She ignored the last, though something in her face changed. "You must tell me if any of the medicines do not work, or do not work very well," she said, aware that her own doubt made the medications more credible. "I cannot always be certain of what the inscriptions say, or what the instructions mean."

"I am pleased that you bother at all, and I apologize for pestering you about the formulae. I felt it was necessary, so long as you have been willing to—" He stopped and looked at her, his eyes softening. "I sound ungrateful, don't I? I'm not. What other European has bothered to assist me as you have? To hear them speak, nothing of those ancient people is of any use today. The only time the other antiquarians set foot inside these walls is when they are in need of attention; they have no wish to give assistance, even when it is theirs to give," said Falke as he slipped his free arm around her waist. As they neared his private wing, he said, "I was reading *Wilhelm Meisters Wanderjahre.* I have done that once a year since I came here. I had a *wanderjahre* ten years ago; that was what convinced me that I ought not to stay safe at home. I admire Goethe; I doubt I should have had the courage to undertake this project without his writings to spur me on."

Madelaine was not unkind enough to laugh, but she said, "But your admirable Goethe remains at home."

"He has very serious work to do," said Falke without a trace of amusement. "He would be wasted here in the desert. His mind is a treasure and one that has not been wholly explored, not by him or any other man."

"Yet you think you are not doing serious work?" Madelaine said, and went on before he could speak. "I'm more gratified than I can tell you that you came here, don't mistake me, and my reasons have little to do with the treatment you offer here: but could you not have practiced medicine less . . . hazardously than you do here? Wouldn't you be able to make the contributions you wish to without imperiling yourself?"

"Women's logic," Falke dismissed affectionately. "How could I have learned about the diseases of the desert had I remained in Germany?" He chuckled as he opened the door to his private wing.

"But why study them at all? That's my point," said Madelaine as she entered his villa. "Is anyone up still?"

"It is after one in the morning," Falke pointed out. "I have a porter at the front gate who must surely be drowsing by now. With Jantje gone, I manage with local nurses, who come during the day only. They are gone from here at sundown, so that they will not break the law."

She stared at him. "Magistrate Numair permits this?"

He rubbed at his chin, rasping at the day's fine stubble. "I don't believe I've inquired," he said with a great show of innocence.

Madelaine stopped, looking at him with real distress. "You haven't asked him? Is that true?"

He put her basket on a standing chest near the window. "Why should I? He would only demand payments I cannot truly afford to give him, payments that he would expect me to increase as time goes by. He would demand the money that I need for medicines. How can I countenance that?"

"But to employ Moslem women—you do employ women, don't you?—without his permission could mean difficulties for them and for you." She put her hand on his arm. "I don't want to worry you, Falke, but I suggest that you swallow your pride and part of your purse to pay the Magistrate whatever he requires, or face consequences you will not ..." Her words trailed off as she saw him staring at the window where the dark of night had made the glass a mirror.

His single laugh was unconvincing. "Look. I was certain you were just there"—he pointed at the window where her reflection ought to have been—"but you're not."

"An angle of the light," she said, wishing she could move without drawing attention to herself.

"No. No, it's not the light. Because there is that engraving behind you. By all rights, your head should be in the way." He regarded the window in fascination. "How remarkable," he whispered, as if any sound would end the moment. "There is no reflection whatsoever."

"An illusion," she said, feeling more uncomfortable.

"No, not that. This is the other. This is what you meant. You said that you underwent a change years ago, but I didn't think it was—"

She interrupted him. "I told you that I became a vampire in 1744, upon my death in Paris," she said, deliberately making her words as unadorned as possible. "Do you believe me at last?"

"Your reflection is convincing," he said, though by the sound of his voice, he still did not believe what he saw.

"Don't be troubled," she said. "Take it as another part of my nature."

"I suppose I must," was his bemused answer as he stared into the glass. "I never noticed before."

"I'm usually not so inept," said Madelaine as she came to his side; she did not bother to look toward the window, for she disliked the sensation of vertigo that always resulted when she could not find her reflection.

"But it is quite remarkable," said Falke, touching his fingers lightly to the window. "If anyone were outside, would he see you?"

"Oh, yes. Just as you see me when you look at me." She leaned her head on his shoulder. "It's not worth bothering about," she told him, wishing it were so. As she kissed the place below his ear where his jaw and neck joined, she said, "Do we go to your bed-chamber?"

"Certainly not," said Falke, his indignation only half feigned. "I am not one to disgrace you, and under my own roof. You will not be subjected to idle gossip, nor will you have to listen while I am called a reprobate. I have set out cushions in the small salon, the one with the herbs. That's a safe enough place."

"Yes, it is. Who would think we had an assignation there? In case anyone should see us, I could say we were making more of these medicaments." Madelaine teased. "Quite plausible. Very sensible."

"It's not that, and you know it," said Falke. He took her hand as he went down the short hall. "I don't want my staff whispering in the morning that there has been a woman in my bed, for that would lead to more questions than you or I want to answer. Neither of us can be compromised now, not without grave consequences." He opened the door to the small salon. "What do you want, Madelaine? Shall I dim the lights or leave them?"

"Leave the candles," she said, noticing the single branch of them on the table with the pots of thyme and rosemary. "The rest can be blown out."

Obediently he made his way around the small room, blowing out the lamps and adjusting the wicks. "According to legend, you ought to see very well in the dark. Is that true?"

"Yes, and bright light is much brighter for those like me. Without my shoes and their lining of my native earth I cannot move over running water without severe discomfort. At night I need not be too cautious, but by day my strength deserts me and I am at the mercy of the sun if I do not prepare." She was tossing aside her fichu and began the complicated process of unfastening the forty-four looped buttons down the back of her frock.

"Don't bother with that," said Falke, his voice becoming much softer. He blew out two more lamps. "I will do it for you."

"As you wish," Madelaine said, smiling. She watched as he finished putting out the lamps. As he came toward her she raised her arms, sliding them around his neck before they kissed.

"You are a dangerous woman to know," Falke whispered as they broke apart. "I was all content to let the desert and the world take its toll of me, and then you . . ." While he held her, he worked her buttons open until her dress was open from neck to below her waist. "Was it deliberate? Making me notice you? Did you mean me to love you? Did you?" With each question he kissed her, the last time with such intensity that he was breathless.

She shrugged herself out of her dress, unheeding as it made a gorgeous puddle of gold-embroidered gauze at her feet. Her slip, of fine lawn, was very simple except for a border of lace at the hem. "I cannot force love on anyone; I would not want to if I could, for it would have no . . . savor for me," she said without any coquetry. "If you love me, it is because you love me, not because I have cast a spell over you."

"I didn't think you had," he said, feeling her tension under his hands.

"Didn't you?" At the very beginning, didn't you think that I might have been like Mesmer, and capable of controlling the minds of others?" Her kiss was quick. "Well," she went on recklessly, "I learned from the selfsame master as Mesmer did; there are those whose minds I could cast into sleep and take what I wish of them while they dream. I have done so many times. It is how most of us survive, though it is like dining on chaff." She saw the shocked look in Falke's eyes. "You would remember nothing of it. And there would be nothing more than a little lassitude to remind you of the dream in the morning." She pulled away from him. "Do you doubt me?" She was halfway across the room from him now, and she paused there to watch him.

Falke shook his head. "No. I do not doubt you. But I cannot imagine you behaving in such a way."

For that instant she wanted to shock him, to see if he would turn away from her. "I do. I must." She stopped long enough to pull her slip over her head; now she was clad only in her corset and stockings. "Can't you accept that?"

He stood staring at her, his neckcloth and collar both undone, one hand sliding the studs out of the front of his shirt. "You are the most beautiful woman," he murmured. "You are so beautiful."

"Am I?" She came toward him a pace or two. "No matter what I am?"

"No matter," he repeated as he unfastened the cuffs of his shirt, setting the links near his low-cut boots. "You could raven in the desert like a jackal, and I would not stop you."

She looked at him with so vast a sadness in her eyes that it frightened him to see her. "So I am one with the jackal?" She unfastened her garters and began to unroll her silk stockings.

"No," he said, trying to conceal his desire for her. "It was a bad choice of words."

"So it was," she said as she tossed the first stocking atop her discarded dress. "A jackal feeds on carrion, Falke. That offers nothing to those who are of my blood. The virtue of the blood is in the life; if the life is gone, then the blood can offer nothing." She pulled the second stocking off and dropped it with the first. "It is life I seek, Egidius Maximillian Falke."

He nodded twice, as he would have nodded to anything so long as she spoke the words, for his need for her grew as he watched her. "Yes," he made himself say.

"I take no carrion; I have no victims. Do I?" This last question was wistful. In the faint light her pale skin had a lustre rich as pearls. "Do I?" she repeated, trying not to dread his answer.

"Not in me," he said, closing the distance between them in two impetuous strides across the magnificent silken carpet. "I am no victim, except for love," he said, going on quickly as he wrapped his arms around her, holding her close so that he could feel her vitality and her yearning. "You are more than anything I have ever known, Madelaine, and I am ... frightened by what I want of you." He looked down into her face, entranced by what he saw in her violet eyes, what he sensed in himself. "We Germans are taught that Frenchwomen are ruinous."

"How gallant," she said sarcastically, then regarded him with simple candor. "Is that what you think?"

"I think that we Germans don't know the half of it, if all French-women are like you." He kissed her, his lips demanding and gentle at once. "I was told to expect caprice and found constancy; I was warned to put no faith in your word but you are completely trustworthy."

"It's the pact. I've tasted your blood," she said very seriously. "There is a bond with that." She leaned against him, her cheek pressed against his shirt where it opened over his chest. "No one like me can ignore that bond."

"It wouldn't matter if you did," said Falke. He loosened the pins in her hair and let it fall over his hands, touching the rich brown tresses as if they were rarest silk. "Dark like the river at night," he whispered. "And twilight eyes."

"Poetry," Madelaine whispered. She slipped one of her hands inside his shirt, loving the texture of his skin, the curl of his hair. "It's been quite a while since I've heard poetry, at least this sort. I'd forgot I like it. How good to remember the pleasure of it." She pressed her lips to his chest where his shirt was open, feeling the beating of his heart. "Does it worry you, the risk you run if we continue as lovers much longer?"

"That I will be like you?" He chuckled. "An odd notion, Madelaine."

"The truth," she said softly, wishing it were not so difficult to speak of how he would change. "You must think of it, because if you are not willing to be a vampire when you die, then we will have to abandon our passion, for your sake as well as mine. And that would be ... painful." She knew he was about to speak, to dismiss her concern; she forestalled him. "I have tasted your blood four times. You are already at risk. If you accept me tonight, your risk will be greater. Another two times together, and unless your body is destroyed or rendered wholly incapacitated, your change will be an irrevocable certainty, and death will not have hold over you."

"I would be a vampire?" He took care not to mock her. "Hardly what a physician should be." He saw the hurt at the back of her eyes.

"You don't believe me, do you?" She started to pull away.

"Don't do that." He tightened his embrace. "What man wants to be a vampire? I want to be your lover."

"The two are linked, Falke." It made her sad to admit it. She slid her other hand inside his shirt. "I want you, but not if you do not want me, and all of what I am."

"I could, in fact, tell you, leave, and you would go?" His amusement was filled with disbelief.

"Yes," she said with utter conviction.

The tone of her voice startled him; he regarded her more seriously. "But you would come again?"

"No," she told him. "Not as your lover, only as your friend."

"I won't let you. I won't have that." Carefully he unfastened the laces of her corset, then eased it away from between them. Her flesh was as intoxicating as the poppy paste that brought enthralling dreams and the end of pain. He pulled her more tightly against him. "What do you want me to say to you, Madelaine?" He kissed her hair, wishing she would face him.

"I want you to say what is in your heart. Nothing else matters." It was difficult to wait for his answer, more difficult to refrain from trying to influence him more than her presence did. "If you want me, then there is nothing that would give me more joy than your love, and I would want you as the living want breath. But if you do not want me, if you cannot accept what I am, then I do not want to remain as an unwelcome lover, bringing you danger and a transformation you abhor."

He touched her face and turned it toward his. "You may be content to release me, but I am not so generous."

She frowned. "I am not generous. I speak of necessity. I know that those who do not truly seek my love, whom I cannot truly love, are not what I need, and as I will not give them gratification, so they will not provide all that I need. Blood without love is less than bread-and-water."

"It must be a difficult life you lead," he said, partly in jest. "And one day you will have to tell me all about it. Just now I would prefer we speak much less." His kiss was insistent, not as gentle as before, and his hands moved over her back and hips with increasing urgency. He went down on his knees, drawing her after him.

"If you decide to be like me, you will have much to learn," she said, as a last sop to her conscience. Then she relinquished her concerns to his kisses and his passion, welcoming the explorations of his fingers and mouth, returning caress for caress as he sought her fulfillment with his own. From the curve of her breast to the arch of her hip, he lavished attention on her, receiving her ministrations with jubilant pleasure.

Long before he probed her flesh with his own, he was raised to a splendid, tender frenzy that was more intense, more encompassing than any experience he had known before. He penetrated more than her body, achieved more than the culmination of their reciprocal desire. In the attenuated instant when both touched the totality of the other, Falke discovered a communion he had never before realized existed, nor hoped to find.

It was much later when he drifted out of the glorious half-sleep that had claimed him; he saw Madelaine seated beside him, her knees drawn up to her chin, her arms around her legs. He reached out to be certain she was not just a continuation of his dream, and was elated to find her. "You're here."

"What?" she whispered as he grazed the back of his hand down her arm.

He did not answer her at first. "Was that part of your nature?"

"If it is accepted," she said in a soft, clear voice, "it can be."

"Then any man is a fool who despises it," he said as he rolled onto his side, and only then realized that he was in his bed. He did not recall getting into it; they had made love on the ancient silken carpet.

"I brought you," said Madelaine, adding as she saw flat disbelief in his eyes, "Another virtue of those of my blood is strength, of a sort." She leaned back against the pillows. "At night, it is no trial to carry you and another like you. Under the sun ... well, we who have died and changed, we do not fare well in the sun."

Falke was more awake now, and his curiosity was roused. "Why is that?"

"I don't know," she said with a short sigh. "My first lover, who made me one of his blood, said that it had to do with earth. Earth is strongest at night, as the sun is strongest in the day. All of us who change to this life eventually learn to line our shoes and our saddles and beds and carriages and the floors of our houses with our native earth so we will not be weakened while the sun is up."

"And if you do not?" Falke inquired when she had been silent for some little time. He traced the line of her shoulder, her breast, the arch of her ribs with a single finger.

"Oh, it depends," she said, looking away from him. "At the least, the sun will burn us as flames burn you. It requires time to recover from such burns, even for those of us who are undead." She brushed her hair back from her face. "Leave one of us in the sun long enough, so that the burns go deep enough to damage us beyond recovery, and we will die as surely as any heretic chained to a stake. Burn us with fire and it is the true death. Break our spines and we die; destroy our nerves and we die. But we cannot take nor give any sickness. We cannot starve. We cannot bleed to death."

"And the Cross?" asked Falke, remembering the harrowing tales of his youth, when those who had thrown off the shackles of death were held at bay by the symbols of Christ.

Madelaine laughed softly. "And holy water? And the Host? And the names of God and Jesus and the Saints? I was born Catholic," she said, "and in some ways I still am, though the Church might not agree."

"But vampires . . ." He said the word with difficulty and disbelief.

"What of them?" She reached over and touched the place on his throat where a tiny speck of blood was. "We are not tools of the Devil." Her eyes grew dark and distant. "I know those who bow to Satan, and I am not of them."

Falke read something in her face that took him aback. "Madelaine?" He wanted to bring her close, to protect her from what she saw in her memories.

She shook her head slightly. "Nothing. It was years and years ago."

Some of the contentment he had felt slipped away from him. "Come here; let me hold you."

Though she went into his arms willingly enough, when they

had kissed, she said, "It's growing too late. I ought to be gone."
There was sufficient reluctance that Falke could not conceal a
smile of satisfaction.

"You may stay, if you wish." He kissed her brow, her eyes.

"That would be very unwise, for both of us. Right now there
are rumors everywhere about us; it would be folly to give them
certainty." She gave herself up to his kisses once more, then
strengthened her resolve. "The Moslems will be called to prayer
within the hour." Her smile was more ironic than any he had ever
seen her make. "Those of us who have changed can feel the sun
better than any other of night's children."

He released her. "Is it so necessary?"

"Isn't it?" she countered as she slipped from the bed. "I have
my clothes here."

"Shall I help you?" he offered, hoping to keep her with him a
little longer.

This time she laughed softly and with genuine amusement.
"That would not speed me on my way," she said, then grew serious
again. "Have a care, Falke. We're neither of us safe here."

"We will prevail," he said, as he had said every day since he
opened the doors of his villa to the sick and injured.

"Do you think so?" she asked as she tugged on her corset.

Falke was puzzled. "Don't you, when you have come so far?"

She did not answer at once, busying herself with pulling on her
dress and fastening some of the buttons down the back of her
dress. "No," she said at last. "I hope I will be able to survive, and
that the cost will not be too high." She leaned over to kiss him.
"But I will hope that you will prevail, if you wish."

Text of a letter from Honorine Magasin in Paris to Jean-Marc
Paille in Thebes.

My cherished Jean-Marc;

*How good of you to arrange to send me that sketched portrait,
for I have had so few mementos I dared display, and my father
took the locket you gave me when he ordered me to have no*

more commerce with you. Tomorrow I will go to have this framed, and I will display it as proudly as I can with discretion. I have often longed for your image so that I could speak with it and pretend you were by me. You say that your hair is much whitened by the sun, and that there are deeper lines around your eyes now, and that your face has been burned quite brown. I will try to picture that as I look at your portrait, and remind myself that since you have seen me I am somewhat changed, as well. I hope I have not acquired lines in my face, but what woman can escape the toll of age? I carry my parasol and use cucumber lotion, but I fear that I am not quite as youthful as I was when you left.

You will find that the hair-styles in fashionable circles have changed very much. I can hardly recognize myself when I look in the mirror, for the new coiffure is so very striking, and such a departure from the way I have worn my hair before, and the resultant apparent alteration of my features is quite dramatic. Aunt Clémence has said that it is very fetching, but I am not yet used to it, and therefore it does not yet seem so to me. When I see you once again you will tell me how you like the change.

My sister has finally produced an heir, but there is concern for the boy, for he does not thrive, being very small and peevish. The infant requires attendants every moment of the day and constant vigils at night. My father has said that he requires me to marry so that he will not have to place all his hopes on this single grandson. Solange has declared that she will have another son before the year is out, but who can say if this will come to pass? I offer prayers for my new nephew every morning, for I do not want to have to argue with my father again about my single state. I have made my choice, and there is nothing my father can do that will turn me from you. Do not think ill of me, though, if I wish you were here with me, for I begin to hope that my father will be more tractable now that Solange has not succeeded as he hoped. My father wishes me to be a mother, not an Aunt, for the sake of continuing the family. Can you think of me as an Aunt, Jean-Marc? It is quite difficult for me.

Your last letter to me took much longer than usual to reach me—nearly five months—and that caused me worry, especially since I had heard that there were still battles being fought in that part of the world, what with the Turks and Russians and French and all trying to keep the peace. I made it my business to discover if there had been any military action where you were and I was informed that Egypt had not been involved in the conflict. I was much relieved, and you may well imagine how I felt, discovering so long after you had left that you might be in danger from such a thing as a war. I beg you to keep me informed on this head. Otherwise I will fret on your behalf.

Georges has just recently left Paris for a while, for his grandfather has finally died. He was a great invalid, you know, living quite removed from society on his country estates. Georges has looked after his affairs for years and years. I have never understood the whole of his riches, though apparently some were gained in foreign trade and the rest from dealings in metals. I have a poor head for such matters. His wealth is legendary in the family, and now it appears that Cousin Georges is to inherit the largest part of it, because he has for so long run the old man's businesses. Georges, as you might think, is beside himself with astonishment. He has said that this was not what he expected, and that he will have to make preparations to alter his style of living to be more in accord with the lands and monies he will now control. Of course Georges has always been comfortable, but now he is going to be quite fabulously wealthy. I am sure it could not happen to a man more deserving than he, and I am confident that he will succeed in enlarging his estate, which would please his grandfather. I have told Georges that I will assist him in any way I can, for he has been so kind to me, aiding me and serving as courier between you and me. I am certain you are as pleased for him as I am. In fact, I have extended your congratulations to him, because I am certain it is what you would want me to do.

Just three nights ago Aunt Clémence and I attended a private concert here in Paris where a recital of the opera Oberon *took place. Weber's music is quite pretty, and the work has had a vogue in London, but I find it is not to my taste. I long for a work about those ancient rulers of Egypt, their wars and their loves, which would capture the wisdom of those amazing men and at the same time offer sublime entertainment. Perhaps when you return you might be willing to seek out a composer and work with him on such an effort. I cannot think of a finer use for your explorations and scholarship.*

You will want to know that I wore that Egyptian necklace at the concert, and as usual I received the most flattering comments on it. Most of those attending said they had never seen anything like it, and when I told them a little of how I came to have it, they were impressed and astonished. One woman, a most dignified old lady, exclaimed over my necklace so persistently that I was almost obliged to give her a hint that I was not quite pleased at the attention she was drawing to herself and my necklace. She took my remarks in good part, but later I heard her say she would not be surprised to learn that the necklace was nothing more than a trinket from the bazaar in Cairo. I made no retort, but there was one in my mind, I can assure you.

The two new dresses I ordered at Christmas have been delivered, and the pale blue muslin is so beautiful it is quite enough to make me shiver with pleasure. You cannot imagine how it becomes me, for ordinarily I am not one who looks well in blue. But this appears to have draped me in a sigh. The muslin is so fine that it drifts as I walk, and the cut of it precisely complements my figure, though I should not say it. I must tell you it is not convenient to have Georges gone just now, for he was promised to escort me to several afternoon fêtes where this dress would be perfect. I shall have to wait until he returns. Luckily the dress is suitable for summer wear, or I should have to put it away until next spring, at which time it would not be as much the first stare of fashion. I have taken advantage of my Aunt to the extent that I have not refused another ensemble she has proposed for me: a fine daytime suite with a long coat for carriage rides that perfectly matches the gown beneath, which is of fine linen. I had not thought I would like a linen dress, for I am old-fashioned enough to think that only farmers wear linen, but it is becoming quite the rage, and it is extremely durable, which in outing costumes must be a consideration.

My Aunt Clémence has also informed me that she is about to

*have another set of chairs done up for the grand salon. I confess
I was surprised, for the chairs she has now are only twelve years
old, but she says that another upholstery is not sufficient, and
she must have new. The upshot of this is that she has said she
will put the current chairs into storage for me against the day
you return and we are faced with having to set up our household.
You, being a Professor, will need to economize on certain items,
and these chairs will help us make the most of what money we
will have. Not that such matters are important to me, but I
know that it is wise to take what advantage I can of such
generous offers as the one my Aunt has made so that you will
not have to overextend yourself when we marry.*

*Just a week ago I went to a country house with Aunt Clémence,
where we were shown a very ancient fortress that is said to date
back to the time of the Romans. It has no roof now, and some
of the walls have fallen, but I found myself thinking as I made
my way around those heaps of stone that I was doing much the
same thing you are, far away in Egypt. I must tell you that I
do not know how you are able to keep your enthusiasm when
the work is so arduous and so monotonous. I would not be able
to endure it for more than a month or two, I am certain. Still,
when we are in Egypt, there will be things to do other than
uncovering stones, won't there? You have written about the
entertainments offered by the Egyptian Monsieur Omat, and the
company of other antiquarians, so that your society is not as
limited as I sometimes fear. You might wish to see this fortress
when you are once more in France. No doubt it will be less
exciting than those mysterious monuments you now explore,
but your skills might be put to use here as well as at Thebes.*

*Now I must close. My Aunt Clémence has sent word that the
landaulet is ready and we must hurry, for her coachman does
not like to keep the horses standing. We are off to Saint Sulpice
for a special service of thanksgiving offered for those who fell
battling the Turks; you may be certain that I will be attentive
at this occasion, and will be praying for your safety. It is my
dearest hope that there will be no more hostilities in that part
of the world, and that those who were victims of the conflict be
accorded the respect due the heros they are. There have been*

*other services, of course, but Aunt Clémence is of the opinion
that this one is more important than some of the grander me-
morials. I am wearing a fetching day gown of a deep lavender,
so that I will not appear too frivolous for such a mournful
occasion. After the memorial, we are going to a supper held by
an old friend of my Aunt's who has asked us to join her and
two or three dozen of her friends for an evening of conversation
and airs on the harp.*

*You cannot fathom the depth of my love for you, dearest Jean-
Marc. Come home soon, and claim your prize in my lifelong
devotion.*

*With constant love,
Honorine Magasin*

March 9th, 1828, at Paris

4

"It was a gift from my father," Rida Omat said in answer to Madelaine's question, preening. "Quite lovely, isn't it?"

Madelaine reached out and touched the little ibis that hung
suspended from the gold chain around Rida's neck. "Yes," she
said in a thoughtful voice. "Yes, it is quite beautiful. How fortunate
that your father would give you so fine a present."

Rida's smile was ingenuous. "Yes, it is quite fortunate. Father
does not give presents to his wives, not like this. Each has jewels
from him, but they are nothing so remarkable as this." She looked
down at the ibis. "He is a very great man, my father."

"Many have said so," Madelaine said, knowing that Rida would
hear agreement in the words. She looked down at the array of
fans she had brought to show Rida. "It seems a shame to have to
conceal something so splendid behind painted chicken-skin." As
she said this she lifted one of the most elaborate fans. "This would
be proper."

"How pretty," Rida exclaimed, taking the fan from Madelaine and looking at the miniature scene painted on the chicken-skin. "This is almost as nice as those little paintings the Persians do."

"It is similar," Madelaine allowed.

"How pretty," she repeated as she took up one of the silk fans. "I must ask my father to get one for me." Her smile was too patent to be convincing. "Do all young European women have fans like this?"

"Not all of them, no," said Madelaine. "But girls making their debut in society have fans like that. The ivory is very fragile, so do not wave it too hard; it will break if you do."

"It isn't very useful if you cannot wave it." Rida turned it over, looking at the pattern. "Still, it's . . . pretty."

Madelaine indicated the oldest of the fans. "This is an antique," she explained. "My . . . Great-grandmother carried it." She picked up her mother's fan and showed it to Rida, at the same time looking at the ibis once more. "A fan like this is a very gracious gift, especially if your hostess is an older woman who would recognize its worth."

"Would it be proper for me to give a fan to a woman?" asked Rida with a lift of her brows.

"To a hostess, most certainly," said Madelaine. "So would a fine scarf, though a fichu would not be appropriate unless you were to stay at your hostess' house for many days. I would suggest that you bring a few pieces of jewelry, nothing too fine, to offer as gifts to your hostesses. It is not quite the sort of thing that is expected, but you have the advantage that you are Egyptian, and therefore you . . ." She saw something change in Rida's face. "What is it?"

"Do you think that Frenchwomen will actually receive me as a guest?" she asked, her voice so plaintive that Madelaine was taken aback. "Who would want me in their houses?"

It was a few moments before Madelaine framed an answer. "There are those who would not; I regret that many would not know how to receive you, not only because you are an Egyptian, but because you are a Moslem. You might find that some of the Europeans are . . . uneducated, and you might be offended."

"But where am I go to in Egyptian society in these clothes and with this fan?" She shrugged, her eyes averted. "I do not question my father's wishes, but I do not know what is to become of me. No Egyptian will offer for me now, and what European will ..." Then she put her hand to her lips. "I'm sorry. I am letting my feelings be overset. It is senseless." She looked down at the fans. "Is there anything more I ought to know of these?"

"Nothing we haven't discussed before," said Madelaine, puzzled at the sudden change of direction in their conversation. "You know how to carry the fan, and you hardly need me to tell you how to flirt."

Rida's face colored. "What makes you say that?" she demanded.

Madelaine was more perplexed than before. "I say it," she told her as calmly as she could, "because you are a very pretty young woman and you have been in society, at least a little. What did you suppose I meant?"

"Nothing." Rida sighed once, then clasped her hands together. "What husband will my father find for me, if he insists that I become so much a European? What European man will offer for me? They are Christians, and they cannot have more than one wife. Oh, that is so foolish!" She flung herself away from the table, then rounded on Madelaine. "How do you bear it, having men who cannot acknowledge more than one wife?"

"They have mistresses," said Madelaine bluntly. "It is a clandestine relationship, and not everyone approves of it, but most men who can afford it keep a mistress, and few denounce them for it." She regarded Rida to try to read her expression. "In some circles, it is considered so correct that if a man does not keep a mistress, he is thought to be odd."

"A man needs many women, to give him many sons," said Rida. "Anyone who thinks that is not true is a fool."

"A man is expected to have his sons with his wife, in Europe. If he has them by his mistress, he is expected to support them, but not to advance them above the sons of his wife, nor is he allowed to have them as his heirs, whether or not he has sons of his wife. If his wife gives him no sons, then his heir is his brother or his nephew." She indicated the refreshments that had been presented earlier. "Would you like anything more, Mademoiselle?"

"I don't think so," said Rida. "Is a man expected to have just one wife and one mistress, then?"

"That's preferable, and respectable in its way," said Madelaine with a slight smile. "He may not keep his mistress long, but he is supposed to support her while he reserves her to his own use. Such a mistress must be faithful to him while he supports her. His children he is supposed to support until they come of age, no matter what his dealing with their mother. Not all men recall that. A man might have several mistresses in his life, but if he has more than one at a time, he is regarded as being wild." She walked down the room and came back. "There are whores, of course, but a man is not supposed to make a mistress of them. He may have a favorite brothel or a whore he prefers, but these are not women he would keep as he keeps a mistress or a wife. He is expected to pay for his pleasure when he takes it, and there is no question of continuing support, or the acknowledgment of children; not that whores in brothels have many children. Most brothel-owners will not permit it. There are street whores as well, who are the most common, but men of quality do not often resort to them; it's not very wise."

This time Rida was shocked. "There are institutions where women are kept for men who are not their leaders or their husbands?" she said indignantly. "It would be better if a man had several wives and did not bother—"

"It is often a question of taste," said Madelaine. "There are things wives and mistresses do not . . . accept, most of them. And there are brothels for boys and men."

Rida laughed. "Well, men are always falling in love with boys, aren't they? But why must there be these institutions? Isn't it something better arranged between them?" She picked up one of the sweetmeats and tasted it. "Boys are boys for such a short time. Sons and wives are a man's for a lifetime." She indicated the fans. "I don't want to spend any more time with these today. I know my father wishes me to become accustomed to using them in the European fashion, but I have learned enough for now. I'd rather know more about these brothels."

"Why?" Madelaine asked, not at all convinced that Yamut Omat wanted his daughter to be told about brothels. "This is not something you are expected to know; it is most improper. Most women of quality do not notice brothels, not to acknowledge them."

"Are these brothels concealed?" Rida inquired, fascinated. "If they are concealed, that would excuse a woman not knowing about them."

"They are and they are not," Madelaine struggled to find a way to describe them to Rida so that she could grasp their workings, though she hoped there would not be many more questions. "They are . . . discreet. It is expected of the brothel-owners that they will not make themselves noticed officially, and if they are flagrant in their work, they must bribe a great many people to continue to operate. If they are too notorious the law closes them down. The French police do not bother to arrest the men—the women are shipped out of the country. They used to send them to the New World, but that's not so easily done any more, and the public does not like Frenchwomen being sent to Africa."

"What curious customs," said Rida, as if she were no longer certain Madelaine was telling her the truth.

"The customs of other peoples are often curious," said Madelaine, trying not to sound too amused or upset. She went to the small sofa near the window and sat down, smoothing the skirts of her walking dress as she did. "Come. Take the chair."

"Another lesson," Rida protested.

"If you'd rather not . . ." Madelaine said, indicating she would abide by Rida's decision. "You must learn how to choose for yourself. Your father would rather you know that than discover the illicit dealings of Frenchmen. European women are expected to accommodate their men, but not to capitulate."

"What is the difference?" Rida asked, sinking into the chair and relaxing against the cushions.

"Sometimes it is difficult to tell," said Madelaine, and laughed once, her tone ironic. "And there is a ritual of sorts to it. If you wish to protest what a man wants from you, it is possible to pout, but not if he is very angry. If he is exasperated then you may cajole him from his ill-humor. There are some men who will seek your opinion honestly, and when they do, you must give it, no matter how strange to do it; a woman who does not give an opinion when asked quickly loses the right to have one." She put her hand to her brow. "It is very difficult. When I attempt to explain it, there isn't much sense to it."

"No," said Rida. "How can you know what is being asked?" She tossed her head, copying the way she had seen Madelaine do it when Professor Baundilet had taken her aside at a gathering some weeks earlier. "What does a Frenchman do when he wants a woman? What would a man do to marry me?"

"It would depend," said Madelaine, who had anticipated the question. "If he were seeking a wife, it would be most proper for him to speak with your father before fixing his interest with you, though in these times, a man is more likely to learn something of the woman before declaring himself to her father." She hesitated. "A man who cares for you would treat you with attention, courting you. He would give you flowers and escort you when you went out. He would invite you and your father to be present when he entertained at home, if you were not to be the only guests. He would treat you honorably and respect your position as well as your family."

"Truly?" She made a valiant and unsuccessful attempt at laughter.

"Yes," said Madelaine.

"But if both loved, wouldn't that be different?" Her voice was higher than it had been.

This was becoming difficult, for she did not want to encourage Rida in her quest for a European lover if such a man would not be acceptable to her father. "It would mean that you might expect more concern for your well-being. Nothing clandestine or seductive would be contemplated, and your suitor would never attempt to coerce you for his own satisfaction." She thought back to some of the young men she had known in her youth. "I agree that such concern is rare, but so is love."

"But if a man is to do nothing but give flowers, how is a woman to know the kind of man he is?" She spread her arms as if to take in the immensity of the question. "Would not a man, if he loved a woman, dare everything for her? And if she loved him, wouldn't she offer him all her love instead of a simper? Wouldn't they both seek the fullness of their love? Wouldn't they have to? Wouldn't they? You say that men do not often seek the real thoughts of women, and then you say you can recognize a suitor by his reserve. What is the sense in that?"

"It isn't always sensible," Madelaine conceded. "It is men's way to make women guess, and then blame women for being too mysterious." She glanced toward the window. "If you were in France I could show you by example. But here, where there are few Europeans, and we do not live as we do when we are at home, I . . ." She rose from the sofa. "Your father would not like me to tell you these things. He wants me to teach you the ways to be a lady: how am I to do that without telling you about what is not discussed?"

Rida stretched out her languorous arms and made a motion to indicate it was all the same to her. "Do Frenchwomen know these things?"

"Yes," said Madelaine, "but they are not talked about openly, not the matters of brothels and mistresses and bastards. Love is thought too personal to discuss except with your lover. Women speak of very few things openly, but their gowns and servants and the progress of their children." She shook her head. "And the recognition their husbands receive."

"You have no husband and no children," said Rida.

"And I am an antiquarian, which is worse than the first two," Madelaine said for her. "Yes. I am rich and well-born, as well, and this is what makes it possible for me to have what little independence I do have. Without my fortune and my place in society—such as it is—I would not be tolerated by anyone."

Rida sat up, imitating the way Madelaine had been sitting. "You are angry?"

"Upon occasion," said Madelaine quietly. "There have been times when I was so furious it made me quite sick. But for the most part, I am more tired than angry."

"Then why not marry and have children? You are a pretty woman, young enough, and your fortune must bring you suitors. Frenchmen care about fortunes, don't they?" This last question was a little petulant, but Madelaine was so caught up in what she was saying that she did not notice.

"Most men care about fortunes," she said gently. "And you are lucky enough to have your father's fortune to compensate for your education."

"Is that wrong?" Rida asked, and this time she was sullen.

"It is the way of the world," said Madelaine. Then she shook her head. "We ought not to speak of these things. We cannot change them. Surely you will learn them soon enough without my help. Your father would not thank me for telling you these things." She did not want to think what Yamut Omat would say to her if Rida passed on any of their conversation.

"My father will know nothing of it. I will do as European women do, and I will do as you said: pout." She thrust out her lower lip. "See?"

"And will your father accept that?" Madelaine asked.

"He will have to. I will not reveal this even if he beats me. He does not do that so often now, for he wants me to be ready to meet his friends often, and if I have bruises, I will not please his friends, or I will seem rebellious, which is worse than unpleasing." She ate the last sweetmeat. "I suppose I should tell him that I am learning to behave as Frenchwomen do; he cannot fault me for that, since he is sending me here for lessons in being a Frenchwoman." She was about to wipe her mouth with her hand and lick her fingers, then remembered what Madelaine had told her and picked up one of the tiny linen serviettes. "How silly to waste cloth for this," she said as she dabbed at her lips. "Is this correct?"

"It is close enough to correct," said Madelaine, finding it slightly amusing.

"How silly," she said, but folded the serviette once, loosely, and placed it on the tray. "Is that right?"

"Yes," said Madelaine. "If you refold it as it was presented to you, it appears that you think they use their serviettes more than once, which is offensive to guests."

By now Rida was laughing. "I have thought for years and years that Europe is a most peculiar place, but now I am convinced of it." She regarded Madelaine with curiosity. "I have ordered a . . . driving coat, is that the word?"

"If you mean something to wear while you are out in an open carriage, yes, that is the word. A proper driving coat ought to have two or three capes. Only men have more, and that has not been high fashion for several years. The English coats were the most elaborate; the English were the first women to wear driving coats." She looked toward the windows. "This is not the proper climate for such a coat, but it is very correct."

"I have ordered three capes," said Rida. "My father warned me that I was not to be seen out driving again without such a coat and a proper bonnet. I haven't yet seen one that looks comfortable."

"Very few of them are comfortable," said Madelaine, and was about to go on when Renenet came to the door. "What is it?" Madelaine asked, unused to being interrupted when Rida was there for her informal lessons.

"Professor Baundilet would like a word with you, Madame. He says it is urgent or he would not disturb you." Renenet bowed, showing as much mockery as deference.

"Baundilet?" Rida asked, the breath catching in her throat. "Does he know I am here?"

"I so informed him, Mademoiselle," said Renenet. "I have asked him to wait for you in the green salon. I will send Brother Gurzin to him if you would prefer I do that."

Madelaine shook her head. "No. If it's urgent, I had better see him." She addressed Rida. "Will you excuse me, Mademoiselle?"

"Of course," said Rida quickly. "I will practice with the serviettes."

"Fine." Madelaine left the salon quickly, following Renenet and wishing that her very superior houseman would not insist on going everywhere at a pace more stately than a butler's.

"Madame," said Professor Baundilet as Madelaine came into the green salon. He took her hand and kissed it, giving her an arch look as he did. "How good of you to permit me a little of your time."

"What's the matter, Baundilet?" she asked him, taking care to be very correct.

"Something I hope you will help me with. It touches the whole expedition, I am sorry to say; we must act quickly: I fear that Jean-Marc has taken it into his head to return to France without delay." When he saw the surprise in her face, he nodded. "Yes, well you might be astonished. I am myself. I do not know what has got into the fellow. He keeps talking about that damned fiancée of his and his need to find himself a suitable university post now that he has some experience of antiquarian expeditions under his belt. It is all the greatest confusion, Madame. I can't get a word of sense out of him."

"So I would gather," said Madelaine, motioning to Baundilet to be seated. "What is it you want me to do?"

"Talk to him. *Talk* to him!" Baundilet burst out, paying no attention to her unspoken invitation and beginning to pace. "The fellow is the greatest fool alive. This is not simply an error of youth. He is prepared to throw his future away on a whim. But he is good at this work and it is not at all suitable to our purposes to have him gone now." He stopped beside the chair she had taken. "He'll listen to you. Any man with blood in his veins would listen to you."

"What an odd description," said Madelaine, thinking it was much more apt than Baundilet could know.

"You know what I mean. You are the kind of woman that a man must listen to for desire if no other reason." He leaned over the arm of her chair a little. "I haven't forgotten: don't say you have."

"I have made a good attempt, and would forget if you were not determined to remind me," she responded sharply. "You were speaking of Jean-Marc."

Baundilet brushed his hand over her shoulder, then, before she could protest, he paced away. "I know he's troubled because he has not found the fame and fortune he was depending upon this expedition to bring him. I'm sorry for it, but I am more sanguine than he. There are universities all over the world that put little stock in this digging up of the past, saying that what we need to know of what has gone before is taught us as religion and all the rest is the province of historians. What can ruins tell us, in any case? That is the argument of many scholars. They are just ruins, you see. Jean-Marc does not agree, and he wishes the academic world to change because it is what he wants." He pushed his hands deep in his pockets. "I don't want to lose Jean-Marc, Madame. I am depending on you to assist me."

Madelaine shook her head. "What difference could I make, Professor Baundilet? I have no authority with Jean-Marc. Undoubtedly you have more."

"Not just now," said Baundilet with the first indication of temper. "I have had in the past, but he is critical of what I have done. In his mind I have worked against the success of the expedition because I did not single him out for praise and favor. He will not heed me, I fear, because of his disappointment. He has also said he does not like what I have been doing in regard to what we have found. He disapproves of certain of my methods."

"What methods has he questioned?" Madelaine asked, thinking of the ibis on Rida's necklace.

Baundilet waved his hand in a vague way. "Oh, he is not consistent on that point. Perhaps you will be able to learn from him." He came and stood directly in front of her chair, close enough so that she could not move without touching him. "You will know what to do, Madame."

"I pray you; move back if you will." Her manner was polite but there was an edge in her voice.

"I want to impress you with my concern," said Baundilet, not giving ground. "I fear you think my worry is trivial, but I assure you it is not." He took her jaw in his hand, deliberately holding too tightly. "You will do this for me, or I will send a memo to Magistrate Numair about you, and you will then find it very inconvenient to remain here. Do I make myself clear?"

"Most certainly," said Madelaine, wondering if she dared turn her wrath on Baundilet; she decided it was unwise.

"And when you have convinced the young idiot to be sensible, I want you to tell me about it, all about it, and show me how you made him change his mind. Whatever you did for Jean-Marc, you will do for me, as a demonstration of your persuasive powers. You will hold nothing back. You'll do that, won't you?" His hand pinched again before he released her.

"I am not about to seduce him, if that is what you intend," said Madelaine, her voice easy and conversational, concealing the disgust she felt. "And I will not make myself your harlot."

"Not my harlot, oh, not that," said Baundilet with mock chagrin. "You are too fine a lady to do that, aren't you? Though you'll cross the orchard at night to that German's villa. "This accusation was made harshly. "Don't lie about it, Madame. Guibert has watched you, and he has told me everything he has seen."

It took all of Madelaine's composure to answer, "If he can see through a stone wall, he is more gifted than anyone I have ever encountered." She rose, though it meant standing too close to Baundilet. "You have no right to watch me. I told you that some time ago. That you continue to watch me is offensive to me."

"But necessary, it would seem," said Baundilet, making no apology for his behavior. "You are spending the night with the German."

"Are you certain of that?" she asked. "You speak as if what I have done is dishonorable; but you do not know what I have done, or if I have done anything, do you?"

"If that German has anything between his legs, you've done something, all right," said Baundilet. "And if you will give yourself to him, then you can give yourself to me." He put his hands on his hips. "If I tell the Magistrate about the cobra in your chest, he will question you about your witchcraft, and in this country, that means you will be stoned to death."

Madelaine did not reveal the fear that gripped her. "You are willing to turn a Frenchwoman over to a Moslem court to be killed? How do you think that report will do on your record, Professor?" She smiled coldly. "Or did you intend to offer a trade—you would provide the necessary bribe to the Magistrate to keep me from being killed so long as I complied with your desires." She saw his expression change. "So that's it."

"It's not—" he began.

"You are free to accuse me now or any time," she said with more bravado than courage, giving her temper free rein. "Go ahead. Under the circumstances, I believe I would prefer stoning to you." She started to push past him, but he caught her arm. "Let go, Professor."

"You owe me this," he growled, and forced his mouth onto hers, dragging her into a suffocating embrace.

Fury made her reckless; with her tremendous strength she broke free of his grip, and then delivered a single, bruising, open-handed blow to his face. "Never try that again, Professor."

He took a step back, one hand where she had slapped him, and regarded her with lambent rage. "I will have you, Madame. I will have you or I will see you dead." He started toward the door, and only then did he see Rida Omat staring at him, her face pale as wax.

Text of a letter from Erai Gurzin at Thebes to the Brothers of the monastery of Saint Pontius Pilate at Edfu.

To my reverend superiors and my Brothers in the Name of Christ, my greetings and blessings;

I thank God that you have allowed your fears for my soul were without grounds and that there is no danger to my vows or my faith while I am in the company of Madame de Montalia. It is the greatest deliverance to me that you are willing to reconsider what I have done, the more so because now calumnies are spoken about Madame that can only bring danger to her. There are those who swear that she is practicing the blackest sorcery, and are seeking to have her before the Moslem courts to be condemned, where she cannot defend herself and where she has no advocate the court would accept.

This is why I am writing to you: I wish to offer Madame de Montalia the protection of our monastery if it should become necessary for her to seek refuge away from Thebes. I believe it is possible she will need such sanctuary if these accusations become more insistent and the bribes of the Professors are no longer enough to convince the Magistrate of her innocence. Should she require shelter, for the sake of Saint-Germain if not Madame de Montalia, I wish to be permitted to bring her there until she can be taken safely out of Egypt.

Whatever you decide, I have already sent word to Saint-Germain, informing him of some of the problems Madame de Montalia has encountered. The letter will not reach him quickly, of course, and that is what troubles me. Madame de Montalia writes to Saint-Germain with great regularity, but it is her way to make light of her peril, and I suspect that she has not revealed

*the whole of her situation to him. It may be that she is not com-
pletely aware of her risks—although she is a most perspicacious
woman—or it is possible that she is reluctant to have to leave
Thebes, for she is fascinated with the ancient monuments.*

*She has been very determined in her labors here. By now she
has made over three hundred sketches of inscriptions and friezes,
another hundred or so rubbings, and her notes cover nearly a
thousand pages. She has said to me that she is convinced that
this is just the merest beginning in the study of the times of the
Pharaohs. While other scholars are saying that twenty to fifty
years will be sufficient to catalogue and record all the old ruins,
she says that there is more under the sands than anyone can
imagine. I am not convinced that she is correct, but I have come
to agree that there may well be more to study than is now
assumed. Any scholar, man or woman, who is so dedicated to
learning that risk means little is one entitled to our respect, and
the records she has made of this expedition are such that they
are worthy of being preserved, no matter what may happen.*

*I implore you to remember the debt we owe to Saint-Germain,
and I ask you to weigh all I have told you in this and other
letters. If you cannot tolerate the presence of this woman, then
inform me at once so that I can try to find other means to assist
her. The servants she employs will not do this: in fact, I fear that
they will be the first to denounce her to the Magistrate if they
believe it would be wise to do so. Those who are part of the
same expedition are in no position to give her more than cursory
assistance, which is true of all the Europeans here, though I am
of the opinion that the Frenchmen would be less inclined to aid
her than some of the others. It is a dreadful thing to anticipate,
the duplicity of friends. She is closely allied with a German
physician, but he cannot hide her, not only because he has no
position with the court, but because their association is private
but not wholly unknown, which would make it especially difficult for him to take her in with safety. She knows few Egyptians,
and which of them would compromise himself defending a
European woman?*

*May God give you compassion and clear vision, and may He
inspire you with the wisdom to know the deepest heart of Christ's*

Love. Surely if we are mandated to take in strangers from the desert we must also open our doors to Madelaine de Montalia.

With faith and the hope of Grace,
Erai Gurzin, monk

At Thebes, the Mass of the Archangels

5

By four in the afternoon, a wedge of shadow provided some relief from the heat; the old temple wall was long enough and tall enough to allow Madelaine to work in comparative comfort, though without her earth-lined shoes she would have been as weak as a newborn calf. She held her sketch pad up, comparing what she had done to the inscription surrounding what she supposed to be a gathering of gods, for most of them had the heads of animals. The cat-headed goddess was not quite accurate, and she had not got the offering on the tray right. She heard a step behind her but did not turn.

"Madame," said Jean-Marc Paille, his voice tense and unhappy. He kept his distance as he spoke. "I must speak with you."

She looked over her shoulder. "Yes; I suppose you must," she said, noticing how distraught he appeared; she gave up her work for the time being, closing her sketchbook and slipping it into her satchel. "So then. What is the matter, Jean-Marc?"

He ran his hands through his hair, disarranging the ribbon that held the unfashionably long locks off his face. "I don't know where to begin."

"The ibis might be a place to start," she suggested as reasonably as she could, and saw him draw back as if threatened. She moved closer to the wall so that she could see his face more clearly. "You told me you had seen her wear it and now I've seen as well. What we need to know is: how does Rida Omat come to have it?"

"I can only guess," Jean-Marc admitted. "I . . . assume Baundilet sold it to her father. How much of the rest he has passed on to Omat I dare not think." He slapped at the image of a ram-headed god, wincing with satisfaction as he abraded his palm.

"So I gather, since she informs me it was a gift," said Madelaine. She cocked her head to the side. "So Baundilet sold it to Omat, or gave it to him, perhaps? Or did Omat hear of the find and arrange for it to be stolen? Or was it stolen without Omat's knowledge and offered to him by the thief?"

"Would the girl wear the ibis, if it were stolen?" Jean-Marc looked at Madelaine, distress rendering his young face ugly. "Is Omat that brazen?"

"Only if he believes it would make no difference to Baundilet, and I doubt that; he is too eager to keep on good terms with Europeans, and stealing from them would not promote that. So did Baundilet give it to him? Or sell it to him? Or arrange for it to be presented in some other way?"

Those were the self-same questions that had been roiling in Jean-Marc's thoughts for many weeks. "I don't know. I don't want to think about it."

"And you can think of nothing else," said Madelaine softly. "Yes; I can tell." She shook her head, her eyes sympathetic. "What now, Jean-Marc? What are you going to do?"

His hands became fists, pressed together in cursing rather than prayer. "I don't know what I can do," he said unhappily. "I am . . . ham-strung."

"At the least," she agreed.

Some distance away from them dust devils rose swaying into the air as the scorching wind stirred for the first time since midday.

Jean-Marc slapped his thighs and then dropped onto the sand beside the wall, leaning against the inscriptions, his forehead pressed against his knees. "I wrote to the university, telling them what I suspected. I thought it would make a difference." He laughed once, harshly.

"And it did not," said Madelaine. "Not as you'd hoped. Ah, Jean-Marc."

He shook his head; his words came out in a rush. "I thought they might question his methods, or at least warn him that he was compromising the expedition. I thought they'd be upset at what he was doing, selling antiquities that way, since he's supposed to provide the university with more for their collection. I expected them to be displeased that he was not giving all his discoveries to them, and was not recording everything he has found. But instead they reprimand me. And they have told me that they aren't going to take any action against me yet, but if I should continue in this way, they will not endorse my work, which would make it very hard for me to obtain the Fellowship I want."

"And it might not help you marry," said Madelaine, settling down beside him. She tucked her skirts around her legs and wished she could wear breeches or inexpressibles instead.

"Oh, that is most surely the case. I have not been able to bring myself to tell her of this latest development, for fear she would then be compelled to break our arrangement. If my fiancée has not been permitted to marry a Professor of Antiquities, think what her father's objection would be if he learned I might never find a permanent post?" He threw back his head and glared up at the sky. "And if Baundilet turned against me, then I would not be able to remain here. He's got too much power with the officials in this district." He rubbed his face. "Sand."

"Everywhere," Madelaine agreed, content to lean against the wall that had been new when Saint-Germain tended the dying out of the House of Life. "I am amazed that the old Egyptians called the country the Black Land for the land after the Inundation rather than after sand."

Jean-Marc did his best to chuckle. "You can't grow wheat in sand," he said, then went on, trying to be arch. "Are you sure that is what they did? Called the country that way?"

It took a moment for her to recover herself, thinking that she had been too incautious with Jean-Marc already. "Well, it was known as Kheme, the Black Land, and the Black Land only describes the area of the Inundation," said Madelaine, trusting that Jean-Marc was too preoccupied with his own misery to notice her gaffe. "What else can the Black Land mean?"

344 *Chelsea Quinn Yarbro*

"Why not?" asked Jean-Marc, shrugging once. "It makes as much sense as other theories. Or it may mean something much different. Does it mean Black Land, or could it be Burned Land, because burned things are black, and this country does burn."

It was tempting to argue with him, but her prudence intervened so that she desisted. "What are you going to do about the objects you gave to Baundilet? Or have you not decided?"

"What can I do?" Jean-Marc asked in desperation. "I cannot challenge him openly, not here in Egypt, and I cannot do it when I return to France, not and keep a post. So I reckon I will have to tolerate what has been done and hope that I will not be subject to this again. But it galls me to think that I will have to overlook such flagrant abuses of the purpose of this expedition, and so much denial of my own work. For all the notice I shall receive for my work here, I might as well have stayed in France teaching Latin and Greek to the sons of rich merchants. I want to haul Baundilet into court, but what court and on what charge?" He put one hand to his eyes. "I hate talking about it: I'm afraid he'll learn of it, and that will be the end of it. I'll be turned off without a character, like some inferior servant, and abandoned here, with no chance of finding a position in this country or anywhere in Europe." He took a pebble and flung it away from him, watching as it disappeared into a mound of sand.

Madelaine started to trace Pharaohnic characters in the sand: joined papyrus buds, an ankh, a serpent, a closed eye, a hawk, a saw-toothed line. "There are my monographs," she reminded him when he had been silent for a short while. "They are carried by Brother Gurzin to Cairo, and they are sent on ships belonging to"—she looked at the version of his name she had written—"a blood relative. They reach France without interference."

"And then?" He did not quite want to scoff, because he respected the work she did so diligently. "What becomes of your monographs, Madame?"

"They are published," she said, and had the satisfaction of seeing him shocked. "Not by a university or a scholars' journal, but by a publisher who has some standing, nonetheless. The publisher is French but located in Ghent, for political reasons."

"Aristos," Jean-Marc sneered.

"Some of them, yes," said Madelaine without protest. "That is where the money comes from, in any case; a few of them have excellent academic standing, and many of them have justly famous collections of antiquities and extensive libraries which serve for subjects and gives the press a good reputation in spite of its unusual situation."

"And they publish your work," he said, making no excuse for the doubt he felt. "As antiquarian writings."

"Of course: that's what they are." Now Madelaine was a little stung. "They have published many other scholars; a few of them have been women." She did her best not to look annoyed. "I have already sent a monograph about our shared find, with descriptions of your share as well as my own; it has been sent to that publisher with instructions that the objects be donated to the university with the most worthy collection of antiquities." Now she could not keep from being amused, for she saw how difficult it was for Jean-Marc to make up his mind. "There were sketches of your items in the monograph, and they will probably try to include illustrations of them, as they will include lithographic plates of the things I've sent them. The monograph should be published before summer."

"You have great foresight," Jean-Marc said at last, the compliment coming unreadily to his lips. "I wish I had been as well prepared, but I never anticipated I would encounter such—"

"Resistance?" Madelaine suggested. "But you see, I knew I would: you are not the only scholar to doubt my abilities because of my sex; and so I arranged this in advance."

"Admirable," Jean-Marc conceded. "You are a surprising woman, Madame." He squinted away to the east, toward the distant cliffs. "It would be a gamble, giving my monograph to you. It could be that it will be ignored without the approval of the university. If your work has been noted at all, then it may be that I will be able to counter Baundilet at his own game. If it goes the other way, I will be . . ." He was not able to finish.

"Yes," said Madelaine as if there had been no break in their conversation. "It is a gamble, and you are risking everything on an uncertain venture. Suppose you accept things are they are now, suppose you do not challenge Professor Baundilet—what then? You will not have the credit you deserve and Baundilet will have a hold over you for all the time you occupy an academic. chair. Won't he?"

Jean-Marc let his breath out very slowly. "He will."

"Do you think, knowing what you do of his character, that he will be able to leave you alone?" She hesitated only a moment before going on. "Because I think he may decide that he will have to make you dance to his tune, if only to know that he can."

"He's not so reprehensible," said Jean-Marc, but with less conviction than he wanted to express.

"I hope you are right. But that is a gamble, a greater one than permitting me to arrange for the publication of your monograph. Since I have already had three monographs published, your information can be presented as complementary to what I have done." She took unmalicious but wicked pleasure in watching him wince. "Aristos look after one another, Jean-Marc," she said, knowing she was making it worse.

For once Jean-Marc had the good sense to hold his tongue. He shied another pebble into the sand. "It's a generous offer, if it's sincere." He glanced at her, but she remained silent. "If I were to do this, when would you want the monograph?"

"In no more than four days," she said. "Brother Gurzin is carrying another monograph and sketches for me; he will leave for Cairo in five days. Do you think you can prepare something in that time? They prefer their monographs to be of good length: at least fifty full pages in standard copperplate."

"That is a great deal of work," said Jean-Marc, trying to calculate how many pages he would be able to write each night.

"But it would be received as your own, and you would have it in print before Baundilet knows you have done it." She stood up. "Well, consider it, Paille. You know when I am going to send my work. If you have something you want sent as well, then bring it to me in four days. If you do not, then I will assume you have decided to deal with your predicament in your own way."

He watched as she pulled her sketchbook from her satchel, then found her pencils. "You are very dedicated, Madame."

"Thank you," she said, already starting to sound a bit remote as she searched for the place on the inscriptions she had been copying.

"Why is that?" Jean-Marc asked, uncertain why he wanted to know.

She had just located her place, but with an exasperated sigh she looked down at him. "I am curious. I have always been interested in ancient places and those peoples who have vanished from the earth."

"Those before the Flood," Jean-Marc quipped.

Madelaine gave him a serious answer. "I doubt the Flood had so much to do with it, or these ruins would be gone or far under water. They are from before the Flood, and they cannot be the only ones." She was prepared to continue to work on the sketches.

"The waters of the Flood retreated," Jean-Marc reminded her.

"These buildings have never known any Flood but the Inundation every year. Look at them. Use your eyes." She gave an impatient gesture. "Go away, Jean-Marc. Work on your monograph. There isn't much time."

The cry of a circling hawk came down to them, but neither looked up; the sound had become so familiar that they scarcely heard it. A second cry answered it from farther off.

He stood up slowly. "I ought to thank you for this."

"Yes, you ought," she said with a faint smile. "And if I were doing it entirely for you, I would be miffed if you did not."

Jean-Marc frowned. "What other reason would make you do this." The fretfulness that had marked his face earlier returned.

Now her smile widened but her violet eyes grew colder. "I am doing it to show Professor Alain Baundilet for what he is, to make him answer for all he has done."

"Oh." Jean-Marc tried to think of something more to say. "Still, it is good to be part of your plan."

"I hope you think so when it's all over," she said, and went on with her sketching.

"Of course," Jean-Marc exclaimed. He waited for her to say something but realized she was too busy with her sketches; awkwardly he started away from her, and before he had reached the end of the wall he was trying to think of how to present his monograph.

Madelaine had listened to him go: she was more aware of his presence than she wanted him to know. When she was certain he was gone, she stopped her work, trying to decide if she had increased or decreased her danger by offering to help Jean-Marc Paille. He had good reason to be frightened, she was certain of that, and even better reason to be angry at the usurpation of his work, but would countermeasures actually succeed? She was still trying to decide when she heard footsteps behind her and turned, expecting to see Jean-Marc back again.

"Didn't mean to intrude, Madame. Just out for an afternoon ride," said Ferdinand Charles Montrose Algernon Trowbridge making his way across the ancient paving stones toward her, doffing his hat as he came. "Thought you might not mind a spot of my company." He saw the sketchbook in her hands. "I'll leave if it ain't convenient for me to be here."

"Don't be a goose, Trowbridge," she said with affection. "You are just what's needed to keep me from megrims." Her smile echoed her words, but it did not last. "The inscription will be here yet awhile."

He faltered, then began, "None of my business; I know that. The thing is, can't help but notice you aren't quite yourself, you see. Troubled, Madame?" Trowbridge asked, concern on his cherubic features.

"Not seriously, no," she said, coming toward him. "And less so now that you are here."

"Gracious as always," said Trowbridge, offering her a slight bow. His fair countenance was ruddy from the heat, and his eyes were little more than slits. "I don't know how you endure it, working here. I think I should faint. At the very least I should require my smelling salts." His voice was droll as he tugged an enormous handkerchief from his pocket and swabbed his face with it. "Dreadful place, but nothing quite like it."

"No place for the unprepared," she said, which was no more than the truth.

He put his handkerchief away. "Sometimes I wonder if it wouldn't be better to cast breeding and position to the winds and put on one of those robes the natives wear. Can't look any more ridiculous in that than I do in this rig, now can I? Not the

done thing, of course, but a fellow can't be blamed for considering it."

"You may try it, if you wish. You won't be censured by me."
She sighed. "I have just been longing for inexpressibles instead
of skirts."

Trowbridge's pale brows raised. "Inexpressibles, is it? Don't let
anyone but me hear you say this: they wouldn't know how to
take it."

"And how do you take it?" she asked, her curiosity enlivened.

He hunched his shoulders. "As a shocking notion that might
be sensible if it weren't so shocking," he told her, winking.

"Then why don't you don a djellaba, if that's the right word,
and I will change these skirts for . . . trousers." She said the forbidden word with relish, enjoying the way Trowbridge did his
best to appear unruffled by her language.

"I'm not here alone, or I might give it a try. Castermere's having
a look around, too. He wanted to talk to Professor Baundilet, don't
you know. I think he wants to arrange for something to take home
with him. His family are partial to antiquities. He's finally leaving
again." He put his hat back on. "His family ordered him. He's
required to take a wife. They don't know about his likes, of course.
Well, a fellow keeps that to himself. He'll have to make arrangements on the side, for it don't do to whip a spouse too often, and
Castermere . . . well . . . Still, he's the sort who keeps his prefer-
ences out of sight. Not the sort of thing you tell Pater or the
family." He considered this, and amended it. "Or it may be they
know, but say nothing. Easier that way, I should think."

"He's been back once to England, as I recall," said Madelaine,
indicating the largest patch of shade. "It isn't much cooler, but
it's out of the sun."

"Thank you kindly," said Trowbridge as he came to stand near
her. "Yes, Castermere went home for several months, about the
time the fever broke out. All of us kept to ourselves during that
siege." He blushed. "Well, I know you didn't. Everyone said you
helped that German physician. You took care of those with the
sickness. Vastly heroic thing to do."

"You needn't keep saying so, Trowbridge," said Madelaine. "And
you can cease faulting yourself for not joining us." She put her

hand out and touched his wrist. "You make too much of what I did. Truly."

"Seems bloody brave to me, if you'll excuse my language," said Trowbridge, then looked down at his scuffed boots. "I told Castermere I'd be going home soon, too. Pater said he won't send money beyond this quarter, so I haven't much of an option, have I?" His smile crumpled at the edges.

To her surprise, Madelaine realized she would miss Trowbridge. "How soon before you depart?" she inquired. At the edge of her eye she saw the heat shimmering off the paving stones.

"Oh, not until the end of May. I was assured I could have until then, so I could finish up whatever studying projects I was doing. Not that I'm doing much of anything other than wandering around the west bank of the Nile goggling at the statues as they're cleared of sand. I haven't looked in the temples. They make me nervous, those temples."

"Small wonder," said Madelaine.

"Are you joking me?" Trowbridge asked, then laughed. "Nothing small about it, Madame. Those cliffs are filled with temples and Great Harry knows what-all. I don't blame the ones who say that we won't know what's there for another twenty or thirty years. It beats me how they plan to move all that sand in that time, let alone record everything they find. More expeditions, that's the answer." He dabbed at the sweat that ran down his cheeks.

"More expeditions, and with more money to hire native helpers," said Madelaine thoughtfully. "And having money for the necessary bribes, naturally. Nothing happens in this place without the proper bribes." If she had not been talking with Jean-Marc earlier, she would not have said this so angrily. As it was, the words came out sharply.

"What do you know of bribes, Madame?" said Trowbridge with an attempt at gallantry. "Not the thing for ladies."

"It may not be the thing," she said with asperity, "but I don't like to think what my life would be like if I didn't pay them." Belatedly she saw he was upset by this. "Not that I present them myself, or call them bribes, for that matter. Oh, no. Brother Gurzin calls upon the Magistrate with a consideration for his many gestures of respect. I do not participate, because women have no place before the Magistrate; Gurzin is tolerated because he is Egyptian for all he is a Copt. A small pouch of coins exchanges hands, very discreetly, and I am permitted to continue to have Egyptian servants in my villa. If I did not do this with some regularity, I would be forbidden to employ Egyptians, and no one would be able to work for me. It is the way of the world here." She scowled. "Fortunately I am rich, or I would not be able to meet Numair's demands. Not that the demands are spoken— heavens, no!—but we contrive to understand one another."

"Hardly seems fair, Madame," said Trowbridge earnestly. "Can't someone in Cairo do something?"

"What?" she asked. "By the time word came up-river, there would be no one willing to work for me, not for any price." That would be inconvenient: she said nothing about the greater dangers of actions that could be taken against her by the Magistrate's court.

Trowbridge took out his handkerchief again. "Does it never frighten you, Madame, this precarious existence of yours?"

She was about to give him a flippant answer, then decided he deserved more than that. She looked directly into his eyes. "Often," she admitted, then turned back toward the wall and the figures of the ancient, enigmatic gods.

Text of a note from Professor Alain Baundilet to Rida Omat, both at Thebes, carried by Ursin Guibert and delivered secretly.

My cherished one,

Don't be ridiculous, little love. You have no reason whatsoever to be jealous. You say that you are convinced Madame de Montalia has taken your place in my heart, but that is wholly untrue. Let me but have an hour with you and I will demonstrate beyond any doubts how foolish your fears are, and how completely I am in your thrall.

You know as well as I do that it isn't wise to approach your father, not yet. He is worried for you, as well he ought to be, and does not want you to be compromised. There is no reason to be angry with him for this, Rida my darling. He is doing what he knows is right for you. He desires to bring you to the attention of many Europeans so that you will be received by them here as an honored guest, as well as you should be. He is attempting to establish you in society before he finds you a suitor, and until he is satisfied he has done this, he will take no application for your hand, not even mine.

He is concerned that I have a wife in France, my little dove, and he worries that I will not be in a position to be the husband you so richly deserve. That is very prudent of him. He is aware that there are Europeans who would shun you if you married a European, simply because you are not European or Christian. An absurd prejudice, of course, but one neither your father nor I can ignore out of our affection for you.

Certainly I know that no woman could be as passionate and giving as you are with me. You are right that my French wife is nowhere near as capable in love-making as you are. She lacks technique and the adventuresome spirit you have in such abundance. I am thankful every day that I have a place in your heart and I am mortified to think that you are not happy with our love.

It would be wonderful, I agree, if there were a way we could be more open in our loving without bringing odium upon you. And I would not like to think that I was the target of unwholesome comments because I have been lucky enough to engage your affections. Neither of us would be able to do as we wish if we were discovered, and I could not bear to end loving you. That is what I fear the most, that we will be compelled to cease meeting and will not be permitted to continue as lovers. So I must still urge that we keep our love secret and admit to no one how deeply we adore one another.

That is why I must occasionally be seen to approach other women: so that my true passion will not be discovered and bring shame to you and me. Surely you understand. I know that Madame de Montalia is not going to accept me as a lover, because I am a Frenchman and married, and she is a Frenchwoman. So she is the one woman it is best I pursue, because no one will remark my interest or her continued refusal. You need not fear that I would act on the things I say to her.

Dearest, most precious Rida, be calm with me. No doubt I should have explained my purpose to you before you saw me with Madame de Montalia, but I thought you would understand what my purpose was. We have such sympathies and our unity is so great that occasionally I forget that you are not experienced in the ways of Europeans. I never meant to cause you pain, and I did not intend to shock you. I must do things that are distasteful to me in order to protect you from scandal. Know that everything I do I do for our benefit, to ensure our love will be able to continue and flourish. When the time is more auspicious, then I will speak to your father, and we will find a way to be together. If it were possible I would obtain an annulment of my marriage, but for a man in my position, that is not wise, and would call into doubt my marriage to you, if you are not willing to convert. In time we will discover a solution to our predicament, never fear.

In the meantime, keep the ibis near your heart. When I found it, I knew it was intended for you, and only for you. Though it may cost me my place as a professor, I was determined you should have it, so I permitted your father to purchase it in order to give it to you, since there was no other way to accomplish the gift. If it were up to me, you would be laden with every treasure in the lost treasuries of Egypt, and all the jewels of the Pharaohs would be yours, though you outshine them all.

Tomorrow I will come to the garden gate at the usual hour. If you have forgiven me, if you understand why I have had to do this thing, then meet me there. I long to be in your arms, to possess you fully.

Tell me you forgive me when we lie together and I will bless these hours of your anger as heralds of a deeper love.

Your pining
Alain

March 18th, 1828

PART V

The sigil of Sanh Zhrman
who-is-
Imhotep
High Priest

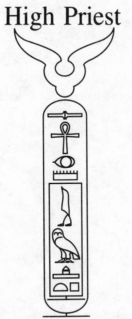

Text of a letter from le Comte de Saint-Germain in Athens to
Madelaine de Montalia in Egypt, dated March 15th, 1828.

Madelaine, treasure of my heart,

*From the sound of it, Paille is frightened, and frightened men
do reckless, desperate things. You cannot trust him now, no
matter what he tells you. I urge you to get free of him. He is
like someone drowning, likely to pull you down if you try to
save him. You cannot help him out of his predicament, and he
can cause you much harm. As unprincipled as Baundilet is, he
is the more reliable of your two colleagues. Do not expose yourself to greater risk, for my sake if not your own.*

*In answer to your questions, without actual sketches I will
not be able to make a positive identification, but I can venture
a guess or two: Hapy is easiest, being the only hermaphrodite;
he is usually shown with streams of water flowing from his
breasts, indicating the Blue and the White Nile. The god with
the hawk head is probably Horus, but could also be Montu if
there is a plumed disk on his head. The cow's horns are for
Hathor, but be certain they are not gazelle's horns, for that
would make her Anukis. The ram-headed god with the crown
and two plumes is Harsaphes, but without the headdress is
Khnum, unless he carries three sceptres, in which case it is probably Ptah. The rat-headed god is Seth. Both ibis and baboon are
sacred to Thoth. The god with the plumes, the flail and the*

phallus is Min. The lion-headed goddess is either Bastet or Sakh-met; if there is a cobra on her head, she is Wadjit. Isis, Osiris, Anubis, Apis, Geb, Nut, Shu and Nephthys you know already, and Imhotep.

If the man you mentioned to me—the young British anti-quarian Wilkinson—is willing to make sketches for you, I would be glad to see them. I can give you a more accurate identification from good sketches than from descriptions, and from what you say, he is painstakingly accurate in his work.

You ask why the figures in murals and scrolls and bas-relief are always shown in profile: you say you have found no excep-tion thus far, and I assure you that you will find none. It was considered to be usurping the right of the gods to show both sides of the face on flat or bas-relief surfaces, and any artist who attempted such a representation was subject to being stoned to death for blasphemy. Such sentences were carried out a few times, as I recall, and the work of the artist obliterated in order to appease the gods and show proper awe for their powers. It was not necessary for such vengeance to be exacted often, for to do such an unthinkable thing was regarded as madness at best. No matter what stylistic changes occurred in the wall paint-ings of the Black Land, that one tradition did not alter, so great was the power of the gods and their priests.

It was Shoshenq, the Pharaoh who founded the Libyan dy-nasty, who made the repairs at Karnak mentioned in the text you sent me, strengthening the defenses where they existed and making new ones where there had been none before. You un-derstand, he had taken the land by conquest and was determined that no one else would do so. There are inscriptions to his honor throughout the new construction. He was a capable, acquisitive, and ruthless man, one who sought power with avidity, and to that end installed his son as High Priest in the temple of Amun-Re; his successors often tried similar ploys with the intention of preventing just the sort of usurpation they had accomplished.

For a time they brought renewed prosperity to the Black Land, but it was fragile and did not last much more than a century, which in the Black Land was not long. By the time Shoshenq III came to reign, the kingdom was divided again. However, the position of foreigners had changed because of the Libyan rulers, and five decades before Osorkon IV made his daughter Shepen Wepet High Priest of Amun-Re, I was at last made a priest of Imhotep, accorded full power and privilege in the Black Land. Eventually, I rose within the priesthood.

Through the night Bathatu Sothos clung to life, certain that the god he had served so long would save him as he lay in the temple sanctuary. As High Priest of Imhotep he had worked to keep the temple from greater Pharaohnic disfavor, and had been rewarded with sufficient funds to rebuild two of the courtyards. The priests who had served under him feared for their futures now that Bathatu Sothos was near death.

"The walls belong to the glory of Neferkare," muttered Bathatu Sothos to the priests attending him as the night wore on. "He restored them for that, his glory, not for Imhotep."

"It does not dishonor Imhotep," said Sanh Zhrman, who had been designated Bathatu Sothos' successor.

"It dishonors his priests, those words that are not truthful," said the dying man. "It sticks in my throat like a fishbone." He looked toward the others, blinking to focus his eyes in the lamplight. "Our scrolls say there was a time when we did not depend on the favor of a stranger to keep our place in the world." The last words faded almost to inaudibility, and his breath wheezed.

Neksumet Ateo, who was only nineteen, made a gesture to protect himself from the spirits of age and disease. "There is no reason for Pharaoh to favor us above others." He looked at Sanh Zhrman as if waiting for the foreigner's endorsement.

The High Priest gestured feebly, unable to speak. Finally he gasped out, "No favor. No favor. Resentment."

"Hush," said Sanh Zhrman, putting his hand on Bathatu Sothos' forehead. "Save your strength."

"Why?" came the answer.

Sanh Zhrman had nothing to say; he motioned to his servant and whispered to him. "I have an errand for you: I want the tincture in the chalcedony jar, the one with the jasper stopper. Will you bring it?"

"At once," said Aumtehoutep, and left the sanctuary swiftly and quietly.

"The others should be chanting," protested Wekure Udmes, who was constantly discontented. He loved grandeur and had felt its lack acutely in the House of Life. Two of his brothers held positions at court, which served only to make his annoyance more complete. "It is not fitting that no one is chanting."

"It is my . . . request. I told them not to," said Bathatu Sothos quietly. "I want peace."

"Peace," scoffed Wekure Udmes, getting up from his chair and beginning to pace. "How can you have peace when there is no offering, no chanting, no ceremony to guide you out of the House of Life." He looked at the others gathered around the High Priest. "We are disgraced, and none of us are concerned. Our High Priest is dying and there is no messenger here from Pharaoh, no mourners from him. How is it none of you seem to notice what has happened?"

"Wekure Udmes, be still," said Sanh Zhrman for them all, though he did not look at the other priest.

"You aren't High Priest yet, foreigner, and I need do nothing you command." His sandals smacked the granite floor, declaring his anger more clearly than his words. He looked at the other priests. "Will you be content to have a foreigner officiate here?"

"They will," whispered Bathatu Sothos.

Neksumet Ateo spoke for the other priests. "Sanh Zhrman has been here longer than any of us, well before the oldest of us can remember. My uncle has told me that he saw Sanh Zhrman here when he was a boy, and that was more than forty years ago. It is said that he has been here since before the temple was built. If he is willing to serve as High Priest, then we are fortunate beyond our deserts." He stared at the floor, embarrassed at his own fervor.

This endorsement did not silence Wekure Udmes. "There are records that say a foreigner has been here for hundreds of years. But the first records tell of a slave, not a priest, something hardly human, to tend the dying out of the House of Life. Because he does it now and is a foreigner, you say he is the same man, but someone must always tend them, and who better than a foreigner? Who can tell which foreigner is which?" He stared at Sanh Zhrman, as if aware for the first time that there might be some credibility to the records for those less skeptical than he. "The description is the same, but descriptions can be altered."

"And have you ever known the priests of Imhotep to alter their records?" asked Sanh Zhrman softly. He gave his attention once again to Bathatu Sothos, placing a cool compress on his face. He knew from the way the old man was breathing that their vigil was almost over.

"They say the slave had scars," Wekure Udmes persisted. "Severe, wide scars."

"I'm sure you've read the description," said Sanh Zhrman without shifting his attention from the High Priest.

"From the arch of the ribs to the base of the pelvis," said Wekure Udmes. "As if all the skin had been peeled away."

In spite of himself, Sanh Zhrman shuddered: it had been more than twelve hundred years since his death by disembowelment, but the memory was with him still. "Yes; that is the description."

Neksumet Ateo felt more confident, and he looked at the other priests gathered in the sanctuary. "You are scarred, Sanh Zhrman. It is a similar scar, broad and white. It is enough."

"Yes," said Sanh Zhrman miserably. He rested his hand lightly on Bathatu Sothos' chest, feeling the faint, failing rise and fall. He nodded at the scrolls of the liturgy for the dying and said to Pama Yohut, who kept them, "I think you had better start the last lines."

Pama Yohut complied promptly. He took the scroll from its place of honor at the foot of the statue of Imhotep and rolled the papyrus open. " 'For every day is completed in accordance with the eyes of the gods, and all things are concluded in their will, coming to the end that has been ordained for them. For those who strive to do the work of the gods, their conclusion is part of their beginning, a facet of the jewel given as life. There is no task that cannot be resigned to the gods, no act that will not be honored—' "

"Sanh Zhrman," muttered the High Priest.

"Yes, great teacher," said Sanh Zhrman correctly.

" '—though the *ba* and the *ka* come with the heart to be judged by Osiris before Maat and Thoth and Anubis—' "

"Do not be swayed from our calling. Do not listen." Bathatu

Sothos spoke so weakly that Sanh Zhrman was almost unable to hear him.

"I will not," Sanh Zhrman promised him.

" '—when rest comes and the journey is ended,' " finished Pama Yohut. He paused with the scroll held open, and only when Sanh Zhrman moved back from Bathatu Sothos did he permit the scroll to close.

At the time, when the ceremony investing me was complete, I amused myself imagining what Mereseb or Sehet-ptenh would have done had they witnessed that event. I had not expected to feel such vindication as I did then. Thinking back now, I am a bit ashamed for the delight I took in my advancement. After almost eight centuries—over half my life at that time—to rise to High Priest: it was a sweet victory. And I suppose that I was justified in my pleasure, or so I tell myself.

By the time he was sixty-nine, Neksumet Ateo had lost half his teeth and his hair had turned white. He squinted now when he read the sacred texts, and the swelling in the joints of his hands had made writing a slow and painful task. He peered up from a five-hundred-year-old scroll as a shadow fell across it. "Sanh Zhrman," he said in his cracked voice.

"Neksumet Ateo," Sanh Zhrman responded. "I am going out of the House of Life, to see who has been admitted there today. Would you care to come with me?"

The old priest knew that Sanh Zhrman's invitation was a rare honor, one accorded to very few of his fellows, but he hesitated, thinking of the heat of the sun and the sight of the dying. "I will know what it is to be out of the House of Life soon enough, High Priest. If I decline, it is not a slight to your generosity of spirit."

"Of course not," said Sanh Zhrman with a fleeting smile. "I did not intend to impose on you, old friend."

"Old, yes; that is the word that governs me: old." He indicated the scroll. "This is the record of a high priest of Imhotep who served here long ago, named Amensis. Part of his writing is devoted to you, Sanh Zhrman, though he does not call you Zhrman. It is you nonetheless."

"Are you certain?" asked the foreign High Priest.

"As certain as any man can be of something so unthinkable," said Neksumet Ateo. "I have been remembering those things that were said of you when Bathatu Sothos died, when I was so very young. Well, they say that with age there comes understanding. Do you believe that, High Priest?"

"I hope it may be so," was Sanh Zhrman's careful answer.

"And I; for I would not like to think myself mad." He leaned his head back, studying Sanh Zhrman through narrowed, failing eyes. "How old are you?"

"Older than most of you think I am," he answered truthfully, an amused light in his dark, dark eyes.

"Where did you come from?" He was perplexed at the quickness of Sanh Zhrman's response, for he had supposed that the High Priest would deny his past.

"From north of Mycennae, in the mountains; I have earth from there shipped to me for . . . reasons of ritual." His smile was swift and heart-broken, gone almost before it began. "My people are gone from there; they have been gone from there a long time. One of the regional princes who paid tribute to the Hittites met us in battle. He fought shamefully, capturing the warriors to serve as cover for his own soldiers, and killing all the rest: women, children, the old and the addled. He offered them all to the gods for his victory over us. He killed my father last, flaying him and then roasting him."

"All bad deeds," said Neksumet Ateo, caught up in what the High Priest of Imhotep was telling him.

"And one he paid for, in time." Sanh Zhrman's voice was colder then than Neksumet Ateo had ever heard it. He had been looking away from the old man, but now he turned back. "Would you like to know the rest of it, or are you content to have a piece of the truth?"

"Why do you tell me?" the old priest blurted out.

Sanh Zhrman's laughter was short and painful; he hesitated before he spoke. "Why indeed? Perhaps because I am weary of concealment. Perhaps, just once, I would like to tell someone."

He looked down at the old priest. "Not even my servant knows these things. One day I will tell him, but ... You are a good man, Neksumet Ateo, and you are loyal to a fault. So it may be that you will hear me out, and when I am through, you will keep what you hear to yourself and earn my ... undying gratitude."

Neksumet Ateo did not answer directly. "I have been a priest of Imhotep for fifty-one years, and I have not seen those years touch you, Sanh Zhrman. From what I have read, you were here in the time of the heretic Pharaoh with his Hittite sun-god and Hittite wife. That was long ago."

"I came here a century before that," said Sanh Zhrman quietly, standing so that the old man could see his face clearly.

"And you were no older or younger then, were you?" asked Neksumet Ateo, sensing the reply.

"No."

For a short time Neksumet Ateo said nothing; then he looked at the High Priest. "Tell me."

Again the faint, stricken smile pulled at his mouth. "I was the son of our King—he was not so great as Pharaoh, but he was greater than many—and because I was born at the dark of the year, I was initiated into the cult of our god." His dark eyes were distant, haunted with his memories. "When I was old enough I was left in the sacred grove, my hands bleeding, waiting to offer myself to the god. He came, of course, and accepted my dedication, for when I grew to manhood, I drank his blood, and became one of his, destined to break free of death." He stopped abruptly and looked at Neksumet Ateo. "That was thirteen hundred years ago; Mentuhotpe, I think, was Pharaoh."

"Your god kept his pact with you," Neksumet Ateo observed.

"Yes; he has." Sanh Zhrman's expression grew distant. "He died, my god, in the battle that enslaved me and half the men who had fought at my side. He died and never rose again, for his head was struck from his body." He regarded the old priest thoughtfully. "It is fatal to me, as well."

"It is fatal to all that lives," said Neksumet Ateo placidly. He was grateful to Imhotep, who had shown his face to him this once.

"The King who took me prisoner had me killed—for winning

a battle that was all but lost." Involuntarily his hand went to the white swath of scars across his flat belly.

"Yet you are alive," said Neksumet Ateo.

"I am not dead," the High Priest corrected him softly.

In all the centuries I served at the House of Life, only Neksumet Ateo had my secret, and he kept it faithfully. When the priests of Anubis came for him, I gave them a glass ring to be buried with him. In that time, my heart, glass was a rarer jewel than diamonds. He left an account of our discussion, but it was sealed and no one read it for many, many years.

Throughout the Black Land unrest continued, growing worse from time to time, never quite bringing about a collapse of the country, but eroding it steadily. It took Shabaka to put an end to the regional disputes and once again reunite the Black Land. By the time Taharqa started building monuments from Nubia to the sea, the country was beginning to flourish again. The Inundations were heavy during Taharqa's reign, and since the little wars had stopped, there were generous harvests for more than a decade.

With Pharaoh in Memphis, the governing of Thebes and Upper Egypt was left to the fourth priest of Amon, a well-born and capable zealot named Montemhet. He was all but worshiped by the people of Thebes, and monuments to his glory were raised all over the city. Unlike many of the rulers of the Black Land, Montemhet was very interested in improving the means by which work was done. Forward-thinking in many ways, he financed projects to improve roads and buildings, and altered the taxation process. He still refused to consider minting coins, for that to him was foreign and reprehensible because the Greeks did it. So Egypt continued with its barter exchange. You will search in vain for Pharoah's face cut in silver and copper and gold like Caesar's.

In the north, Pharaoh was being hard-pressed by Esarhaddon, King of Assyria, who took Memphis for two years until Taharqa came with an army raised in Upper Egypt to reclaim his capital.

All this strengthened Montemhet's position for a time, but nothing could save him from treachery; whether it was the supporters of the Nubians or someone closer, the only time I saw Montemhet was after he had been poisoned and brought to the House of Life in the vain hope he could be saved.

Under the sun-disk pectoral Montemhet's chest was cold and slick. His breath was shallow; air hissed in and out of him. He watched the High Priest closely. "You are a foreigner; I have heard about you," he said at last.

"So is Pharaoh," Sanh Zhrman said as he bent to examine the man. "Do you know how you came to be ill?"

"Poison," spat the fourth priest of Amon.

"Yes," said Sanh Zhrman. "But do you know how you were made to eat it?" He waited, knowing it was a mistake to demand an immediate response. "If you cannot remember, there is no error in saying so."

"I do not think I can remember," said Montemhet, selecting each word with care. "There is nothing that comes to mind."

"Might you have been given a little over a long time?" Sanh Zhrman continued his examination.

"I noticed nothing until yesterday," said Montemhet. "And then I felt there was a scorpion in my vitals."

"Yes," said Sanh Zhrman, straightening up. "That is unfortunate."

"Does unfortunate mean deadly?" Montemhet challenged.

Sanh Zhrman looked away, then met Montemhet's gaze. "I fear in this case it does."

"How soon?" Montemhet did not need to have Sanh Zhrman's reply; there was something in his stance that said more than any words. "Tomorrow? Will I at least have tomorrow?"

"I think so, if it has not progressed too far; I cannot be certain of the day after." He moved back from the table where the fourth priest of Amon lay.

"Is there nothing you can do?" asked Montemhet seriously, his ashen features filled with resolution.

Once more Sanh Zhrman took a short while to answer. "I don't know. It is a difficult matter. If I were certain of the poison there might be something I could give you that would . . . delay it." He made a quick, final gesture. "It would not stop death from taking you, and it would not diminish the pain much, but it would give you two or three days more."

"Why must you be certain about the poison?" This time Montemhet made himself sit up, watching Sanh Zhrman with narrowed eyes.

"Because if I treated you for one poison and you had been given another, it might well be that the poison would be doubled in its potency and you would die before sunset." He said it in a flat, steady voice, but there was something in his face that revealed his concern.

"Give me the treatment," said Montemhet at once.

"No," protested Sanh Zhrman. "If I am wrong—"

"If you are wrong, I will die more quickly and with less suffering than I will in any case. If you give me two more days, I will apprehend the traitors who did this to me." He slapped his hand on the surface of the table, but the blow lacked force and the emphasis it was intended to convey was lost.

"And it will be said that I killed you," Sanh Zhrman reminded him. "What would happen then, do you suppose? How many priests of Imhotep would answer for my mistake?"

"I will order protection for the House of Life," said Montemhet. "Send me a scribe and the order is given."

Sanh Zhrman frowned as he said, "Very well."

He died that night, in spite of the tincture he drank. The poison had too great a hold on him. Toward the end he sent word to the guard that he was leaving the House of Life and would be at the Temple of Osiris, to discover through their oracles who had given him poison. It was a generous thing to do, for it meant that none of us in the House of Life were accused of killing him. Not long after that the Assyrians returned and made war the length of the Black Land. Eventually they were defeated, but they changed Egypt, for the victory over the Assyrians was gained by a Pharoah who employed Greek and Carian mercen-

aries. Psammetichus I stated it was so that the army would not have too much influence in the court, but that was not the reason: he feared Egyptians more than he feared foreigners. He maintained his capital in the north and claimed that the Black Land was unified once more. To some extent his strategy worked, for Necho II was able to repel Nebuchadnezzar II and to build up the fighting ships at the mouth of the Delta.

It was not long after that Nitocris, the Divine Worshiper of Amon at Thebes—you would call her High Priestess, I believe —agreed to adopt Ankhnes Neferibre as her successor. It was a pragmatic arrangement, promoted by Pharoah and the Divine Worshiper to their mutual benefit. Both women were long-lived, and between them they served as deputies for the royal family in Thebes for well over a century.

It was when Ankhnes Neferibre was about forty that there was a new outbreak of trouble in the House of Life, for the priests were accused of selling magic potions to those who had money enough for them. At first the rumors were inconvenient, but then they became insistent and dangerous. Ankhnes Neferibre ordered me to answer for all the priests of Imhotep.

She was seated when Sanh Zhrman came to her, and her slaves stood around her to show the extent of her importance; her wig was enormous and elaborate, her face as expressionless as a statue. When the High Priest of Imhotep had made proper obeisance, she indicated the place he could stand. "Have you brought me an answer, Sanh Zhrman?" The omission of his title was her reminder that he was being held personally accountable for his information.

"I have made many inquiries, Divine Worshiper, and I do not yet know which of my priests, if any, have done the things they are accused of." He spoke openly and without the usual persiflage required at so formal an audience.

"And what conclusions have you reached, Sanh Zhrman?" She had a decorative flail in her hand, but the way she moved it showed the intensity of her feelings. "There are those who are afraid to

eat or drink because they are certain that your priests have supplied deadly substances to their enemies."

"It is not so, Divine Worshiper," he said as calmly as he could.

"It is so," she insisted. "It is a known thing. It is certain that
the priests have overstepped the bounds that they have observed
for so long, all because you are not able to master them." She
glared at him.

"Because I am a foreigner?" he suggested lightly, refusing to be
goaded. "It is a reasonable explanation, if you believe the insin-
uations."

She rose, her head coming up as far as she could raise it without
shifting her wig. "Listen to me, Sanh Zhrman: there is to be no
more treachery."

"Rather address that to Amon than to me, Divine Worshiper,
or to Pharaoh." He showed no lack of respect, but there was
something in his stance that irritated her.

"You are not of the Black Land, and yet it has been allowed for
you to rise to High Priest of Imhotep. What better way to bring
down the might of Kheme than through your temple, where all
men seek healing?" She flicked her ornamental flail once more.

Sanh Zhrman made a second show of submission. "It is true
that I am not of the Black Land, but I am not of any people who
are known to you, Divine Worshiper. I am the last of my people
and I have found a haven in the Black Land that I was most
fortunate to encounter. Why should I profane such a gift when
there would be nothing but loss for me?"

"What a facile tongue you have," said Ankhnes Neferibre, her
large, kohl-lined eyes sharp and critical. "I was warned about you
before."

"Why should that be, Divine Worshiper?" Sanh Zhrman asked
with genuine curiosity. "I have kept to the temple; I do not do
anything that is not appropriate to the priests of Imhotep. It is
my task to care for those who come to us for help." He put his
hand over the pectoral he wore; it was his personal sigil, the
eclipse disk with upraised wings.

"I have been told that you are not what you seem." She rose
from her throne, a small, angular woman with features that had

once been pretty but were now sharpened by age. As she took two steps toward him, she remarked, "They say you play the harp."

Sanh Zhrman blinked. "Yes."

"It is for women to play the harp," said Ankhnes Neferibre.

"It has not always been so," said Sanh Zhrman carefully, recalling a time not more than three centuries past when women had not been permitted to learn any musical instrument except the flute. "I learned some time ago."

"A foreigner who plays the harp." She laughed, and the rest of the courtiers laughed with her. Her eyes flicked over him as if searching for weaknesses. "What injury scarred you, High Priest?"

"An old one," said Sanh Zhrman.

"No insolence," Ankhnes Neferibre snapped.

"None was intended," Sanh Zhrman assured her, his tone deferential. His sense of unease was growing stronger, but he dared not acknowledge it in any way.

She took another step toward him, then turned her back on him. "I am not satisfied that your priests are blameless. You would defend them against me; I doubt that you would consider them responsible for such acts even if you knew about them." She held up her hand, the flail flicking lightly. "I will withhold judgment about you for a time, but your priests are to be watched. You will not oppose me."

It took tremendous determination for him say to her, "As you wish, Divine Worshiper," when he wanted most to protest.

"As I wish," she agreed.

Which is how we came to have spies from the temple of Amon in the House of Life. There were four of them in the next two years, and each one created more dissension than the last. There was nothing I could say to the Divine Worshiper that would make her change her mind on those rare occasions when she would receive me in her audience room. She was certain that the root of the evil was in the House of Life, and she was going to find it if she had to invent it for herself; eventually it came to pass. As the distrust grew in the Temple of Imhotep, some of the acts Ankhnes Neferibre sought began to occur; at first it was possible to cast out those who broke their vows, but it became increasingly difficult as all the priests grew more secretive.

I do not know when the plot was laid, but I know it was inevitable. A few of those who were discontented found allies with others, and soon they decided that in order to bring the House of Life out from the suspicions and recreancy that had become standard fare in the temple, they would be rid of me, so that another High Priest could rule. I suppose I should be grateful to all the forgotten gods that they chose knives as their weapons.

Denin Mahnipy, as leader of the group, was the first one through the door of the High Priest's private study. He held his knife ahead of him like a torch, as if the blade would give off light. When he was satisfied that the room was empty, he motioned to the other three waiting in the hall to join him. "Hurry," he whispered as he reached to pull the door closed.

"Where is he?" hissed Wanket Amphis as he looked around the room; like most of the priests of Imhotep he had never entered the chamber before and his curiosity was almost stronger than the thrill of danger.

"Out of the House of Life," muttered Kafwe Djehulot. "He goes there every evening." He stared at the shelves with their profusion of jars and vials. "When does he do this?"

"At night, or so I have been told," said Wanket Amphis brusquely. "We must conceal ourselves." Hide was a word that he could not bring himself to use because it sounded too cowardly.

"Yes," said Kafwe Djehulot, looking around for a likely place. "Where is his manservant?"

"He is at the market; I saw him leave not long ago." Denin Mahnipy nodded toward the door that led to the High Priest's sleeping chamber. "In there."

"But if he does not come in quickly?" asked Kafwe Djehulot, his determination fading quickly. "What if he does not . . ."

"He will come there to change his clothes," said Denin Mahnipy with more patience than he felt. "It has been his habit for years."

"We can take him if we must," said Mosahtwe Khianis, who was the largest of the four, almost as tall as Sanh Zhrman himself.

"Into the sleeping room, then," said Denin Mahnipy. "Keep your knives ready and say nothing."

"What if we're found out?" asked Kafwe Djehulot, nervousness making him stammer.

"We will not be found out," said Denin Mahnipy as he stepped into the sleeping room, pausing a moment at the austerity of the place: a single, narrow bed placed on a chest, a cluster of oil lamps, a simple chair, and a rack of rolled papyrus scrolls. There was no gold, no ornaments to reveal the high position occupied by the man who slept there.

"The priests will join with us," said Mosahtwe Khianis, his voice as implacable as the sun.

"Be quiet," warned Denin Mahnipy, who had heard a sound in the hallway. "Get ready."

The four fell silent, each of them tightening their holds on their knives, their attention on the door.

As he came through the door Sanh Zhrman hesitated, his head slightly to the side, his dark eyes clouded. He was still. Then, as if making up his mind, he stepped through the door, reaching to pull off his black headcloth. Before he could toss it aside, he hesitated again, turning toward the door of his sleeping room, alert and strangely feral.

Wanket Amphis stumbled out of the sleeping room, his knife held behind him. He lowered his head. "Your pardon, High Priest. I . . . I was curious. I . . . did not intend . . ." He let his words trail off.

"Intend what?" Sanh Zhrman asked when Wanket Amphis did not go on.

". . . nothing . . ." Though his voice was muffled and his posture deferential, Sanh Zhrman remained alert.

"Are you alone?" he asked quickly.

"Yes," said Wanket Amphis, speaking more forcefully. "There is no one else to blame." In the same breath he swung his arm, knife angled to sink deep into Sanh Zhrman's side.

With this as a signal, the other three burst through the sleeping-room door, their knives up, reaching for the High Priest.

Sanh Zrman, who had not suffered a serious injury in nearly a thousand years, was more surprised by the pain than by the attack. He staggered, sinking to his knees as the knives bit into him, and felt his blood slick on his hands. The four men bore him down, their knives busy.

"Cut his throat," panted Mosahtwe Khianis. "That's sure."

Through his agony, Sanh Zhrman heard the order and felt three hands move toward his neck. He steeled himself, then brought up his arm with such impact that Kafwe Djehulot was slammed back into the first set of shelves hard enough to make half the contents topple and crash around him.

The next to feel Sanh Zhrman's wrath was Denin Mahnipy, who was lifted from his feet and flung down onto the table in the center of the room; three of the table legs broke under the impact. Denin Mahnipy sprawled in the wreckage.

Wanket Amphis spun toward the door, looking now to escape. He felt bloody fingers close on his arm, and in the same movement, he was tugged around into the door-frame of the sleeping room. He felt his shoulder and ribs crack before he lost consciousness.

Mosahtwe Khianis could not believe what he saw: he lashed out with his knife two more times, and felt the blade enter deep into the High Priest's flesh, yet Sanh Zhrman was not stopped. Before Wanket Amphis slid to the floor, Sanh Zhrman had rounded on Mosahtwe Khianis. "No," muttered Mosahtwe Khianis as Sanh Zhrman, now shining with blood as with lacquer, stumbled toward him, trying to wipe his eyes clear.

"Traitor," said Sanh Zhrman as he threw imself at Mosahtwe Khianis, hands closing around his throat, fingers fixed.

Desperately Mosahtwe Khianis attempted to break free, but succeeded only in backing himself into the far wall with Sanh Zhrman still throttling him.

Neither combatant noticed that the door had been opened, that Aumtehoutep and two senior priests stood there, watching in horror as the fight continued.

"My master!" exclaimed Aumtehoutep as the first stupefying impact of shock left him.

Mosahtwe Khianis made a noise as he floundered against the wall; his face was a mottled shade of plum.

"The High Priest is bleeding!" shouted one of the priests with Aumtehoutep; with that he shouldered his way into the room and signaled to the other priest to come with him. "They carry knives," he said to the other priest.

Aumtehoutep moved faster than the two senior priests. He reached Sanh Zhrman and straddled him, trying to pull him off Mosahtwe Khianis. "My master, my master, think what you are doing," he cried.

In his daze of pain and outrage, Sanh Zhrman barely understood what his servant said. Then his hurt welled up, and he let go of Mosahtwe Khianis. Where his strength had been enormous he was now filled with weakness. He put one bloody hand onto the broken table. "They were waiting for me."

"You dealt with them," said Aumtehoutep, his face impassive.

"I suppose so," said Sanh Zhrman, trying to get to his feet. It took Aumtehoutep's help to rise and remain standing. He closed his eyes. "How many wounds?"

The older of the senior priests looked up from where he was examining Kafwe Djehulot. "We have not counted them, High Priest." From his attitude, it was apparent that he feared the wounds were fatal.

"Yes," said Sanh Zhrman in a fading voice. His head rolled back. "Aumtehoutep."

"Yes, my master," said the manservant.

"Take me . . ."—there was a faint, ironic light in his pain-racked dark eyes "—take me out of the House of Life."

For thirty-nine days I lay in the courtyard out of the House of Life and listened to the priests chant against my death. Denin Mahnipy and his men were sent to Ankhnes Neferibre, and she ordered them drowned. Someone found the account of Neksumet Ateo. So when I entered the House of Life once more, my name was in a cartouche with the cartouche of Imhotep, and I was a god.

A century later I had left the Black Land for the north, traveling to my homeland before coming to Athens. In my homeland I was as much a stranger as I had been when I first arrived at the

House of Life. Though the place restored me, it did not bind me, and I left it with more sorrow than regret.

It might be wise for you to consider departing, as well. I have ordered my yacht in Cairo to wait for you. There is a bed over the good earth of Savoie in the main cabin, and two chests of it in the hold. My captain will follow your orders without question. I will depart for Crete in four days, and will wait for you there.

Do not forget that Egypt is Africa, not France; that Africa is a place where everything is devoured. There are great treasures in those cliffs, and there are riches and glory for those who find them, but there is death there as well. The tombs have waited in that valley for three thousand years—they will wait a little longer for you to find them, my heart, as I waited to find you for almost as long. If you leave for a year or a decade or a century, Egypt will still be there. As will I. And I will love you when all the hidden wealth of Egypt is nothing more than dust.

Saint-Germain
(his seal, the eclipse)

April through July, 1828

Text of a letter from Ferdinand Charles Montrose Algernon Trowbridge in Thebes to his father, Percy Edward Montrose Dante Trowbridge, in London.

Esteemed Pater,

In accordance with your wishes, I have arranged passage from Cairo, departing there July 19 on the ship Duchess of Kent, *which is bound for Barcelona before heading home. I have already made arrangements to leave for Cairo in May, mid-month, for Thebes, as you know, is more than four hundred miles from Cairo, and cannot be reached in a day. True, the current is at our back, but it is not the swiftest passage. The felucca will also bring my goods, such as they are, so that they may accompany me back to England.*

Let me tell you that I am reluctant to go at this time, for I have developed quite a fascination for this place. It is rather an unusual experience, actually, for I've never fancied the delights of scholarship. Now I realize that once I am married there will be no dispute if I wish to return here once the family has been started. Yet that is not the way I would like to conduct myself. Yes, Egypt can be a hellish place, and I have complained of its many difficulties before, yet it is the beginning of the world, or so it seems to me, and I can stand the heat and the sand if I gain some little comprehension of these amazing monuments. Here, in the shadow of colossal statues that dwarf the excesses in Rome, I have come against a mystery that does not yield readily to my application of logic and study. Here and there, a phrase, a name, gains my attention, but it does not last, it cannot last. I cannot imagine what it must have been like only twenty years ago, when these stones were entirely mute, for we had no translation of their language. Now, since Champollion has done so much for us, it baffles me that so few antiquarians have come here to reap the rewards of his efforts.

No, I am no scholar, merely a curious fellow with a tolerable education. I have no wish to add to the collected writings about this place, but I do have interest in it, nonetheless. I admit I did not expect to be captivated by this country, and my first affinity for the place came through my interest in Madame de Montalia. Well, what sensible man would be unmindful of the charms of so gracious a lady? It is still astonishing to me that she is willing to become my friend. Then the spell of the place overcame me. Now I am truly intrigued, and not as a curiosity or a place where the people put up enormous statues, and temples of such grandeur that no words can express it, or not entirely. Egypt is filled with mystery and I want to know what lies beneath the façade of the place.

Perhaps I will come back later, but I know part of the spell will be broken, for I will not be able to give myself to it as I can now. I will have a wife and children who will hold my thoughts as much as these monuments. If you had seen the Pyramids or these tremendous statues and walls and temples, you might know why I complain to you. But you do not, you do not know this place, and it is senseless of me to attempt to explain.

When I reach home, I will endeavor to comply with your wishes and to enter into the spirit of your plans. I will be delighted to see my sisters and my two nephews, and I hope you will tell Mater I will bring her several bolts of cloth when I return. Arrangements are being made to purchase cloth and some brass platters and urns when I go down-river. I will make certain that these are packed and stowed properly so they will arrive intact and unblemished.

Please inform my sisters that I regret I cannot bring them ancient treasures. Even if I had found them, I would not feel it proper to send them. I know many others who would not agree, but I have come to share the concern Madame de Montalia has expressed in regard to the dispensing of these treasures; if it is ancient, it is an object of study, part of a body of work that is what Egypt used to be. If it were still what it was, there would be less pressing reasons to want to keep the discoveries intact; but since we do not know these ancient people except by the things they left behind, we do them and ourselves dishonor if we permit their work to be scattered. If that is a radical notion, then consider me a radical. Never thought I'd say that about myself, come to think of it, that I'm a radical, and about something so strange as tombs and temples in this infernal place. I cannot tell you how much I love these stones. I never thought I should, and now that I do, I am the most disoriented man—meaning no pun.

I suppose Daffodil Peg has foaled again. I'll want to see what she's produced when I get back. You said her '25 colt-foal went for a cool fifteen hundred. Not too shabby for a yearling, fifteen hundred. It will be good to see a proper English Thoroughbred again; these desert horses are beautiful, but wispy, not up to English country and use. Give me a good hunter any day. Both the horse and I will be the happier for another hand and more bone.

My fond regards to Mater and my sisters, with the assurance that I will be prepared to dance attendance on them; my greetings to the staff and senior staff, especially the servants who have served me before; if Sheffley is still in your employ, please put him in charge of my horses if it is convenient; pray inform my friends when they might be likely to find me at home, so that you will not be pestered until after my arrival. My affectionate respect to you, sir.

Your most obt. son,
F.C.M.A. Trowbridge

April 2nd, 1828, at Thebes

1

Now that most of the sand had been cleared from the outer courtyard, Madelaine had a better idea of the size of the temple. It was not as enormous as she had thought at first, but she saw that it had several different areas dedicated to various aspects of healing, or what she hoped were various aspects of healing. Aside from stores of jars and linen bands, there was no reliable indication that anything happened here. It might be part of the Temple of Anubis, where the dead were made into mummies. She shook her head. Was the place where she stood now actually once that courtyard Saint-Germain had called out of the House of Life, or was it something else? Was this not the temple of Imhotep, but of some other god, or goddess, or perhaps a building that had nothing to do with religion? The only answers lay under the sands.

Using the large broom, she cleared more of the sand away, looking at the stones and bas-relief the length of the wall, wishing she were more expert in the language of the ancient Egyptians. It was tantalizing, knowing a few of the sounds, but almost none of the sense. These people, she thought, were so far away, and so unlike what she had expected. Everyone spoke of gifted and austere men living in a rich, chaste world, offering prayers and sacrifice to gods as incomprehensible as Jehovah would be to the Egyptians who bowed down to Pharaoh. But Saint-Germain told another story, one that changed, ebbed and flowed with the fortunes of the Black Land. As she moved the broom, she tried to concentrate on everything she saw, but knew her attention was wandering.

Then a few of the stiff, dried roots that made up the broom snagged on a little outcropping, and her attention once again focused. She dropped onto her knees and began to work at the sand as if she were a dog digging up a bone. She had not often felt as excited as she did now, knowing she was on the brink of something new, something so very ancient it was brand-new. One of her fingernails tore, but she continued to clear away the sand, first with her hands, then with her arms. Something was waiting to be found, she could sense it. She dug more industriously. She knew Lasca would complain to her of how badly she treated her clothing, but now it was as nothing to her: clothes could be replaced. Nothing could replace what was under the stones.

Within an hour, there was enough space cleared for Madelaine to kneel in the sand and clear away enough room to open the low door she had found: the compartment was almost as tall as Madelaine, and as wide, the square obvious only once she had seen it.

The door groaned, though not as loudly as Madelaine anticipated, sliding on a trough of beads and half a dozen brass rollers about as long as her middle finger. There were three shelves inside the chamber, with lined-up jars on two of them, the third with a number of figures of men and creatures, and the combinations of men-and-creatures that were seen everywhere in these artifacts. Madelaine stared, knowing she was a fool to waste the light so that she would not have enough at the end of the day to complete her sketch records for what she found. If she were a man, she would appoint two diggers to sleep here with her and would bar the way with her body, but being a woman made it impossible for her to do this; none of the Moslems would hesitate to kill a woman if her death would bring a rich reward. She rocked back on her heels, digging into her satchel so she could get started. She gave a single, vexed cry.

"Did you find something?" The voice was friendly enough, for Baundilet was always friendly. "What are you being so secretive about?"

"I ... I"—it was foolish to dissemble, and so she did not bother—"I thought there was something in the wall. It turns out I was right," she answered, loathing what she knew would come next.

"Was that the noise I heard"—he beamed at her—"just now?"

"Ten minutes before," said Madelaine, wishing she could have concealed the sound of the door opening. "I was irritated, with the afternoon fading. I've been staring." She indicated the open door, her face softening though her thoughts were cold. Having Baundilet so near these things was profane, giving her a disgust she kept out of her face in order not to warn him. "Magnificent, isn't it? That carnelian jar alone must be worth a small ransom."

"Um," said Baundilet. "I suppose it must. Yes." He had squatted down beside her and now he let his hand rest on her shoulder. "Quite a serendipitous find." He tweaked the short, sensible ribbons of her straw bonnet. "A wonderful discovery. I can think of no reason why we should not celebrate, with this find. It changes things for you, for me, doesn't it? Time to reassess where we stand, wouldn't you say?"

Madelaine moved away from his hand. "Oh, I doubt it," she answered. "I think it's more a case of being able to make a few pragmatic requests. You see, I am as aware of the opportunity here as you are."

"How do you mean?" He was not so sanguine now.

Madelaine looked directly at the open door. "I am prepared to continue to excavate this part of Thebes and Luxor. I am fascinated by this place. It captivates me, these records of those vanished people. I have funds of my own, as you know, and I do not mind working without . . . your assistance. In fact, I begin to think I would prefer it. Paying you so handsomely to be allowed to sketch inscriptions for you is not as equitable as you like to believe."

Now Baundilet's smile was gone. "It's not unusual for members of an expedition to pay for the privilege of being part of the explorations." He spoke abruptly. "No one requires you to pay me."

"No one requires it? *You* require it," snapped Madelaine, her large violet eyes eloquent. "Without your approval, the Magistrate Numair would deny me permission to excavate anywhere near here. Without your tacit endorsement I would not be accorded the limited approval I am given here. Without your consent, I would have to go up-river, perhaps to those temples they say are in the Nubian desert. If I went north to Lower Egypt, I would not be given the opportunity to do exploration myself, which is the very reason I came. As difficult as it is for a female antiquarian to work here, I cannot convince myself that it would be easier between the First and Second Cataracts, or in the shadow of the Great Sphinx."

"You're not an opera singer, Madame, to display such petty temperament." He showed her his teeth. "You purport to be an antiquarian scholar. Well, there is an enormous country here, and there are monuments for over a thousand miles. Go find one to your liking: I won't stop you."

Madelaine looked over her shoulder at him. "But my protest is about these monuments, Professor Baundilet. This is about the enigmas that are hidden under the sand and in the cliffs. It is about study, Professor. I'm convinced that this discovery is part of a greater treasure that requires the expedition to continue, to explore and examine intact—not in the manner you managed it so far." She straightened her back, finding more energy than she usually experienced while the sun was up, and that surprised her; she knew it came from ire. "This discovery will receive appropriate credit and full recording, if I have to purchase every piece of it myself. And before you attempt to come up with another attempt to control what I may publish, as you have been attempting to control the work of other members of this expedition, let me warn you that I will record this discovery in detail, including anything that is missing in the morning."

Baundilet decided to brazen it out. "It would seem you do not trust me, Madame; why is that? Surely a woman like you does not listen to rumors." He was trying to calm her, to give her charm instead of answers, but it would not do for Madelaine.

"It would seem I do not," she said, her urbanity greater than his. "Under the circumstances, you will agree I have reason. Your publications give me to fret, Professor Baundilet."

Baundilet's eyes did not smile now, but his face still beamed. "Publications. Oh, yes, publications. I believe I understand. And now I know where my trouble has originated. How much you have made my affairs your affairs, Madame. I find that to be one of the principal arguments against having women on expeditions, aside from the poor quality of their intellects."

To his amazement, Madelaine chuckled. "Have I said something that distresses you? You are trying very hard to put me off my point, striking out that way. Do you try to bully everyone, Professor Baundilet? Is that how you have advanced in the world, through shaming those more timid than you are?" She remem-

bered the look in Saint Sebastian's lean, cruel face before he let
his pack loose on her father, before Achille Cressie smashed Rob-
ert de Montalia's face with a burning metal brazier. "I have seen
worse than you can do, and I am still here," she said with great
dignity.

Baundilet read something in her face that warned him to be
cautious. "You will have your amusement, Madame," he said,
starting to get up.

"I prefer you on your knees, Professor, at least until this is
settled. It might be regarded as a whim, nothing more than a little
feminine caprice. Afterward we will see." She rose, walking to
the door, taking a quick inventory of the contents, then she looked
over at Baundilet. "Post de la Noye here, with two diggers. You
might want to have him make an inventory while you are arranging to guard the site. In the morning, if anything is missing,
you will have to report your loss to Magistrate Numair, won't
you? Because this will serve as evidence."

"Evidence from a Christian woman?" Baundilet scoffed, growing seriously angry. "What damage could that do, except to
your—"

"Coming from a Coptic monk," said Madelaine, letting the question settle in. "You didn't think I was alone, did you?" She pre-
tended she did not see the fury in Baundilet's eyes, or the way
his glance scraped over her as if to shred her clothes.

"Where is that fellow?" Baundilet insisted, breathing heavily as
he got to his feet. "I will deal with him."

"Not very wise," said Madelaine, doing all she could to maintain
her composure; mentioning Brother Gurzin had been a wild
chance, since he had left that morning carrying more letters for
Madelaine, including one to her dearest ally, who was now in
Athens. Always the monk was ordered to leave undetected, but
this time Madelaine hoped more fervently than ever that Erai
Gurzin had been careful. Tomorrow morning, when he would
surely be missed, then it would be regarded as prudence, her
own sensible action to protect the Coptic monk. "The Moslems
respect most Christians and Jews as People of the Book. Those
who live holy lives are as revered being Christians as are Moslems
and Jews. If Gurzin has a good reputation—and you know that

he does—the Magistrate would not be adverse to hearing testimony from him." She gestured as if to reassure her missing colleague. "If you make any move against me, I have a full report of my participation in this expedition, and the journal is in safe hands. Your work, your dealings will not go unscrutinized." She made herself look Baundilet directly in the eyes, hoping that he could not realize how difficult this was for her. "Have I made myself clear, Professor Baundilet?"

"You have stated your case," replied Baundilet, his tone going flat. "It appears we have reached an impasse."

"That is up to you," she said, and made herself walk away from the place as if the discovery was protected and she was in no danger. Only when she had made her way through the larger temple did she let herself lean against one of the papyrus-shaped pillars and tremble.

The next morning, shortly after her gallop from her villa to the temple, Madelaine was bemused to see that Yamut Omat had arrived with a small retinue of European friends. He was effusive in his pleasure and made a thorough inspection of the new areas, making several observations about the superior quality of the objects that had been found. He made a point of addressing Madelaine at once, bowing over her hand in perfect form and presenting her with a small rose that was already wilting in the heat.

"Professor Baundilet has informed me of your great discovery. A most remarkable man, Professor Baundilet. He has said that you are to be given the credit for this discovery. He has said that you are entitled to it, having made the discovery wholly on your own. What liberality! Isn't that gallant of him?" Omat beamed and this brought about several clever little smiles.

"Not hard to see how it happened," whispered one of the English expedition, a ruddy young man with hairy arms and an energetic mustache. "Still, it's the ladies for you."

Baundilet showed up then and made a great show of kissing Madelaine's hand. "It is most remarkable. Here is this beautiful, accomplished woman who has made an amazing discovery, truly the most devoted antiquarian anyone has as part of any expedition." He almost tweaked one of her coffee-dark curls, then thought better of it.

Omat clapped his hands and said a few crisp words. His servants set about erecting a tent near the place in the wall where Madelaine had made her find. "It is nothing much, for so great a moment, but a little champagne and a bite to eat, well, this is a festive occasion, isn't it?"

"Is it?" Madelaine said softly, looking at Jean-Marc Paille, who stood somewhat apart, his hands deep in his pockets, his face like a thundercloud.

"Never would have thought that side of the wall would yield very much," said one of the English party. "Still, it goes to show."

"What a delightful notion," said Baundilet with a pointed look at Madelaine. "To have Omat offer you this tribute is an honor indeed."

"Indeed," Madelaine echoed, knowing that Baundilet was doing all he could to make it appear she was his mistress and the credit for her discovery was a romantic gift Baundilet was giving to her. She ground her teeth.

"Omat is fine at his entertainments," said Enjeu. He had developed a morning cough in the last few months, and he had lost flesh. "Makes the place almost worthwhile."

"Almost?" de la Noye inquired, reaching for another square of round flat bread filled with ground nuts, onions and goat.

"More gold and a sop from Baundilet would be welcome," Enjeu growled, then hitched up his shoulders. "Well, tonight there'll be women at his villa, no doubt, and pipes." He draped his arm over de la Noye's shoulder. "That pretty one, with the eyes and the breasts, Nadja? She's the one I think is very special."

"Omat might give her to you," said de la Noye after he had thought about it, then threw back his head and laughed out loud.

Madelaine hung back, trying to hold her temper. At last she was satisfied she would probably not spit in Baundilet's face, and she started toward the pavilion, her mind on what she would do to stop that infuriating rumor; as she reached the half-open flap of the tent, she felt a light touch on her arm. "What?" she started, and turned to see Trowbridge.

"I know he's lying," said Trowbridge with his usual sincerity. "I know you would not do that. I know you love that physician. I know that." He was still holding her hand anxiously.

Thank goodness for Ferdinand Charles Montrose Algernon Trowbridge, thought Madelaine as she stared down at how his hand held hers. "You're very kind."

"He's the most beastly fellow, saying those things about you," he announced, but discreet enough to keep his voice low.

"It's not what he says, it is what he implies." She had heard whispers since she was a child and had learned what terrible erosive power a soft, often-repeated tidbit of gossip could possess.

Trowbridge looked up sharply as de la Noye laughed suddenly. "I've a mind to draw his claret, but ... I've never been much of a fighter." He admitted this wretchedly. "Oh, Great Lord Harry, Madame, what is he up to?"

She made a gesture as if brushing away crumbs. "He's trying to make it appear that I am his mistress. He wants everyone to think it is so. Then, you see, he wants to convince me that since they believe it already, I have no further reason to resist him." Her voice grew brittle.

Trowbridge turned quite pink. "You wouldn't do it, would you? I know I'm not a catch, but if you'd do me the honor, I'd put a stop to what he's saying." He hesitated. "I could call him out, if you said you'd ... you know ... marry me. I might not be too good with my fists, but I'm thought top hole for my shooting."

"I don't require such a sacrifice," said Madelaine, touched by his affection. "And it would make no difference no matter what. I will have to find another way." She took his hand sharply. "No," she said softly. "No. There is no reason to do this, not here, in this place." She had intended to say something about the temples and their antiquity, but Trowbridge interpreted it another way.

"Ah, yes. This is a country of strange laws. Just so." He put his hand on his paunch. "The warning's well taken, Madame."

She laughed once, determined to get away from the site as quickly as possible. The night before she had been certain that she had managed her conversation with Baundilet successfully; now she knew that she had made several crucial errors. As she made her way past the pavilion, she heard Baundilet drink to her captivating eyes again.

As she reached her villa, she was less agitated, but it was an effort for her to speak about what Baundilet had done. "I should have known he would find some ploy like this. I should have done something about it." She unfastened the ribbons of her bonnet and flung the simple hat aside.

Lasca, helping her change from her morning clothes to her afternoon at-home dress, knew better than to comment.

"He wants what I've found, not just to get the credit for it, but to *have* it, to make it his. He is determined to make it his." She sat down on the edge of her bed. "I can't decide which has made me angrier, his insistence that he take charge of the discovery or that he is determined to make me his mistress because he dislikes intelligent women." She thumped the pillow beside her, her face softening a bit. "Trowbridge was all for finding an excuse to fight a duel for me, which is touching but foolish. If Falke had been with me, he would have ended up shouting at Baundilet, but that would do nothing." She leaned back, but her whole body was as tight as a drawn bow. "There's a dhow headed for Cairo in a week. I think it would be wisest if you were on it. Saint-Germain is sending his yacht to Cairo. Someone should be there to meet it."

"Madame!" Lasca expostulated, a world of indignation in that single word.

"It would be wise," repeated Madelaine. "And I would not have to worry about you. If I should go north now, it would not be remarked upon. It is known that Baundilet and I are displeased with one another. If I left Thebes for a time"—even saying it was difficult—"no one would think much of it." She glanced at Lasca. "It is better you leave, so that when I depart, I have only myself to fend for."

"But it is not right that you should be left alone." Lasca knotted her hands together. "Madame, if you are not pleased with my service, or if you fear for my courage, you have no reason to; I swear to you that—"

"If I doubted your courage, I would not have brought you to Egypt," said Madelaine in her most composed manner. "But now is a time for sense. A wise person does not compound problems, which having you here would do. As to Saint-Germain, his last letter said he would send his yacht, and I am serious that someone must meet it." She sat up. "He's very splendid, Saint-Germain. He has a beautiful yacht and you will want a little time to establish yourself aboard."

Lasca's eyes were hot, sullen. "I do not want to be sent away like a disgraced cousin."

"You're not that." Madelaine took a long breath. "If I must leave covertly, I will have to be sure I will be protected when I reach Cairo. I cannot entrust just anyone with getting me out of this place . . . alive."

"Alive?" Lasca repeated, turning pale.

Madelaine looked away from her servant. "As I am now."

Text of a letter from Honorine Magasin in Poitiers to Jean-Marc Paille in Thebes.

To my very dear, dearest friend Jean-Marc;

Never in my life has it been so difficult for me to set pen to paper to write to you. Never in my most terrifying nightmares have I imagined the anguish I feel now, but as a good Christian woman and one who has loved you for so long and so sincerely, I must tell you of the changes in my feelings and my life. I never thought that in any length of time my bond with you could possibly weaken, or that I could falter in my love.

Yes, I fear my feelings have changed. I have discovered that I cannot sustain my attachment to you as we have done until now. I have asked for guidance, for I cannot express the contempt I feel for my weakness, though we are told women are weak creatures. My confessor has said that you are wholly without blame in this, but that you permitted me to continue to correspond with you when my father had forbidden it. He has said that silence will not be sufficient, and therefore I must impart to you the events that have led to the writing of this letter, and my most earnest supplication that you will not despise me too deeply when you have finished reading it.

As I have informed you, my Cousin Georges has recently in-

herited money and land. The bequests were generous and very accommodating in regard to the condition to the Will left by his Grandfather. He is most deserving of such good fortune, as you will certainly agree, for he has been so very much our friend in these long months when we have had to rely entirely on his discretion and assistance. It is of Cousin Georges that I must speak now, for I am in a most difficult position, and I need your kindness and understanding.

My father has been attempting to find a husband for me, this time with much greater determination than he has previously displayed. He had almost settled with a crony of his who is obscenely rich and has decided that it is time he had a family. He is fifty-two, a dealer in dyes who takes snuff so there are crumbs of it on the fronts of his shirts. My father all but offered me on the auction block, issuing the most dreadful ultimatum. He wanted me to accept this friend of his or be disinherited. That was the only bargain acceptable to him. You may well imagine how distressed I was, for my father's intentions were expressed with great determination and it was apparent from his language that there would be no way to dissuade him as Aunt Clémence and I have been able to do in the past. It has been much more difficult for me here, because while I was in Paris I did not have to see my father every day, did not live under his roof and listen to his words with my breakfast. He has been increasingly obdurate, and his manner reflects this inflexibility.

I understand that his disappointment at Solange's recent miscarriage has been great, for her physician has recommended that no more attempts at producing heirs be made, for she has proven to be too weak for the rigors of child-bearing. In these sad circumstances, my father has become more militant in regard to his determination to have grandchildren. He has informed his son-in-law that the inheritance will be halved. He has made the demands of me I have already briefly mentioned.

As you may suppose, I wrote at once to Aunt Clémence and she wrote to Georges. Both of them arrived in Poitiers at the first opportunity, traveling from dawn until dusk every day. Aunt

Clémence said it was fortunate that the coach was not damaged, so quickly they came. She attempted to reason with my father, but to no avail. He was so churlish as to refuse them rooms in his house, and they were obliged to put up at the posting inn until they were asked by Georges' good friend Henri d'Erelle to stay with him, which made my father furious, as he has never been able to secure an invitation from Monsieur d'Erelle, though he has tried.

Aunt Clémence was closeted with my father on three separate occasions, but at last had to admit that she could not persuade him to withdraw his demands of me. She and I mingled our tears, and for one evening we discussed how I might flee this place, get aboard a ship bound for Egypt and seek you out. But I have not been in foreign lands, except Italy, and I fear I should not know how to go on without you to guide me. After long discussion, we realized that we must be more pragmatic.

As it turns out, Aunt Clémence imparted much of this to Cousin Georges, imploring him to use what influence he might have with my father to change his mind. The result of this discussion is that Cousin Georges offered for me on the most favorable terms, and assured my father that any inheritance my father should choose to leave would be regarded as trust for his heirs. He could not accept my father's insistence that his name be changed to Magasin. Georges is of a better-born family than we are, in any case, and it would be most unfortunate if he were to lower his station in life to keep my father in a pleasant mood.

I know you will think me a light-hearted trifler and one who has earned your odium forever, but I hope you will consider the predicament I have been in, with the prospect of having marriage with my father's crony forced on me. I know I am not as firm in my affections as I wished to believe, and it may be that I will rue my decision as you go on to fame and glory, but I must tell you, Jean-Marc, that I have done all that I might to stand against the demands made upon me, and now that I cannot resist without being wholly cast off by my family, I have done what I believe is the wisest thing for everyone concerned,

*for I have a great and abiding fondness for Georges, and have
had since we were children. It is true that he offers me advancement and position, but so did the suitor my father selected for
me, so it is not as if I am wholly worldly in my choice. Georges
and I have a good understanding of each other. It is not at all
the passion you have roused in me, but I begin to suspect that
such passion can be a dangerous thing, as the Church warns us.
Passion leads to many sins by its very nature, and in marriage
it can bring about suffering, for I have seen this many times.
When I think of you I ache, but in time that will lessen, and
my caprice will fade. I know when that comes I will be grateful.
I know that Georges will care for me and never give me cause
for worry. He knows I comprehend his need for the company of
men and that I will not berate him for keeping company with
them. He has promised that he will not make many demands
on me once we have two children, which is most satisfactory to
me. Georges is a brilliant catch, even my father has allowed
that, and his place in the world assures me an improved situation in life. I have seen how the world goes on during my stays
in Paris, and I have come to accept that a woman must look
out for her own interests if she is not to be at the mercy of her
father and her husband until she dies.*

*You and the memory of loving you must be the greatest trea-
sure of my life. Georges is so kind that he is permitting me to
keep the necklace you sent me, and your letters. He has also
said that you must come to visit us when you return to Paris.
He is willing to help you find a suitable position until you join
another expedition to Egypt, as you surely must do.*

*If you can find it in your heart to forgive me, I will bless your
name, for I most humbly beg your pardon for what I have done
to you, and the useless hopes I have raised in your breast. There
is no act of contrition for what I have done save the regret that
must always be as an inward stain, a wound that never quite
heals. What consolation you may gain from knowing that my
heart will be blighted for loss of you, please take.*

*The 19th day of October has been set for our nuptials, here
in Poitiers. My father has said it will be the grandest wedding
since the Emperor was banished. In spite of what I have done*

*to you, believe that you will always have a place in the secrets
of my soul.*

> *With chagrin,*
> *Honorine*

April 24th, at Poitiers

2

They had ridden for almost an hour and the heat was now an
enormous palm pressing down on them. The cliffs rang with the
sounds of their horses' hooves and the distant clatter of digging
on the river side of the bluff. The ground was rough and broken,
and even the single track of roadway was rutted and littered with
stones.

"We'd best rein in!" Trowbridge shouted. "Wilkinson's party is
supposed to be around here somewhere." He was red as a brick
and sweating profusely, but his smile was still eager. "Good of
you to give me such a slice of your morning, Madame."

"And good of you to take me around the west side of the river,"
she countered as she pulled her sweating mare down to a walk.
"Why did they make their buildings so huge, do you think?" she
asked as they passed another seated colossus.

"Trying to impress people, I suspect," said Trowbridge. "That's
why people do many things. Only natural to strut." He cleared
his throat and made a gesture toward the cliffs with his lightly
gloved hands. "There's temples all through here, so they say."

"And more we haven't uncovered yet," said Madelaine, a frown
settling onto her brow under her dashing hat with the hussar's
crown.

Trowbridge brought his bright bay alongside Madelaine's pink
roan. "You're troubled, Madame?"

"Oh, it's nothing for you to concern yourself with. Nothing at
all." She smiled, the anxiety gone. "It's going badly because of

squabbles. I am not blameless, I know that. But there is so much to do here, and so much to learn, and there isn't time."

"Have you and Professor Baundilet come to some compromise?" Trowbridge asked shrewdly. "Have you? I haven't seen any evidence of cordiality; that's my reason for asking. Have you worked something out between you? I haven't been aware of any sign of it." He made a point of not looking at her.

She gave a quiet laugh. "No, no cordiality, I'm loath to report," she said. "He would like me to leave, and it may be necessary for me to go, if Baundilet persuades Omat and Numair that I do not belong with the expedition. Baundilet has a great deal of influence with Omat, who in turn has great influence with Numair. Between them, my position isn't very good." She squinted ahead toward a north-westward-bending canyon. "Has any digging been done there?"

"A little, I've been told," said Trowbridge, adding, "Some of the diggers tell us that there are tombs back in the cliffs."

"But they do not know for certain where these tombs are," Madelaine finished for him. "Ah, how many times have we heard that tale." She let her horse trot a short way, going up the canyon. Was this the place where that poor girl had been hung from the cliffs? What a hideous place to die. Was this the place where—what was the child's name?—had been brought to perish in the sun. "Hesentaton," she said without realizing she had spoken.

"Beg pardon?" said Trowbridge, his small eyes growing as round as they could. "What did you say?"

Madelaine pulled in her mare to a walk and used that to gain a few seconds to think. "A name, I believe. Egyptian. I have been tyring to think what it might be, a name or another sort of word. My command of the language is nothing more than passable, and this at last sorted itself out."

Trowbridge actually seemed relieved. "Puzzling over the gods and eyes and birds, trying to say them right. Must say, I don't envy you that task, but I know the sensation. Finding your way around unfamiliar words. Yes. I remember I had a dog once when I was just a pup myself. Nothing much to speak of by way of breeding, but he took to me; dogs do that from time to time. His name was Pomeroy, but I was never able to get it right, not while

I was a child, and I called him Pryboy. Makes no sense, and it ain't any more difficult to say Pomeroy than Pryboy, but for the life of me it took me a year to learn it straight." He took his crop and pointed to the edge of the cliffs high above them. "Feel the heat off them. It's worse than a smithy."

"True enough," said Madelaine, looking around and realizing with some alarm that they had come a considerable distance into the valley. "Where is Wilkinson, Trowbridge? Isn't this where we were supposed to find him?"

His small eyes got narrower. "I haven't the vaguest. A rum thing. His note was on my desk last night, all full of little sketches and something about the jars you found in that wall: I was sure he'd have someone waiting to show us this thing he's found. That's what he's done in the past." He pulled his hat off and wiped his brow. "It was such an urgent note. You'd think he'd be impatient to see you."

The wind blew over them, dry and scorching, the breath of a furnace or a dragon.

Madelaine swallowed, her mouth suddenly parched. There was a cold finger on her spine and a hot pinch under her corset. She rose in the stirrup and looked around. "I don't see anyone." There was a slight quaver in her voice.

"No more do I," Trowbridge agreed, an edge in his second. He wheeled his horse and looked back toward the river. "Wilkinson!" he shouted, holding his bright bay as the horse reared in protest at the noise. "John Gardner Wilkinson!" He let the bay spring ahead, then pulled him into a stop, listening for response.

Madelaine let her mare move up to the bay. "I don't hear anyone. I don't see anyone." She kept her voice low and clear, fighting a rising sense of dread.

"I don't understand it. Not like Wilkinson at all to leave us guessing. Not at all the thing to bring us out here this way. Wilkinson's a bit mad, but he's not a fool. The meeting's his idea. He set the time in the note." His face darkened. "I'll have something to say to him when we catch up with him, I may tell you. It's one thing to drag me out here, but quite another to disaccommodate you."

"No need for indignation until we find out if Wilkinson was the actual author of the letter," said Madelaine, appalled by the suspicions that flooded her mind.

"Not the author?" Trowbridge challenged incredulously, turning in the saddle. "What bloody—beg pardon for my tongue—nonsense is this? You're a reasonable woman, Madame. You can't believe—"

Madelaine interrupted. "That Wilkinson did not send the note? Yes, I do," she said, thinking it was unfair: she had lived little more than a century, had escaped the Revolution and the guillotine, and now her life was threatened because of some two-thousand-year-old jars. "I am thinking that we have been lured into a trap."

"But who? A trap?" Trowbridge looked around the canyon again. "It isn't possible, Madame. Who would play so dastardly a trick as this?" He suddenly fell silent as the enormity of their danger became apparent to him. "But it is no trick."

"I'm afraid it's not," said Madelaine, her eyes hardening. She forced herself to ignore the fear that gnawed at her, trying to think of winning free, springing the trap. Saint-Germain had lived her, walked here. He had survived it. There was earth in her shoes. She had to think.

"*Merciful Savior,*" Trowbridge whispered.

Madelaine closed her eyes to shut out the stones around her. She did not look at Trowbridge as she said very softly, and with an assumption of confidence she did not feel, "I may have an idea. Don't say anything, just listen. Pretend to fix your cravat or adjust our stirrup leathers or something similar, so that we will not appear to be conversing."

"As you wish," said Trowbridge promptly, and swung his leg forward and pulled up the flap of the saddle. "Carry on, Madame."

"We have to assume someone is watching us. We have to assume we were lured out here for a reason. Thus we must anticipate what those watching us will assume." Under the brim of her riding hat her violet eyes were dark and cold as scarabs carved in obsidian. "We must try to get out of this canyon. As long as we are here we are in a cage." She bent nearer to him as if he needed her help with the stirrup leather. "We can't make it apparent that we know what's happened. We need to make it appear we do not realize our danger. We must do something amusing. Challenge me to a race. Make sport of it. Then go straight toward the river. It's a south-east line to the Nile once you go around that bluff." The cliffs now seemed to her to be twice as large as when she had first ridden into the canyon. She did her best to ignore the shadow of outstretched wings as they passed over her.

"Oh, God's teeth," whispered Trowbridge. "I've a neat little pistol, but it is back in my quarters. I ought to have brought it."

"You weren't to know you'd need it," said Madelaine, trying to keep him from this useless self-chastisement. She shaded her eyes with her hand and looked around the valley again. She raised up, using this to cover getting a more secure seat. Most of the time she did not mind riding sidesaddle, but here, in this place, she wanted to straddle her mare. "Wilkinson, are you there?" she shouted, then said to Trowbridge, a trifle more loudly than necessary. "Where is the infernal man? You told me he would be here."

"I thought he would," said Trowbridge, picking up on her lead. "His note said one in the afternoon, and it's gone twenty minutes after." He shouted for Wilkinson, and waited again. "He must not hear us."

"How is that possible?" Madelaine asked, knowing better than to attempt a laugh. "He's as bad as the rest of them: he gets his head into an inscription or a painting and he loses track of everything else. I do it, too." She pulled her reins in, her hands sweating in her thinnest riding gloves, though not entirely from the heat.

"I've half a mind to leave him to his studies," Trowbridge said, giving Madelaine a quick, subtle gesture.

"Why not? It's almost time for the afternoon lie-down. I don't want to stay out in the heat of the day. So much sun makes me feel quite sick," she said honestly.

Trowbridge clapped his hat back on his head, making a show of irritation and restlessness. "Well, what do you say to an impromptu race, your mare against this gelding? It's not a bad course for a good run; say around the bluff and toward the road. First one to the road wins." He touched the brim of his hat with his crop. "Say ten pounds?"

"Are you making a wager with me, Trowbridge?" Madelaine

asked, so grateful to him that she decided she would arrange for a special entertainment for him before he went home. He was such a sweet man: whoever became his bride would be more fortunate than most. She wished him happy. And she would miss him when he was gone.

"Not the proper thing to do, I know, but considering where we are, who's to object?" he called, making it a challenge. "Around the bluff to the road: what do you say?"

She gave a look around the canyon one more time, hoping to discover their watchers but appearing to determine the course. "No shortcuts. We must keep to the road," she said, knowing that the ground here was treacherous and they could not risk being tossed if their mounts went down. As hazardous as their predicament was, unhorsed it would be catastrophic. "All right then—ten pounds. We race."

He kneed his horse closer to hers as if lining them up, but used it to say to her, "They are probably ahead of us. That bluff makes excellent cover and blocks our escape." A trifle more loudly, he said, "No forcing off the road, and no blocking the way."

"Yes, I noticed that." She agreed with his assessment, but was afraid that there might be more than one watcher, and they might be in a crossfire. Her next words were spoken softly, accompanied by indications with her crop that meant nothing. "We'll have to stay close together. Never more than a length apart, and closer if we can." It was risky to ride at speed over rough ground so near to each other, but their circumstance was more dangerous than the hazards of the road. "Watch for tripwires or—"

"Muzzle flashes," he said with a determined nod. "Right you are." And with that he set his spurs to his bright bay's sides, hollering loudly to urge the horse on.

Madelaine used her crop to set her mare galloping, leaning into the ride to help the horse balance; the bright bay was roughly two lengths ahead of her. She squinted as the hot wind swiped at her eyes and suddenly carried her hat away. Her mare shied at the blowing hat and veered to the side, giving a squeal of protest. As Trowbridge lengthened his lead, Madelaine used her crop again, driving the mare to the limits of her speed. They could not afford to permit too much distance between them, for that exposed them both. Madelaine's hair blew around her face, sometimes masking her eyes.

The bluff loomed up on their right, glaring fulvous yellow in the shine of mid-day. Trowbridge waved his crop, pointing toward a place about half-way up the side of the stone slope and shouted something Madelaine could not hear over the sound of the horses.

And then there was a shot.

Trowbridge lurched in the saddle, flopping forward onto the pommel with a grisly scream. He locked his arms around his horse's neck as the bright bay sped on, panicked by the shot and Trowbridge's blood flowing down his flank.

Madelaine shouted, trying to force more speed from her mare. But the horse had already reached her limits did not have it in her to give, and no matter how she strained, she could not reach the gelding and the wounded man riding him.

There were two more shots, and Madelaine's mare went down screaming and thrashing. Madelaine was already dazed from the second ball, which had left a long welt along the side of her brow and into her wind-disheveled dark hair, and did not feel the impact as she fell from the treacherous side-saddle to lie not quite unconscious in the full might of the sun. She could not turn over: her face was toward the disk of the sun.

After struggling to her feet, the mare tried to follow Trowbridge's gelding, pain and frenzy driving her some considerable distance before she suddenly slowed to a walk, then staggered, giving a few hard coughs. Then her knees buckled and she collapsed. High above her, the first vulture rode on the relentless wind.

Four times Trowbridge was almost thrown from the saddle, which only terrified the bright bay more. The horse was sobbing for air, his coat flecked with foam and dark with sweat. In spite of the heat, he kept running, his mouth wide, his heart pounding so fiercely that Trowbridge could feel the beat through the saddle flaps, though he could not tell what the pulse was.

The carriage road lay ahead, and beyond that a stretch of irrigated land and the Nile. Trowbridge was dimly aware of these things but he could not see them clearly. His arms ached—he thought it must be from this odd way he was riding, clinging to the bay like a monkey—and when he laughed, there was blood in his mouth. Something was desperately wrong, he knew that. His side felt as if someone had clapped hot metal to his body, and neither his arms nor his legs were working properly. He was distantly aware of tremendous danger, and of jeopardy not only to himself but Madame de Montalia. Madame de Montalia. Madame de Montalia. There was something—

At last it came to him, and he cried out in anguish that was greater than his hurt. She had fallen. She was not behind him. There had been shots.

He knew then: he was wounded. As if in confirmation the ravening pain increased as if an enormous cat had fixed its teeth and claws in him. And Madame de Montalia was not behind him. God, he thought as he tried with what little strength he had left to bring his horse under control before the poor creature ran himself to death, God please, let me live long enough to help her. Let me do that. Just that. I'll come after, and gladly, I promise. He repeated the words to himself as he dragged on the off-rein, hanging on as the bright bay finally dropped to an exhausted trot.

It was a little later—he did not know quite when, for he had drifted in and out of consciousness as his horse plodded down the road toward the place where the statues were being cleared—Trowbridge was aware of voices and shouts. He tried to raise his head and discovered it was too much effort. He tried to answer, but all that he could achieve was a bleat that was half an oath. He felt people around him, heard the local dialect and French, and then, mercifully, English.

"Good God, man. You're hurt." It was Symington, who had arrived just two months before, fresh from Cambridge.

Orders were being babbled, and more diggers arrived to assist; hands pried his arms from around the horse's neck; he felt himself levered out of the saddle.

"You've been shot," Symington declared, stupefied. "This man," he said to the rest, "has been shot." He looked to the other members of his expedition who had joined him. "He needs a physician."

"Lost a lot of blood," said one of the others, though Trowbridge did not recognize the voice.

Through the miasma of pain, Trowbridge whispered, "German."

"Did he say German?" asked Symington as he knelt beside Trowbridge and pulled off his muslin cravat to stanch the flow of blood. "German?"

"German physician on the other side of the river," said one of the men.

"Yes," Trowbridge muttered, his agony increasing as Symington applied needed pressure to the wound in his side. "Falke." Then he made himself open his eyes and look directly at Symington, though the man appeared to be in a fogbank. "Tell him. Soon. As he gets here." He swallowed, ignoring the metallic taste of his own blood. "Madelaine." In some distant part of his mind, he realized this was the first time he had used her Christian name. "Tell him. In the valley." He was dizzier, and it was difficult to speak at all. "She's shot."

"Are you saying there's a second victim?" Symington demanded, his eyes now very grave.

"Get Falke," wheezed Trowbridge. "Now."

"We'll tend to it right now," said Symington, making a sign to one of the English antiquarians. "And hurry," he said softly.

The man nodded once. "I'm on my way. I'll have him back quickly as you can say knife." He made a sign of encouragement and raced off toward the boats tied on the short wharf.

"He is very bad," said the chief digger, shaking his head as he bent over Trowbridge. "A pity."

Trowbridge reached out with the hand that hurt less and tried to grab the front of Symington's waistcoat. "Madelaine." There: he had said it twice. "Save her." It was strange, he thought as he laced his fingers with Symington's. There was less torment now, as if repeating her name was anodyne. He was no longer alarmed at the blood soaking his clothes.

It was not easy for Symington to answer. "We'll do our best, old man. My word on it. We'll tell the German as soon as he arrives, as soon as he's seen you." He looked up, trying very hard to keep from stammering or breaking down, for he could see that Trowbridge was almost gone. "Did anyone notice where he came from? If there's a woman out there, somewhere, we'd better find her . . ."

"Watch for the vultures," the chief digger recommended.

"No," said Symington. He blinked back tears. "No. We must find her. I gave my word."

The diggers exchanged soft words and harsh glances, and the oldest English scholar there said, "Quite right."

"It is lie-down time," said the chief digger. "If she is out there, she will not be alive for long."

Trowbridge had no more strength left to hold onto Symington's hand. His eyes fluttered open. "Find," he breathed. "Her."

"Yes," Symington promised gently, knowing that Trowbridge could no longer hear him, that his open eyes saw nothing.

Text of a letter from Professor Rainaud Benclair in Paris to Professor Alain Baundilet in Thebes.

My dear Professor Baundilet;

Some months ago one of your colleagues wrote to me to make certain claims as regards the conduct of your antiquarian ex-pedition that at the time were dismissed as the discontented whining of an ambitious man dissatisfied with the rigors of the antiquarian life. We informed him at the time that he was not to make such irresponsible allegations again, and sent him on his way with a warning against repeating this error. At the time it seemed to be the most sensible thing for us to do, the course circumspect and prudent men ought to follow when queries of this nature arrive. We acted in a responsible and well-considered manner, or so we thought.

Then it was brought to our attention that the Eclipse Press in Ghent had recently published an extensive monograph by an adjunct to your expedition, Madame de Montalia. This mono-graph deals with the work she has done as a member of your expedition, and is in part a journal of a year on the expedition, with notes for each day's work, where it was done and who has done it. The monograph, a handsome volume of 144 pages with some superb etchings, is entitled: An Antiquarian Journal of the Excavation of Pharaohnic Thebes and Luxor: Twelve Months, *and has begun to receive some serious attention in various universities in France and England. Madame de Montalia is a concise writer and her presentation is direct and clear. Surely you must be proud of the quality of her work, for the standard it sets might well serve as a model for many another such publication. While this Eclipse Press does not always exercise good judgment in the varieties of subject matter which it chooses to print, there is no denying the level of scholarship achieved there. That is one of the aspects of this matter which serves to make it delicate.*

It appears that Madame de Montalia, in the journal portion of her monograph, assigns credit and discusses work done by members of your expedition that have not been similarly reported in your own writings. While we naturally expect a degree of internal variation due to the natural differences of observation and opinion of diverse persons, there are a few crucial consistencies which we believe are lacking in regard to your work when compared with hers. This is the source of our dilemma, for as your sponsors we do not wish to question the statements you have made, nor are we anxious to scrutinize the methods you have employed to continue your work where the arrangement is an Egyptian one. Still, the allegations of Madame de Montalia are specific and her records appear to be most conscientious. It is the manner in which her refutations are presented that have led to some concern, for to us, as the sponsors of your work, it would be a most lamentable development for your credibility to be cast into question, for it would reflect badly upon all of us. Doubtless you are as distressed by this as we are, and are prepared to assist us in ending the doubt that Madame de Montalia's writings have cast on your expedition.

Your recent communication about the newest discoveries there are awaited with true enthusiasm here, for we believe this may well be the most significant find since Champollian translated the Rosetta Stone and gave us access to the language of those by-gone peoples. Your observations will be welcome as soon as you are prepared to send them, and we are equally anxious to view these splendid artifacts. Your crucial role in bringing these treasures to light will speak in your favor as regards this other matter, I am certain of it.

We repose utmost faith in you, and do not mean to question your integrity, for a man of your position must clearly be an honorable man. However, we do believe that there have been occasions when you may have been more zealous than necessary about establishing the role you have played in the work of your expedition. We do not wish to cause you embarrassment of any kind, yet this monograph has appeared and there are those who seek some explanation of the various contradictions in your works.

We propose one way to resolve these differences and submit it to you for your consideration. We have decided that a point-by-point comparison of your various antiquarians' journals will reveal how this misunderstanding came about, and will make it less arduous for all involved to have these questions answered. The journals of LaPlatte, who has supervised your diggers, would certainly help our inquiries as much as those of Paille, Enjeu and de la Noye. Perhaps we will interview Claude-Michel Hiver as well, for we have been told that he has recovered enough to lecture from time to time. The more thorough the comparison we make, the more totally we can answer your critics. We trust that you will be prepared to send your journals by return packet, and we in turn state that we have arranged for comparative publication at the end of the year. Your assistance will speed the happy day when there are no more doubts or confusion in regard to the work of your expedition.

We anticipate the joyful occasion when this issue is laid to rest and you are completely vindicated.

With sincerest personal regards as well as professional respect,

> *I remain*
> *Professor Rainaud Benclair*

May 9th, 1828, at Paris

3

He leaped off the flat-bottomed boat that was used to ferry supplies and men from one side of the Nile to the other before the boatmen had secured it to the short wharf. His jacket was over his arm, he had neither tie nor cravat, and he carried his physician's satchel along with a second case of salves and bandages. Egidius Maximillian Falke was pale as his shirt; his blue eyes burned like the heart of a furnace. "Where?" he demanded in the local dialect of the first person he saw.

"The English was taken to—" the thin, bent boatman began, only to have Falke shove him away and hurry toward the knot of Europeans he saw not far off.

As he rushed up to the group, a sober young man with a prominent adam's apple held out his hand in greeting, saying, "You must be Falke; I hope you speak English, for I'm sorry to say I have no German." He stood carefully between Falke and a covered shape on the road behind him.

"Some. I am better in French," he said, his pronunciation hesitant and stilted. "Where is the messenger?" He started to push Symington away, but was detained.

"I'm Roland Symington. I . . . did what I could for your friend." He would not move.

"Thank you." Falke was more than brusque. Then he saw the stark expression in Symington's eyes and his tone changed. "Is he—I gather he . . . is dead."

"Shot; in the right side, just above the waist. Ribs broken inward, worse damage." At last he moved and nodded toward the figure. "He gave me a message. He said someone named Madelaine was still out there—we think in one of the canyons—"

"Madelaine." Then the enormity of it struck him; Falke howled with rage and desperation, his head raised to the sky, his eyes all but shut. "No!" He closed the distance between himself and Trowbridge's body in six faltering steps, then dropped to his knees, letting his satchel and case fall. "He was a hero. A hero," he repeated. He lifted the cloth, his face now impassive as he studied the damage the bullet had done. "Struck from the side and went deep. There was nothing to save him," he said quietly, then turned to Symington. "Is that all? That Madelaine was out there?"

This was becoming worse and worse, thought Symington. "He said . . . she was shot." He spoke the words as kindly as he could, as if that would make them less hideous.

"Shot?" The word was barely audible, but the anguish in his face was eloquent.

"We're trying to discover where they were," Symington told Falke, offering this as a mitigation of his grief. "We're going to search in a while."

Falke seemed not to have heard him. "Shot. Oh, *mein Gott.* I must look for her. At once. Madelaine. I want two donkeys," he said to Symington, his voice rising. "This moment. Tell me what direction he came from and I will follow the traces—"

"On this ground?" Symington was apprehensive, fearing that the German physician would break down. He said sensibly, "How can you follow the traces? Look at it. It is too hard; you'll never—"

This time Symington was interrupted. "I will follow Trowbridge's blood. He lost almost all of it: that will be my trail."

"His blood?" Symington had been pale but now he went ashen. "Good Lord, man, you can't mean that."

"I have never meant anything more in my life." He reached out and seized Symington by the lapel of his waistcoat. "Get me the donkeys. Or do you want that brave man to have died for nothing?" He glanced toward Trowbridge, then back to Symington. "No one need come with me."

"It is difficult, don't you know? Three hours from now, there'd be no questions. It's the heat of the day," Symington said unhappily, and Falke winced, for he remembered what Madelaine had told him of the danger of the sun. "The diggers won't search until it is a little cooler. I don't think they'll venture into the valley until more of it is in shadow." He looked uneasily toward the shrouded figure of Trowbridge. "But I'll see if some of them will come before then. Two hours; sooner if I can arrange it."

"Sooner," Falke said quietly, making it a command.

Symington nodded, then stepped back, breaking free of Falke's grip. "I'll see to your friend." The offer was compensatory, an apology for his inaction.

"His name was Trowbridge, Ferdinand Trowbridge," Falke said, then burst out. "The donkeys, man! Bring them."

A few of the other English antiquarians had seen this exchange; one of them came to Falke's side. "They're just coming, sir."

"Danke." He shouldered his satchel and picked up his case. "I am grateful," he told Symington, but neither Symington nor Falke himself believed that.

Symington cleared his throat. "We'll get him out of the sun. Your friend. Trowbridge."

"Good," said Falke, looking around for the donkeys. "Can you spare me water?"

"Of course," said Symington, deeply relieved to have something he could do that would not be looked upon with contempt. "Three skins," he offered, and clapped for the chief digger, issuing sharp orders in the local version of Egyptian Arabic.

"There is an English chaplain in Thebes, I think," said Falke to Symington. "Send for him."

"Yes. Have to do that." Symington nodded repeatedly, as if that made his word more certain. "There's the donkeys now." He took a deep breath as one of the diggers brought two donkeys, full water skins slung over their Egyptian saddles. As Falke swore and mounted the larger of the two, Symington came up to him one last time, holding out the reins of the second donkey for Falke to lead with. "We'll search for you, don't doubt it. If you haven't returned by evening, we'll put lanterns on the donkeys and continue the task until we find you." He stepped back. "Godspeed."

"Amen to that," said Falke, nudging the white, long-eared animal to a bone-shuddering jog, keeping a firm hold on the lead rein as well as those for his mount. As he rode, he watched the dusty road, following the dark splatters already soaked into the earth. Without being aware of it, he prayed.

Overhead the sun had slipped past the zenith, beginning to sink toward the west. It hung, huge and unforgiving, over cliffs that sang in the heat. What little wind there was, was parched and smelled of dust.

Though her eyes were closed, Madelaine could see the sun

through her lids; the light intruding, burning her lids before turn-ing her vision to a dancing red. That girl hung on the cliffs. How dreadfully she must have suffered. Madelaine's clothes had pro-tected most of her body for a time, but the light muslin was not sufficient to keep her from burns that were starting to become blisters. If she were able to turn over, she knew there would be a little relief, no matter how painful it would be to lie on the burns, but she could not move; the sun pinioned her as surely as if she were nailed to the ground. There was nothing to distract her but the cry of vultures and the occasional, fleeting shadow of their wings passing between her and the sun. Mut and Atum-Re, she reminded herself. Both of them gods in the Pharaohnic pantheon, both a part of the Egyptian soul. The good earth of Savoie in her shoes gave only the most feeble assistance to her as the brazen face of that most ancient god slowly, inevitably, leached the life from her.

She could last the day, she was fairly sure of that, but she would be burned and weak. Possibly in the night she could crawl to shelter under the rocks of the cliffs; they were some distance away, but if she were not too enervated, she might be able to get there before the sun rose again. Where she lay few of the cliff shadows reached, and so she would be directly in the sun soon after dawn. She knew beyond question that she would die before noon on the next day if she could not get out of the sun.

To die the true death so soon! If she had been able to shed tears she would have cried for it. She consoled herself thinking that tears would be painful as acid on her burned skin. There were blisters rising on her face and hands now, and her lips were so chapped and cracked that she doubted she could speak a word without agony.

Be patient, she told herself. Someone will come. Her next ironic thought was that the only person who would know where to look for her was the person who had shot her and Trowbridge. When the afternoon was a little older she expected her murderer to arrive to finish his work. In her weakened state she would not be able to stop him. She could not afford to hope that Trowbridge had got away.

Three vultures dropped lower in the sky, circling over the body of Madelaine's fallen mare. Their cries brought more birds to hover over her.

What if it was not Baundilet? she asked herself. It might be someone else. There were those who distrusted and disliked her. She resolutely shut out the first sounds of the vultures landing to begin their feast. If Baundilet were truly the one who sought her death, he would not come himself; he would sent a deputy: Guibert, perhaps. Or Suti, who thought she was an abomination. Abomination, she thought, seeking to keep her thoughts diverted from the pain that spread over her body as the burns increased. Abomination: that which ignores or acts against omens.

More vultures landed to devour the horse, and squabbles arose between the birds; harsh shrieks and indignant gobblings echoed through the canyon.

The worst part of dying here was leaving Saint-Germain. Though they could not remain long together, knowing he was in the world was cause for joy. To lose his love now, that was more difficult than all the rest. She thought of his face, his dark, compelling eyes that had enthralled her from the first time she saw him, of his compassion and kindness and love. How little time they had together as lovers, and yet how well those few hours sustained her. And when she came to his life, their bond was strengthened though they lost their capability to love one another. She would never hear his voice again, nor see that swift, ironic smile that fascinated her.

The secrets of the temples of Luxor and Thebes would remain unrevealed for her, which was suddenly so infuriating that she wanted to yell her protest, though there was no strength in her for that. She had only begun! Just one century, and it was over: too soon, too soon! There was so much more to do, so many discoveries lying hidden in the sands, waiting to be revealed once again. She would not know if she had found Saint-Germain's House of Life.

She would never see Falke again, or lie beside him, her head pillowed on his chest, feeling the rise and fall of his breath in sleep. He was near and that made it worse, for that nearness prompted longing. How sweet it was to love him, to feel the life of him, to accept the gift of his desire and answer it with rapture.

She would not share wakened passions with him, kiss his mouth, open her body to him. The pang that passed through her was as much from desire that would never be fulfilled as from the blisters that ruptured and blackened on her forehead and lips.

A vulture landed near her, for she felt the wash of its wings and smelled its carrion stench. It gave a grating cry, then took off once more, disappointed to find its prey still breathing.

It was arduous to keep her mind away from the heat and sun and injury that were taking possession of her, but she strove to think of other matters. If she let herself be caught up in her own hopelessness, she would be too despondent to take action during the night; that was her only chance of survival. She made her thoughts drift through the years. She had been born one hundred and three years ago; she had risen from her grave eighty-four years ago. There had been so much to learn, so many places to go. She had not done enough, not nearly enough to be ready for the true death. She wished she could doze, but with the sun branding her, this was not possible.

There was a rattle in the distance.

Madelaine listened, trying to determine the location of the sound. It was like a rockfall. Was the assassin finally coming?

Another distant sound, mingled with the caws and screams of the vultures.

This time she knew the clatter was rocks, from the south-eastern end of the canyon. Someone had been digging in the cliffs down at that end of the canyon: she recalled that she and Trowbridge had remarked on it when they had ridden into this trap.

Trowbridge. Fear for him enveloped her. Remorse for bringing him into danger followed after.

She tried to turn her head, whimpering at the pain that lanced through her face and neck at the attempt. The graze left by the ball blazed with renewed severity. She bit the inside of her lip, but could not hold it without making the hurt more intense.

Hoofbeats. She heard hoofbeats.

Who were they, she wondered in a sudden flare of dread. Was this a rescue or was this the coup de grace, the last triumph of her killer?

Falke saw Madelaine's fallen horse as the vultures plundered the body and his heart slammed in his chest. He urged his donkey onward, his blue eyes narrowed to slits as he peered ahead. The tawny rocks cast their glare into his eyes, and he slowed to a walk.

She could not speak, and moving was such torture that Madelaine had to take her single chance carefully. There was a rock under her left hand; it had pressed into her palm since she fell. To grasp it pulled open blisters on the back of her hand. She dared not move against this pain for it would rob more of her little remaining strength.

"Madelaine!" Falke shouted, knowing as he did that if she heard him it was not likely she would be able to answer. "Madelaine!"

If taking hold of the cup-sized stone had been grueling, lifting it was excruciating. She summoned every bit of reserve within her and tossed the stone as far as she could. It landed near her foot. She held her breath.

At first Falke was not certain he had heard anything more than another outburst of temper from the vultures, but then he realized the sound had come from a different direction, and he shaded his eyes as he perused the canyon floor. He admitted to himself for the first time since he set out that his impossible hope might not be entirely lost. His shout as he caught sight of Madelaine's pitiful figure rang off the canyon walls and set the vultures hurtling into the sky while the two donkeys brayed in protest.

Falke's voice. Madelaine was certain it was her imagination. How could Falke be here? She tried to cry out, and gave a soft, anguished wail.

Her voice was so pain-racked that he ought not to have heard it, but he did. He thudded the donkey with his heels and dragged the second beast after them, forcing the two almost to a canter. As he drew nearer he was aghast to see the burns and weeping blisters, the puffy and partially ruptured eyelids and cracked lips. He pulled the donkeys to a halt, reaching for the nearest waterskin as he flung himself out of the saddle, pausing only to secure the donkeys to medium-sized boulders before scrambling over the rocks to where she lay. "Madelaine. Madelaine," he repeated over and over as he knelt over her, shielding her from the sun with his body. "Heilige Baptist! Oh, my love, dearest dearest love." He bent to kiss her, but held back, knowing that the lightest touch would cause her more torment. "Mein Gott. Your face. Your hands . . ." He was too much of a physician to be able to deceive himself: she had been ravaged by her ordeal. Desolation welled within him even as he opened the waterskin and patted a few drops of it on her mouth.

"Not water," she grated, trying to open her swollen, blistered eyes.

"Yes. Yes, water," he said, reaching for more. "You must have water."

"Life," she muttered.

"Yes." He pressed his fingers to her lips, trying to be as gentle as possible, but his haste made him clumsy and he accidentally touched her face. "I'm sorry. Christ! Madelaine, I'm sorry."

She made no sound, but the trembling that shuddered through her was testimony to her suffering.

"No, no, sweet love, Madelaine, dearest." His hands shook so much that he did not trust himself to put more water on her poor bleeding lips. "I didn't bring opium or . . . anything else for the pain." He hated himself for this lack. "I have ointments, but you . . . not ointments, the way you've been burned." He smoothed her hair, taking care not to touch any part of her face or to press down.

She saw the desolation in his eyes, and knew that he did not think she would live. "Find shade," she made herself say, though the sound she made was a travesty of speech.

He leaned closer. "No, no, cherished Madelaine. No. It would hurt you too much." He wanted so to find a place where he could kiss her, just graze her skin with his mouth, but was afraid to attempt it. "I'll shelter you here. Others are coming."

Hurt blazed up her arm as she made herself reach out to take his hand. "Find shade." This time the words were a bit clearer.

"Don't ask that of me." He put his hands on either side of her head, but would not make contact with her. "I can't do it, Madelaine."

Lying with his shadow across her, Madelaine felt a faint stirring of energy. "You must," she said. "Please."

He could not answer her; he was torn between his desire to protect her and the need to treat her. With infinite care he put his finger to her lips. "The pain would be unbearable."

She tightened her hold on his hand. "Danger here."

This held his attention. He glanced swiftly around. "I don't see anyone."

"Cliffs," she said, and gave a racking cough.

"You were shot at by someone hiding in the cliffs?" He half-rose, then dropped back down to keep her in shadow. The floor of the canyon was so very bright, so hot. He remembered what she had told him about the sun and its capacity to burn her, to kill her. There were other things she had said as well, and those things he forced from his thoughts.

"Yes." She was exhausted now, so much that breathing was an effort. The only reason she did not release his hand was that it was too much work.

Never had it been harder to think clearly, and never had it been more crucial. He turned from side to side, searching the cliffs more, for some indication of who was there. He had to act, but how? His shirt and waistcoat were sticking to his body, and now he knew he had to protect himself as well as Madelaine from the sun. "I don't want to hurt you. I want you to live."

The tiny lift of one shoulder was supposed to be a shrug; if her face had not been so burned she would have encouraged him with a wry smile. "Yes."

This time when he looked toward the southern cliffs he looked for the nearest outcroppings of tall rocks and boulders where a little respite from the sun could be found. He kept repeating to himself, "Calmly, calmly, calmly," though he was far from it. At last he saw what he was seeking: three tall hillocks, one surmounted by an enormous tumbled stone. There would be cover at its base. There might also be room enough for the two donkeys. But it was some distance, and he was not certain he could carry her so far, or that she could endure to be carried. He dared not try to put her on one of the donkeys, for she was too weak to hold herself in the saddle and if she fell . . .

Some of this was in his touch, in his eyes. Madelaine muttered,

"Over your shoulder."

He moved closer to her. "No. Oh, no, Madelaine. It would be—"

"Over your shoulder," she murmured.

Neither had the strength to argue; he realized that this was the only course available to him, repellent though it was. "I will try not to hurt you," he said very softly. "I must go get the donkeys. Then I will come back to you. I"—he had to choke down bile before continuing—"will lift you over my shoulder. I will try not to make it worse than I must."

"I know." Rough as her tone was, it caressed him. "Go." She steeled herself against the renewed onslaught of the sun, and while she lay exposed to its implacable brilliance she closed herself off from all else but resistance of its puissant enormity.

Then Falke was back, dragging the donkeys behind him, calling to her, warning her. His hands were gentle, and he set himself against his own aversion to the terrible pain he gave her. "Hang onto my waist," he said through clenched teeth when he had her over his shoulder. "You'll bounce less." To help her, he took her wrists and held them in the hand that did not lead the donkeys.

In the shadow of the outcropping there was a sheltered hollow, large as an armoire, protected from sun and prying eyes alike. Falke eased Madelaine from his shoulder onto the hard earth, then turned to secure the two donkeys at the entrance of the hollow, taking a little time to give each animal some water before he returned his attention to Madelaine, moving reluctantly because of what he feared to see. Death was fierce in the desert, and Madelaine especially vulnerable if even half of what she had said about her nature was true. And if what she said was true, his mind went on, he would be as vulnerable as she if he attempted to restore her.

She could open her eyes a little more now that she was protected. "Thank you," she told him. "It is a beginning."

He came to her side, his medical satchel open. "Lie still. I will think of something to ease your hurts." It was a vain promise, and he sensed she knew it as well as he. "I will."

"I will heal," she whispered. "Now I will heal."

"Yes," he lied, knowing that there was no remedy for burns like hers.

"I will." She moved so that she could lean her head on his arm. "In time."

His eyes were so filled with tears that he could not see her clearly. "Yes, my dearest love." He had to find something in his case. There had to be something he could do; he turned it over in his thoughts again, and found as many fruitless answers as he had before. She had warned him that he was at risk, that they had been too close too often; to give her his blood might save her but he dreaded what would come after. But she was dying. He had nothing in his satchel, in his case to help her.

There was a flicker of violet in the depths of her swollen lids. "Help me."

Nothing tortured him more than that simple request. Of all persons to fail, he had failed her. He had no more promises for her. In his misery he touched his mouth to hers, as much to keep from speaking as to express his love for her. To his amazement she answered his kiss, though her lips bled from it. "No, Madelaine," he said, drawing back. "It will make it worse."

"Yes," she answered. "Love me."

He stared at her, taken aback at what she said. "I . . . it's not possible. Your burns . . ."

She was insistent. "Love me."

"It isn't possible," he said, stammering.

"Falke." She had managed to force her eyes half open. Blood ran from her eyes in place of tears she could not shed. "Love me."

Intense desire flooded him even as he shrank back from something so agonizing to her. The burns that disfigured her, the welt on her temple, none of it mattered, not even his own malignant transformation into her life, for it was Madelaine and he loved her from the very core of his heart. "I've hurt you enough already," he whispered.

"Then love me." She lifted her head a little. "Or am I too hideous?"

"No," he said quickly. "No." He kissed her a second time, and this time he needed more will to keep from gathering her close to him. In confusion he tried to move away from her. "I have bandages."

"Leave them," she said, less breathlessly than before.

"Madelaine ..." He knew he ought to cut her clothes off her and examine the extent of her burns, then bandage them, but now he was afraid of what he wanted beyond that. As if his hands belonged to someone else, he saw them unfasten the neat riding coat in soft muslin. Gently he peeled it off her shoulders, then began to unbutton the shirt beneath. He was astonished at how keen his need for her had grown. He tossed her shirt aside. "Your corset was some protection."

"At last. Corsets are useful for something," she murmured, moving her arm a little so that he could reach the back to unfasten the lacings.

"I mustn't do this," he said, frowning as he continued to remove her clothes. Passion for her was strong in him; he did not think of his own death, so remote and unreal, but the immediate possibility of hers. "I don't want to ..." He stared at her breasts, the skin reddened, the nipples erect. "Madelaine, I don't ..." The touch of his fingers, his arms, his mouth was annealing, the first mending of what would be a long recovery. He was so careful, so tender, his movements slow, delicate, verging on adoration; his passion burned more brightly than the sliver of sunlight on the far side of the hollow.

There was rapture in her, and esurience, under the vitiation and pain. To be cradled in the curve of his body, held so that she would not be scratched or pressed, gave her renewed hope. When she moved over him, taking him inside her, she welcomed the tremor of approaching fulfillment. The world, which had been agony, and the sky now shrank down to the sweetness of his flesh and the kindness of his love. As their ecstasy grew, she pressed closer to him, until her lips touched his throat and they lost themselves in unexpected exaltation.

Text of a letter from Erai Gurzin in Thebes to Saint-Germain on Crete.

My revered teacher and master,

She is safe and hidden. Were it not for the German physician, this would not be so. She was left in a canyon to die, but he was warned of it by a young man who lost his own life bringing the message. Falke has returned her to a deserted building to the north of Thebes, and is hiding her there.

I must warn you that she has been severely burned. Much of her face peeled away, and Falke has said he fears she will be scarred. She has said she will not, and I believe her.

On her orders, I have made inquiries about those who might wish her ill, and the evidence continues to point most directly to Baundilet or one of his creatures. I have no certain proof of it, but if I had to swear that Baundilet was truly innocent of the actions against her, I could not do it. So I will continue to regard him as her enemy and take appropriate measures. Because of all that has happened, I continue to fear that she is in great danger. Were her whereabouts known, I would not be able to ensure her safety. Only Falke and I visit her, Falke to care for her as well as to show his devotion. I am not satisfied that her hiding place is so secure that we do not need more guards for her, but that would increase the risk that others would discover the place, and so Falke and I have kept it to ourselves.

Madame de Montalia has ordered me to return to Cairo in order to lodge an official complaint with the French diplomats there in regard to Baundilet's conduct, but your orders are that I should remain with her, and until you countermand that, I will do as you have instructed. As soon as she is well enough to travel I will take her up-river to Edfu, where Baundilet will not be able to find her; I will keep her there as long as is necessary for her safety, or as long as she will permit me to protect her. I have met few such self-sufficient women as Madame de Montalia.

As to whether Baundilet can be tried in Egypt, I do not think it is likely, for Europeans are not often brought before Egyptian Magistrates. Numair, the Magistrate here, is venal enough that another generous donation from Baundilet's university would assure his freedom. Then, too, Baundilet has had many dealings with Yamut Omat, who would protect him if Madame de Montalia attempted to bring him to court. If there is to be any satisfaction for his actions, it will have to come from Europe, I suspect, and that does not appear to be possible. Whatever satisfaction she seeks, it must be in other ways.

Let me confess to you, my esteemed teacher, that I underestimated Madame de Montalia, not just in her scholarship and determination, but in the strength of her character. I supposed from the first that she would grow weary of what she undertook here, and would demand amusements, like those English-women who want to ride with the Bedouin. You told me that I had not the measure of her, and that is true. I ask your pardon as I shall ask hers for having so little respect for her, and will pray that in future I will not be similarly blinded.

I will send you word of her improvements, and inform you of Baundilet's actions. As much as it is possible to guard her, you may repose all confidence in my fealty to that task. If you have considered coming to her yourself, I must remind you that the price is still on your head and those who opposed you have long arms and longer memories. It is difficult to hide and watch over her; it would be impossible to protect both of you.

May God bless and guide you, and may He restore Madame de Montalia for her sake as well as your own.

In the Name of God
Erai Gurzin, monk

May 13th, 1828

4

In the lamplight Madelaine's face no longer looked raw and peeled. Soft, new skin was emerging from the burns and blisters. The furrow at her temple was gone; a single fine raspberry line remained, though it was fading. She could smile without effort, for her mouth had healed. "I said there would be no scars."

"Because of what you are," Falke said, sighing once. "Or so you claim."

"Because of what I am." She kissed the curve of his jaw. "Without you, I would still be suffering, if I were alive at all."

He moved back from her and took a step toward the shuttered window. "I must get back, Madelaine. I had meant to be here just for an hour, and look: the sun is down."

"I'm not supposed to look out the windows," she said, and there was a little petulance in her voice.

He turned toward her. "You must not be seen. If anyone found you here, it could—"

She raised her hands in mock surrender. "I know. Between you and Brother Gurzin, I haven't been allowed half a day to forget it." She wandered back to her couch. "I wish I had work to do. I've explored the basement here, which was probably part of an older building once. But it's not the same. There are walls filled with bas-relief not far from here. No one has sketched them yet. It is like a feast where I am not permitted to dine."

He came behind her, wrapping his arms around her waist, his face against her hair. "You must be careful, Madelaine. I could not bear to lose you."

She made a complicated gesture. "I realize the dangers. I know it is wise to remain here, to recover, to regain my strength. God knows I never want to go through such ..."

"Shhh," he said softly.

"But I'm bored," she said reasonably as she turned in his arms to face him. "Falke, can't you understand that? You and Gurzin are wonderful to me. I am grateful, truly I am. But I am being stifled. I am bored."

"I can't bring you books, dearest love. I'm being watched, and it is hard enough getting away to visit here without being noticed. If I brought books, or carried them, those who watch would become suspicious."

"Then bring me something to write with. Bring me pens and ink and paper. Let me have something to *do*." She kissed him again, this time with more urgency. "Other than this."

He grinned in mock outrage. "Bored with this, are you?"

"Never," she said seriously. "But no one can make love every hour of the day. Besides, you are at risk now, and you have not said if you wish to become vampiric and walk again after dying. If you would rather not, then we cannot love each other in passion and blood again." Her violet eyes held his blue ones. "I won't give you my life if it is not what you want."

"But you will not love me, either," he said, dropping his hands from her.

"I must not," she said, her eyes still on his until he looked away.

His jacket was across the only chair in the room, and he retrieved it. "I do have to leave." The smile he gave was tentative, an apology he did not know how to make.

She nodded, a warmth under her ribs that was neither pleasure nor pain but a disturbing amalgam of the two. "Will you come tomorrow?"

"I won't have much time." He chuckled softly. "Truly. I will not be able to remain long." He stood silently, staring at her with desire and chagrin in his face. "I'll try to bring you paper and ink."

"And a pen," she said, the sensation growing stronger.

"Yes. A pen." He hesitated, then turned toward the narrow entrance to the ancient building. "Tomorrow."

"I will be here," she said, doing her best to make her words humorous.

He was about to say something more, then kissed his hand to her and slipped out the door, taking care to mask his coming and going by drawing a curtain across the door before opening it.

She listened to the sound of his horse trotting away, her face showing no emotion. She put the bolt into place with melancholy thoughts. He would not accept her gift, she knew it already. He would not want to come into her life when he died. And so they would not be lovers again. She let her breath out slowly, as if that would make it less a sigh.

There was nothing better to do, so she continued the repair of the embroidery on one of the large cushions strewn around the little chamber. It was one of the few skills she had learned from the Sisters of Sainte Ursule that continued to be of use to her.

The single lamp made it impossible to match colors accurately, but since the chamber was never opened to daylight she decided it did not matter. With care she picked out the old frayed strands and set her needle with silken floss.

The small Dutch clock on the low brass table had chimed one when Madelaine stirred from her task. "Gurzin?" she called out softly.

There was no answer, but in the garden a single crunch of gravel brought her fully alert. Securing her needle in the embroidery, she moved the pillow aside and stepped back, out of the soft light of the lantern into a small alcove where a poignard was hidden.

Someone fumbled at the door, unable to move it because of the heavy wooden bolt on the inside. Then there was a tentative knock. "Madame?" The voice was quiet, shaking, very young.

Madelaine took the poignard and moved out of the alcove. "Who is it?" she asked quietly, knowing that what she was doing was reckless.

"Madame de Montalia? It's Rida Omat," came the quavering answer. "Will you let me in? Please?"

"Rida?" Madelaine hesitated, wondering how the Egyptian had found her. "Are you alone?"

"Yes." She sniffled. "I'm so scared."

It was foolish to let her in. There was no reason to suppose that Rida came alone. Madelaine stepped into the shadow of the curtain that covered the door and pulled the bolt back, but did not open the door. "Push inward," she said. "I am armed."

The heavy door swung inward and Rida Omat slipped into the curtained part of the room, leaning against the door at once to close it. As Madelaine slipped the bolt back into place, Rida burst into tears. This was a steady, convulsive weeping that racketed through her, exhausting her.

Madelaine tucked her poignard into her sash and went to Rida's side, putting an arm around her, though she knew that Rida found such familiarity with an Infidel offensive. "What's this? What's wrong?"

"I'm frightened," she sobbed, and pushed away from her, seeking out one of the enormous cushions and flinging herself onto it.

"Whatever for?" Madelaine asked, coming to her side. She would rather have learned how Rida had found her, but knew she would have to calm her before she could get such an answer. "What is the matter?" There were a number of smaller cushions and Madelaine drew up the nearest to sit on it.

At first all Rida could do was weep, but then she struggled to control herself enough to answer. "I'm pregnant," she said finally.

"Pregnant?" Madelaine repeated, knowing the severity of penalties given in this country to young women who did not remain chaste. The strictures against illicit lovers were far more binding for Moslem women than for Europeans. "But how is it possible?"

"It is possible the way it is always possible," she said suddenly, angrily. "They will stone me to death for it. My father will not stop them. He will curse me." Though she continued to weep, she sobbed less.

"But what lover . . . who?" It was the question she should never ask. It was sufficiently humiliating to Rida for Madelaine to know of the pregnancy; to know the identity of Rida's lover was intolerable.

"He . . . he said he would marry me. He said it would be all right to have two wives, that it wouldn't matter." She mopped her eyes with her sleeve.

Madelaine sat very still. "Baundilet." She was certain of it even before Rida cried out that he was French. Who else would be so cruel, she wondered sardonically. Who else would behave so egregiously? "Does he know?"

"I thought he would be pleased." She became very still. "He told me he could not aid me. That was all, that he could not aid me." The color drained from her face. "He wouldn't speak to me again. He said he could do nothing. He walked away."

Hearing this, Madelaine longed for the opportunity to expose Baundilet for what he was, reveal his rapacity and greed and malevolence. "When?"

"Today. Earlier. Near sunset." She embraced the cushion she lay on. "He wouldn't talk to me at all."

Madelaine looked down, studying her hands. "And why did you seek me out? How?"

"Everyone said you had been lost in the desert and died." She began to rock as she spoke. "I was so worried for you, dying out there in the wastes. But I heard one of the French servants say someone had found you. So I bribed the servant, and he took me to another servant, and I bribed him, and he took me to the old woman who told me where I could find you. I gave her a jewel."

"I see," Madelaine remarked, knowing she owed Rida a response. What old woman knew where she was? Who else had she told? She would have to speak to Gurzin in the morning and find out.

"My father does not know yet, I don't think. But when he does, he will disown me and give me to the Magistrate." She shivered. "I am a dead woman."

"Not yet," said Madelaine, her face determined. She rose and walked around the confines of the little chamber. If only she were not alone here. With a servant or a guard, she could act. As it was, she was forced to remain with Rida until Brother Gurzin arrived, and that lost her the precious advantage of time.

"What am I to do, Madame? Can you tell me?" Rida's eyes flooded with fresh tears. "I do not want to die."

"Few of us do," said Madelaine, stopping near the shuttered window. A night bird shrieked, and its alarm was taken up by others. "Something is disturbing them." As she told herself sternly that the birds might be upset by any number of things, she grew apprehensive. She glanced at Rida. "Were you followed?"

"No," she said, shuddering at the thought.

"Are you certain?" Madelaine asked, and did not wait for an answer. "Something is bothering those birds."

"Rats. A dog, a cat." She lay on the cushion, her knees drawn up to her chest, her face stark with terror.

Madelaine shook her head, motioning for silence. "I don't think so," she mouthed as she moved next to the shutters, listening.

A goat bleated nearby, and further off a dog began to bark.

"It's going away," Rida muttered. "Good."

In the next instant the shutters were bludgeoned open with three tremendous blows of a sledgehammer, and Professor Alain

Baundilet stepped through the wreckage, Ursin Guibert at his side. "Well," he said as he looked from Rida to Madelaine. "We can finally settle this."

Rida screamed and shrank back, her eyes immense. *"No! No! No! No!"* When she backed against the wall, she yelped and tried to make herself as small as possible.

Madelaine moved her poignard so that the folds of her skirt concealed it. She wished she had regained more of her preternatural strength to use against this dire man. She remained standing, watching him levelly.

"Pick her up, Guibert," said Baundilet, pointing at Rida before he turned, now holding the sledgehammer as if it were a cane and he was parading on the boulevard. "I heard a rumor that said you were not dead."

"No thanks to you." She was pleased at how steady she sounded.

"Suti is not as good a shot as he said he was," Baundilet said, dismissing her comment with a lift of his brows. "How did you manage to survive, though, out in that canyon?"

"I was fortunate. I found some shade." Looking at him, having him so close to her, made her feel queasy. "How did you find me?"

"Why, I should think it obvious; I had Guibert watch the girl. When she left her father's villa, Guibert followed you and I joined him when he summoned me." He waved his hand toward Guibert, who had dragged Rida to her feet and was taking a cord from somewhere in his capacious sleeve to bind her hands. "Not too tightly. And make her stop that squawking."

Madelaine started toward Rida. "Don't hurt her any more."

Guibert affected not to hear her and carried on with his task. "I'll gag her, Professor," he assured Baundilet as he sank one hand in Rida's hair, tightening his hold. "If you're quiet I'll let go."

Rida's keening stopped at once.

"Much better," Baundilet approved. He strolled toward Rida. "What a stupid, vain creature you are. How do you contrive to be so foolish?" He slapped Rida and Madelaine shouted in protest. Baundilet rounded on her. "She at least has the excuse of stupidity. You are proud and obstinate, Madame, which is inexcusable. You're intelligent enough to keep away from matters that do not concern you." He reached out and caught her by the shoulder. "You wouldn't be persuaded and you wouldn't be warned and you wouldn't be sensible. What was I supposed to do with you?" He tightened his fingers, relishing the force he exerted. "You've only yourself to blame for your predicament. You know that."

Madelaine would not give him the satisfaction of wincing or trying to break away from his grip. She had survived the sun; there was nothing Baundilet could do she could not endure, she told herself.

"It's a pity, having to be rid of you. It doesn't matter about her, but you are interesting. You have some aptitude for antiquarian scholarship, which is surprising. Aristos are usually interested in ancient things only if they can hang them on their pedigree." He chuckled at his own humor.

Rida pulled at the cords that held her, trying to break free. "I loved you. I have lost everything because of you."

He looked over his shoulder, not bothering to face her. "You threw yourself into my arms. You wanted me far more than I wanted you. I am human enough not to be able to refuse a woman who comes to me that way." His eyes flicked back to Madelaine. "You never accepted my offer, Madame. I still do not understand why."

"I find you repugnant," said Madelaine as if she were ordering tea. "And your treatment of Mademoiselle Omat shows that I was correct to do so." The poignard was still in place; she moved the folds of her skirt so that it would continue to be concealed.

"Touché," Baundilet said, his smile hardening to a grimace. "You might as well say your worst."

"Because I will not be able to speak again?" Madelaine suggested. "Is that what you plan? You intend that both Mademoiselle Omat and I should vanish?"

Baundilet favored her with a gallant little bow. "You have already vanished. There have been three searches for you, all of them unsuccessful. Rida Omat will simply be one of those countless girls who disappear from their fathers' houses. I may offer a reward for her return, to assuage Omat's distress a little." He signaled Guibert. "Bring her to me."

Rida whimpered as Guibert shoved her toward Baundilet. "You

do not need to treat her so shamefully," Madelaine said, adding to Rida, "You have no reason to cower. He is not worthy of it."

Baundilet released his hold on Madelaine's shoulder and with deceptive languor, he slapped her twice, the second time with such force that she reeled but would not fall. "I do not want to hear more of this," he rapped out, his mendacious bonhomie giving way to anger. "You are not to speak to Rida again. Do you understand me?"

"I hear what you are saying," Madelaine told him, moving her hand into her skirt again, covering her poignard.

Guibert looked directly at Baundilet. "What do you want me to do now?"

"The river's probably best. When they find the body, they'll think she drowned herself for shame." He saw the horror in Madelaine's eyes and smiled.

Rida bent over, retching and moaning.

"You are another matter." He stepped back and looked her up and down, his eyes rapacious. "And you have a great deal to answer for, not just the accusations you've published, but your conduct on this expedition. You've brought trouble with you from the time you arrived at Thebes. And now, since you're already dead, there's no need to be too nice about the details. You need not perish at once."

"Salacious and insolent," Madelaine said contemptuously, trying to find an opportunity to use the weapon she carried. "Do you want to debauch me, or is humiliation what you'd prefer?" She spat on him, raising her head with pride as he bellowed.

Baundilet's visage darkened in fury, and he reached out for her again. "You *poissarde*! Arrogant aristo! You *liante* whore!" He dragged her close against him, smashing at her with his fists while he tried to kiss her.

And Madelaine took the poignard and pressed it with all her strength into his back, just below the ribs, angling the long, narrow blade upward. "Rida! Get away!" she shouted as Baundilet howled and struck out at her again, cursing her in the lowest terms. One blow caught her by the ear; her head rang from it but she did not stumble. She held onto the hilt of the poignard, refusing to release it until Baundilet's voice faltered and he leaned on her, blood running from the corner of his mouth. His eyes glazed and he was sliding down her body, grasping at her breasts, her waist, her thighs as he collapsed, ending in a sprawl at her feet.

"Oh, Great Christ." It was an oath as much as a plea. She trembled and had to reach out to steady herself against the wall. Baundilet was dead and she had killed him. She had taken her poignard and made him dead. Her vision wavered and her knees no longer supported her well. Only then did Madelaine realize that Guibert had not come to Baundilet's rescue, and that Rida was still in his grasp. She had no other weapon but could not bring herself to tug the poignard from Baundilet's back. As she looked away from Baundilet, she met Guibert's eyes, and froze.

Guibert had pulled Rida Omat onto her feet again and was standing against the wall, away from Madelaine's struggle. He had his arm across Rida's body, laying claim to it. For many long seconds no one moved. "This alters matters," Guibert said when the silence had become unbearable.

"But how?" Madelaine asked, making no attempt to hide her anxiety.

Guibert stood a little straighter. "What will you ... But you can't stop me." He pushed Rida behind him. "She's mine. I've earned her. All the time Baundilet was rutting with her, I knew about it, and I knew he was deceiving her. She's not a whore, to be used that way. She's a virtuous girl and he knew it. I owe her something for standing by while Baundilet ruined her." There was another little silence. He coughed. "I have a house—nothing grand, but nothing shabby, either—near Beni Suef."

Madelaine was deeply confused by what he said. "Why do you tell me this?" she asked when Guibert volunteered nothing more.

"I will take her there, and marry her. She can't go back to her father; they'll kill her. It's better she come with me. You will not stop me. I will see that she is not harmed. She will not be stoned. We will have the child tended to." He made no attempt to see if Rida agreed with any of this.

" 'Tended to' means sold," Madelaine pointed out.

"It would be necessary," said Guibert without apology.

"Is this suitable to you, Rida?" Madelaine screwed up her courage to ask, knowing that Guibert might not be reasonable if he disliked her answer.

"I will go with him," Rida whispered.

"I work with many Frenchmen," said Guibert. "Other Europeans as well. She'll not be wasted like most Egyptian women. I'll need her help, and she will need mine." There was a tinge of pride in his tone now, and a satisfaction. "My father kept an inn at Marseilles, and I know how to assist travelers. Rida will come to like the work."

Madelaine knew she was in no position to cavil. With Baundilet dead, she had no hope of remaining in Egypt. "And I?"

"You are dead, Madame. You are a European woman. What can you do?" He indicated Professor Baundilet's body. "You cannot remain here, certainly."

"No," she agreed, shuddering as she looked down at Baundilet once again. "I have not healed. Travel now would be difficult." She did not add that travel over water would be grueling with her burns still tender.

Guibert achieved an eloquent shrug. "You'd better not stay here," he said casually. "When he is found, there had best be no trace of you. Find another place to heal." He reached back and took Rida's bound wrists, pulling her to his side. Carefully he released her. "You'd best go now. Leave me to deal with this place. Find that Coptic monk of yours or the physician—have them hide you until the hue and cry dies down, and then leave." He patted Rida on the shoulder much as he might pat a favored horse. "As long as you stay away from Egypt, Madame, you may count on my continued silence. If you come back, I won't be able to protect you and I will not try." His quick, feral smile had no trace of malice.

"What are you going to do?" Madelaine demanded; she was caught in the horror of Baundilet's death and could not think far beyond it.

"I will make it appear there was a falling-out with grave robbers. It won't be difficult. Baundilet was known to sell antiquities from time to time"—this time his sarcasm was angry—"and when I am through, it will seem that there was an argument."

Madelaine closed her eyes and nodded. "Very well." When she opened her eyes she resolutely avoided the body of the man she had killed. "I will keep my word: I will leave by morning. You will not see me again while you live."

Guibert gave her a crisp salute. "That shows good sense." He pointed toward the broken shutters. "Go out that way. I don't want to know who you will seek out. Just leave."

"Yes," Madelaine said. She felt a great sadness come over her, for herself, for Rida, for Egypt, perhaps for Baundilet as well. She held out her hand to Rida, but the young Egyptian woman would not touch her. "Good-bye," she said to the girl.

"Good-bye," said Rida, as if speaking to a stranger.

Text of a report from the Magistrate Kareef Numair.

Regarding the discovery of the body of the Frenchman Professor Alain Baundilet: an anonymous message was given at the court five days ago informing us of the murder of Professor Alain Baundilet, who had been the leader of the French antiquarian expedition working on the ancient monuments of Thebes under the sponsorship of two French universities. The message was not regarded when it arrived, for statements against the Europeans are common here. The message was put with many such others and dismissed. But the next day Professor Merlin de la Noye of that expedition called upon the court to help locate Professor Baundilet, who was missing. Since one of the members of the expedition had already disappeared, it was deemed of some urgency to investigate the Professor's absence.

To this end, I sent for Yamut Omat, who has been friend and confidant to Professor Baundilet, and received his report as given with his hand on the Koran, that he had no knowledge of the location of Professor Baundilet, but was himself troubled over the disappearance of his daughter Rida. Because the other French antiquarian who was missing was also a woman, it was thought at first that there might be some association between all these events. With the intention of determining the truth of such a supposition, I authorized three officers of the court to conduct an investigation.

It had been rumored for some time that Professor Baundilet was dealing in the sale of antiquities to Europeans. While this is not against the law, as Magistrate I have stated that I do not look favorably on the sale of such articles except to Egyptians. Yamut Omat has made it apparent that he and Baundilet had several such dealings in the last three years, and that he, Baundilet, apparently also dealt with others. One of the officers spoke to the other members of the expedition, one of whom has said that he suspects that the same persons who killed Professor Baundilet also killed Madame de Montalia, for she was outspoken in her criticism of those who sold antiquities.

The body of Professor Baundilet, naked and severely mutilated, was discovered three days later in a remote building where it is said witches have lived. The condition of the body was poor because of the time since the death and the heat, but from certain indications it has been determined that he was likely the victim of a certain well-known group of grave robbers, and it has been speculated that he and they had a falling-out, and they killed him. It is a reasonable supposition, and one that is consistent with what we know of Professor Baundilet as well as the robbers in question.

Therefore it is my conclusion that Professor Baundilet met his death at the hands of grave robbers during an attempt to buy or sell antiquities, and I will so inform the French government and the sponsoring universities.

Let me caution those institutions that if they wish the expedition to continue, they must appoint a new leader at once and be certain that the requisite monies are paid for permission to continue to excavate the ruins at Thebes. If these things are not done, I will have no choice but to rescind permission for the expedition to explore.

In the name of Allah the All-Glorious,

Kareef Numair
Magistrate

5

A splendid Baltimore clipper rigged for yachting waited at the end of the little jetty, as out of place among the dhows and feluccas and markabs as if it were not a ship at all but an exotic invention. The *Eclipse* had arrived the evening before and everyone in Edfu had come to stare at it.

"There is Savoie earth in the second stateroom," Roger explained to Madelaine as he helped gather her few things together. Sandy-haired, blue-eyed, middle-aged, he was dressed in the dark hammer-tail coat that marked him as the very superior manservant he was. "You will be comfortable there."

She smiled at him, but her eyes were tired. "Thank you."

Roger looked at her with concern. "Are you truly well enough to make the journey? Gurzin tells me that you are, but after such burns, you might want a little more time."

"It's not that," she said with a tiny shake of her head, the line of a frown forming between her brows. "I am ..." She opened her hands to show she did not know how to describe her feelings. "But I want to be gone from here. Brother Gurzin has been most attentive and the monks have been at pains to help me, but they do not want me here. I am an embarrassment to them, because I am a European, and a woman, and ... the rest of it." She picked up her shawl lying on the single chest in the room. "It's as well for me, too, leaving here."

"You have dreams and memories?" Roger suggested with kindness. "Those with long lives have more dreams and memories than most."

"Nightmare and hauntings is more like it," she responded shakily. "I waken at dawn, remembering how Baundilet died, or fearing I am back in the desert." She pulled the shawl open and swung it around her shoulders. "I need other skies for a time. Little as I want to admit it, I need to leave these wonderful monuments for a time. I ... have lost my perspective. I need to see Saint-Germain, to get my bearings once more." Her sketching satchel was leaning against the chest; she picked it up and shouldered the straps.

Roger took up the larger satchel and slung it over his shoulder. "He is on Crete, waiting for you. If there were not still a price on his head in Egypt he'd be here himself." He opened the door for her. "The monks are at prayers; I have given them your farewell."

She was able to chuckle as he said that. "Which is your very genteel way of saying they are glad to be rid of me. My departure can go unnoticed. Quite proper of you, Roger." As she followed him out into the narrow hall, she hesitated. "I should give a donation or—"

"It has already been done," Roger assured her.

"Ah," Madelaine said ruefully. "Of course. You arrived with a pouch of gold coins, didn't you?"

"My master provided a gift, as he did for Niklos Aulirios." They were almost to the side door. He stopped in front of the door to Erai Gurzin's cell. "Do you wish to leave him a note?" he suggested.

"Oh, yes," said Madelaine, then hesitated. "It would not be correct for him to receive it, would it?"

"Marginal," said Roger. "Gurzin has taken a vow to remain at the monastery for the rest of his life, so it would not be seen as too critical. But he would not be encouraged to accept it, if that is your question." He looked directly at her. "What do you wish?"

"I don't want to cause him any unpleasantness, not after all he has done for me." She did not open her small satchel. "Will they permit him to receive a letter, do you think?"

"From Saint-Germain, most certainly. You may include your thanks in that." He stood, allowing her to make her decision.

"Probably that would be best." She looked at the cell door for a moment, turning away with a short sigh. "Then I will wait until I am on Crete to tend to it. After all he has done for me, I ought not to make his life here more difficult." She put her hands to her face. "I'm a little frightened to leave the monastery. I haven't been outside its walls since I arrived; I've walked in the garden at night, but haven't been further than that." As she said this she recalled the centuries Saint-Germain had lived at the Temple of

Imhotep, out of the House of Life. Her stay here had given her a taste of the limits of that life, and it distressed her. "I keep expecting someone from the expedition or the Magistrate's court to be waiting for me."

"I will go first, if you like." Roger opened the door and stepped out into the glowing morning light. "Everyone is at the river."

"Staring at the *Eclipse*," Madelaine finished. "Well, she is worthy of being stared at." Her hands were shaking, so she folded them into fists as she walked into the narrow alley. She and Roger were quite alone there. "All right. I will follow you."

Roger inclined his head. "As you wish." He started toward the street, keeping close to the walls of the monastery. "This walkway is more ancient than the avenue ahead," he told her as they went. "It was here when the great temple of Rameses III was new, and it remains. How unfortunate that you could not examine what is left of the temple. There are carvings on it that are more impressive than most." They had reached the avenue. "If you look to the right, you can see part of the temple. No one has done work to restore it, or excavate it. The inscriptions are secondary to the friezes. Saint-Germain has copies of many of its bas-relief inscriptions and the writing on the pylons and columns inside." He led the way onto the street which was almost deserted. "Few of the Moslems frequent this area because of the monastery."

"You are determined to distract me, Roger," said Madelaine, knowing his easy flow of conversation for what it was.

"And to provide you with a more favorable impression of this place. You are now halfway between Thebes and the First Cataract. This is Upper Egypt, and you have not been able to explore it."

At the first crossing, a caravan was proceeding away from the town, toward the desert. Camels and donkeys shuffled along, urged by riders who sang and swore at them. Two of the men made the sign against the Evil Eye as they caught sight of Madelaine.

"Do not be offended, Madame," Roger said to her calmly. "They do that for all Europeans, who they believe to be devils." He stood patiently while the caravan passed, then crossed the street. "Europeans are not much seen here in Edfu. Most of them go to

Philae, which is more beautiful but less instructive." He continued to regale her as they made their way toward the Nile. "The Inundation is just beginning. We will ride it down-river to the sea, and sail to Crete."

"And Saint-Germain will meet us there." She could not help smiling. "It's worth crossing water to see him."

"He would say the same of you." They had reached the jetty and Roger led her through the small crowd that stared at the majesty of the *Eclipse.* "Stay with me, Madame. And do not pause to speak with anyone." He offered his arm to her, a courtesy he would not extend in Europe, where it would be impertinent. Here in Egypt, she took it gratefully.

"Who is the captain?" she asked as they reached the gangplank. "I want to address him properly."

"His name is Araldo Uliviero, of Palermo. You will not have met him before." He stepped onto the gangplank and led her aboard. "You are the most welcome guest of le Comte de Saint-Germain," he greeted her formally as she stepped onto the deck.

"How elegantly done," she marveled with the ghost of a smile, then she looked up at the man in captain's garb who came from the foredeck.

"Madame de Montalia," Roger introduced, "may I present Captain Araldo Uliviero to you."

As she curtsied, he touched his hat-brim. "Welcome aboard, Madame," he said, and kissed her hand. "It is an honor to have you with us." He was polite and correct, but there was a curiosity in his eyes that sprang from the knowledge this passenger was the occasion for their voyage and the special concern of his employer. "Roger will show you your stateroom. We have most of your goods aboard. We will stop at Thebes to retrieve the rest of your belongings and will then continue to Crete." He executed a perfect short bow, then added, "We cast off in fifteen minutes."

"I am at your disposal, Captain Uliviero," said Madelaine. She turned to Roger. "Well, lead the way, please."

The statement was larger than she had expected, and as Roger stowed her satchels, he said, "Under the mattress is a layer of Savoie earth, enough to counteract the water. Rest. I will call you late in the afternoon."

She tried to laugh but the sound caught in her throat. "I appreciate all this, Roger."

"You are still not wholly recovered from your ordeal, Madame," Roger said with great care. "I know the signs. You will need rest."

"Yes. Thank you." She removed her shawl and draped it over one of the two chairs in the stateroom. "Will the captain remark if I do not take meals with him?"

"No. I have said you have a predilection to seasickness and will probably keep to your cabin. He knows that my master never eats while on the water, and since you are known to be of his blood, he probably assumes the weakness . . . ah, runs in the family." His eyes glinted but he did not smile.

"You are very practiced, aren't you?" Madelaine asked, sensing the comfort of her native earth already.

"After so long a time, it would be strange if I were not," Roger answered, bowing again before leaving the room.

Madelaine did not bother to do more than remove her frock. In her slip and corset, she lay down on the bed and succumbed to the restoring power of her native earth as the *Eclipse* set off down the Nile.

With the swell of the Inundation to carry them, the Baltimore clipper had made good speed. By sunset, they had reached Esna, which was almost halfway between Edfu and Thebes.

"There are some fine ruins in that town," said Roger as they slid past it on the rising Nile. "From the later times, or so my master has told me; from the times after the Greeks came to Egypt. He was no longer here." He leaned against the rail and looked out at the darkening hills. "One day you must let him show it all to you, when he can come here safely."

"And when I can come here safely," Madelaine added. "I never thought I might not be welcome in Egypt."

"That is because you forgot it is two countries, and the one you seek is gone." Roger looked out over the river, where the water was alternately slate blue and faded gold. "Not so many years ago, I went to Gades; I was born there. Now it is Cadiz. The city I knew has not existed for centuries, and I could not find it again, no matter how I searched for it." He looked up at the sky, where the first stars were showing. "Even they change, over time."

Madelaine stared up at the sails and the stars beyond. After a while, she asked, "When will we reach Thebes?"

"According to Captain Uliviero, we should be there by mid-day day after tomorrow. We will load your things and be off again at sunset. Captain Uliviero has permission to sail at night: Europeans are required to tie up unless they have a writ from the Khedive's council. Egyptians can sail all night if they have the skill to do it." He indicated the western bank. "No place there large enough to tie this ship, so we must go on."

"Captain Uliviero must be very skilled," said Madelaine with an ironic smile.

"Of course," Roger said, catching her tone. "Will you stay up tonight, or are you going to rest some more?"

"Rest, I think. I want to be prepared for the day after tomorrow." It was not entirely true; she was more fatigued than she thought she would be and she needed more rest. "If I have to go ashore, I—"

"No. That can't be allowed," said Roger apologetically. "The Magistrate might take it into his head to demand you appear to be questioned, and we cannot permit that to happen. You will remain aboard the ship and the crew will tend to bringing your belongings. The ox-carts have already been arranged and we have confirmation from Jean-Marc Paille that he will supervise the loading of your sketches and other material. He was very eager to assist you. He can deliver messages for you, if you wish to contact anyone. He said he owes you a debt of gratitude."

Madelaine smiled slightly. "He doesn't, but it is flattering to think he might." She came and stood beside Roger at the rail, staring down into the river, seeing only the lights reflected from the sky and the running lanterns. "I may have one or two notes to be delivered, and it would be pleasant to see Jean-Marc before I leave Egypt." There was no trace of her reflection on the Nile, and she had to steady herself against the vertigo that threatened to overwhelm her.

"Are you all right, Madame?" Roger inquired.

"Yes," she said after a moment. "Quite all right." She looked down at the Nile again, to prove to herself that she could. "But I am worn. I'll say good-night."

"Do you want to be wakened for Thebes?" he asked as she started away from her.

"Yes. Yes, call me an hour or so before we arrive there, so I may prepare myself." Would Falke come if she sent word? The only way to have an answer to that would be to ask Jean-Marc to call upon him, carrying her letter. With failing hope she returned to her stateroom and spent the next three hours trying out several versions of the message that might bring Falke to her. When at last she abandoned the work, she was no closer to a form she liked. She trusted that sleep would help clarify her thoughts, but it did. Not that night, nor the next.

When Roger knocked on her stateroom door, she was already half-awake, her mind active. She rose and sponged herself before she dressed, taking care to choose her most attractive frock, a soft linen gauze in a muted shade of rose, the sleeves not quite as lavishly belled as fashion now required, but generous enough to be acceptable. Her hair was loosely knotted and instead of a bonnet, she had a chaplet of silken flowers. To keep off the worst of the sun, she carried a delicate parasol. When she appeared on deck, she had the satisfaction of seeing Captain Uliviero raise his eyebrows in approval. She approached him, not quite smiling. "I thank you for your fine sailing, Captain; I have hardly noticed any motion, so well do you handle this ship."

Uliviero beamed at this praise. "Saint-Germain sets high standards for his crew. I am pleased to serve you, Madame." He indicated the first few buildings on the east side of the river. "We will be at Thebes in half an hour, unless we must reduce sail for more river traffic."

"I recognize a few of the ruins from here," she said, and felt a pang of nostalgia. How much she wanted to go ashore and walk in those ancient places one last time. "They are so beautiful, so fascinating." She stood on the foredeck as the Baltimore clipper nudged up to the wharf, and watched as the sailors trod down the gangplank with Roger. She wished she could go with them. Just one more walk in the little temple she had discovered, one more chance to find out if this were the House of Life. Impossible and unwise though it was, she yearned for it.

Roger came back with the first ox-cart, and as the men unloaded it, stowing her possessions in the hold, he talked to Madelaine. "I have delivered your notes to Jean-Marc Paille, who has promised to pass them on at once. He wished me to tell you that no matter what the rumors may be, he is certain you never sold antiquities. He has told the Magistrate that you are on record opposing the sales Baundilet made."

"He did not need to do that," said Madelaine, feeling an odd gratitude to Jean-Marc. "I am pleased that he has done it, of course, but I do not think it was necessary."

"I doubt he shares your view. He seems determined to keep you from any tinge of guilt." He read the sudden pallor of her face. "He knows nothing of that, and I am sure he would not blame you if he knew."

"Possibly," she said, recalling how furious and frightened Paille had been when he learned how Professor Baundilet had abused his trust. She pulled herself together. "Is he planning to visit the ship before we sail?"

"He sends his regrets, citing the burden of work. He believes it would be best if he did not. I did not press him, Madame. He is willing to carry your letters, and perhaps that is all the risk he can accept now. He told me he wishes to correspond with you about the discoveries the expedition is going to make." He paused. "I must return to your villa. Your servants have been eager to assist. I think they are eager to be away from the villa."

"My reputation must have deteriorated more," said Madelaine, trying to make light of it. "Well, many of them did not approve of me in any case so now they can think themselves justified in their opinions, and I suppose some of them were taking payments from others to report on what I was doing. All the more reason to go elsewhere." She looked toward the road that led to her villa. "Thank them for me, if it seems wise."

"I will be proud to do that," said Roger, who then bowed and hastened away.

Madelaine stepped back to give the sailors greater access to the gangplank. She went back to the foredeck, strolling languidly, occasionally pausing to look out at the Nile, not wanting to admit she was waiting for answers to her letters, especially one in particular.

The afternoon dragged on and most of her goods were aboard the *Eclipse* before an Egyptian youth came to the gangplank and handed a letter to one of the sailors, saying it was for Madame. He was gone before the sailor could summon her, and so he gave her the letter with no additional information to offer. Madelaine took the letter and went back to the foredeck, breaking the seal with anticipation as she closed her parasol.

When she had finished reading, she stared out across the water for some little time, the letter still open in her hands.

"Falke?" Roger asked as he came up to her.

"Yes," she said, not turning to him.

He took a step nearer to her. "Will he come?"

"No."

Roger did not speak at once. "Does he say why?"

She shrugged and let go of the letter, watching it rise and sail over the river, a paper bird fluttering toward its distant nest. Her eyes never left it as long as it was in the air.

"All your goods are aboard. Captain Uliviero is preparing to cast off," Roger told her a short while later; there was a question implied in his words.

"Fine," she said distantly, no longer able to see the letter.

"Shall I tell him to go ahead?" His faded blue eyes were full of sympathy, and his voice was gentle.

"Cairo, then Crete," said Madelaine, making it her approval. She moved away from Roger, walking toward the prow of the clipper. In the late afternoon light she was glowing with all the colors of sunset. Her violet eyes were distant, glazed with unshedable tears.

Sails unfurled, and caught the first evening breeze. Wind filled them, tugging the *Eclipse* toward the heart of the river to ride the coming flood away from the mysteries of the ruins of Thebes toward the sea and Crete and Saint-Germain.

* * *

Text of a letter from Yamut Omat to Jean-Marc Paille, both in Thebes.

To my dear Professor Paille;

I must congratulate you on your promotion to head of the expedition. I felicitate you on the increased size of your staff, for surely five more antiquarians will make the work of the expedition much more remarkable than what has already been done. This is an unmistakable sign of confidence in your work, which must be very pleasing to you. After the unfortunate incidents with the late Professor Baundilet, you must feel vindicated that the universities have found that your complaints were soundly based.

Your tale of the perfidy of your former fiancée is lamentable, and a very shocking thing, but men who live long know that women are ever feckless creatures and given to fits and starts that serve only to discredit themselves and drive men to madness. It has ever been thus, and no man of good sense puts faith in women, or surrenders his heart to them, for surely they do not know the treasure you have given them, and they will disdain it from vanity and ignorance. You say that she gave you no warning of this change of heart, and that you are shocked that she would permit the need for riches to come to dominate her life so completely. How can we comprehend them? I share you bewilderment: I have yet to learn why my daughter has fled with the men who killed Professor Baundilet, for that is what the Magistrate has determined happened. What could have possessed her to do that? If she had been in their company, how could she have witnessed the atrocities committed on the Professor and still wanted to be with them? As a father, I am filled with dread for her fate, but as a man, I curse the very existence of women because they are so wholly at the mercy of their emotions. I have cast her out of the family, and I recommend to you that you cast this faithless harlot out of your heart and count yourself lucky that you learned of her venality before you married her, for surely she would put horns on you for the sake of a bauble or a night at the concert hall.

In regard to Professor Baundilet, I must tell you I think his usurpation of your work and the work of others quite unforgivable. I confess I was ignorant of these activities; had I known of them, I would have been less inclined to extend my hospitality to him, or consider him a proper friend. It troubles me to think what might have become of you as a scholar if his peccadillos had gone undetected, for you would not have been able to achieve the position you now occupy and which you so richly deserve. Your exoneration and his condemnation should serve as a worthy example for all antiquarians, and give pertinent warning to everyone that such chicanery will not be tolerated in the field. I applaud your detemrination in making the matter public, for that was a great risk for a man in your position to take. You are to be commended for your courage.

There is a matter, however, which I hope you have considered, which is the qustion of having these treasures you discover leave Egypt. I am troubled by the number of monuments and other items that have been spirited off to Europe and America and other places. As an Egyptian, I cannot believe that this is correct. I am determined to do all in my power to keep these great discoveries in this country, where they belong. I cannot see why the Germans should have a better collection of Egyptian antiquities than can be found in Cairo. To that end, you and I must have some discussion on the nature of your discoveries and your willingness to permit me to purchase these items for reasonable prices. I found Professor Baundilet most understanding on this issue and I am sure your good sense will guide you to a conclusion not unlike my own. You may use the funds I give you to expand the work of your expedition and to extend the areas you are permitted to excavate. With what has been found in the last six months, you must be very eager to have the right to dig in those sites at Luxor that appear to offer the greatest possibilities. You are in the strongest position in terms of the qualifications of your staff, and with support you might achieve those ends without too much money being spent on bribes and other such demands.

Only tell me that you will review this offer. I do not want you to feel I have put any undue pressure on you to accept these

*dealings, but you must surely understand that I am very inter-
ested in adding to my collection as well as protecting the arts
and artifacts of the old Egypt. You can make this aspiration of
mine a reality.*

*I have arranged an entertainment for the end of the week. I
hope you and your staff will come, including the new members
who have only just arrived and must be eager to know more of
the Europeans living here in Thebes. With the English group
working on the west bank and you on the east, this is surely
the most exciting time for all of us. While it would not be correct
to say that you and they are in competition, I am aware that
the presence of both groups has done much to spur the efforts
of each. At the gathering you will be able to obtain the kind of
information you want in a setting that will promote goodwill
and understanding. The entertainment will give all of you the
opportunity to compare notes and to enjoy a pleasant little
concert as well as two superior meals. You are familiar with
my entertainment and I hope you will look forward to this one
as much as I look forward to having you here.*

*My own carriage will call for you. Pray tell the driver if you
wish more of your staff brought with you. And while you are
here, I will save an hour or so for a little conversation. I am
hoping you will have arrived at the terms by which we will
conduct our private business by then.*

*With my very best wishes and the anticipation of doing busi-
ness that is satisfactory to us both in the near future,*

*Cordially,
Yamut Omat*

July 18th, 1828

Epilogue

Text of a letter from le Comte de Saint-Germain in Praha to Madelaine de Montalia at Montalia in Savoie.

My dearest heart Madelaine;

You cannot blame yourself for Falke's death. He chose to walk into the desert when he became ill, you did not force him to go. That he hid himself so well and burned so utterly is proof he knew what he was doing. You offered him our life and he refused it; it has happened to me so many times that I have lost track of the number. You admired his courage for taking on the work he did, yet it was that courage that led to his death, not your love for him. It is not your burden to carry, my love; it does not belong to you, and if you try to assume it you will destroy the memories you have of the man.

So now, with Jean-Marc Paille's latest report, you are itching to go back to Thebes. It will take time before it is safe for you to go there, as it will take time for the price to be gone from my head. In a decade or two, you can probably arrange to accompany another expedition and work there without too much risk. For the time being, you will have to be content with the ruins you find in Savoie and Provence, such as those ancient stone houses and the abandoned hill forts. They may not be as impressive as the stones of Egypt, but they have a history of their own which has a spell to cast, if you will permit it.

I have thought about your question, why I never have given

445

you a bondsman as I gave Niklos Aulirios to Olivia, as I have Roger for myself, and before him Aumtehoutep. I can find no sensible answer, and so it must be the answer of my heart: that you have your bondsman already, that I can relinquish you to no one, not even a guardian bondsman for you brought me a rebirth I had lost hope of finding. It is foolish: you are so much a part of me that I cannot endure releasing you to another. No, I am not jealous of your lovers, not thus far in any case. But a bondsman is another matter, and I find I am your bondsman as I was and will always be your lover, though we cannot be lovers as we were.

For as I am your bondsman so I am your lover, now and ever; nothing will alter that, nor would I wish it to. That is the triumph you have, and it is mine as well. All the rest of it, the four thousand years, the learning, the fortunes and friends won and lost, the blood that is life itself, is meaningless without loving you, and that will sustain me through all the years to come, through our separations, through the true death itself.

> *Saint-Germain*
> *(his seal, the eclipse)*

June 17th, 1831, Praha, Bohemia